Fire for Joy
Book 1 in the Ashborn Chronicles
Hal Rowan

Contents

To those who taught me that joy is worth chasing, and that anyone can be anything they set their mind to, no matter your origin.

Part 1 - Born of Stone and Flame

Rivals in the Gutter

A rock struck Halfa between the shoulders, hard enough to stagger him. He grunted but kept moving, the battered crate digging into his ribs. Another stone clattered against the wall to his right, sending flecks of mortar into the muck. Behind him, laughter rose, sharp and hungry, too thin to be anything but boys.

"Drop it, stonehead!" someone jeered. "Leave it and run!"

Halfa said nothing. Words only made you a target in the Dock Ward.

He shifted the crate higher, feeling the slick wood scrape against his bruised palms, and pushed forward through the rain-slicked alley. His boots slipped once on a patch of fish guts, but he caught himself before he could fall before they noticed him falter.

Another boy darted ahead, cutting him off. Halfa lowered his shoulder and barrelled through, sending the smaller body skidding across the cobbles. The boy cursed but didn't rise.

The others didn't follow.

By the time Halfa crossed the open market, the laughter had thinned into silence. Only the gulls screamed now, wheeling overhead like they smelled blood.

The merchant glanced at him. Grunted. Tossed a copper into the mud at Halfa's feet. No thanks. No respect. Just transaction.

Halfa stooped, picked up the coin, and tucked it away. He turned without a word, boots squelching through the filth, and disappeared into the alleys again.

◈

Halfa Schoona had learned to fight before he learned to speak in full sentences.

Not because he liked it. Because the Dock Ward didn't want for words.

The city's filthiest corner had no patience for the slow-tongued or soft-hearted. Its streets were a language of fists and elbows, of knowing when to duck and when to bite. Halfa's words always came late. They were too thick in his throat, too big for his mouth. Fists were faster and fists got you fed.

Grayspire was built on stone and regret. Every brick had blood under it, and every alley remembered things best left forgotten. The city didn't creak; it groaned. Still adjusting to the gravity of its deeds.

By the time he was eight, Halfa had earned a reputation. Not for cruelty or for winning. Just for surviving.

Halfa didn't want to hurt people. Not really. He just didn't know what else to do with the part of him that kept breaking things. No one had ever taught him how to build.

He was tall as a man by ten, shoulders wide as a cart axle, with calloused palms and a stare that could stop a dog mid-charge. No one knew where he'd come from. No one asked. Rumours filled in the blanks. Some said he was half-ogre. Others swore they saw him eat a rat whole. Most people pointed and whispered at him as he passed, as if he were scraped off a ship's hull.

He was a Goliath, though no one in the Dock Ward used that word. Too fancy. Too foreign. To them, he was just "that big bastard" or "the stone kid. " His skin was pale, not sickly but weathered like sun-bleached granite, with faint speckles like lichen across his shoulders. Most days, he looked like he'd stepped out of a mountain, slab-muscle and silent fury. No one in Grayspire had seen many or any Goliaths, and even fewer had seen one that didn't come swinging first.

Most Goliaths didn't live in cities. They didn't kneel, didn't bargain, didn't bow. Those who stayed in Grayspire were usually exiles, mercenaries, or wanderers who never made it back up the mountain. People said they were proud. Halfa knew better. They were heavy. Heavy with silence, memory, and things they couldn't name.

The truth was simpler. And lonelier.

Halfa had no parents. No real name. Just the one he'd given himself.

Halfa, always seen as "half" by people. Half-man. Half-wit. Half-monster. Never whole. Never enough.

The second name came later, scrawled by a drunk dock clerk into a shipping ledger. The man had slurred "Schooner" into "Schoona," then shoved the boy a job chit and told him not to lose it.

Halfa liked the way it sounded. Schoona. Heavy. Solid. Like something that didn't move unless it wanted to.

He kept the name and the job.

Halfa's bed was a pile of damp cloth stolen from washing lines, stashed in a half-collapsed tenement wedged between a fish smokehouse and an abandoned chapel. The floor sagged, the roof leaked, and the whole place reeked of brine and rot. He slept with his back to the wall and his hands curled into fists. He shared it with no one and fought to keep it that way.

The Dock Ward had no mercy for boys like him. Salt clung to every surface, doors, crates, skin, and dreams. Fish guts choked the gutters. Gull cries split the morning air like war horns. The smell of blood never quite washed away, no matter how much rain fell. It rained incessantly, offering no relief.

Halfa made coin where possible. Carrying crates. Hauling barrels. Sweeping up broken glass after tavern brawls. Starting a few brawls himself, when the price was right. His size got him noticed. His silence earned trust.

"Big lad. Don't talk. Does what he's told. " That was enough to be useful.

Being useful meant fewer kicks. Fewer cuffs. Sometimes, it meant bread.

Sometimes.

But being noticed came at a cost. Every coin job meant someone else went hungry. Every fistfight meant someone held a grudge. And every night, when the sun slid behind the masts and the streets turned meaner, Halfa wondered if he'd wake up with a knife in his ribs.

He didn't fear dying. He feared dying without ever having mattered.

He didn't know what he wanted from life. His life lacked purpose.

And yet, day after day, he kept moving, silent and stone-faced. A question in broad shoulders and broken boots, the kind no one wanted to answer. A shadow the Dock Ward learned not to chase.

Then, one morning, the tide shifted.

And Halfa met someone who didn't flinch when he looked him in the eyes.

It started like any other muddy morning in the Dock Ward.

The sky hung low and grey, like the gods had rolled over in their sleep and pulled the clouds down with them. Rain had come and gone in the night, leaving the cobbles slick with fish oil and yesterday's piss. Halfa was already at the docks before the shouting began, his shoulders aching from hauling rope spools for a crooked merchant who paid in dried eel and insults.

A wagon rolled in, creaking, spice crates stacked high and swaying, fresh off a cutter from Dreskar. The air changed. Even the gulls noticed. A dozen dockhands circled like sharks around bleeding chum, eyes fixed on the foreman shouting for workers.

Halfa moved. Fast. Direct. He always did.

But someone else moved too.

A shadow split the crowd. It was leaner than Halfa, but with the same unmistakable bulk of a Goliath. Pale stone skin with a bluish undertone, jaw too broad for his grin, and eyes that sparkled like someone who liked the damage he caused. Another Goliath. Halfa had never seen another one up close before, only heard whispers of their kin. Yet here stood one and he was just as big, just as sharp, but smiling as if he owned the street.

Halfa stopped.

So did the other boy.

In the Dock Ward, Goliaths were rare. Two was a problem. It meant people started locking doors and counting coins. It meant something was about to break.

The dockmaster, who was balding, red-faced, and soaked in fish stink, looked between them his face looked like he'd walked through vomit.

"Only need one of you," he muttered. "Ain't runnin' no bloody circus. "

Halfa said nothing; just raised his hand.

The other boy stepped forward, cocky as a prince. "I'll do it. "

His voice flowed rhythmically. Smooth, confident. Like he enjoyed hearing himself speak. He turned, just enough to flash a grin that didn't reach his eyes.

Halfa's jaw tightened.

The dockmaster didn't care. He'd already lost interest. "Sort it out, then," he grumbled, waddling off.

The moment he was out of earshot, the boy turned to Halfa and smirked.

"Didn't know there were two of us in this hole," he said. "You got a name, or should I just call you Boulder?"

Halfa shrugged, unmoved.

The boy stepped closer, unafraid. He wasn't as tall. Not as broad. But he carried himself like someone who'd never lost a fight badly enough to learn humility.

"Not a talker, huh?" He studied Halfa like a smith sizing up a stubborn piece of ore. "Alright then, Boulder. Let's see who wants it more. "

He dropped into a fighting stance, feet apart, fists up. There was no proper technique, just familiarity. This wasn't a bluff.

Halfa didn't respond.

The boy raised an eyebrow, lips twisting into something halfway between a smirk and a sneer. "You gonna fight, or stare at me till I fall asleep?"

Still, Halfa didn't move.

Then, just as the boy turned away, dismissive, Halfa stepped forward.

No warning. No words. Just weight, rage and silence.

He tackled the boy into a stack of spice crates.

Wood cracked. Spices exploded into the air. Cinnamon, pepper, and salt, mixed with sweat. The scent hit like a punch to the face, dizzying and sharp.

They hit the cobbles in a tangle of limbs and fists.

They fought like they'd been waiting their whole lives for this.

No opening shouts. No circle drawn. Just limbs flying, bodies crashing, breath coming in harsh, wet bursts.

The crates shattered beneath them, splintering across the dock. A sack of saffron burst open, dyeing the air gold and bitter. Cinnamon mixed with salt. Blood with sweat. Spice with fury.

Halfa swung first, wide, heavy, unforgiving. Like a tree learning how to fall.

Gronk ducked it and drove a fist into Halfa's ribs, then another to the side of his jaw. Fast. Wild. Laughing as he moved.

The noise brought a crowd. Not a big one, the usual mess of kids, dockhands, gull-feathered fishwives, and old men with nothing better to do than watch two titans knock the silt out of each other. Fights weren't rare in the Dock Ward. But this? This was worth pausing for.

Halfa didn't notice the onlookers. He barely noticed the pain.

There was no rage in him. No heat. Just the cold rhythm of movement.

Step in. Swing. Absorb. Repeat.

He took a jab to the cheek, then rammed his forehead into Gronk's with a sickening *crack*. The other boy staggered back, grinning even as blood ran from his lip.

"You hit like a mule," Gronk spat, circling. "Statue-boy's got legs after all. "

Halfa blinked, breathing hard.

This wasn't like other fights. This wasn't about coin, food, or survival.

This was... something else.

He didn't know what.

They traded blows again. Halfa's fists were like anvils, Gronk's like knives. The wood beneath them creaked with every shuffle. Shouts rang out. People placed bets in muttered tones. Somewhere, someone started playing a tin whistle in rhythm with the fight, because, of course they, did.

Gronk ducked low, drove a shoulder into Halfa's gut, and pushed him back toward the seawall. Halfa slid, boots scraping across the fish-slick stone.

"Thought you were stronger," Gronk teased, panting. "You look like a damn statue, but you hit like a drunk dwarf. "

Halfa stepped back into the fight, grunting as another punch clipped his temple. Then he landed a left hook that spun Gronk sideways into a stack of rope coils.

The crowd roared.

Blood now dripped from Halfa's eyebrow. Gronk's eye was swelling. Every inch of them ached. Still, neither stopped.

The blows slowed. Not from a lack of will, but from wear, like blacksmiths hammering cooled iron. Still determined. Still locked in rhythm. But burning out.

Then, between jabs, Gronk let out a breathless laugh.

"This is fun. "

Halfa froze. Not from pain. From confusion.

No one ever called fighting fun.

Gronk grinned, even with blood on his teeth. "Name's Gronk," he said, swinging again. "You ever figured out how to talk?"

Halfa caught the next blow on his forearm. Grunted. "Halfa. "

Gronk blinked, almost impressed. "Halfa? Half of what?"

The answer came as a left hook that almost dropped him to his knees.

He coughed, spat blood, and laughed again. "Yeah, alright. I like you. "

Halfa didn't respond. His knuckles were raw. His head throbbed. He didn't like this. He didn't hate it either. It just *was*—a rhythm he understood better than sleep.

Pain and silence. Fists and breath. Something to do with his hands.

Sensing no winner would come soon, the crowd peeled away, shaking heads, and muttered curses about broken spice and wasted time. No knives had come out. No one was dead. Just two boys hammering out a question neither could phrase.

That's when the dockmaster came storming back.

"Oi! What the hell is this mess?! Get gone, both of you, 'fore I call the Watch!"

Gronk wiped his chin and spat a streak of red into the gutter. "Guess we're not getting the job. "

Halfa didn't move.

Gronk turned to walk away, paused after a few steps, tossing a look over his shoulder.

"You coming, Halfa or whatever? There's a bakery on Fish Street that throws out day-old loaves if you ask real nice or look real scary. "

Halfa stood there for a long second, jaw clenched, blood trickling into one eye.

Then followed.

❖

They talked a little on the walk to Fish Street.

The Dock Ward was waking up around them, slow and sullen. Vendors were unlocking carts, grumbling over crates of spoiled shellfish and wilted leeks. Gull cries pierced the air like thrown knives. Laundry lines snapped above narrow alleys, heavy with last night's rain.

Halfa's lip was split and swollen. Gronk's right eye had puffed up into a fat purple bruise. They looked like they'd brawled their way through a tavern. In a way, they had. The entire city was a tavern if you looked at it sideways.

They didn't walk side by side. Not exactly. But neither walked behind.

Time and weather had beaten the bakery, which was tucked into a crooked alley and leaned as if punched repeatedly. Its chimney already belched smoke into the sky, coughing it between the eaves like an old man with a grudge.

The sign above the door had rotted through, leaving no name, no symbol, only a warped scrap of wood swinging on one chain. But the smell of bread didn't care about names. It filled the street like a promise. Warm. Yeasty. Alive.

Gronk approached like he owned the place.

He banged on the back door three times, sharp knuckles on older wood, and then leaned against the frame like a boy with no cares, like someone who hadn't bled on the cobblestones minutes ago. He looked over at Halfa with that same cocky grin.

"You're gonna like this," he said. "Old lady's got the heart of a salted slug, but she hates waste more than she hates us. "

The door creaked open. An old halfling woman squinted up at them. She wore a flour-dusted apron and had forearms like rolling pins.

"You again," she said.

"Me again," Gronk chirped, all mock-innocence. "Looking my best, too. "

Her eyes shifted to Halfa. "This one new?"

"Barely," Gronk replied. "Hits like a carthorse. Doesn't talk much. "

Halfa didn't blink.

She stared at him a beat longer, then huffed and vanished into the shadows of the bakery. A few moments later, she returned with two thick, lopsided loaves that were still warm. The cracked crust whispered steam into the morning air.

"Only 'cause I hate waste," she muttered, shoving them into Gronk's arms.

He winked. "You love me. "

She slammed the door.

They sat on the stoop beside the bakery, backs to the brick wall, bread in their hands, bruises on their faces, silence between them.

The first bites came fast, ripping through the crust with teeth still aching from punches. No talking. Just breathing, chewing, and swallowing.

Halfa hadn't eaten since... yesterday? Maybe longer. Hunger blurred the days. All he knew was that this was warm and not stolen.

After a few mouthfuls, Gronk spoke, his mouth still half full, voice muffled.

"You don't enjoy fighting, do you?"

Halfa didn't answer right away. He tore a hunk from his loaf and chewed slowly. "No. "

"Huh. " Gronk took another bite. "You're good at it. "

Halfa stared ahead at nothing. "That's the problem. "

The words surprised him as he said them. He rarely spoke unless forced. But they felt true, and they didn't need to be explained.

Gronk nodded like he understood. Maybe he did.

They sat there a while longer, chewing in rhythm.

Then Halfa asked, "Why do you?"

"Fight?" Gronk shrugged. "Because people don't mess with you when you scare 'em. You hit someone hard enough. He stops talking. Stops laughing. Stops making that face like he's better than you. " He paused. "You ever noticed that?"

Halfa nodded. He had.

Gronk tilted his head, curious. "Where'd you learn to fight like that?"

Halfa swallowed. "Didn't. "

Another bite. Another breath.

"Just... had to. "

Gronk chuckled. "Yeah. Me too. "

They fell into silence again, but it was easier now. Not heavy. Not empty. Just two boys letting the world pass around them without asking for anything.

After a time, Gronk leaned back against the bricks and stared at the patchy clouds above. "If I ever get out of this city, I'm gonna buy a horse. Big one. With teeth. Name it Thunderclap. "

Halfa frowned. "Why a horse?"

"Because nobody laughs at a man riding a horse named Thunderclap," Gronk said, eyes still closed, grin wide and tired. "Also, I could trample a few nobles on the way out. "

Gronk had a dream. Thunderclap and horses and a way out. Halfa didn't. Not yet. But sometimes, when he saw a child with eyes like his, or heard an old song about stone-blood warriors, something inside him stirred like a map trying to redraw itself from memory.

For the first time in what felt like forever, Halfa smiled. Just a twitch. But real. "Gronk?"

"Yeah?"

"...thanks for the bread. "

Gronk opened one eye and studied him. "Thanks for not knocking out my other tooth. "

They sat like that until the city got louder, until footsteps rose in the alleys, and dock bells clanged in the distance. Eventually, they stood without speaking.

◈

They didn't speak as they walked.

Not out of discomfort. Not anymore.

It was just... quiet.

Halfa's limbs ached. Every step reminded him of a blow taken or given. His lip was cracked, and the skin around his eye was bruising. He could still taste the blood in the corner of his mouth.

Gronk walked with his hands in his pockets and a half-loaf under one arm, humming something tuneless. His eye was almost swollen shut, but he didn't seem to mind.

The Dock Ward moved around them. Back to work. Back to noise. No one cared that two boys had bled on the stones this morning. No one asked if they were alright. No one remembered.

That was how Grayspire worked. It swallowed people whole and spat them back out with new names, new bruises, fewer teeth.

But as they crossed a crooked bridge over the canal, its boards warping with salt and time, Halfa glanced at Gronk.

And for the first time in his life, he wasn't sure that he was alone in the world.

He didn't have a word for it. He didn't need one.

They reached a fork in the road near a collapsed warehouse. Gronk slowed, then pointed with his chin toward the western lane. "I'm off that way. Got a place, sort of."

Halfa nodded.

Gronk didn't offer an invitation. Halfa wouldn't have accepted one. That wasn't how this worked. This wasn't a story with heroes and bonds and vows. It was just two kids trying not to drown.

Despite that, before he left, Gronk gave him one last look. Not a grin. Not a smirk. Just... a look.

"We'll see each other again," he said.

Halfa didn't answer.

Gronk didn't wait for one.

He turned and walked off, his boots slapping on the wet stone.

Halfa stood a moment longer. Then turned the other way.

Not side by side. Not together.

But not alone.

Shadows of the Same Shape

Ten years later, the Dock Ward hadn't changed, but Halfa had. He'd learned to speak by then. Bargain, threaten, and even laugh sometimes, primarily because of Gronk.

Halfa and Gronk moved through the Dock Ward like shifting landmarks. Two walking walls of muscle. One quiet. One loud. They were impossible to miss. Few made the effort.

Since that first fight, their friendship had grown and grown, as well as their physiques.

Some people called them "the Goliaths. " Yetta, a halfling dockside food vendor, called them "Stone and Fire".

Seven and a half feet tall, Halfa was all blunt muscle and silent as stone. He wasn't merely big; he was as wide as a doorway. Street-warping. The figure people remembered even if they never saw his face.

Other people decided who they were long before Halfa or Gronk had a chance to. Halfa had chosen nothing. Not his name or his strength. Not even the quiet that followed him like a cloak. The city had given him a shape, and he'd worn it. Yet, a part of him felt that a different form was hidden underneath. Something better.

They didn't always walk together. But when they did, streets seemed to bend. People parted. Shopkeepers paused mid-shout. Guards took notice, and gang lookouts whispered warnings. It wasn't just their size; it was the rhythm of them. Silent tension braided with violent promise.

They took odd jobs where they could.

Hauling crates for taverns. Guarding shady dice dens. Running interference when a merchant needed leverage, but not the Watch. The work wasn't clean. The pay wasn't fair. But it fed them.

They didn't always speak while working. Halfa didn't like wasting words, and Gronk preferred saving his voice for when it mattered—for laughter, for shouting, for fighting. What they shared wasn't friendship. It was something older. A pact without words: stay strong, stay seen, stay standing.

Halfa worked to survive.

Gronk worked to be seen. To create his own inviolable realm.

The city learned to move around them.

And the streets—well, the streets started talking.

One morning near the old smokehouse, they passed by Yetta's cart.

Yetta was a halfling built like a stubborn memory. She was short, broad, and always covered in flour, no matter the hour. Her eyes were sharp as fishhooks, her voice rough from years of shouting over street markets, and her generosity came edged with the kind of threats that kept people honest.

It was still early, lantern-light clinging to the gutters. The air stank of salt, ash, and river sludge. Yetta stood behind her battered food stand, spooning sourbread stew into chipped bowls with the focus of a sculptor.

She didn't look up as they approached. "You're late," she said. "Soup's been done since sunrise."

Gronk chuckled. "I didn't know we were expected."

"You're not. That's what makes you late."

She handed him a bowl without asking. When she got to Halfa, she studied him a moment longer, her weathered face unreadable beneath streaks of soot and steam. Then she handed him one, too.

"Careful, big fella," she said, her voice like a stone rolled over gravel. "You've got kind eyes. That's dangerous in this part of town."

Halfa blinked. Gronk elbowed him in the ribs. "She thinks you're the soft one."

"I *know* he is," Yetta said, ladling more stew for a waiting dockhand. "He's the one who listens."

Gronk laughed. "And I'm the one who talks?"

"You're the one who enjoys being seen. " She nodded toward a drunk snoring against a barrel. "World's full of shadows, boys. But you two—Stone and Fire? You're not hiding. You're casting your own. "

Halfa frowned. "That bad?"

Yetta shrugged. "It's power. Could be good. It could be terrible. Depends who decides what you are. "

Halfa didn't respond.

But her words stuck longer than the stew.

◈

As they walked away, Gronk finished his bowl in three long gulps and tossed it onto a heap of broken crates. "I like her," Gronk said, wiping his mouth. "She reminds me of my gran. If my gran could cook. And hated everyone. And if I'd ever met her. "

Halfa carried his bowl a little longer, sipping the broth in slow pulls. He didn't smile, but he didn't scowl either.

The city stretched ahead of them, loud and cracked and waiting. Somewhere out there, work needed doing. Someone needed hurting. Or protecting. Or both.

They walked into it. Not side by side. But not apart.

And behind them, Yetta watched the backs of two boys the world was calling by names they hadn't chosen.

◈

The job came from a spice merchant with a busted nose and a twitchy left eye. He found them near the fish docks, counting crates like they might vanish if he blinked wrong.

"Some street rats've been lifting from my stall," he said, voice low, breath sharp with clove and nerves. "Don't want the Watch involved. Just want 'em scared off. "

Gronk grinned before the man finished speaking. "We can do scary. "

Halfa's jaw tightened. "They're kids?"

The merchant shrugged like it didn't matter. "Thieves are thieves. "

The coins were real. Not much, but clean silver. Gronk took the pouch and bounced it in his palm like it weighed more than it did.

That night, they waited near the stall, which was a crooked table tucked into an alley that reeked of fish scales and cumin. Lanterns flickered against the damp stone. Halfa sat still as a statue. Gronk leaned against the wall, humming under his breath.

Just after midnight, two shadows crept in. Small. Fast. One older than the other, maybe thirteen. The younger couldn't have been over ten. Barefoot. Rib-thin. Moving like they'd done this before.

They didn't go for coin or spice. Just the back crate. Dented. Mislabelled.

Gronk moved first.

Silent. Fast. Efficient.

He grabbed the younger one by the collar and yanked him off his feet.

"Didn't your mother teach you not to steal?" he growled, holding the boy aloft like a grain sack. The kid kicked at the air, wide-eyed, limbs flailing like a snared bird.

Halfa stood. "Put him down. "

Gronk turned, surprised. "What?"

"He's a child. "

Gronk's grip didn't loosen. "He's a *thief.* "

The boy's face said everything—mud-smeared, terrified, hollow-eyed. Halfa didn't see a criminal. He saw himself. Ten years ago. Cold. Hungry. Trying not to die.

"Let him go," he said again, stepping forward.

Gronk's brow furrowed. "This is the job. "

"No," Halfa said. "The job is sending a message. This isn't a message. This is fear for fun. "

For a heartbeat, it looked like Gronk might argue. Might squeeze harder. But something shifted in his eyes. He dropped the boy into the mud with a splash.

The kid hit the ground hard, scrambled backward, and vanished into the dark before either of them could say a word.

They stood in silence.

Gronk didn't move. Just let the coin pouch dangle from his fingers.

"We taking the money or not?" he asked after a slight pause.

Halfa nodded his head. "Better us than the merchant. "

◆

The next morning, the Dock Ward smelled of old wine and new regrets.

Halfa passed by Yetta's cart as the mist still clung to the cobblestones. She was stirring a massive pot with her left hand and swatting gulls with her right.

When she saw him, she tilted her head. "I like a man who doesn't hit children. "

Halfa blinked. Said nothing.

She reached below the cart and pulled out a half-loaf, still warm. Crust golden, just beginning to harden.

"No charge," she said, handing it over. "Don't make me regret trusting you. "

He took it. Nodded. Walked on.

For the first time in a long while, the bread didn't taste like survival.

It tasted like a choice.

◆

The job came a week later.

A slick-haired man with rings on every finger and too much scent on his collar approached them. He didn't give a name, just the promise of coin and a message that needed delivering.

"Tavern owner," he said. "Behind on payments. You know the type. Think a sob story makes them special. "

Gronk lit up. "So you want him scared?"

The man smiled. "Scared, bruised, or rattled. I don't care how you do it. Break a chair. Break a finger. Make sure he remembers who he owes. "

Halfa looked at the pouch of coin the man offered. He didn't touch it. Gronk took it without hesitation.

They waited until just before the last call.

The tavern was quiet, with warm light spilling through grimy windows, the hum of conversation low and tired. A few locals nursed tankards in the corners. The place felt... small. Honest. The kind of tavern that existed on thin margins and thick regulars.

Halfa had been here before. Once, after a long night, heaving barrels uphill in the rain. He remembered the ale being cheap, the stew watery but hot.

The bartender spotted them as soon as they stepped inside.

"I don't have it," he said, hands raised before either of them spoke. "I used it for medicine. My wife's lungs; she couldn't breathe last week. I didn't have a choice. "

He was pale, with deep creases under his eyes and a hitch in his breathing. His hands trembled against the edge of the counter.

Gronk slammed a fist into the bar. Not hard enough to break it, but enough to make the lanterns jump. "Wrong answer. "

The few patrons scattered. A chair scraped. A door creaked. In seconds, they were alone.

Halfa stepped between them. Quiet. Heavy.

"We're not here to hurt you," he said.

Gronk scoffed. "Yes, we are. "

Halfa turned, keeping his back to the bartender. "He's not a threat. He's a man with a sick wife. You want to hurt someone for that?"

Gronk's jaw flexed. "Someone paid us for that. "

"Then they can come do it themselves. "

Behind him, the bartender made a choked noise—half sob, half thank you. He pressed something into Halfa's hand without looking. A few copper coins. All he had.

Halfa left them on the counter.

"Tell them you said no," he said. "Tell them we didn't listen. "

Then he turned and walked out.

Gronk lingered a moment, then followed. He didn't slam the door, but he didn't close it gently, either.

◈

Outside, fog coiled around their boots. The smell of brine curled in the air. Gronk struck a match and lit a cigar made from rolled dock weed, exhaling a slow ribbon of smoke into the street.

"You're getting soft," he muttered.

Halfa stared ahead. "I'm getting tired."

"Of what?"

Tired of being a thing, not a person. Tired of not knowing what I'm meant to be.

He didn't say it. But he felt it. And the feeling was starting to ache more than the bruises.

"Of hurting people who don't deserve it," he said instead.

Gronk leaned against the wall, eyes hooded behind a haze of smoke. "Everyone deserves it more than us. You just haven't figured that out yet."

Halfa didn't reply. He didn't have the words for what he felt, only that he felt it like a stone pressing on his ribs.

They didn't speak again that night.

◈

The next morning, Halfa passed by Yetta's cart as the fog clung to the stones. She didn't greet him; she just handed him a bowl of thick oat stew and a strip of eel.

It was... surprisingly good. Rich, spiced, and oddly comforting. Halfa frowned at the bowl like it had tricked him. Maybe Yetta had decided to be merciful. Or maybe his standards were just lower.

She slipped him a folded scrap of parchment.

"That barkeep's kid came by for stew," she said. "Said his mum is breathing better. Said he owes you his father's life."

Halfa said nothing. But this time... he didn't look away.

The job sounded easy. Too easy.

Guard duty. One night. A warehouse stacked with crates too valuable to leave unguarded. No names were offered. No details given. But the man who hired them flashed real coin and swore it would be warm, quiet, and simple.

"Nothing ever happens there," he'd said. "You just need to be seen. "

Halfa and Gronk took the job.

The warehouse sat near the edge of the Ward, close to the piers, but removed enough that no one stumbled past by accident. It was squat, wide, and reinforced. Built with the paranoia of someone who didn't trust locks alone.

Inside was warmer than expected. A small fire crackled in a brazier. A pot of stew sat on a crate nearby, half-eaten by the last shift. Rats moved in the walls, but not much else did.

For the first few hours, they ate and talked in short bursts. Gronk filled the silence with stories Halfa didn't ask for; tales of near-brawls, exaggerated jobs, girls he'd never quite kissed. Halfa listened with the patience of stone.

Then, just after midnight, the quiet cracked.

A window above creaked open. Halfa turned toward the sound just in time to see shadows drop from the ledge. Three of them. Fast. Young.

Teenagers, barely more than kids. Clumsy but determined. One held a dented crowbar. Another had a cloth satchel clutched to their chest.

They didn't look dangerous.

They looked desperate.

Gronk stood up, cracking his knuckles. "Well, well. "

Halfa stood, too. But instead of charging, he raised a hand to stop him. "Wait. Let's ask. "

Gronk's lip curled. "Does it matter?"

Halfa looked at the kids who had backed into a corner, eyes wide, trembling. One stepped forward.

"We need medicine," she said. Her voice cleared the silence. "For the orphan house. There's nothing left. "

Gronk exhaled through his nose. "Cute story. Still theft. "

Halfa didn't move. "What if it's true?"

Gronk looked at him like he'd grown another head. "We're not a charity. "

"No," Halfa said. "We're not monsters either. "

He walked to the nearest crate and pried it open with his hands. The lid groaned, then gave. Inside, there were rows of bandages, vials, and sealed jars. Clean, organised, expensive.

He turned back to Gronk. "We let them take it. "

Gronk stepped forward. "That's not our call. "

Halfa didn't flinch. "It is now. "

A beat passed. Gronk stared at him. Not furious. Not amused. Just... studying.

"You're gonna get us blacklisted. "

"Maybe. "

Halfa stepped aside.

The kids didn't wait for permission. They moved fast, filling the satchel with as much as it could hold. One paused, met Halfa's eyes, and whispered, "Thank you. "

Then they vanished into the shadows.

❧

They didn't talk on the walk back.

The streets were quiet, fog creeping through gutters like something alive. Every lantern was dim, every window shuttered. The Dock Ward was sleeping, or pretending to.

At the corner near Yetta's cart, they paused.

She didn't speak.

She handed each of them a cup of tea. Hot. Bitter. Heavy with dock root.

"You boys are changing," she muttered, almost to herself. "Careful which way. "

Halfa looked down into the steam.

He didn't know which way he was heading.

But for the first time... he cared where he ended up.

◉

The job came from a man neither of them trusted.

He wore too much perfume, smiled with too many teeth, and spoke like every word was an apology he'd already gotten away with.

"A message," he said, voice oily. "One of our taverns has forgotten its place. The owner is late on dues. Burn a chair, scuff some walls. Make it loud, but not too loud. "

Halfa was about to ask a question when he heard Gronk say, "We'll do it. "

The coin was already in his hand.

Halfa frowned.

Gronk gave a shrug like it was nothing. "Easy coin. We've done worse. "

Halfa didn't argue. Not out loud.

But something in his gut turned over.

◉

They arrived just after midnight.

The tavern's shutters were closed, and it was dark. No lanterns in the windows. No noise inside. Halfa recognised the place as The Gull's Wing. A decent corner pub. Cheap ale. Rooms upstairs for merchants passing through. He'd eaten there once. It was quiet. Clean. Kind.

"This doesn't feel right," Halfa muttered. "Another tavern. "

Gronk pulled a scrap of oil-soaked cloth from his belt and wrapped it around a shard of broken wood. "We're not here for right. "

Halfa stepped closer. "What are we doing, Gronk?"

Gronk crouched beside a rain barrel, dipped the rag in the oil, and lit it with a flint. The flame caught quickly.

"Couple broken chairs. Maybe a scare in the alley," he said. "Enough to make 'em listen. "

Halfa watched the flame flicker in his friend's hand. "This isn't you. "

Gronk didn't look up. "Don't tell me who I am. "

Then he turned and tossed the torch.

It hit the wall near the back door. Flames licked at the timber, caught a straw mat, then roared—up the frame and through the cracks.

The wood drank the fire like it had been waiting for it.

"Shit," Gronk muttered, stepping back as heat rolled out like a punch to the chest.

The back door blew outward, blown from its hinges. Smoke poured from the frame. Inside, fire climbed the banister like a dancer.

Halfa swore. "Too fast. "

"Place was empty," Gronk said. "It's fine. "

Then they heard the scream.

High. Human. Hoarse from smoke. The building had gone up like kindling.

Gronk's eyes went wide. "No—no one was—"

He lurched forward toward the flames—just as the ceiling above them gave a crackling shriek.

A beam, still burning, sheared loose.

Halfa lunged.

He grabbed Gronk by the shoulder and shoved him back hard—just in time.

The beam crashed down between them, embers exploding across the street.

Another scream. Weaker. Above them.

Halfa didn't wait. He ran, jumping over the collapsed beam, hoping the rest of the ceiling didn't come crashing down.

🔥

The fire swallowed him the moment he stepped through the ruined doorway.

Smoke choked the air, thick and greasy. Heat pressed in from all sides, alive and snarling. Halfa moved through it blindly, coughing, one arm over his mouth, the other outstretched.

He kicked through a half-collapsed chair, tripped over a fallen beam, and shoved aside a table already crackling with flame.

The stairs loomed ahead. Burning.

He took them two at a time.

At the top, curled near a window, trying to breathe, was a girl. Maybe twelve. Hair singed. Face streaked with soot and tears.

"I can't..." she rasped.

Halfa swept her into his arms.

Then the ceiling groaned.

A rafter cracked.

Snapped.

Fell.

He threw himself forward, and something inside him broke open.

Not a bone. Not a thought.

Something deeper.

The fire... *moved*.

It curled around him. Licked his arms, his shoulders. It should have burned. It should have ended him. But it didn't.

It *welcomed* him.

Heat pulsed under his skin. His heartbeat thundered, not in fear, but in tune with the flame.

The smoke parted.

The fire flinched.

And Halfa ran.

Down the stairs. Through the wreckage. Out into the street.

He stumbled into the open air, the girl still clutched in his arms. Smoke coiled off his back. His shirt had burned away. Ash streaked his skin, but he was unscathed.

The girl sobbed. But she was breathing.

Halfa collapsed to his knees, gently lowering her to the cobblestones.

Gronk stood frozen a few feet away. His eyes were wide. His mouth moved, but no words came.

"You were—" he finally managed, "—on fire. "

Halfa coughed. Wiped his mouth with the back of his hand. "She was inside. "

"You walked through it," Gronk said. "You *should be dead*. "

Halfa looked down at his arms. Smoke still curled from them like a ribbon. Beneath the grime, his skin shimmered red.

"I had to. "

For a moment, neither of them spoke. The girl coughed beside them, curling into herself, soot streaking her cheek.

Gronk stepped forward. His voice, when it came, was different. Small.

"You saved me. "

Halfa blinked. "What?"

"If you hadn't shoved me back when the fire jumped, I would've been under there. You didn't have to. "

Halfa didn't know what to say. It hadn't been a decision. Sheer movement. Just instinct.

"I couldn't let you burn," he said.

For the first time in a long time, Gronk looked at him with something close to softness.

But then his gaze shifted.

Down.

To Halfa's arms.

To the smoke, still rising.

"What the hell are you?" Gronk whispered.

Halfa didn't answer.

He didn't know.

The Watch bells rang in the distance—two quick peals, followed by silence. Somewhere, someone had seen the fire.

He wondered if they'd come for the girl. Or for him. Possibly both. Perhaps neither. Maybe they didn't know what he was, either.

Halfa and Gronk didn't wait to be found.

They disappeared into the alleys. The girl was left safely in the arms of a cloaked stranger who had rushed from a nearby door. She would live. That was enough.

The city swallowed them in shadow.

Once they were clear, they walked in silence. Not side by side. Not together. The Dock Ward loomed around them, wet with mist, flickering with torchlight. The air stank of seawater, burned wood, and oil.

Halfa's skin still steamed. His hands ached, not from injury, but from something deeper. Something shifting.

They stopped beneath the overhang of a broken stairwell where the smoke couldn't follow. Rain pattered above them, soft and cold.

Gronk lit a cigar with shaking fingers.

He took a long drag. Then another. Then looked at Halfa through the curl of grey.

"You saved me," he said again. This time, it sounded less like gratitude. More like confusion.

Halfa said nothing. He didn't know how to answer a thank you that came wrapped in fear.

"I've seen you take punches. I've seen you lift barrels no man should lift. But this..." Gronk's voice dropped. "You *walked through fire*. You didn't flinch. "

Halfa stared at the ground. A puddle there caught his reflection. The flicker in his eyes wasn't just torchlight. It was something deeper. Something inside.

"I didn't know I could," he said.

Gronk exhaled. "That makes it worse. "

The silence between them settled like ash.

Gronk asked again.

Not loud. Not angry.

Just a whisper. But one that would echo for weeks.

"What the hell are you?"

Halfa didn't answer.

He couldn't.

He looked away, jaw clenched, steam curling from his forearms like breath in the cold.

Gronk didn't press.

Didn't ask again.

Didn't walk beside him.

They moved on through the alleys. Not enemies.

But not brothers anymore, either.

◈

By the end of the month, Gronk was taking jobs without him.

Halfa didn't blame him. But every time he found the tenement quiet, it felt like the silence had teeth.

It wasn't loneliness, exactly. It was like something had been constructed and later dismantled.

No explanation. No goodbye. Just mornings when Halfa woke to find the corner where Gronk sometimes slept cold and empty, and evenings when Gronk returned with bruised knuckles and coin he didn't talk about.

Halfa didn't ask why.

Gronk didn't offer a reason.

And the silence between them grew. It wasn't loud, wasn't hostile. *There*.

Gronk became sharper. More dangerous. He laughed harder but smiled less. The jobs he brought back from the edges of the Ward reeked of desperation, coin for bruises, silver for silence, names that no one wanted to say aloud.

Halfa stayed quieter. The jobs he took were simpler. Delivery work. Load-bearing. Protection gigs that didn't ask questions. He didn't trust himself to do more. Not with the fire still curling in the back of his thoughts like a sleeping dog that had learned to bare its teeth.

It had hurt no one. Not yet. But he could feel it waking. Watching. Waiting for something. He just didn't know what.

◈

One evening, Halfa returned to the tenement behind the old smokehouse just after dusk. The sky was the colour of rust, and the streets smelled of stale wine and boiled fish. He passed Yetta's cart without stopping.

She didn't call out.

She watched him go with a squint and a sigh.

Inside, he sat alone on his bedding, threadbare blankets over cracked floorboards, and stared at his hands. They looked the same. Calloused. Broad. Steady.

But he remembered how they had glowed.

How the fire had coiled around his arms and not burned him.

It had opened a path through smoke and flame like it *knew* him.

He hadn't told Gronk.

Halfa had told no one.

But Gronk had seen it. Had seen *him*—and something in his eyes had changed.

They still walked the same streets. Drank the same water. Passed Yetta's cart on the same mornings.

But they no longer walked side by side.

Not because they couldn't.

Because they didn't know how.

It wasn't bitterness. Nor betrayal.

It was the space between lightning and thunder.

You hear one.

Then you wait for the other.

And sometimes... it never comes.

Fire and Joy

The fire had changed everything. No one said it out loud, but the shift was there, hanging in the alleys like smoke that wouldn't clear.

Halfa found an old warehouse dock, half-collapsed and empty, where the river lapped softly against the pylons. Rain fell in sheets, soaking him where he sat on a rusted anchor chain, but he didn't move.

His skin had cooled. His chest hadn't.

Not pain. Not fear. Something else.

He lifted his hand. No flame. No heat. The memory of it—real and alive, threaded through the space between his fingers. The fire hadn't fled.

It had moved with him.

He clenched his fist. Focused. Breathed in deep. Called to it. *Just a spark. Just a flicker.*

Nothing came.

He should've been afraid. Maybe he was. But more than anything, he felt the weight of it settle inside him. Not power. Just potential. Like a storm waiting for a name.

What if it came back? What if it didn't?

What the hell are you?

Gronk's words echoed, not as an accusation this time, but as something closer to the truth. Halfa didn't know.

But the fire did.

It had known him.

The rain eventually stopped.

The questions didn't.

Halfa stopped working. Not entirely, but enough for people to notice. Enough that regulars at Yetta's cart whispered questions and looked twice when he passed. He wandered more. Ate less. Slept with one eye open, half-expecting his hands to glow again in the dark.

They never did.

But he sensed it within him, like a serpent. Coiled and ready to strike. The heat. The tension. Fire that hadn't burned him, but hadn't left either. It was like holding your breath without realising, like walking through fog that pressed in even when it didn't touch you.

Gronk didn't stop. He surged. Louder. Bolder. Hungrier.

They met again in the alley behind the old smokehouse, back where it had all started. Same cracked stones. Same fish stink in the air. But nothing felt familiar anymore.

Halfa arrived late. His coat drawn tight against the sea wind, shoulders tense. Gronk was already there, pacing, eyes bright, grinning like he'd swallowed a lightning bolt and wanted the world to see it crackle through his teeth.

"They want me," he said before Halfa could speak. "The Blackjaw Syndicate. "

Halfa said nothing. He didn't need to ask who they were.

Everyone in the Ward knew Blackjaw. They scrawled their cracked jaw symbol on alley walls like a brand. Smuggling. Protection. Gambling. Debt collection. Where the Watch wouldn't go, Blackjaw already ruled.

"They want me as an enforcer," Gronk said, puffing up. "Top rank. A crew under me. Real coin. Proper respect. I wouldn't just be surviving anymore. I'd be *something*. "

"There's someone rising through their ranks," Gronk said, quieter now. "Name's Valka. She doesn't shout. Doesn't fight for the fun of it. But people clear a path when she enters a room. "

Halfa frowned. "Never heard of her. "

"You will," Gronk said. "Word is, she's cleaning up the Blackjaws. She is cutting out the loose ends, the hotheads, the casters. "

"Casters?"

Gronk nodded. "Mages've been turning up dead. Dock Ward, Gutbridge. No blood, no burn, and no trace. "

Halfa felt a flicker in his gut, but said nothing. He had seen the bodies, as had most of the Dock Ward.

"She's not one of them," Gronk continued. "Doesn't trust magic. Thinks it makes people lazy. Unstable. She says she needs muscle, and she'll deal with the mages. "

"And you're good with that?"

"I'm tired of waiting for scraps, Halfa. She's offering purpose. Power. Something bigger than ducking elbows in alleys. "

"She's offering a war," Halfa muttered.

"She's offering not to lose one. "

A beat passed. Gronk's smile faltered. Just a little.

"You think you're better than this?" he asked, voice sharpening. "I have done this for us. This is how we survive. "

"No," Halfa said quietly. "I just... don't want to become something I can't come back from. "

Gronk's jaw tightened. "You already are. "

Halfa looked at him, really looked, and saw something different. The grin was still there, but menacing now. Not joy. Not mischief. Hunger.

"You walked through fire," Gronk went on. "You carried that girl out like the flames *obeyed* you. You think the Watch is gonna see that and hand you a badge?"

"I didn't ask for the fire. "

"No. But you've *got* it. And I'm offering you a way to use it. "

Halfa looked down the alley, past the shadows. Torchlight flickered in the corner. Somewhere, someone played a flute—wild, fast, off-rhythm. It didn't belong here. It sounded like dancing, like joy where none should live.

"I'm not coming," he said.

Gronk was silent.

Then he breathed in deeply and stepped back. The grin didn't return. Something colder took its place. Disappointment. Maybe even grief.

"Then don't stop me. "

Halfa didn't move. Didn't speak.

He watched as Gronk turned and disappeared down the alley.

Behind him, painted fresh and red, was the Blackjaw sigil.

A crude, cracked jawbone. Still dripping.

A mark Gronk hadn't needed to speak to claim.

◈

After that confrontation, Halfa could feel his fire rising deep in his chest.

He found a stretch of rock near the edge of Grayspire's southern bluff that was flat, wind-swept and empty. The kind of place no one went to unless they wanted to be alone.

Halfa rolled up his sleeves. His palms were scarless. The soot had long since washed off. If not for Gronk's eyes, he might've convinced himself it never happened.

He clenched his fist. Focused.

Nothing.

He tried again—breath held, jaw tight, digging for whatever had cracked open that night.

Still nothing.

"Come on," he muttered. "I know you're in there. "

He punched the rock. Stone and pain.

He sat back, breathing hard, arms resting on his knees. The wind tugged at his coat, and for a moment, he thought he saw steam rising again. But it was only the mist off the cliffs.

"You showed up when I needed you," he whispered. "Is that it? Is that how this works?"

He let his head fall back, eyes closed.

"Do I have to be angry? Afraid? Am I supposed to burn to protect or burn to destroy?"

A long silence followed. No fire answered. No heat stirred.

Just the wind and the whisper of waves far below.

Halfa stood. Brushed the dust from his hands. "Fine," he muttered. "Be that way. "

But as he walked back toward the city, something stayed coiled in his chest.

Not gone.

Just waiting.

He didn't find fire. Only questions.

Was it blood? Magic? An inheritance he didn't know he'd earned? Or something worse, something broken open by grief?

◊

Halfa walked.

No goal. No route. Just movement.

His boots scuffed through puddles slick with fish oil and lamp soot. The Dock Ward was curling into itself for the night, smoke rising, voices dimming, shutters closing with the finality of survival.

Grayspire wasn't a city so much as a conversation. One shouted, whispered, and sang through alleys, arches, and underground halls. It had never belonged to one people, one god, or one king. It belonged to time and chaos. Every generation reshaped the city, each brick a testament to arguments settled in sweat and blood.

No one ever mapped Grayspire successfully. Not really. The alleys moved. The rooftops shifted. A cart could vanish for days and reappear on the wrong street. Locals didn't trust maps, they trusted their instincts, routines, and gossip. Especially in the Dock Ward, where knowing the right shortcut could mean the difference between safe passage and a blade in the dark.

Gronk's words echoed in his skull. Not sharp like knives. Heavy like chains.

"Then don't stop me. "

Halfa hadn't.

He just let him go.

So he walked. Out of the alleys, out of the stench, out of the places where his name carried weight or warning. His feet moved faster than his thoughts. Past crooked signs and flickering torches. Past familiar doorways and bruised memories.

Eventually, the Ward changed.

The air lightened. The streets widened.

Here in the Trades Ward, the city didn't slouch; it stood. Straight-backed. Lanterns dangled from wrought-iron balconies. Bright-painted shutters gleamed in the twilight. Flowers bloomed in boxes without being stolen. People moved as if the ground beneath them *belonged* to them.

Halfa wasn't built for painted corners and narrow lanes. Every step reminded Halfa that he belonged on docks and crates, not cobblestones and colourful buildings.

People claimed they built Grayspire on the skeleton of a long-dead god. Others claimed its foundations were older than the mountains. Whatever the truth, the city had moods. Fog hung heavier in certain corners. Streets curved where no architect had planned them. Doors slammed on windless days. And sometimes, if you listened, the cobblestones muttered.

He was about to turn back when a flicker caught his eye.

Not a torch. Not a Watch lantern.

A banner.

Silk, bright red and edged with gold, fluttered from a narrow archway nestled between a music shop and a dye vendor. A series of low walls enclosed a wide courtyard beyond it, open to the sky. More banners swayed overhead: saffron, indigo, and emerald, strung from corner posts and struts above the walls like festive sails. Tiny metal charms sewn into their hems sang when the wind passed.

Above the arch, a glass sigil caught the light.

A stylised flame wrapped in ribbons.

Thessira. Our Lady of Joy.

Halfa stopped.

At the far end, partially hidden behind flowering trellises, stood the temple itself, a simple stone structure with sunlight-painted glass. A violet door separates it from the rest of the world.

Music drifted from the courtyard. There were tambourines, hand drums, and flutes that moved like dancing feet. But not rigid. Not rehearsed. Alive. Messy. Beautiful.

He stepped closer, almost without meaning to.

From within, laughter spilled, uncontrolled and unapologetic. Not the mean, barked kind he knew from the docks, but something rounder. Lighter.

He watched a child spin barefoot across the threshold, arms flung wide. A woman nearly tripped over her own skirt, falling into the arms of a dwarf who caught her and dipped her low with a bow. Both of them were grinning like fools.

No guards. No coin demanded.

Just a violet door.

Halfa's shoulders dropped. His jaw loosened.

He didn't understand what this place was.

Only that it was not the world he came from.

So he stepped inside.

◈

No one flinched.

That was the first miracle.

He was a giant, grime still on his boots, soot on his cuffs, scars and silence in his stride, and no one backed away. No one whispered. No one braced.

A halfling woman in a red scarf walked up to him, smiled, and handed him a clay mug filled with something hot and spiced.

"Welcome home," she said simply, as if she meant it.

A human bard nodded to him mid-verse and changed his melody—slower, softer, tuned to Halfa's stillness. A barefoot dwarf spun past with a flurry of skirts and gave him a wink before vanishing into the rhythm again.

He was the only Goliath in the room.

And it didn't matter.

No one asked what he could lift.

No one asked what he could break.

No one asked where he'd come from.

They just... made space.

◈

Halfa found a corner and sat. He wrapped both hands around the mug like it might anchor him to the moment. The steam curled around his face. The heat touched his skin, but didn't feel like fire this time. It felt like peace.

The room pulsed with music. Unstructured, wild, joyful. Dancers tripped and caught each other and laughed at every stumble. Children dashed overhead, throwing flower petals off the balcony. A pair of old women clapped a hand drum and a pan out of sync and didn't care.

It was messy. Alive.

And Halfa didn't feel like a weapon here.

He felt... like someone.

He didn't know the name for this feeling. But he knew what it wasn't:

It wasn't fear. It wasn't duty. It wasn't survival.

It was joy.

Unafraid.

Unapologetic.

And for the first time in a long while... he didn't want to leave.

❦

The temple was quiet.

Not solemn. Not sacred.

Just... *quiet*.

The kind of stillness that made Halfa's breath feel loud. He stood near the back stairwell, boots already on, a satchel slung across his shoulder. He'd moved like a ghost. Avoided the creaky boards.

He had taken nothing that wasn't his.

Only what he brought in.

Which wasn't much.

He planned to leave before anyone realised just how much he didn't belong.

❦

The spiral candles burned low in the hall behind him. Their glow didn't reach the exit.

But the hallway light did.

And in that light stood Serelion. They were tall, spare, and quiet as the moon. Their elfin features were elegant but unreadable, with fine-boned edges and stillness that made others speak more softly.

They had sharp features and sharp eyes—but a voice like distant rain.

Elves in Grayspire were a quiet presence. Long-lived and long-watching, they didn't rush or rattle like the surrounding city. Most drifted through noble houses, artist enclaves, or the rarer temples—like ghosts that had lingered. They spoke softly, carried stillness, and saw the city as something temporary. Even its tragedies.

Serelion stood. Not blocking the door.

Just... waiting.

Halfa froze.

Serelion didn't speak.

They tilted their head slightly like a man watching an animal decide whether to bite or bolt.

"I wasn't—" Halfa started.

"You were," Serelion said, gently.

A pause.

Then: "But that's alright. "

Halfa shifted his weight.

He hadn't expected kindness. Or confrontation. He'd expected no one to notice.

Or care.

He met Serelion's gaze. "You're not going to stop me?"

"I don't believe in stopping people," Serelion said. "Not when they're walking away from pain. Only when they're running from themselves. "

Halfa looked away.

His hand flexed on the strap of his satchel.

Serelion stepped closer. Not enough to threaten. Just enough to be heard.

"We're not a prison, Halfa. You can leave any time. "

They smiled, small, tired.

"But if you walk out that door tonight, I hope it's because you *want to go somewhere*, not because you're afraid of what staying might make you feel. "

Halfa didn't answer.

He didn't move.

Not for a long time.

Eventually, Halfa turned around, moving back into the temple.

And Serelion didn't follow.

They just stood there, watching the moonlight fade across the tiles.

❦

The temple didn't change Halfa overnight.

Nothing ever had.

But it gave him space.

No one asked him to break anything.

No one paid him to threaten anyone.

No one feared him.

And no one expected him to prove he belonged.

Instead, they asked soft questions like,

"Would you like to help hang the silks?"

"Would you like to stir the incense pot?"

"Would you like to light the lanterns tonight?"

Halfa, always told, never asked, agreed. Every time.

❦

The next time Halfa visited the temple, rain slicked the stone steps of the temple, turning every surface into a trap for the careless. Halfa climbed anyway, slow, deliberate, letting the weight of the storm press into his shoulders. Thunder rolled above like an argument among gods.

The door to the temple creaked open before he touched it.

She stood just inside, lantern in hand, the flame haloing her face in gold and shadow. Young—maybe twenty, with a narrow half-elfin build and a cloak several sizes too big. Her hair was damp from the rain, braided tight and tied with a sea-blue cord. She didn't look surprised to see him. Just curious.

"You're soaked," she said. "Come in before you ruin the floors. "

Halfa blinked. Not the welcome he expected.

The temple interior was quiet but not empty. There were rows of flickering candles lining the walls, and the scent of sea salt incense clung to the air. Carvings of Thessira, goddess of joy, loomed from the stone.

She led him in without asking questions. No fear. No hesitation.

"I'm Marin," she said as they passed the shrine, still holding the lantern like it was part of her. "I help with the grounds, light the candles, and sweep the salt. You here to pray or to hide?"

"Neither," Halfa said. "Needed high ground. "

Marin glanced at him sideways. "Well. You picked the highest ground in Grayspire. "

She didn't ask about his name, scars, or the faint scent of burned leather clinging to him. She just walked, the lantern swinging low.

"Storm's not letting up tonight," she added. "You want dry clothes or something warm? Speak to Serelion. They have blankets stashed behind the altar. "

A pause.

"I won't tell them you tracked mud on the marble. But only if you wipe it up. "

Halfa cracked a smile despite himself. The girl had a spine. Grace, too. The kind born from walking on holy stone in bare feet.

◈

It was not a feast day, yet the temple radiated festivity.

Rain had come earlier, light and steady, but the courtyard stones were already drying. The air smelled of salt and oranges. Dozens of lanterns lined the outer walkway, their flames steady despite the wind. Halfa leaned against a pillar, half in shadow, watching her.

Marin moved from lantern to lantern, relighting the ones that had dimmed. She carried a bundle of reeds for wicking, a bit of flint, and a piece of dried lavender, which she kept behind her ear, "For blessings," she'd told him.

The others had gone inside. Evening meal. Chants. Marin had stayed behind.

And the light had stayed with her.

Halfa had watched lanterns sputter when Serelion passed by, blink out entirely when one of the junior acolytes walked too fast. But with Marin, they flared brighter. Not wildly. Not all at once. But. . . *noticeably*.

One by the prayer stones sparked to life before she even reached it. Another, near the herb garden, flickered until her hand brushed its base and settled into a warm, unwavering glow.

She didn't seem to notice.

She hummed her off-key melody, barefoot, smiling at nothing, completely unaware that the light bent toward her like flowers to the sun.

Halfa crossed his arms. Watched in silence.

"She loves you," he muttered under his breath.

Thessira—Lady of joy, laughter and holy mischief—favoured Marin. Halfa had no proof. But he could *feel* it.

The rain softened as Marin danced through it.

In how candles near her never guttered, even in the wind.

Her joy felt less like a choice, and more like a gift Thessira gave to the rest of them *through* her.

"You light this place better than the lanterns," he whispered, though she couldn't hear him.

Then, as if on cue, the last lantern on the far pillar flared.

Marin turned, saw him watching. Grinned.

"That one's always stubborn," she called. "Must be in a good mood tonight. "

Halfa smiled. Just a little. "Maybe it likes you," he said.

"Well," she replied, adjusting the lavender behind her ear, "who wouldn't?"

He swept floors with a broom way too small for him.

He strung banners from the rafters, his head brushing the ceiling beams.

He carried tables like they weighed nothing and set them down with a gentleness few expected from someone built like a stone wall.

Most nights, Halfa didn't make it back to the tenement.

The others started nodding when he passed.

Some smiled.

One morning, a young acolyte quietly handed him a flower, red with yellow tips. Halfa tucked it into his collar with a grin before darting away.

He left it there all day. Didn't know why. Just did.

Over time, Serelion taught him the temple's little rituals.

How to grind the incense into soft powder without letting it clump.

How to balance the lanterns so their flames danced without flickering.

To fold the silks so they fall like water.

They worked in silence often. Not the stiff kind. The kind showing silent communication.

One evening, as the sun bled orange over the temple's tiled roof, they sat together on a bench in the garden. The sound of music trickled through the shutters, faint tambourine beats, someone laughing off-key.

Halfa turned the lantern in his hands, watching the etched lines catch the light.

Serelion didn't speak for a while. Then: "Do you know what the spiral means?"

Halfa shook his head.

"It's not a path to the gods," Serelion said. "It's a path to yourself. Every step inward is a question. Every turn is an old hurt. The centre? That's the flame. And when you reach it, if you do. . . you bring something back with you, or leave something with the flame. Not treasure. Not answers. Just. . . peace. "

Halfa looked at the lantern again. "Does everyone make it to the centre?"

"No," Serelion said gently. "And not everyone walks out with the same light. "

They leaned back on the bench, hands resting in their lap. "Thessira doesn't promise safety. She doesn't promise ease. She offers joy, but only to those willing to carry it through the darkness. Not as a shield. As a torch. "

Halfa's fingers curled around the lantern's handle.

"Some fires destroy," Serelion said. "But the right one? It clears space. It leaves warmth. That's the fire we choose. That's Thessira's fire. "

Halfa didn't answer. He didn't know how.

So he just... lit the lantern.

And for the first time, he felt proud of the silence that followed.

☙

Children started trailing behind him like ducklings. They climbed his arms like trees. One painted a flower on the outer temple wall, wide and bright, right beside the entrance. No one erased it.

So Halfa began tucking a real one into his shirt each morning. A small thing. Red, yellow, or both. It made no sense.

But it felt like something true.

☙

It happened in the courtyard.

One of the Thessiran kids, Marell, the one with the cracked tooth and the permanent jam stains, was playing too close to the outer gate when the shouting started.

A merchant. Drunk, loud, angry. Spilling coin and fury in equal measure.

"Stupid little rat—watch where you run, gods-dammit!"

Marell backed up, stammering, hands up.

The man raised a hand.

And Halfa was already moving.

The violet door against the stone as Halfa stepped between them. No words. No warning. He grabbed the man's wrist mid-swing and twisted. Not hard. Not cruel. Just... final.

The man howled and dropped to a knee.

"You strike one more child in this district," Halfa said coldly, "and I'll take the hand that does it. "

A beat.

Then another.

Then silence.

The man scrambled away, cursing, disappearing into the street crowd without looking back.

Halfa stood motionless for a second.

Then turned to check on Marell.

And found Serelion watching from the doorway.

❦

They said nothing until they were alone in the hallway.

Serelion didn't shout.

Didn't scold.

They asked, softly: "Would you have hit him?"

Halfa didn't answer.

"You were right to step in," Serelion added. "But we don't protect joy with rage, Halfa. "

Halfa's jaw clenched. "He was going to hit a child. "

"Yes. And you stopped him. I'm proud of that. " Serelion's voice dropped further. "But joy is not protected when fear takes its place. "

Halfa looked down at his hand.

Still clenched.

Still ready.

"I don't know how to do this," he whispered.

Serelion smiled, tired, kind and unshaken. "Good. Then we can learn together. "

❦

Months later, Halfa started hearing whispers.

Low voices at street corners.

A name muttered in the shadows.

Rumours like oil slipping through cracks.

Gronk.

"He's the one who runs Fishbone Alley now. "

"He made a bookie eat his own dice. "

"I heard he took out two Watchmen and didn't flinch. "

At first, Halfa tried not to listen.

But the stories grew.

And the name spread.

Gronk was no longer a bruiser with fists and fury.

He was a figure. A symbol. A threat.

◈

The Blackjaw Syndicate had always been part of the Ward's bones, embedded in the rot and routine. But now, they weren't content with lurking. They were claiming.

They started subtly.

First, it was "protection" for food carts and market stalls—coin for "safety".

Then came the dice games in shuttered taverns.

Then, the debts.

Followed by the bodies.

Halfa saw the signs.

A crude cracked jaw sigil began appearing more frequently.

Etched into wood. Painted in fresh red. Burned into the sides of crates.

It didn't mark territory. It marked ownership.

◈

The temple was safe. A different world.

But even that safety couldn't make him deaf.

He heard merchants say they used to see "the two giants" together.

He heard a gambler mutter, "One of them vanished after a fire. The other took over the Wards. "

Halfa saw how the children stopped dancing as freely outside.

How Yetta's cart stayed open later than it should have, her eyes sharper than usual.

How Serelion folded their hands more often during prayer.

The Blackjaws were growing.

And Gronk, his Gronk, was their spearhead.

Halfa hadn't seen him in months.

But he saw his wake.

And it made something stir inside of him.

Responsibility. And fear.

It was a good evening.

One of those rare ones where the city seemed to exhale.

The bells of the Trades Ward chimed soft intervals as dusk bled into the sky. Children in ribbons chased each other through the temple courtyard, shrieking with laughter. The kitchen ovens glowed with warmth, and the scent of bread and cumin drifted through the air like a lullaby.

Halfa carried a basket through the garden filled with fresh herbs, two goat-cheese wheels and still-warm bread. One loaf was already missing a corner, thanks to a particularly sneaky halfling acolyte.

The grass felt soft under his boots.

The air was light.

For a moment, everything felt... earned.

He rounded the garden wall.

And stopped.

There, on the outer wall of the temple, beside the painted flower some child had lovingly daubed months ago, was a mark.

Fresh.

A cracked jaw.

Crimson. Still wet. Dripping like it had been painted with blood.

Halfa froze.

The basket sagged in his arms, bread tilting, herbs spilling. He didn't notice.

The wall had always been simple stone, aged, cracked and warm in the sun. And beside it, the bright red-and-yellow flower had bloomed defiantly against grey.

Now, that bloom was cut in half by violence.

It wasn't just a mark.

It was a message.

He saw it in the slant of the brush. In the dripping boldness. In the way, it sprawled too large for subtlety.

Gronk had done this.

Maybe not with his own hands, maybe not in the dead of night, but the message came from him just the same.

We haven't forgotten you.

You don't get to walk away.

We know where you sleep now.

Halfa's fingers clenched around the basket until the bread crust cracked.

Inside, the music swelled. A song about sunrise over the drowned city of Marrowdeep, high and lilting, sung by a child in a voice full of pride and too many missed notes.

Someone laughed in response. A drumbeat picked up. Feet thudded on the wood in a wild rhythm.

Behind him: Joy. In front of him: a warning.

The contrast made his throat close.

He turned away from the wall.

Didn't say a word. He didn't call for help. Didn't ask who'd seen it.

He just walked inside, the basket crushed in his arms.

❦

That night, he didn't dance.

Halfa sat cross-legged in the sanctuary's far corner on the smooth stone floor, arms resting on his knees, staring into the circle of candles laid out in evening prayer.

There were seven flames. One for each tenet of Thessira: joy, freedom, defiance, kindness, colour, courage, and choice.

Halfa didn't know which was which.

Didn't care.

He watched them flicker. Each flame was a little different. Some leaned left, some right. One sputtered in a draft. One stood impossibly still.

None of them went out.

He sat in that stillness, letting the warmth brush his cheeks, letting the questions swirl where answers wouldn't settle.

The cracked jaw on the wall had felt like a blade aimed at his centre.

But these flames, this silence—felt like a shield.

◈

A quiet rustle of fabric broke the stillness.

Serelion.

They didn't speak right away. They lowered themselves beside him with the same ease they did everything, knees folded, hands resting in their lap. Their saffron robes shimmered faintly in the candlelight, catching the flickers like silk set to song.

They didn't speak.

Didn't offer comfort.

Didn't pry.

Just breathed beside him.

It was enough.

Eventually, Serelion's voice came soft and steady.

"You're not only afraid for yourself."

Halfa didn't look over. Just nodded.

"I'm afraid for *them*."

His voice cracked at the edge.

Serelion nodded gently. "That is the right fear."

They let the silence sit for a moment before adding, "But even the right fear must be guided. Not ruled."

Halfa's jaw tightened. His hands curled slowly, quietly, into fists.

"If I don't act... if I wait too long...."

Serelion turned slightly toward him, their voice low and sure.

"You will act. When it's time. When it's yours to choose. But joy isn't weakness, Halfa. Rage without joy, that's wildfire. It consumes everything, even you."

Halfa blinked slowly, the candles doubling in his eyes.

"And what if... what if I can't come back from it?"

That was the truth of it. The fear inside the fear. That he might lose himself again, not in the heat of battle but in the burn after. That whatever fire lived inside him wasn't just a gift—but a hunger.

Serelion didn't hesitate.

They placed a hand gently on his forearm. Their skin was cool.

"Then we will build the path back with you. Brick by brick. Step by step. Together. "

Halfa didn't move. Didn't speak.

But something in him shifted—a breath he hadn't realised he was holding, released. A muscle unclenched. A root extended through the stone.

The candles flickered.

But none of them went out.

⸙

A few days later, Halfa journeyed through the city alone.

It wasn't a mission. He needed air that didn't carry incense and laughter. He needed to hear the city's breath again, to listen to the tension in the stones, the warnings in the wind.

He bought more lantern oil, tucked the bottles into a thick canvas satchel, and turned toward home.

That's when he saw it.

Tucked into a narrow side alley off Trades Street, wedged between a dying fruit stall and a leaning post for lost notices, was a battered food cart cloaked in patched canvas.

Steam rose from a dented pot.

The smell hit him first. Salt, spice, and something fried.

Then the voice.

"Hey, Big Flame. Still carrying flowers in your collar and lookin' like thunder in a tunic?"

Halfa blinked.

He turned.

Yetta.

The same halfling who'd once handed him warm loaves with a muttered, "Don't make me regret this. " Same dusting of flour on her sleeves. Same squint like she could size you up in two seconds and still be generous.

Halflings were Grayspire's glue. They ran kitchens, operated markets, whispered in the right ears. Rarely rulers, but always present. Underestimated but vital. In the Dock Ward, they were survival embodied. Sharp-eyed, fast-footed, and generous if you earned it. Like Yetta. Like the bread that had kept Halfa warm on frosty nights.

Yetta grinned up at him, ladle in hand, eyes sharp as ever.

"You gonna say hi or stare like a love-struck giant?"

Halfa smiled.

Small. But real.

"Hi, Yetta. "

She laughed, the sound crackling like a pan over fire.

"Heard rumours," she said, giving the pot a stir. "Bad ones. Got a few friends down by the docks still. One of 'em says the Blackjaws have a new muscle man. That wouldn't be your old shadow, would it?"

Halfa's jaw tightened.

He nodded once.

Yetta's smile dimmed, but only slightly.

"You watching your back?"

"Trying. "

She leaned forward, dropping her voice. It didn't lose its humour, but something *steelier* threaded through it.

"Well, listen close. I know things. Quiet alleys. Safe rooftops. Which carts can carry a ten-foot lump across the harbour without drawing eyes. You need to vanish? I can make it happen. "

Halfa blinked. "Why are you telling me this?"

Yetta didn't answer immediately.

She turned the flame under the pot down, then ladled a dumpling into a scrap of cloth and handed it to him.

Still hot. Still made with care.

Then she met his eyes.

"Because I've seen fire before. The kind that burns and the kind that cleanses. "

She shrugged.

"You're both. And I like the second kind better. "

She waved him off before he could speak.

"Now get outta here before I get sentimental. I've got stew to stir and people to intimidate. "

Halfa didn't argue.

He held the dumpling like it was something precious, nodded once, and turned back toward the temple.

The warmth lingered in his hands long after he'd eaten it.

◈

The cracked jaw had been scrubbed off the temple wall.

Someone had taken a stiff brush and soap to it. The red was gone. The lines blurred. But the stain remained.

The stone still held the memory.

Halfa stood before it now, arms folded across his chest, head bowed slightly. The late-afternoon light spilled through the garden trees, casting long golden shadows across the stone. The flower beside the mark still bloomed, a little bruised, a little bent, but whole.

Like him.

Serelion stepped beside him, folding their hands behind their back. They didn't speak right away.

They rarely did.

"They're getting close," Halfa said.

Serelion nodded.

"Yes. "

Halfa shifted his weight, the gravel crunching underfoot.

"What happens when they get here?"

Serelion's gaze didn't leave the stone.

"Then we show them that joy doesn't kneel. "

A soft breeze stirred the garden silks above them. The flower at the base of the wall shivered but didn't fall.

He couldn't sleep.

Halfa couldn't sleep.

The temple walls were too still. Too warm. Every creak of wood or breath of wind stirred his instincts, expecting fists, fire, or footsteps. But there were none. Just silence. The kind he didn't trust yet.

He found himself in the main hall, pacing slow circles around the spiral on the floor. His steps were bare. The cool stone calmed something in his heels, even as his chest stayed tight. He traced the lines of the spiral with his eyes like it might give him an answer if he walked it long enough.

A match struck behind him.

Marin stood there, a small beeswax candle between her fingers. She stepped into the hall without speaking. Didn't ask what he was doing. She didn't need to.

She knelt and placed the candle at the outer edge of the spiral.

Halfa frowned. "Who for?"

"No one," she said. "Sometimes joy doesn't need a reason. "

He watched her sit cross-legged beside it. The flame flickered gold against her cheeks.

"You ever wonder," she asked softly, "if the fire inside you is meant for burning... or warming?"

Halfa didn't answer right away. He stared at the candle. "I'm not sure. " Thoughts of his own literal fire inside come to mind.

"Maybe understanding *is* the use. " She smiled. "Some fires don't want to hurt anyone. They just want to glow. "

Silence again.

Halfa settled.

Not to pray. Not to speak.

To be by a small flame that didn't need a reason to burn.

The Cost of Peace

It arrived just after dawn. Slipped through the temple's front gate by a man whose eyes never stopped moving.

He was small and sharp-eyed, dressed in neat clothes stained enough to pass unnoticed. The only thing remarkable about him was his hands, inked from knuckle to wrist with symbols, dots, and lines arranged in a code anyone from the Dock Ward would recognise.

Blackjaw tattoos.

He didn't speak. Bowed slightly, handed a folded letter to one of the temple keepers, and walked off into the fog.

◈

The parchment was thick. Clean. Expensive.

The handwriting was elegant, slow, deliberate, looped like someone had practiced the art of seeming respectful.

The message was brief.

To the Joyful Custodians of Thessira's Temple,

We respect your space and your sanctity.

The Blackjaw Syndicate believes joy should flourish, even in a hard world. But the streets are changing. Gangs, merchants, and jealous temples are all sniffing at your steps.

Let us offer you our protection.

One gold per tenday.

In exchange, you stay safe.

Your joy remains undisturbed.

Consider it a tithe for peace.
In Joy and Strength,
Gronk

◊

After the reading, a thick silence filled the room.

They sat in the upper garden, gathered around the stone prayer table beneath the hanging lanterns. Early sunlight filtered through the silk banners overhead, casting saffron and rose-coloured shadows over the paper like it was softening the blow.

It didn't.

Several of the temple's elders frowned.

One of the younger acolytes, still new, still unsure, rubbed at their arms and asked what everyone else was thinking.

"Is it a threat?"

"It's a performance," Serelion said, folding the letter neatly along its crease and setting it aside like it was nothing more than a flyer for a local bakery. "One designed to look like generosity. "

Their voice was calm. Even. But Halfa saw the tension in their fingers.

"And it's signed Gronk," someone muttered.

Halfa's heart didn't skip.

It *tightened*.

He had tried not to think of Gronk for the last few weeks. He wasn't afraid of him, but he felt that perhaps he was afraid of being left behind. He was fearful that he had just stood still while the world moved on without him.

He hadn't seen the name in writing before. Somehow, that made it worse. More final. Like carving a childhood memory into stone and watching it twist.

Peering up at him from the edge of the table was a halfling girl, about twelve, her eyes wide with wonder.

"He's your friend, isn't he?" she asked.

Halfa didn't answer.

Not yes. Not no.

He watched the wind catch the edge of the parchment and lift it slightly, just enough for the light to catch the signature at the bottom.

In Joy and Strength.

It was mockery.

Or maybe it wasn't.

Perhaps, somehow, Gronk still believed it.

That thought chilled Halfa more than the threat itself.

A little later, in the mid-courtyard, Halfa knelt beside a cracked stone bench. One leg had splintered near the base, a slow crumble from too many rainy seasons.

Marin crouched opposite, inspecting the damage with her usual scrunched-nose focus. She tapped the fracture with a knuckle.

"We could patch it," she said.

Halfa shook his head. "Won't hold. "

She gave him a look. "Everything's cracked, Halfa. Doesn't mean you throw it out. "

"If the base is broken, the weight wins," he said. "You tear it down. Build new. "

Marin ran her fingers along the break, tracing the fault line. "Some cracks can still hold joy. "

He huffed softly. "You sound like Serelion. "

"Then maybe I'm learning. "

She reached for the mortar, scooping a generous dollop into the groove. Halfa didn't stop her. He handed her a trowel instead.

They worked in silence, side by side. Not hurried. Not solemn. Steady.

As the afternoon light slanted through the prayer flags overhead, Marin said, "This is what peace feels like, you know. "

Halfa glanced at her.

"Fixing something," she said. "Together. Not because it's perfect. Just because it's worth the effort. "

He didn't reply. But he stayed until the mortar set. Fixing now seemed a lot better than tearing down.

Marin squinted at the broken bench like it had insulted her ancestors.

"Was this always crooked?"

Halfa leaned forward. "Or maybe the rest of the world tilted. "

"Very philosophical," she muttered, brushing stone dust off her hands.

They knelt together, mortar bucket between them. Halfa stirred it while Marin checked the sealant lines with her thumb.

"You've done this before," he said.

"Used to rebuild broken things. Before I joined the temple. "

She hesitated. "Turns out joy still needs hammers sometimes. "

He passed her the trowel.

"You think it'll hold?" he asked.

"The bench?" She shrugged. "Maybe. "

She tapped her chest. "But it's not really about benches, is it?"

He didn't answer. She didn't expect him to.

A quiet pause passed, filled with birdsong and grit.

"I used to think I had to fix everything alone," Marin whispered. "Now I think... maybe it's enough just to try. With someone who stays. "

They sat a while longer, letting the stone settle and the silence stretch. Then Marin stood, brushing grit from her hands.

"Come on," she said. "You look like you haven't eaten since the last fire. "

Halfa gave her a look. She raised an eyebrow. "There's a vendor near the lantern square who doesn't overcharge for soup. If we walk fast, we might beat the evening crowds. "

He didn't argue. He just followed.

◊

The streets were quieter this time of night—Grayspire asleep under a sky too big for its own good. Rain had threatened all afternoon, but never quite committed. The stones were damp. The alleys hummed.

Halfa kept pace beside her, hands in his coat, shoulders hunched more from habit than cold.

"You're too tall to sulk," Marin said. "Makes it look like the buildings offended you. "

Halfa grunted.

Yetta's cart sat at the corner of Benthook and Sailor's Gate, where it always did when the city hadn't outlawed it *this week*. The halfling stood behind the griddle, sleeves rolled high, apron already stained with at least five sauces and one possible magical spill.

She spotted them and grinned. "Well, look what the storm washed in. You two bring coin, or just opinions?"

"I brought regret," Marin said. "And a stomach. "

"That'll do. "

Halfa watched quietly as Marin leaned on the cart's edge, ordering without looking at the menu.

"Two onion pies. One with extra pepper root. And none of that vinegar relish this time, or I swear I'll bless your oil to burn everything. "

Yetta winked. "You love the relish. "

"I *tolerate* the relish. Like I tolerate this city. "

Halfa tilted his head. "You know Yetta too?"

Marin smirked. "Everyone knows Yetta. And anyone with taste comes back. "

Yetta cackled. "I'm a culinary institution. Ask your stomach in an hour. "

She dropped a coin with flair. "And he's paying. "

Halfa blinked. "I am?"

"You owe me for that hole you punched in the pantry wall. For emotional damages. "

Halfa sighed and dropped a second coin beside hers.

Yetta snatched both. "Now *that's* divine partnership. "

They ate on a barrel nearby—Halfa crouched, Marin perched on the lid like a gargoyle in a scarf.

"I don't get it," Halfa said eventually, between bites.

Marin didn't look up. "You're going to have to narrow that down, sweeting. "

"You run a temple. You talk about joy and light. But you swear like a dockhand and threaten soup carts. "

Marin snorted. "That *is* joy. You think Thessira wants smiling statues and dancing bards all the time? Joy's messy. Loud. Sometimes it bites. Sometimes it's hot food when you didn't ask for it, and sometimes it's making sure the right people get punched. "

Halfa considered this.

"I'm good at the punching part. "

Marin smiled, soft and dangerous. "I know. "

Yetta passed by, dropping an extra sauce pouch in Halfa's lap when Marin wasn't looking.

"For your friend," she whispered. "She needs it. "

Halfa stared at it.

Then emptied it into Marin's pie.

She paused.

Raised an eyebrow.

Took a bite.

"...still hate it," she muttered.

Halfa shrugged. "Still yours. "

They ate, they laughed, and for a little while, the threat waiting beyond the temple walls felt a little further away.

◊

Gronk didn't send another letter.

Two nights after the parchment arrived, the temple's evening celebration was in full rhythm with flutes whirling through candlelight, laughter rising like smoke from the garden fires and a circle of dancers spinning in the sanctuary's open court. The scent of spiced tea and orange peel lingered in the air.

And then....

The doors opened.

Not kicked.

Not slammed.

Just... opened.

Gronk entered; he projected an air of entitlement.

He had changed little, and somehow, that made it worse.

Broad-shouldered, still cocky, still grinning like he knew how this was going to end. But now there was a cracked jawbone inked on his left shoulder, outlined in black and silver. It peeked from beneath the cuff of his sleeveless coat, flashing like a dare.

He was flanked by two men, silent, lean, all scars and tension. Each wore leather vests marked with subtle signs of allegiance: scratched symbols, club hilts, bone-threaded cuffs.

They didn't look at the art on the walls.

Didn't notice the warmth of the hanging silks.

Didn't smile.

◊

In the garden, Halfa was lighting candles beneath the columbine arch when he heard his name.

"Halfa!" Gronk's voice echoed across the temple like a laugh at a funeral. "You still sweeping floors in this little joy box?"

Halfa turned.

The wind shifted. The candle's flame in his hand flickered, then snuffed out.

Gronk opened his arms like they were brothers at a reunion.

"There he is. The big man himself. "

Halfa didn't smile. Didn't move.

Gronk looked around like he was shopping.

"Nice place," he said, turning in a slow circle. "I get it now. It's clean. It's bright. Pretty people dancing. No one screaming. " He glanced at one of his men. "Bet the food's even better than fish gut stew. "

He was toying. Playing it all off as a joke. Making everyone a witness.

Marin stepped forward, barely waist-height to Gronk, her voice clear and tight.

"This is a place of peace. If you're here to threaten—"

"Threaten?" Gronk put a hand to his heart. "Lady, I'm protecting you. "

Gronk turned back to Halfa.

"You think I'd let any other crew shake down your little candle club? No chance. I got my boys watching the alleys. Cleaning up the filth. You should thank me. "

Halfa's voice came low. "We didn't ask. "

For the first time, Gronk's grin slipped. Just a fraction. "You didn't have to," he said.

The garden quieted. The music drifted softer from within the temple.

For a heartbeat, no one spoke.

Then Gronk's tone shifted, like he was trying to find something buried in the silence.

"I miss this," he said. "Miss you. "

He gestured vaguely between them.

"Don't you?"

Halfa looked at him.

There were a hundred answers in his chest.

None came to his lips.

What could he say?

Yes?

No?

Please stop before I have to stop you?

All he managed was, "Why are you doing this?"

Gronk stepped closer.

Close enough that Halfa could see the line of an old scar on his jaw. One Halfa had given him. One they'd laughed about over stolen bread and gutter wine.

His voice dropped. Low. Honest.

"Because this world doesn't give peace for free. If you want joy to last, someone's gotta bleed for it. I'm just making sure you don't have to. "

Halfa felt the rage again.

Not wild this time.

Controlled.

The fire, contained like a shut furnace, licks the edges without spilling.

"You think this protects me?"

"I think it could," Gronk said. "If you let it. "

And then there it was—something real in his eyes. Just for a moment. A flicker of the boy from the alley. The one who split loaves with him. The one who stood shoulder to shoulder during a dozen meaningless jobs and made them mean something just by being there.

That boy was still in there. The boy who didn't see power as the only way to survive.

Buried. But breathing.

Halfa didn't move.

Didn't speak.

Didn't stop him.

Gronk clapped him on the shoulder. Hard.

"You'll come around," he said.

Then he turned.

Walked back the way he came.

"You always do. "

His two men followed—silent wolves behind a smiling king.

◈

After Gronk left, the tension didn't break.

It settled.

Like dust. Like ash. Similar to a bruise that you don't notice until hours later when you try to move.

The music inside the temple resumed after a pause, but softer. Uneven. Like someone had forgotten the rhythm. The dancers returned to their steps, but the laughter that followed felt thinner.

Halfa remained in the garden.

He stood exactly where Gronk had left him, shoulder still tingling from the weight of that final clap—friendly, performative, patronising.

Final.

He didn't go back inside.

The others trickled past him. Acolytes murmuring nervously. A child clutching a flower. A pair of elders were deep in hushed conversation, glancing his way and not quite hiding it.

No one asked him what had happened.

No one had to.

The wind stirred the garden's hanging silks.

A lantern rattled against its chain.

A petal blew across the path.

The columbine arch, still half-lit with candles, swayed slightly with the breeze.

Halfa finally moved.

He crossed the garden slowly, boots quiet on the stones, and sat on the low bench beside the central fountain. His reflection rippled in the water, a broad face, tired eyes, shoulders pulled tight with restraint.

He stared at it.

The face of someone who hadn't fought.

Who had let a friend walk in and bend peace like it was his to shape.

And hadn't stopped it.

But what would fighting have meant?

A public brawl in the temple courtyard?

Fists against an old friend's grin?

Fire rising in the place that had taught him joy, and perhaps control?

No.

Not yet.

Halfa closed his eyes and leaned back.

The stone was cold beneath him. The night settling in. Rage still there, but quieter now. Like a tide pulled out, waiting to return.

Not washed away.

Just... held.

He didn't light another candle.

Didn't speak a word.

He just sat with it.

Gronk's words, like lingering smoke, remained.

"You'll come around. "

He watched his oldest friend walk away, not like a stranger, but like someone who had rewritten the script and expected Halfa to follow. For a breath, Halfa wanted to call out. Say something. Anything. But what do you say to someone who has already rewritten your ending?

The courtyard emptied, but Halfa stayed rooted, staring at the place where Gronk had vanished into the fog. The silence pressed in. At last, without knowing if he was running toward something or away from it, Halfa made his way to the rooftop, the only place high enough to breathe.

◈

Marin found him on the roof.

He wasn't hiding, not exactly. Just staring out over Grayspire's skyline like it had insulted him.

Marin hauled herself up the ladder behind the chapel wall, her scarf flapping in the sea breeze like a defiant banner.

"You keep glowering at the moon like that," she said, "and it might file a complaint. "

Halfa didn't answer.

She didn't expect him to.

She sat beside him anyway. Legs crossed. Pulled a battered flask from her belt and took a sip before offering it to him.

He took it. Didn't drink.

She snorted. "Afraid I poisoned it?"

"No," he said. "Just don't want to owe you twice in one day. "

"Smart boy. "

Among Goliaths, strength was proven on the climb, not in the sitting. Mountains were for standing on, not reflecting. They proved strength through challenge, not stillness. But Halfa had never lived on a mountain. He'd learned to find height wherever he could. Rooftops, watchtowers, temple domes. Places where he could observe the world he didn't understand, and wonder if there was still a place for him inside it.

The city below sparkled, soft torchlight and festival strings. Laughter carried up like incense on the wind. Somewhere, a band played out of tune. Fireworks popped like far-off thunder.

Somewhere in the distance, a bell rang three times, not the hour bell, but the long, flat clang of the Daggerpull Watchtower. It meant something had gone wrong near the river. No one looked up anymore. In Grayspire, alarms were background music.

Marin watched it all for a while.

Then: "You ever wonder why a Joy Goddess needs guards?"

Halfa glanced at her. "No. "

"Well, she does. " She leaned back on her elbows. "Because joy's not a song. Not really. It's a rebellion. A fight. A middle finger to every shadow that says you're not allowed to feel alive. "

Halfa looked away.

"Joy," she said, "is what you cling to when everything else is burning. "

He didn't respond.

But she could see the way his jaw shifted.

"People think I'm soft," Marin muttered. "But you've never seen me take someone's kneecaps for threatening my temple's pantry. "

Halfa snorted.

It was small. Barely audible.

But it was there.

Marin looked at him sideways.

"You're built for war," she said. "But that doesn't mean it's the only thing you're good for. "

He said nothing.

And that, too, was an answer.

⨐

There was music in the courtyard.

Not the kind that demanded dancing, just soft flutes and a worn tambourine tapping out a rhythm that pulsed like a quiet heart. The sky above the temple of Thessira was ink-dark, scattered with stars. Lanterns swayed between the columns, their golden light flickering across silk banners that hadn't yet caught flame.

Halfa sat at the edge of the garden, elbows resting on his knees. Watching.

Marin was lighting lanterns along the walkway. Her steps were light, her robe trailing behind her like a wind-drawn thread. She hummed a half-melody, off-key but confident, stopping now and then to adjust the angle of a flame so it would dance right.

She caught his gaze at one point and grinned. Just a flash of teeth in the lantern glow.

He smiled back.

He wasn't sure what this was between them, but it felt like something trying to grow in burned soil. Maybe foolish. Maybe needed.

She didn't wave. She didn't need to. That smile had become a kind of greeting between them. One that said: *We're still here.*

She made her way over, barefoot and quiet, holding an unlit lantern in both hands.

"This one's stubborn," she said, lifting it. "I've tried three matches. Nothing. " A pause. "Think you've got anything warmer?"

He raised an eyebrow. He had never seen her not be able to light a lantern. "You want me to burn the temple down?"

She gave him a look. "Just a lantern. "

He hesitated.

She waited.

Halfa looked at the little brass lamp, then at her face, calm, open, utterly unafraid.

"Alright," he said. "I'll try. "

He cupped his hand beneath the wick. Closed his eyes. And this time, he didn't search for anger.

He thought of the music.

The off-key humming.

The flower she once tucked behind his ear.

The smile she gave him in passing, like it belonged to him and no one else.

Warmth stirred in his chest. A gentle heat. Not rage.

Joy.

A thin ribbon of fire shimmered to life in his palm.

Marin's breath caught—surprise flickering across her face—but she didn't move.

She held steady, eyes wide, watching as the lantern bloomed into light.

When he looked up, she was smiling again. Braver now. Warmer.

"I knew it," she breathed. "You're blessed. "

Then, without warning, she leaned forward and cupped his cheek in one hand.

A brief touch. Soft. Sun-warm.

Before he could say anything, she stood and turned away—walking back into the night, holding the lantern like it was sacred.

Halfa sat in the quiet.

Cheek tingling.

Heart, too full for words.

He sat there long after her lantern light disappeared into the shadows.

The flame was gone, but a strange ache settled behind his eyes, like heat pressed too long against stone.

He flexed his hand. No glow. No burn.

Sometimes he wondered if the fire had always been there, passed down like old bone or blood. A birthright he didn't ask for, but couldn't give back. At other times, it felt like a curse earned through choice alone. He hadn't decided which version scared him more.

A slight tremor he couldn't explain.

He shook it off. Told himself it was nothing.

But part of him wondered, how much of me does it take?

$$\oint$$

The next morning, Halfa rose early. He had slept little.

The fire inside him wasn't gone, it never was. But last night it had curled low instead of rising. And in that quiet, he'd found something steadier than rage.

Resolve.

He walked along the outer wall before the sun crested the rooftops. The stain where the cracked jaw had been painted was fading, scrubbed twice already. But the grooves in the stone still remembered.

Every Blackjaw mark was a promise: this space has been seen, judged, and priced. And if peace refused to pay, war would come dressed in business. The Syndicate didn't break walls first. It broke rhythms. Made deliveries run late. People went missing. Made fear feel like an accident until it didn't.

$$\oint$$

Later, in the kitchen, Halfa found Bilbin muttering to himself over a cauldron of onion stew. Bilbin was the temple's cook.

The halfling was barely four feet tall, with a nose like a beak and tufts of white hair that shot out like dandelion fluff. Age hadn't softened him—it had just made him harder to argue with.

He stood on his step stool, his hand awkwardly steadying a chopping board. A thick cloth wrapped around his hand. It looked fresh.

"Damn turnips," he muttered when Halfa approached. "Always been the rebellious type."

Halfa didn't respond.

He reached out, and gently lifted Bilbin's hand.

The gnome swatted him away, more pride than pain.

"I slipped," he said. "Chopping too fast. No mystery. "

Halfa said nothing. Just waited.

Bilbin grumbled and leaned back against the spice shelf.

"They came at night," he muttered. "Two of them. Said I was late with my coin. Said maybe my fingers worked better than my memory. "

"Blackjaws?"

Bilbin didn't confirm. Didn't have to.

"Told me not to tell anyone. Said it was just business. Said I was lucky they left me my hands at all. "

Halfa exhaled slowly.

"Why didn't you tell Serelion?"

"No. This temple's peace matters more than my hand. " He paused. "You're angry. I can see it in your shoulders. "

Halfa looked at him. Really looked. "I am angry. But not at you. "

He remembered the tavern, the first time the fire had flared without warning, when power had felt like panic and awe at once.

He remembered the bluff, fists raw from stone, waiting for a flame that never came. Wondering why it had chosen him.

And now he knew.

It hadn't chosen him for revenge. It hadn't chosen him for rage.

It had chosen him for this.

For bruised hands and brave silences.

For a temple stubborn enough to dare kindness.

When Joy Burns

Morning light spilled through the garden silks, soft and golden. The temple was stirring, quiet conversations, aromas of warm bread drifting from the kitchen and tambourine taps echoing from the sanctuary like the city's heartbeat had softened.

Halfa crouched beside a boy of maybe eight, his fingers carefully guiding the child's small hands as they lit a new lantern.

"Hold it steady," Halfa said, voice gentle.

The boy nodded, tongue peeking from his mouth in concentration. The flame caught, flickered to life. He beamed.

"I did it!"

Halfa gave a rare half-smile and nodded. "You did. "

Behind them, Bilbin was humming in the kitchen, the familiar staccato clatter of his spoon tapping the cauldron. "Not too much garlic," he warned the pot. "We're feeding followers of joy, not scaring off the next batch of acolytes. "

From the garden wall, Marin called over, "Scaring them might be better for them than you feeding them!"

Bilbin snorted.

The temple laughed—a ripple of sound, small and shared.

Marin danced barefoot through the garden path with a ribbon in each hand, trailing colour behind her. The child ran after her, the lantern forgotten in favour of play.

Halfa sat still for a moment longer, letting the warmth seep into his shoulders. The kind of morning that demanded nothing from him. The kind that felt earned.

He didn't know how long it would last. Maybe an hour. Maybe a day. But he knew better than to believe it would stay untouched.

There was always something coming. That was his understanding of life.

Still, for that moment, he let himself want it. Not just the quiet. But the right to protect it.

The coin was small.

A single gold piece.

But it clinked too loud when Serelion placed it in the offering bowl.

It echoed in the hall like a judgment.

The leaders of the temple stood in a quiet half-circle near the altar. The morning light had turned sharp through the high windows, with less warmth, and more blade.

"It's a test," Serelion said, their voice calm but tight. "Not a surrender. "

They let the bowl sit there, untouched, as if hoping someone might knock it over and end the conversation.

No one did.

Halfa leaned against the far wall, arms crossed, the shadows deep across his face.

The parchment still sat folded on the altar behind Serelion. He didn't need to look at it. He knew every word by heart now.

Let us offer you our protection... One gold per tenday... In exchange, you stay safe... Your joy remains undisturbed.

Acolytes murmured behind him, their worried tones seeping through.

"It's just for now. "

"We're not the Watch, we can't fight them. "

"Serelion knows what they're doing. "

"It's only one coin. "

Only.

That word itched like grit in Halfa's teeth.

"They don't want gold," he said, finally.

The room went still.

"They want obedience. The coin is just how they measure it. "

Serelion didn't argue. They nodded, folding their hands in front of them like someone preparing for the weather.

"And if we refuse," they said softly, "then they take more than gold. They take people. And they'll start with the quiet ones. The kind ones. "

"Let them believe we are harmless," Serelion said. "Let us protect ourselves with patience. "

Halfa didn't respond.

He stared at the coin.

Its surface caught the sunlight and shimmered, bright and clean.

But to Halfa, it already looked tarnished.

◈

Later that day, a man in a grey coat came by. One of the quiet ones. A Blackjaw ledger-man.

He didn't speak.

Just nodded once and took the bowl.

The coin was gone.

And the temple felt different.

Not louder.

Not colder.

Just... *less*.

As if a thread had snapped somewhere beneath the walls, and no one was brave enough to ask what it had been holding up.

Serelion said nothing as they took the bowl. But later, Halfa caught them alone in the sanctuary, rearranging the prayer silks not for worship, but for distraction. Their movements were too careful. Too precise. Like someone trying to keep their hands busy so they wouldn't shake.

◈

They started showing up near dusk.

Two men. It was always the same two.

One leaned against the outer temple wall like he owned the stones, idly flicking a small knife open and closed. The blade clicked with a rhythm too regular to be random.

Click.

Click.

Click.

The other chewed on something red, and spat it out onto the cobblestones, leaving stains like little wounds.

They said they were there for protection. That word again.

But they never looked at the violet door.

They looked at the dancers.

The acolytes.

The young ones.

Marin flinched when she passed them. So did others. Halfa saw it. The way shoulders hunched. The way eyes dropped. Joy grew quieter, not snuffed out, but shaded. The temple was still singing, just *not as loud.*

◊

Halfa stood in the garden one evening, arms crossed, watching them over the archway wall.

They didn't know he could see them from this angle.

The knife flicked.

The red-stained man laughed at something Halfa couldn't hear.

And Halfa's hands curled into fists.

He didn't speak.

Not yet.

◊

That night, after the last candle was lit, he found Serelion in the sanctuary, refolding silks with quiet care.

"They're watching," Halfa said.

Serelion didn't ask who. They only sighed.

"I know. "

"They're not guards. They're circling. "

"Yes. "

"Then why…" Halfa stepped closer, fire stirring low in his chest. "Why aren't we doing something?"

Serelion's fingers paused, holding the fold in place like it was a fragile truth.

"Because lashing out in anger is to let them choose the moment. "

Halfa stared at them. "They already chose it. They're hurting people. "

"Not here," Serelion said. "Not yet. The temple is still a sanctuary. And if we burn the world down now… do you think the rest will run?"

Halfa said nothing.

Because he didn't know.

But his silence wasn't agreement.

It was something darker.

Something growing teeth.

He stepped away from the silks.

The air around him felt heavier than fire.

"They're not going to stop," he said.

Serelion looked at him with tired eyes.

"No. They won't. "

They folded the last silk and set it on the altar.

"But we will choose when to step forward, and how. "

◆

The garden was nearly dark.

The last few lanterns burning low. A hush had fallen over the temple, late enough that the children were asleep, early enough that the musicians hadn't begun tuning again.

Halfa was finishing the final loop of his patrol around the outer walkway when he heard it—

a breath that didn't belong.

A quiet, broken exhale.

He turned the corner and stopped.

Marin stood beneath the columbine arch, backlit by the last of the lantern light.

Her tunic was torn at the shoulder.

Her lip split and crusted with drying blood.

Her hands trembled so violently she couldn't hold the lantern she was meant to light. It lay at her feet, unbroken, but cold.

Halfa's heart clenched.

Not in shock.

Not in rage.

Guilt.

She wasn't just another acolyte. At the temple, she was the first person to call him a friend and mean it without hesitation. She danced barefoot in the courtyard. Sang off-key and too loud during evening prayers. Gave him wildflowers wrapped in broadcloth and told him he needed "more colour" in his life.

She was light; in a place that gave him permission to stop burning.

She *knew* him. She knew his fire, had guessed it, somehow.

And now she was shaking.

Because he hadn't stopped them.

He'd promised himself this temple would stay safe. That joy would hold here.

And now joy had a split lip.

He remembered fire once, as a child. Not in his hands. In the city. A butcher's shop burned after a gang dispute. He remembered the way the light danced against brick, the way the grownups didn't scream, just... moved slower. As if the fire had already decided who mattered. That was the first time he felt fear and awe braided together.

Halfa moved toward her slowly.

"Marin.... "

She didn't flinch. Didn't meet his eyes.

"They cornered me," she whispered.

Just those three words.

She didn't need to say more.

She didn't need to say *who*.

He already knew.

The fire didn't ignite, not yet.

But something inside him clicked.

Like a pressure plate.

Like a trigger.

His hands were already curling into fists, but he kept his voice soft.

"You're safe now," he said.

Marin nodded once. A small, jagged motion.

Then, wordlessly, she stepped away, leaving the lantern behind.

She didn't cry.

She didn't stumble.

She just moved like someone trying not to shatter.

Halfa watched her go.

And in the silence that followed, he looked down at the unlit lantern on the stone path.

He didn't pick it up.

❦

The rage didn't come with fire. Not yet. But it curled inside him like smoke—low and thick, coiling around his ribs. It whispered to him with Serelion's calm and Marin's sharpness: *If you let this stand, she'll never laugh again.* Not here. Not anywhere.

He turned toward the garden wall, shoulders tight, blood humming in his ears. On the other side, just past the carved stone and faded vines, the street waited. So did the people who had come for violence dressed in silence.

The lantern in the shrine hadn't been lit.

And neither had he.

But the spark had come.

❦

The two Blackjaw enforcers were exactly where Halfa expected them, outside the temple's back wall, leaning near a cluster of barrels like this was their territory.

The knife-flicker was still at it.

Click. Click. Click.

The other one, the one with the red-stained lips, was laughing about something Halfa didn't hear. He didn't need to.

They didn't see him coming.

Not until the knife stilled mid-flick.

Not until the laughter died in a half-swallowed sound.

Not until the surrounding air changed.

He was on them like a storm.

The first one turned, eyes widening just as Halfa's fist connected with his ribs. The man flew backward, smashing into stone so hard the impact spider webbed across the masonry.

The knife clattered from his hand, and he lay, unmoving.

The second man moved faster.

His blade came up, flashing in the lamplight.

Halfa's hand caught his wrist mid-swing. Squeezed.

Snap.

The scream was cut short by the fire.

It poured from his mouth like a dragon's breath, a searing torrent of white-hot flame aimed low and fast. It caught the man's cloak, then his chest, then his hair. His shout turned into a screech as he dropped to the ground, rolling, slapping, trying to smother what wouldn't be smothered.

The fire danced like it was joyful.

But there was no joy in this.

Only rage.

Pure. Focused. Deserved.

◈

Halfa stood over him, breathing like a war drum. His chest heaved. Fists still clenched. His skin shimmered with heat, not blistered, not burned, but radiant, as if the fire had kissed him in thanks.

He didn't look at the bodies. Not yet.

His fists were still warm, his breath thick with smoke. And inside him, the fire coiled tighter, but not in rage, but in something harder to name.

Guilt? Relief? Power?

He stared at his hands. Scarred, stained, steaming. Uncontrolled, the fire within him sought release in his rage. The emotion had taken over.

"What are you becoming?" he whispered. The fire didn't answer. But it didn't leave either.

The attack had felt justified. They'd hurt Marin. Threatened the temple. But standing over their broken forms now, fire still warm on his skin, Halfa couldn't shake the feeling that he'd just poured oil on a city already lit at the edges. The Blackjaws wouldn't take this as justice. They'd take it as a challenge. And the temple, already too visible, too bold, had just become the symbol of his defiance. Maybe his fire had protected what mattered. Or maybe it had drawn a target so bright even joy wouldn't survive what came next.

His knees buckled slightly, just once, the way old scaffolding leans after bearing too much weight. The fire hadn't drained him. It had hollowed him. Like something had reached inside and pulled at the part of him, he was still learning to protect.

The alley flickered with light. Smoke curled around him. His shadow leapt across the stone like a creature unleashed.

And then—

A movement. Behind him.

◈

He turned.

Marin stood at the edge of the garden.

She had followed him.

Or wandered. Perhaps something else had drawn her here.

The lantern she'd dropped earlier was in her hands again, though it wasn't lit.

Her face was streaked with dried blood. Her eyes were wide, unblinking, and locked onto his.

She didn't scream.

She didn't speak.

She saw.

Saw what he had done.

Saw what he was.

Halfa didn't move.

Neither did she.

Then, slowly, Marin bent down.

She set the lantern on the stone path.

Stood.

And walked away.

No words.

No judgment.

Silence.

And that was worse than anything she could've said.

When it was over, Halfa stood alone.

The alley glowed with the dying embers of fire. Both men did not move. The stone beneath Halfa's feet was scorched black. His shirt was half-burned. His hands singed. The air reeked of ash and blood.

He didn't feel triumphant.

He felt sick.

Like something had been torn out of him.

Or maybe let out.

Something that wouldn't go back in.

◈

The alley was quiet now.

The only sounds were the drip of water from a cracked gutter, and Halfa's own breath—slow, heavy, uneven.

He stood motionless beside the scorched stone, smoke still curling from his shoulders. His hands shook—not from pain, not from fear, but from something harder to name.

He wasn't angry anymore.

He was empty.

His fire had gone, but it had taken something with it. Something he couldn't name.

◊

Footsteps approached from the temple garden.

Soft. Measured.

Serelion.

They didn't speak at first. They looked at the bodies, the wall, the scorch marks blackening the cobbles. Then at Halfa.

Their expression was unreadable, as always, but something in their eyes... *hurt.* Not disappointment. Not even fear.

Grief.

"They won't stay quiet after this," Serelion said softly.

Grayspire never shouted bad news. It whispered it. From window shutters. Through butcher paper notes tucked in temple steps. By sundown, every gang lookout would know a torch had burned on temple soil, and very soon, someone would price retaliation.

Halfa's voice came low, scraped raw. "You think I care?"

"Yes," they said. "That is why you did this. "

Halfa turned toward them fully. His shoulders were still tense. The heat still shimmered off his skin.

"They made this choice," he said. "Not me. "

Serelion nodded slowly. "And now they'll make another. Because fire never ends things. It only opens new doors. "

He didn't answer. His fists remained clenched. But the rage had burned itself out.

All that was left was the cost.

There was a long silence.

Serelion stepped beside him, looking up at the sky. No stars. Clouds curling like smoke overhead.

"You didn't lose yourself," they said at last. "You did what no one else here could. "

Halfa's jaw worked. "That doesn't mean it was right. "

"No," Serelion agreed. "It just means it was necessary. "

Halfa didn't answer right away. He stared at his hands. The flames were gone, but they still felt warm.

"It didn't feel like losing control," he said. "Not at first. "

Serelion stayed silent.

"It felt like. . . finding something. Like I'd stopped pretending to be anything else. I didn't *want* to hurt them, not exactly. But when I did—it felt clean. Simple. "

He looked up at the flickering sanctuary lights, where children slept behind closed doors and soot still clung to the arches.

"What if the fire's the truest thing about me?"

Serelion's voice was soft. "Then it's not your enemy. It's your language. "

Halfa frowned. "That makes it worse. "

"Not if you choose the words. "

He stared at the flames again. "I don't know how. "

Serelion didn't answer right away. Then, gently:

"Then keep speaking. Until it says something worth keeping. "

Halfa had made his way back into the temple and back up to the rooftop. Hours had passed, and he hadn't moved. Hours had passed, and he stayed in reflection.

His body was wrecked from the extreme use of fire. This had been something that he had never even come close to before.

And then, small footsteps.

Halfa turned.

Marin stood at the top of the ladder....

She looked different now. Not in body, but in bearing. No longer trembling. No longer afraid.

She walked toward him slowly and stopped just a pace away.

"I'm sorry," she whispered.

Halfa blinked. "For what?"

"For walking away. For... not saying anything. " She swallowed hard. "I didn't know what I was looking at. I didn't know how to understand it. "

He opened his mouth. Closed it.

"But now I do," she said. "You protected me. You chose me over... everything else. Over rules. Over peace. " Her voice shook. "Thank you. "

Halfa didn't answer. His throat was thick.

But he nodded, just once.

Marin stepped closer and, without asking, reached for his hand.

It was still warm.

Still trembling.

She held it anyway.

The fire had burned.

But it hadn't destroyed everything.

❦

Later, Halfa sat alone near the Spiral, sleep unable to take him, even through his exhaustion. A lantern lay beside him. He set it upright, opened the casing, and placed his hand over the wick.

A flicker, he thought.

He inhaled slowly. No rage. No grief. Stillness. He reached inward, not like grabbing a weapon, but like drawing water.

Nothing.

He tried again. He concentrated on the pleasant memory of a good night, feeling warmth in his gut. Marin's smile. The temple children running barefoot across the courtyard.

For a heartbeat, there was a spark—then a hiss, and the lantern shattered as a tongue of flame burst from his palm, uncontrolled. He jerked back, burned but not hurt, and the glass scattered across the stone like shards of failure.

Halfa crouched beside the wreckage, breathing hard. The fire had come. But not the way he wanted.

It was supposed to be gentle. Enough to light the wick. He might have been stupid to try so soon after his outburst. He thought he might be able to control it through his emotions. Now, he wasn't sure anymore. Or he lacked emotional control.

He looked down at his hand—skin unmarked, but trembling.

I don't understand you, he thought. *I don't know where you come from. Or why you chose me.*

There were no names. No stories. No one else with fire behind their ribs. The flame came when it wanted, and it burned what it touched. He didn't know if it was magic, a curse, or something his blood had carried from the moment he was born.

All he knew was that wanting to be gentle didn't make the fire less wild.

The Fire We Choose

The next morning, Halfa needed to find Gronk.

Not to fight. Not yet.

He needed to talk to him. To see if words still meant anything—if there was a way to stop what was coming.

He was exhausted from the use of the fire, but his anxiety and adrenaline kept him going at full speed.

He paced the temple courtyard, boots crunching gravel, breath sharp in the cold air. The lanterns were still lit from the night before, their soft glow swaying in the breeze.

But Halfa's mind was already outside the temple walls—out in the alleys, the taverns, the yards where Blackjaw enforcers waited for an excuse to move.

Grayspire was a sprawling thing. Twisting, cracked and angry. Gronk could be anywhere.

Halfa stopped. "Who would know?" he muttered. "Who knows where he is?"

He turned toward the back steps, already moving.

Yetta.

◈

"Bramble Yard," Yetta said without looking up from her stew pot. "Third pit past the tannery. Gronk is there. "

Halfa hesitated. "How did you know what I needed?"

She stirred once. "Word travels fast through Grayspire. Now go. "

Gronk was alone, crouched by a low firepit, poking at the ashes of a half-burned poster. The fog hung heavy. His silhouette was little more than smoke and shoulders.

Halfa stepped through the gate without a word. The gate creaked. Gronk didn't flinch.

"Figured you would come," he said.

"You sent bruisers to a temple," Halfa said. "To *our* temple. "

Gronk rose. "I didn't send them," He said, looking at Halfa, "but you killed them. "

"They hurt Marin. "

Gronk's jaw flexed. "That's what they do. They put pressure on until it cracks. I didn't think you'd crack first. "

"Keep your enforcers away from the temple. "

Gronk spat into the ashes. "You think they will leave you alone after you killed two of them? What kind of message will that send. They will use you as a message. "

"The Thessirans don't want this. It wasn't them. It was me," Halfa said. "They want peace, not blood. "

"And you believe that'll matter?"

"I believe it matters that we try. "

Gronk looked at him then, really looked. "That fire I heard about... You holding it back, or waiting to let it loose?"

Halfa didn't answer.

"You always had that slow-burn temper," Gronk muttered. "Could cook a man alive without raising your voice. "

"Call your boys off," Halfa said. "Or set them on me alone. That's all I'm asking. "

Gronk tilted his head. "You're not asking. "

"No," Halfa said. "I'm not. "

The silence stretched.

"I'll talk to them," Gronk said at last. "Can't promise they'll listen. You killed two of them. "

"They started it. "

Gronk nodded once. "I'll remember that. "

His eyes narrowed. "If something happens to that temple, it won't be on my orders. I can't say the same for Valka. She won't take this lightly... but I'll try. "

"Make sure you do. " Halfa said, then turned into the fog.

Who was Valka? He thought. Halfa had remembered Gronk bringing her up in his plea for Halfa to join him, but didn't know much else.

◉

He took a breath that didn't comfort him. Stepped off the warehouse steps and into the street...

And a hand went for his belt.

The kid couldn't have been over nine.

Barefoot. Quick. Sharp-eyed.

A blur of elbows and dirty fingers.

Halfa caught the wrist mid-swipe. Not hard. Not cruel. Just... firm.

The boy froze.

Big eyes met bigger ones.

"Try someone slower," Halfa said quietly.

No judgment. No anger.

The boy bolted. Gone in a breath, like fog in torchlight.

Halfa watched him vanish into the crowd, then looked around.

◉

"Oi! You with the shoulders!"

The voice cut through the street noise like a blade used too many times, still sharp, but chipped.

Halfa turned.

A man in the grey-and-crimson Watch uniform strode toward him, boots too clean for cobbled grit. Lean, wiry, and wound tight. Goatee trimmed. Posture puffed up like a cock with a badge.

He stopped in front of Halfa and tilted his head back far enough to look like he hated doing it.

"Papers?" the man snapped.

Halfa blinked. "Papers?"

The Watchman sighed like this had already ruined his day.

"Dock registration. Labour clearance. Identification. You do speak Common, right?"

Halfa reached into his coat and pulled out a slip of merchant work authorisation—battered, salt-smudged, but legitimate. It hadn't been used in some time.

The Watchman didn't take it.

Glanced at it. Then back at Halfa.

"You're half a building," he muttered. "You always that big, or you swell in humidity?"

Halfa didn't answer.

"You got a name, Stonewall?"

"Halfa. "

"Halfa what?"

"That's it. "

The man snorted. "Figures. "

Finally, he plucked the slip from Halfa's hand, glanced at it, and then flicked it back like it offended him.

"Passing through?"

"Lived here my whole life. "

"Weird, I haven't seen you before. You're basically a living advertisement to stay out of crime. "

Halfa tucked the paper away. Turned to leave.

"One more thing," the Watchman said.

Halfa paused.

"Name's Dot. Senior Watchman for the East End. You cause trouble, I'll know. And if you *are* trouble.... "

He smiled, thin and sharp.

"...I'll make sure everyone else knows too. "

Halfa looked at him, unreadable. "Duly noted. "

Dot's smile twitched, just enough to show the disappointment of someone who hadn't gotten the rise they wanted.

He folded his arms as Halfa walked on, the crowd folding closed behind him.

The city moved like a current, one Halfa pulled against as he made his way back to the temple.

Shouts echoed from fish carts. Gulls wheeled overhead, snapping at the bones in midair. Lanterns glowed behind soot-slicked glass. The scent of smoke, yeast, and river oil hung in every doorway.

Then came the smell that stopped him: bread. Marin might like something different for once. And the chat with Gronk and then with Dot had made him hungry.

He followed it to a battered cart tucked between a cracked statue and a leaning tenement. The sign swinging above read: "Rye & Respite–Three coppers a slice, one smile included. "

Behind the cart stood a halfling woman, flour-streaked, sleeves rolled up past solid forearms. She looked at Halfa like someone guessing if he was a customer or a warning.

"Well," she said. "You don't look like a bread man. "

Halfa tilted his head. "No?"

"More like a stone wall someone taught to frown. "

She sliced a wedge from a loaf recently pulled from the coals and offered it across the counter.

"Still, you're staring like you ain't eaten since sunrise, and I don't sell bread to ghosts. "

Halfa reached for coin.

"Didn't say it cost anything," she added.

"Your sign did. "

"Signs lie. " She winked. "So does this city. "

He took the bread.

Salt and smoke. Dense. Warm.

It reminded him of something.

Of stew on frosty nights. Of Yetta.

"You look like someone trying not to be seen," she said. "That's hard when you're six-and-a-half feet of mystery. "

Halfa chewed slowly. "Taller than that. "

She laughed. "You find something good in this city; hold on to it. There's rot in every corner, but the flowers still grow. You just have to stomp harder. "

He placed two silvers on the cart.

The halfling blinked. "That's too much. "

"Signs lie," Halfa said.

He turned to go.

"Oi," she called after him. "Try not to rain on the good folk. You've got storm eyes. "

He didn't smile.

But the bread sat warm in his chest.

He glanced back once before disappearing into the alley. Raised the bread in a quiet nod. The baker's eyes widened slightly, and then softened. She didn't speak. Wiped her hands and leaned into the cart like she'd won a fight no one saw. For a moment, it wasn't about fire, or power, or protection. It was about a kindness given and returned. It was about choosing to leave something warmer than you found it.

◈

As he passed a narrow alley, he heard the sound before he saw it.

Raised voices. A woman's sharp breath. A man saying "Don't walk away from me. "

Halfa turned.

Beside a stack of crates, two men had a woman cornered. One too close, the other blocking the exit.

Halfa crossed the street without speeding up.

The first man saw him coming and planted his feet like he was already was angry.

"This ain't your business," he growled.

Halfa looked at the woman. Then at the man's hand on her arm.

"Let go," he said.

Flat. Cold. Absolute.

The second man laughed. "You her brother or her dog?"

Halfa kept walking.

The first stepped into his path.

"You deaf, stoneface?"

He reached—

And Halfa caught his coat. Lifted him clean off the ground.

The man kicked once. Then stilled.

The second man reached toward his belt.

Halfa stared at him.

He didn't draw.

The woman slipped free and vanished into the street.

Halfa lowered the man, hard. Then turned and walked away.

No thanks. No praise.

Silence behind him.

He preferred it that way.

◊

He didn't need thanks.

He needed the quiet in his chest to stay quiet a little longer. It seems the impending Blackjaw attack had him on edge, although he doubted that he would have let that happen on any day.

Halfa turned from the alley, the thugs slinking into the fog behind him. The woman was already gone. No words, no thanks.

He took two steps before he noticed the figure watching from across the square.

Dot.

Standing beneath a leaning archway, half-shadowed by a shuttered seamstress shop. Arms folded. Not moving. Not intervening.

Watching.

Their eyes met for a moment.

Dot gave the smallest tilt of his head. No approval. Not anger. Just... *notation*. Like a man adding a number to a ledger he planned to use later.

Then, the moment broke.

Dot vanished into the street, heading towards another member of the Watch.

Halfa said nothing. But something about the way Dot had stood there, still as ink on a warrant... stayed with him.

A few minutes later, they arrived.

Two Watch officers arrived, crimson and grey uniforms slicing through the crowd like razors.

The first was a dwarf, broad-shouldered and barrel-chested, with a braid thick as rope and a face carved by years of storm-weather Watch work. Her eyes were steel, sharp and fast, and she wore her helm beneath one arm like it owed her something.

Sergeant Brannig Barrelshield.

The kind of dwarf who didn't shout unless it mattered, didn't blink unless she meant to, and didn't waste time on fear.

The other was Dot.

Enough said.

Dot's eyes lit up like someone finding a stain they'd predicted.

"Well, well," he drawled, arms folded. "I knew you'd be trouble. "

Halfa stood still. Unmoved. Unafraid.

The dwarf officer gave him a once-over.

"Name?" she asked.

"Halfa. "

She nodded, glanced down the street to where one thug still groaned against a wall.

"Witnesses say you broke it up," she said. "Stopped something from getting worse. "

"Or started it," Dot added helpfully.

The dwarf ignored him.

"Any magic used?"

"No," Halfa said.

"Any bones broken?"

He shrugged. "Maybe. "

She considered this.

Then nodded.

"I'm recommending a probationary enlistment. "

Dot and Halfa spun to face her, incredulous.

"You're what?" They said.

"City needs shields more than hammers," the dwarf said. "He didn't escalate. He ended it. "

"Give him a badge and a mop," Dot muttered, but there was less venom now. More calculation. "Let's see how long he lasts. "

The dwarf turned back to Halfa.

"Name's Sergeant Brannig Barrelshield. Give it a few days while they try to find something big enough for you, and report to the Watchhouse. "

Halfa gave a brief nod.

"Understood. "

Brannig moved on. Dot lingered.

"Don't think this makes you *welcome*," he said, stepping closer. "You're a stone I plan to trip on. Eventually. "

Halfa didn't flinch. Didn't blink. Didn't respond.

That silence? It said more than Dot wanted to hear.

◊

As Dot stormed off into the chaos, Halfa stood alone again.

But this time....

He wasn't drifting. He had orders. A place to report to. No peace. But something like direction.

And maybe that was the next step forward.

If he made it through the day. Or the week.

There was music in the courtyard.

Not the kind that demanded dancing, soft flutes and a worn tambourine tapping out a rhythm that pulsed like a quiet heart. The sky above the temple of Thessira was ink-dark, scattered with stars. Lanterns swayed between the columns, their golden light flickering across silk banners that hadn't yet caught flame.

Halfa sat at the edge of the garden, elbows resting on his knees. Watching.

Marin was lighting lanterns along the walkway, her steps light; her robe trailing behind her like wind-drawn thread. She hummed a half-melody, off-key but confident, stopping now and then to adjust the angle of a flame so it would dance right.

She caught his gaze at one point and grinned. A flash of teeth in the lantern glow. She didn't wave. She didn't need to. That smile had become a kind of greeting between them.

Bilbin sat near the main doors, a bowl of stew in one hand, a half-carved turnip in the other. A group of temple children had gathered around him, demanding stories. He resisting. Failing miserably.

"Did I ever tell you about the eel the size of a cart that tried to bite off my foot?" he said, stirring his stew like it might reveal the beast at the bottom.

"You said it was a boat last time!" one child cried.

"Ah, but you didn't let me finish that one either," Bilbin grumbled, shaking his ladle. "Now, hush. Respect your elders or I'll cook you into the next pot. "

They laughed and piled closer.

Up on the balcony, Serelion leaned on the rail, watching it all. Their saffron robes rippled slightly in the breeze. They looked tired, but content. Eyes soft. Hands loose. They glanced at Halfa and gave him a slow, quiet nod. Not a command. Not even a request.

Just: *Yes. This.*

Halfa nodded back.

Someone tossed flower petals from a second-floor window. They drifted down in lazy spirals, catching the light like embers not yet lit.

The temple smelled of clove bread and old incense and oil for tomorrow's lanterns. It smelled like home.

Halfa didn't speak. Didn't need to.

◈

Marin found him later in the spiral hall, sitting cross-legged where the lines of the path met.

"Can't sleep?" she asked.

Halfa shook his head. "The fire's too loud. Even when it isn't burning. "

She didn't tease. Sat beside him, knees brushing.

"Sometimes I light a candle just to remind myself it doesn't always need a reason," she said. "It can glow just because it wants to. "

He stared ahead, unmoving. "Do you believe that?"

"I want to. " She smiled. "Maybe joy is stubborn like that. Quiet, but stubborn. "

They sat in silence, the air warm with unspoken things. Then Marin pulled a taper from her pocket, struck it with a flint, and lit a flame between them.

"Let it be enough for tonight. "

This was what joy looked like.

Not loud. Not wild.

Only people. Safe. Together.

◈

The kids had tucked themselves into the side benches, passing sugared fruit and sticky root pie. Bilbin had flour in his hair again. Serelion sat by the far window, watching the sky change from blue to gold to ash.

Halfa stood nearby. Watching.

Quiet.

"Hey. "

Marin waved a slice of bread at him.

"You're officially no longer the temple's most brooding occupant. That honour now belongs to the broken lantern in the back room. "

Halfa almost smiled. "It was always a close competition. "

"Come sit," she said. "Pretend you don't hate us for five minutes. "

He did.

He sat between Bilbin and a snoring kitchen apprentice, and for a few long minutes, he didn't feel like a weapon in a room of glass.

He felt. . . part of something.

Not safe. But *present*.

Later, as the room settled into warmth and crumbs, Serelion stood. Raised their cup.

No sermon. No speech. Just a sentence.

"If the spiral ends here," they said, "may we walk it in joy. "

They looked at Halfa. And nodded once.

Halfa held the look a moment longer. There was something behind Serelion's eyes, a quiet hope, or a quiet fear. He wasn't sure which. And that uncertainty haunted him more than fire.

The laughter resumed.

But Halfa felt the shift.

Outside, the wind picked up.

And something cold followed it.

The silence in the sanctuary the next morning was different. Heavier. The usual laughter during lantern polishing had gone quiet. Softer, hesitant music drifted from the side chamber. Even the children walked a little slower, glancing over their shoulders like shadows had grown longer overnight.

Halfa stood in the garden, arms folded, watching the gate.

Not because he thought someone would come at that moment.

Because he knew someone would.

Serelion emerged from the side corridor, robes unusually plain. Their expression unreadable as always, but something about their stillness gave Halfa pause.

"You decided?" he asked.

They didn't nod. Didn't speak. They simply opened their palm.

In it sat the coin.

Last week's payment.

Still gleaming. Still untouched.

"We do not buy joy," Serelion said.

Then they dropped the coin into the pond.

It sank without a sound.

◊

The kitchen smelled like flour and burnt oranges.

Bilbin stood on a stool behind the kitchen bench, sleeves rolled, apron already dusted with so much flour it looked like he'd arm-wrestled a sack of grain and lost.

He spotted Halfa lurking in the doorway and grinned.

"There you are, lad. Come to sulk or sabotage?"

Halfa raised an eyebrow. "I was walking. "

"Well, now you're baking. " Bilbin gestured grandly. "We've a Thessiran loaf to spiral before dusk. Festival tradition. All hands required. Even grumpy ones. "

Halfa stepped in and hesitated near the counter.

Bilbin shoved a bowl toward him. Dough already rising. "Get that folded, longwise. You'll be coiling it into a spiral. "

Halfa looked at the sticky mass. "I've never done this. "

Bilbin nodded solemnly. "Perfect. Thessira loves a mess. "

Halfa followed his lead.

Badly.

He folded it wrong. Let it stick. Tore it once. When it came time to spiral the thing onto the baking sheet, it collapsed halfway into a loose knot that looked more like a trampled rope than a sacred pastry.

He stared at it.

Then at Bilbin.

"Looks like a drunk snail. "

"Looks like *you* tried. " Bilbin beamed. "Which is better. "

Halfa muttered, "Better than what?"

"Than pretending you didn't care. "

They slid the loaf into the oven. Bilbin adjusted the flame—*just so*—then hopped off his stool and started wiping his hands.

"You know," he said, "people always think joy means laughing. But sometimes it's just. . ." He shrugged. "Showing up. Letting something take shape even when you don't know how it ends. "

Halfa said nothing.

But he watched the oven.

Watched the spiral rise.

Bilbin caught the glance and smiled to himself.

◉

The temple was full of warmth, considering the current atmosphere.

Not heat—though the ovens glowed, and the hearth crackled—but genuine warmth. The kind that filled the corners. The kind that made rooms feel smaller in a good way.

They were all there.

Marin had commandeered the centre table, feet up, scarf askew, gesturing wildly with a cup of cider as she told a story that Halfa suspected was mostly lies and entirely true.

Bilbin had made too much bread again. There were four spiral loaves instead of two. One slightly burnt. One shaped more like a horseshoe than anything sacred.

"I let Halfa help," he said proudly.

"I *can see that*," Marin replied.

◉

Later that day, Halfa stood at the edge of the garden and looked to the city beyond.

He didn't feel dread. He felt clarity.

The kind that only comes after everything else has been stripped away.

He made his way through the lower streets that evening, hood pulled low, boots silent on the stone. He visited three corners, two old cellars, and one forgotten stairwell behind a shuttered gambling den.

He found faces. Some familiar. Some were scarred. All tired.

Men and women who once fought beside him for scraps before Gronk's rise. Before the Blackjaw swallowed them all. Some owed him nothing. Some owed him pain.

But a few still remembered what it had felt like before fear had taken root.

"I won't promise coin," Halfa told them, standing in a half-collapsed storage room with a broken lantern swinging above.

"Only cause. "

Most walked away.

But not all. A few stayed.

Knives. Clubs. Rusted mail stitched into leather. Refusal, not greed, fueled those burning eyes.

Halfa met their eyes, one by one.

Not soldiers. Not saints.

People who refused to kneel.

And for the first time in a long time, he felt the fire inside him rise, not to destroy, but to defend.

This time, they would not stand alone.

The Fire Goes Out

It was a moonless night.

The kind of dark that made even lanterns hesitate.

Darkness that made Halfa's bones feel older than he was.

He stood near the garden gate, not as a guard on duty—as a man with too much on his chest and nowhere to put it. The courtyard was quiet. Not fragile. Soft. A flute somewhere inside. A child laughing in their sleep. Marin's voice, faint from the kitchen, teasing someone about sugar and secrets.

The air smelled of ash and cloves. The silks above him stirred. And yet... he did.

He shifted his weight again. Rolled one shoulder. Then the other. His coat sat wrong. His breathing was shallow. Every motion felt like it came a second too late—like his limbs were being whispered instructions instead of knowing what to do.

The fire wasn't burning in him. But something was. A weight. A hum.

A warning.

He blinked hard and looked down at his hands. They weren't glowing. Not visibly. But the cracks in his knuckles—where the fire had poured from just nights ago—still tingled. Faint warmth. Like metal that had once been molten.

He flexed them. Winced.

"Not now," he muttered. "Not tonight. "

A wind passed through the garden. It smelled like oil.

Halfa went still.

Not incense. Not lanterns.

Pitch. Accelerant.

He turned toward the southern alley. Listened.

Nothing. Not yet.

But the silence had changed. The stillness wasn't resting.

It was a breath held tight.

Behind him, he heard a chair creak—Bilbin, muttering in the kitchen. Marin's footsteps pattering across the flagstones. The soft scrape of Serelion's prayer beads shifting in their lap.

Everything he loved was behind him. And everything coming for it... was not.

He didn't know what he was yet. Protector. Soldier. Something worse. But he knew this: if something came for the temple tonight, it would go through him first.

Halfa reached for the door bolt.

He didn't lock it. Not yet.

He laid his hand on it—calm. Waiting.

And whispered, beneath his breath:

"Please. "

Whether it was to the gods, the fire, or himself, he didn't know.

Then, the first torch flew.

۵

The torch arced high.

It crashed into the garden wall with a mix of fire and pitch, coating the stone in a black flame that hissed and spread too fast to be natural. A second torch followed—through the stained-glass window above the sanctuary doors. Thessira mid-dance shattered in reds and blues. A third hit the silk canopy near the herb beds. It ignited.

Red turned black.

Yellow turned to smoke.

And still—no shouts.

No demands.

Just movement.

They came like a wave.

From the alley. From the rooftops.

From the shadows between stalls and prayer stones.

Twenty of them. Maybe more.

Blackjaw enforcers in worn leather, painted jawbones across their chests. Clubs. Blades. Torches.

No uniforms. Only purpose.

Halfa moved before they reached the gates.

He didn't run.

He *stepped*—like a storm steps off the coast.

The first enforcer vaulted the low wall.

Halfa opened his mouth.

The fire *erupted*.

It poured from him like breath turned to vengeance—white-hot and absolute. The man didn't scream. There wasn't time. One heartbeat he was mid-lunge; the next, he was ash and armour falling through flame.

Halfa didn't stop.

Another came from the side—knife high. Halfa ducked low, drove his fist up at the man's chest. Flame *exploded* out of his fist as the punch connected. The body dropped, smoking.

His breath came fast. Too fast. But he kept going.

A third struck from behind. Halfa twisted, back arched, and *willed* the heat through his shoulder blades. Flame burst outward in a ripple—*like wings*. The attacker fell back, hair alight, screaming.

And still—they kept coming.

From behind the trellis.

Up the sanctuary stairs.

Through the smoke.

Halfa's allies—the few who had answered his call—met them in scattered formation. Rusted swords. Chain mail patched with rope. Some were cut down quickly. Others held their ground, shoulder to shoulder, in front of the temple doors.

Halfa surged through them all like a drawn blade.

Tonight's fire felt different.

It was slower to answer him.

Hotter when it came.

Less... shaped.

His fists were still lit. His breath was still scorched. But each movement cost him. With each strike, the once vibrant glow on his arms flickered, like his inner fire, though spent, refused to yield.

He struck.

He burned.

He *pushed* them back.

But in the pauses between, his hands *shook*.

Just a little. Just enough.

He didn't understand it. Not really. Grief, not rage, fueled this fire; it had listened. But only just. There were moments in the fight where it felt like trying to breathe water. Like it wasn't his to call, just something that tolerated him. No one had taught him how it worked. There were no stories, no other fire-blooded Watchmen, no priests with heat behind their ribs. Only him. And the growing certainty that the power in him was older than magic—and lonelier than he wanted to admit.

Snap!—a banner pole cracked overhead.

Thunk!—a club struck stone near his head.

And then he heard it.

A voice. High, sharp.

"Marin!"

Halfa turned.

Across the courtyard, past the cracked fountain and the spilled spice cart, he saw her—robes torn, sweat across her brow. One hand on a limping child. Another guiding a second—frozen with fear, eyes too wide for their face.

She was moving toward the temple door.

Too slow.

A Blackjaw stepped from the smoke behind a pillar—blade raised.

Halfa *moved*.

But the fire stumbled. His legs *dragged*.

"Marin!" he roared.

The attacker struck.

But not with the blade.

He thrust her hard against the stone wall. Marin crumpled. The kids screamed.

Halfa reached them in seconds, the attacker fleeing into the smoke.

He knelt by her—hands trembling, unsure.

"Marin?"

She groaned.

Alive!

Alive!

Blood on her temple, eyes dazed—but moving. Breathing.

He turned to the children. "Inside. Now!"

They ran.

Marin pushed herself up with a grunt. "You're late. "

"You always say that. "

"I'm always right. "

Halfa helped her to her feet. Her legs wobbled, but held.

From across the courtyard, another shout, "Oi! Overgrown matchstick!"

Bilbin.

He was on a table by the kitchen door, wielding a ladle like a sword, apron smoking, shouting obscenities loud enough to shame the city.

"I've fed fish with more bite than you!" he hollered. "Come on then! Step into the soup, cowards!"

Two enforcers turned toward him.

Halfa shouted—"Bilbin! No!"

But the old gnome stood his ground.

The first attacker raised a torch.

The second lunged.

Halfa reached—too far. Too slow.

But before the torch could fall, something slammed it aside.

Serelion.

They moved like wind through silk—staff in hand, striking low. The first enforcer stumbled. The second reeled. Serelion didn't speak. Didn't rage. They stood between Bilbin and the flames, eyes full of moonlight.

The attackers hesitated—then retreated.

Just for a moment. But it was enough.

Halfa stared.

Then dropped to one knee.

His fire flared in warning.

His limbs shook.

He couldn't stop the heat from leaking out of him anymore. Couldn't keep the cracks in his arms from glowing. His breath came in short bursts. His vision swam.

Not now.

Not *yet*.

Marin placed a hand on his shoulder. "Breathe. "

He tried. He really did.

❂

The fire was dying.

Not extinguished—shifting. Pulling back like a tide, leaving behind only embers and wreckage.

Halfa stood at the edge of the garden, chest heaving, fists unclenched but still glowing faintly at the cracks. The rage had spent itself. The heat still hung in the air, thick as oil, but the momentum was gone.

Blackjaws staggered away from the threshold in ones and twos, clutching burns and broken pride. Some dropped their weapons. Others vanished into the smoke. The charge had faltered.

And then—footsteps.

Heavy. Measured. Familiar.

Halfa turned.

Gronk emerged from the alley at the south wall—alone.

His coat was soaked through with rain and smoke. Soot streaked his face. But he wasn't charging, and he wasn't smiling. His jaw was clenched, his shoulders high with tension.

And his eyes—his eyes weren't angry.

They were afraid.

He took one look at the burning silks, the shattered prayer stones, the broken remnants of joy—and stopped in his tracks.

"Gods," he muttered. "What did they do?"

He hadn't ordered this.

Halfa saw it in the way his fists curled and uncurled. In the way his gaze flicked to the children huddled in the far corner. The way his breath caught when he saw Marin collapsed near the garden wall, Serelion kneeling beside her, shielding her body with their own.

Halfa stepped forward, barely able to keep his knees from buckling. "You said you'd try."

Gronk didn't answer.

He looked around—really looked. At the shattered sanctuary. At the flame-eaten banners. At the bruised faces of Halfa's allies—still standing. Still fighting. Still *there*.

Then he shouted.

"BLACKJAW! STAND DOWN!"

The sound cut through the garden like a hammer blow. Every enforcer within earshot froze.

Gronk stepped further into the wreckage, boots crunching on burnt tile. "You heard me! Drop your blades. Get out. This wasn't the deal."

One bruiser near the arch hesitated. Another—older, scarred, with blood on his mouth—started to speak.

Gronk's voice cracked like thunder.

"I SAID OUT!"

And they went.

Not all. Not immediately. But enough. They looked at him the way old dogs look at the leash—angry, uncertain, but unwilling to bite.

Halfa didn't move.

He watched Gronk call back the storm with nothing but his voice. With the force of memory. Of shared blood and shared streets and something older than power.

The courtyard went quiet again.

Not peaceful—never peaceful—but quiet enough for the garden to remember what it had been. Once.

Gronk turned slowly.

Faced Halfa.

His voice, when it came, was lower. Rougher.

"I didn't call this."

"I know. "

"I told them to wait. "

"I know. "

"They didn't. "

"I know," Halfa said. And meant it.

Gronk nodded once. A slow, tired gesture.

"I tried," he said.

Halfa looked at him—really looked. At the crack running through the bridge of his nose. The way his coat sagged with rain. The weight on his spine.

"You did," Halfa said quietly. "It just wasn't enough. "

Gronk opened his mouth.

And the world shifted.

◊

The fire had gone still.

Smoke twisted up from the courtyard stones, soft now, as if even the ash didn't dare speak. The Blackjaws were withdrawing—slow, uncertain, angry. Not broken. Not beaten. But leashed.

Gronk stood in the garden, shoulders tight, watching them funnel back through the temple gates. They didn't speak. They looked at him. Waiting.

Halfa felt it too.

They weren't gone.

They were waiting for their real leader.

The air shifted.

A ripple—like heat off of stone, except cold. Too cold. The garden's haze stilled.

And then she was there.

Valka.

She stepped through the outer gate like a shadow blooming into form. No fanfare. No storm of boots or shouted orders. Just presence.

She was tall, wrapped in long dark layers that shifted like smoke. Her hair was braided with silver thread. Her eyes gleamed like obsidian glass, cold and reflective.

And when she walked, the fog parted.

Not because she moved through it—but almost because it was afraid of her.

Gronk saw her—and didn't flinch.

But Halfa saw something else in his stance.

Resignation.

Valka stopped just inside the courtyard. She took in the ruined silks. The scorch marks. The burned flower beds.

Then she looked at Halfa.

"You're brighter than they said," she said. Her voice was low, smooth, controlled.

Halfa grunted.

Valka smiled. Not kindly.

Her gaze shifted to Gronk.

He didn't move.

"Your orders were clear," she said. "Pressure. Contain. Influence. Not incineration. "

"I didn't order the breach. "

"You didn't stop it. "

Gronk clenched his jaw. "I called them off. "

"After your little wildfire here tore through a dozen of them. " She stepped closer, past a toppled prayer stone. "Tell me, friend—are you still in control of your part of this syndicate, or are you just its mascot?"

Halfa stepped forward. Power stirred inside him. The last reserve of his fire wanted out.

"You need to leave," he said.

Valka's eyes flicked back to him.

"You don't have the strength left to bluff," she said calmly.

And she was right.

But Halfa didn't back down.

He let the flame flicker in his palm—dim, unsteady, but real.

"I don't need strength," he said. "Only purpose. "

The fire flared.

Valka raised her hand and gestured.

The world... shifted.

Halfa's flame went out.

Not snuffed.

Stolen.

It vanished with a whispering *hiss*, drawn into the space between her fingers like steam pulled into ice.

Halfa staggered, a half-step—but it was enough.

Valka lowered her hand. "You burn with rage. I can taste it. Powerful, yes... but raw. Unguided. You lash out because you don't know how to hold it. " Her gaze sharpened. "I do. "

Gronk moved—not fast, but deliberate. Planted himself between them.

"This isn't the place. "

"No," Valka said. "But it is the time. "

She turned to the Blackjaws, still waiting beyond the temple gate.

"Take him," she said, voice calm, gesturing at Gronk.

And they obeyed.

Six stepped forward. No hesitation.

"Valka," Gronk growled. "Don't do this. "

"You spoke out of turn. Acted without clarity. Cost us territory, lives, control. " She paused. "But worst of all, you showed weakness. "

The enforcers surrounded him. He didn't fight.

Halfa took a step forward, fists curling again.

"No," Gronk said, without looking back.

Valka leaned in close. Whispered something into his ear.

Whatever it was, it turned his face cold.

He nodded once.

Then, the Blackjaws dragged him away.

Not chained. Not bound.

But beaten.

And Halfa stood at the edge of the scorched garden, breath shallow, hands trembling with what little magic he had left.

Valka turned once more, looking at the ruin.

At Serelion, now upright and silent.

At Marin, injured but alive, tucked into the arms of a frightened acolyte.

Her gaze swept across them before she flatly announced, "Consider yourselves warned. "

She turned and effortlessly melted into the fog.

And this time... the Blackjaws followed.

The courtyard was still burning, but the war was over.

The Blackjaws were gone. Valka's voice had cut through the smoke like a blade through silk, and the city swallowed them up again—quietly, with no echo.

Halfa stayed where he was.

He didn't chase them. Didn't raise his voice. Didn't move.

The fire inside him had not gone out.

It had... sunk.

Into his bones, the cracks in his skin and into the hollows of his chest where the shouting used to live.

The temple of Thessira, once bright with banners and wild with laughter, now smouldered in silence. Cracked beams leaned like broken limbs. Ash clung to the garden like snow that hadn't learned how to melt. The spiral tiles of the sanctuary blackened and brittle beneath soot and blood.

Halfa stood in the centre, and he could not breathe.

Not from smoke.

Not from pain.

The intensity of the fire, purpose, and fury within him had reached a point of no return.

And now it had left him hollow.

He took one step.

His knees buckled.

A hand caught him.

Soft. Steady.

Marin.

Her robe was torn at the hem. Her face was streaked with ash. But she was there—alive—and holding him with a strength she didn't have earlier that day.

"You're not done," she said quietly, like it was a prayer. "So you don't get to fall yet."

Halfa didn't answer.

He let her guide him—half-stumbling, half-carried—back into what remained of the sanctuary. The roof had caved in near the east wall. One of the prayer alcoves still stood, smoke-stained but intact. Serelion waited inside it, robes scorched, eyes unreadable. They had laid out what little remained: blankets, water, a low bench that hadn't turned to ash.

They said nothing as Marin helped Halfa lower himself down.

She set a damp cloth in his hands.

He didn't use it.

He just held it.

Because holding something—anything—was easier than holding nothing.

The silence stretched.

Only the crackle of settling beams. The low hiss of distant embers.

Serelion poured water into a clay cup. Passed it over.

Halfa stared at it.

"I don't feel like we won," he said, finally.

"We didn't," Serelion said.

The words were not cruel.

Just true.

Halfa took the cup. The clay was warm from Serelion's hands. He sipped. The water tasted like smoke. Like a memory.

He set it down and leaned back against the wall, the cracked plaster pressing cold into his shoulders.

Then, murmured: "I thought she was dead. "

Marin sat beside him. Her knees drawn to her chest, arms wrapped around them. "You moved like I was. "

Halfa's throat tightened.

"I would have burned the entire city if you hadn't breathed again. "

"You nearly did," she said. But there was no accusation in her voice.

Only awe.

Only understanding.

Serelion folded their legs beneath them and studied the ruin.

"This place will not be what it was," they said. "But maybe that's not the worst thing. "

Halfa stared at the spiral on the floor. Half of it gone—burned away. The other half charred but visible. It looked like a question no one had finished asking.

"I felt strong," he whispered. "Stronger than I ever have. Like I could rewrite the sky. Like the fire wasn't a weapon—it was me. But then..."

"But then it left you," Serelion finished.

"No," Halfa said. "It stayed. That's the worst part. "

He opened his hands.

Tiny cracks ran up his forearms, like spiderwebs of gold and ash. They pulsed faintly with warmth. Not dangerous. Not blinding.

Just... there.

"It didn't take everything," he said. "But it didn't leave much, either. "

Marin reached over and placed her hand on his.

"You're still here," she said. "That's what matters. "

He looked at her.

Really looked.

Beyond the fading bruises. Not just at the way her braid had come undone.

But in her presence.

The fire had saved her.

But she had also come back to him.

Serelion stirred, adjusting a torn piece of silk draped across the bench.

"You asked once," they said softly, "what the fire was for. "

Halfa nodded.

"I still don't know. "

Serelion looked up at the fractured ceiling. Smoke drifted through the hole like a ghost still looking for its home.

"I think," they said, "it's for clearing space. "

Halfa frowned.

Serelion smiled. Just slightly.

"Some fires destroy. But some... clear the rot. Burn the lies. Make room for what needs to grow next. "

He closed his eyes.

Let the words settle.

The cracks in his arms didn't hurt. Not now.

But they glowed.

Like a warning.

Or maybe a map.

He wasn't sure which yet.

Marin leaned her head on his shoulder. He didn't flinch.

"You don't have to decide what it means tonight," she said. "Tonight, you just have to rest."

Outside, a single bird sang—confused, maybe, by the dawn light peeking through the smoke.

Halfa listened to the birdcall drifting in through the smoke-streaked roof—thin, hesitant, as if the world itself was unsure how to begin again. But it was singing. That mattered.

The quiet wrapped around him like a second skin, and he let it. Let it fill the hollow the fire had carved. Let it remind him that not everything had burned.

His eyes closed; the memory surfaced, less a wave, more a held breath.

He thought of Bilbin's ridiculous stories, told with a ladle like a sceptre and a pot of stew as an audience. Of Serelion's quiet grace, their words soft enough to mend stone. Of Marin's off-key humming and the way her laugh always rose half a second before she meant it to.

He remembered the temple as it had been—messy, stubborn, full of colour and warmth. A place that had danced before it burned.

And for the first time since the flames, Halfa felt something ease inside him. Just a little. His shoulders dropped. His fists loosened. He exhaled, slow and ragged, and didn't brace for what came next.

He wasn't a weapon at that moment.

He wasn't fire, or fury, or even grief.

Just a man—scarred, scorched, but still here.

A man who had burned everything to protect something that mattered.

And now, somehow, had to learn how to protect what remained.

◊

The days blurred.

Time passed in flickers of candlelight and whispered voices, in the weight of damp cloth on his forehead, in the quiet scrape of Marin's footsteps and the stillness Serelion carried like a blessing. Halfa drifted between sleep and waking, never fully in either. The fire that had once roared through him now curled low, banked like coals beneath ash.

And then—he dreamed.

He stood on the shore of a black sea. No moon. No stars. Waves the colour of ash and a horizon split by flame. Something smouldered at the edge of the water. He walked toward it. The sand beneath his feet hissed with heat.

There—on the shore—Gronk.

Not the warlord. Not the boy. A man, crouched and shaking, blood in his teeth and firelight in his eyes. His back bore lashes not from Halfa's fists, but from something colder. Something deliberate. He looked up.

"You left me," Gronk said.

Halfa stepped closer. "You chose the path. "

"I chose us," Gronk said. "And you turned me into memory. "

Then he was gone.

The shoreline shattered like glass. The sky folded into flame.

Halfa screamed—but no sound came. Only fire.

And then he wasn't on the shore anymore.

He was on a mountainside.

Snow stung his face, but he didn't feel cold. Only hunger. Not for food, but for something nameless. His hands glowed beneath his skin—lines of molten orange like veins of buried truth. Around him, stone figures rose—taller than towers. Giants. Fire-touched. They stood unmoving, faces turned to the sky.

He shouted to them.

None answered.

But they watched.

Watched as the fire in him flared higher than the peaks.

Watched as it twisted.

Watched as it consumed not just the mountain, but the sky itself.

And then—

A hand.

Outstretched. Commanding.

The fire recoiled.

Snuffed.

He dropped to one knee, coughing soot, breath torn from his lungs.

Before him stood Valka.

Alive. Whole. Drenched in shadow and frost. Her fingers still glimmered with the remnants of magic—a quiet, pulsing force that wasn't rage, but restraint.

She didn't speak. Didn't need to.

He opened his mouth to question—but the dream unraveled.

The mountain burned away.

The sea returned.

The fire inside him screamed once more—and then collapsed.

He awoke with a gasp.

The temple ceiling hovered above him—cracked, scorched, but still standing. Lantern light danced in the rafters. Somewhere nearby, someone hummed—soft and off-key. Marin.

The fire in his chest stirred.

Not in fury. Not in grief.

In curiosity.

He touched his ribs, as if expecting to find the brooch there.

Only breath remained.

And for now, it was enough.

Part 2 - What Survives the Flame

The Spark Beneath

The light filtering through the cracked temple ceiling was pale and brittle. Morning, maybe. Or something like it. Halfa didn't move. Not yet.

His body ached, not with the sharp, urgent ache of fresh wounds, but the dull, marrow-deep kind that settled in once your purpose was done and your body remembered how to hurt. The fire inside him was quiet. Not gone. Just... low. Banked. Like it knew better than to rise without being asked.

He shifted slightly, joints protesting. His fingers moved without glowing. That felt like something worth noticing.

A shadow passed across his face.

"Good," came a voice. "You're not dead. That would've made this paperwork a real bastard. "

Halfa blinked once and turned his head slowly.

In the doorway stood Brannig Barrelshield, with her arms folded and helmet under one arm, her face carved with the same expression of don't-you-dare-make-this-my-problem as if someone had chiselled it there decades ago.

She looked around the scorched temple, took in the blackened beams and the ash-layered floor, and nodded once, like she was confirming a hunch.

"You look like shit," she said.

Halfa pushed himself upright, every motion slow. "Feel worse. "

"Good. Means you probably won't argue too hard when I tell you what's coming. "

He didn't answer right away. The silence hung. Brannig let it.

Then, quietly: "How long?"

"Three days," she said. "Give or take. You've been in and out. That witch-friend of yours," a nod toward where Marin had left a cup beside his cot, "kept the fire from eating you inside out. And Serelion's done more quiet talking over your body than most priests do over the dead. "

Halfa looked down at his hands. The cracks were still there. Glowing subtly. Faintly. . . him.

"I saw her," he said. "Valka. "

Brannig grunted. "You and half the East Ward. "

"She stopped me. "

"Yeah," Brannig said. "And you're still breathing. That makes you special. Or lucky. Or stupid. Maybe all three. "

She crossed the ruined floor, each step heavy with authority and creaking armour. She stopped just short of his cot and tossed something onto his lap.

A folded tunic. Grey and crimson. Watch colours.

The badge gleamed against the fabric like it was daring him to laugh at it.

"It won't fit," Halfa muttered.

"Didn't think it would," Brannig said. "Tailors are working on something in canvas and spite. But in the meantime, that's yours. "

Halfa looked up. "After all this?"

"You think I make promises I don't keep?"

He held her gaze. Said nothing.

Brannig shrugged. "I heard what you did. So did Dot. He won't admit it, but he filed the report himself. Left out some of the screaming and burning, but the gist is the same: you held the line. Not for coin. Not for blood. Just because someone had to. "

She gestured at the surrounding ruin.

"That's Watch work, like it or not. "

Halfa picked up the tunic. Heavy. Too narrow through the shoulders. It smelled like dry cloth and rust.

"It's been more than a few days," he said.

Brannig smirked. "And you think I forgot? You think the city stopped spinning while you napped in your crater?"

She turned to go. Paused at the archway.

"Uniform fitting at noon. Dot'll be there. Try not to punch him unless he swings first. And Halfa," she glanced over her shoulder, voice softer, almost human, "you don't have to burn to belong. "

She left before he could answer.

Halfa sat in the silence that followed, the tunic in his lap, the badge catching the morning light.

He didn't want to be the weapon they called when things went wrong. He wanted to choose when to act. Who to stand beside. Reason to fight. This is why he had agreed to join the Watch. It was time to act.

Outside, the temple was still a wound. But it wasn't bleeding.

He stood.

Time to remind the city that it hadn't burned him down yet.

◈

The uniform didn't fit.

The tunic squeezed his chest like it was afraid of him. The boots pinched his toes, and the belt hung off his waist like a joke written by someone half his size and twice as proud. Yet when Halfa caught his reflection in the cracked mirror above the washbasin, he didn't look away.

He looked like someone trying to believe in second chances.

From the doorway, Brannig Barrelshield watched him wrestle with the collar. Her arms were folded, helm tucked beneath one arm, braid tucked tight along one shoulder.

"You'll stretch it out by breathing," she said. "Or tear it clean through. Either way, we'll find you something less stupid before next week. "

There wasn't a smile on her face, not exactly, but there was warmth behind her words.

Brannig had signed the parchment that turned him from an oddity into a probationary Watchman. Halfa didn't understand why—not fully—but he didn't question it. He didn't question much anymore. Only listened. Watched. Endured.

Dot, however, had not smiled.

He hadn't stood when the paperwork was signed. Just glared from behind the captain's desk, fingers twitching like they itched for a blade or a reason.

"You're on probation," he'd said. Flat. Icy. "You so much as scowl at the wrong person, you're gone. Raise a hand without a direct order; you're gone. Speak out of turn, and I'll bury you in red tape until the rats learn your name. "

Halfa had stood silent.

Dot had leaned forward then, lowering his voice to something meant to crawl into a man's spine. "I don't care what you burned before you got here. But I see it in you. That same flicker. Fire wearing a badge. And let me be clear: The Watch isn't a forge. It's a wall. And walls aren't supposed to burn. "

Then he'd turned and walked out of the room, the air behind him going colder.

Now, back in front of the mirror, Halfa adjusted the collar one more time.

He didn't feel like a soldier. Or a guard. Or a wall.

❦

Training came easy.

The drills were simple: formations, patrol patterns, restraint holds. Nothing about learning Watch protocols was hard compared to the Dock Ward. What was hard was holding back.

Holding the fire.

He was paired with Sergeant Brannig Barrelshield for his first month. Dot had protested loudly, but Brannig had insisted. "He needs discipline," she said. "And I've seen what happens when men try to beat the fire out of someone like him. I'd rather teach him how to bank it. "

It had been two weeks since the fire in the alley, and the bruises on his record were still fresh enough to sting.

She didn't raise her voice. She didn't throw her weight around. But when Brannig spoke, people listened.

She trained like someone who had fought wars without swinging a blade. Every movement intentional. Every word earned. On the third day, after Halfa blocked three strikes too slowly, she barked, "You're not a hammer lad; you're a storm cloud. You don't have to strike, simply make 'em believe it'll rain. "

Halfa had paused at that.

She didn't say it like a joke. Or like she feared him.

She said it like it was a truth she respected.

He started watching her more closely after that, how she carried herself through the Lower Market, how she spoke to people with authority but never arrogance. She didn't bark orders unless she had to. Didn't draw her weapon unless someone truly deserved it.

She didn't flinch when someone cursed her in the alleys. And she didn't flinch when they thanked her, either.

When someone trusted him, Halfa didn't know what to do with it. It felt heavy in his hands. But not in a bad way. Like something breakable you wanted to carry carefully. As proof you were more than muscle.

Halfa had once thought the Watch was just another chain. Another tool of power in the hands of men like Dot. But with Brannig, it was different.

She made it feel like a choice.

And that meant something.

During drills, she corrected him without sarcasm. During rounds, she let him speak when he wanted to, and let him keep silent when he didn't. And on the rare nights they patrolled the wharves together, she'd hum old dwarven ballads under her breath, not for him, but for herself.

He respected her before he even realised it.

And that scared him a little.

◊

Dot made it his mission to unravel everything Brannig built.

Every shift roster seemed like a joke at Halfa's expense. One day, his shift stationed him beside a flooded alley behind a tannery, the stench so thick it clung to his clothes for hours. The next, a decrepit tenement with crumbling stairs and broken windows, where every knock on a door came with a curse or a spit in the face.

Backup never came on time.

Orders were vague.

Routes changed without notice, and Halfa was always told last.

But he didn't complain.

Because Dot was watching.

Always watching.

He hovered near training drills like a vulture, arms folded, jaw tight. When Halfa spoke to a merchant too kindly, Dot would scoff. When Halfa stood still in a fight and let his presence speak louder than fists, Dot would mutter things like, "Should've sent a dog; at least they bark. "

But something strange happened.

The other Watchmen noticed.

They saw Halfa lift a wagon off a trapped child in the Market Square, his shoulders straining, legs braced, the wood groaning with every inch. They saw him calm a mob outside the Bucket of Bones without a single blow, just a few words spoken slowly and quietly. Without hesitation or fear, they saw him walk into danger.

They started calling him *The Wall*.

At first, it was between drills—a half-joke muttered with a grin. But the name stuck. Gained weight.

One morning in the mess hall, a young recruit handed Halfa a plate and said, "Here you go, Wall. " No fanfare. No teasing. Said it like it was fact.

Halfa didn't respond right away. He took the plate. Gave a nod. And sat.

No one laughed. No one explained.

But the silence that followed felt easier than it used to. For the first time, he didn't mind it.

Dot did.

During courtyard drills, he barked across the stone, loud enough for everyone to hear. "You think that name makes you better than orders, Stoneface? Think it makes you special?"

Halfa didn't blink. "No, sir. "

"Expecting applause?"

"No, sir. "

Dot stormed forward, boots crunching across sand and broken gravel. He planted himself toe to toe with Halfa, his chin tilted up like a dagger waiting to slip.

"Wipe that smug silence off your face," he snarled, "before I reassign you to graveyard latrines and let the ghosts figure out what to do with you. "

Halfa said nothing. Just met his eyes.

The silence was louder than any shout.

Later that evening, in the mess hall, Brannig handed Halfa a battered tin mug filled with tea.

She didn't sit. Sipped her own and leaned against the post beside him.

"He's not angry because you're dangerous," she said at last. "He's angry because he can't get you to lose control. "

Halfa stared down at the dark surface of the tea.

"Isn't that what he wants?"

"No," she said, her voice dry as dust. "He wants to control the fire. But you're not controllable. And that scares men like him more than any flame. "

Meanwhile, after his shifts in the Watch, Halfa would return to the Temple of Thessira to help with the rebuild.

Halfa arrived after dusk, still in uniform, sleeves rolled and collar open, his badge tucked deep into one of the inside pockets. He didn't wear it here.

The temple was quieter these days. Not solemn, but thoughtful. Where once there had been lanterns strung like stars, now there were scaffold poles and baskets of salvaged stone. Where prayer flags once danced, there were rope lines and rebuilt beams.

And yet... it was still the Temple of Thessira.

Laughter still drifted through the courtyard. Children still raced barefoot along the spiral path, now half-sketched in chalk until tiles could be laid again. Marin stood by the garden wall, a ledger under one arm and a smear of paint across her cheek. She was arguing with a carpenter twice her height and winning. Bilbin sat under a crooked arch, instructing two young acolytes on how to stir paint without summoning a spirit of mild inconvenience.

Halfa moved toward the half-constructed entryway, where the new outer gate had been built from old wood. He knelt beside the frame and began checking the joints, one by one, in a slow and deliberate manner.

Marin noticed him eventually and wandered over, a roll of parchment tucked under her arm. She didn't greet him with words, bumped his shoulder with her knee as he adjusted the hinge brace.

"You keep coming back," she said.

Halfa tested the weight of the latch before answering. "I never left. "

Marin snorted softly. "You did. You had to. But you're here now. " She sat beside him, legs stretched out in front of her, boots dusty from the scaffolding. "You ever think about staying with us for good?"

He looked at her, brow raised. "I'm here every day. "

"Yeah," she said, bumping his shoulder. "But I mean *staying-staying*. No half a foot out the door. No 'just helping with repairs. ' You're already part of this place. Might as well admit it. " Halfa looked down at his palms. The cracks that once glowed with flame were now just faint lines, like old lightning scars on weathered stone. He flexed them once, then ran a thumb along the new frame.

"I'm not a builder," he said.

"No," Marin agreed. "But you're learning. "

She stood with a groan, stretching her arms overhead. "Help me move the tiles before Bilbin yells about 'joy alignment' again. Last time, he made a kid cry with a measuring string. "

Halfa followed her, wordless but steady. They worked side by side as the sky deepened to violet, shifting stones, redrawing the spiral that had once marked the heart of the temple. It wasn't perfect, not yet. But every stone they placed was a word in a prayer. Every hammer swing, a quiet hymn. It wasn't for the goddess. It was for those who persevered. For what had survived.

And for what might still grow.

Somewhere near the centre of the spiral, Marin slipped. She cursed, softly, reverently, and Halfa smirked.

"Thessira will forgive you," he said.

"She better," Marin muttered. "Or she's getting a lopsided spiral and a shovel to the ankle. "

Bilbin overheard and barked a laugh from across the courtyard. "Threaten a goddess again, and I'll write a hymn about it!"

Someone dropped a lantern. A child shrieked and chased a ribbon into the dusk. Marin laughed. Halfa, tired, covered in dust, did too.

And for a moment, there was no fire in his chest. Just warmth. Real and rooted. The kind that didn't need to burn to be felt.

As they rested, Marin wiped her brow with the back of her hand and nodded toward the garden wall.

"We're going to plant something new there," she said. "Not to forget what burned. Just... so we have something to water. "

Halfa looked at the wall, blackened at the top, cracked in the middle, but still standing.

He nodded.

"I'll bring the shovel. "

◊

They were supposed to clear a condemned building in the Lower Quarry District. It was just a routine walkthrough to ensure no squatters hadn't broken in again.

Three Watchmen moved ahead, new recruits, laughing too loudly, kicking rubble aside with more swagger than caution. Halfa followed last, eyes sharp, senses bristling. Something felt wrong.

He paused at the threshold.

The air wasn't stale enough.

The broken window on the second floor wasn't like that yesterday.

And someone had left a boot print in the soot by the back wall. Fresh. Deep. Wrong size.

Halfa raised a fist. "Hold. "

The recruits turned, confused.

He stepped forward and knelt by the door. The hinges weren't rusted like the others. These had been oiled. Recently.

Brannig appeared beside him a moment later, silent as falling gravel. She scanned the frame, then the alley beyond. No words. A quick nod.

She pulled the rookies back. Halfa motioned them behind the cover of a split stone wall.

Brannig tapped once on her badge. Backup signal.

They waited.

Three minutes later, two figures emerged from the rear of the building. Neither were Watch, both armed, one with a crossbow half-raised.

They saw the uniforms too late.

By the time they hit the ground, Brannig was already turning back to Halfa.

"Good call," she said.

Halfa didn't reply.

But later, in the mess hall, one recruit passed him a mug of tea without being asked.

And Dot, watching from the shadows near the stairwell, didn't say a word.

◊

The Lower Market always danced on the edge of chaos.

Copper, not gold, built fortunes there. Dice games in the shadows, cheap wine in leaky bottles, shouting matches over spoiled apples or bent nails. The Watch didn't always bother unless someone bled.

That night, someone did.

A call came in just past dusk. Brannig and Halfa arrived to find two gamblers shouting, a third already bleeding from the shoulder. The air smelled of smoke, sweat, and old vinegar. One man waved a dagger with the urgency of someone cornered by regret.

Brannig raised her voice. "Grayspire Watch! Weapons down!"

The man spun toward her, blade shaking in his grip.

"Drop it," Halfa said. Calm. Solid.

The gambler spat. "You can't tell me what to—"

Halfa looked at him.

He didn't move.

Didn't posture.

Just... looked.

The dagger clattered to the cobblestones.

Brannig gave a low whistle. "Told you. Storm cloud. "

They processed the men quickly, Brannig handling statements while Halfa kept watch. A woman from a nearby stall gave Halfa a chunk of bread as they marched the prisoners off. No words, just a nod.

Back at the Watchhouse, Brannig cornered Halfa near the training yard, rolling her shoulder where a bruise had darkened beneath her armour.

"You know," she said, "you keep this up, I might recommend lifting your probation early. "

"I don't want rank," Halfa said, sipping water from a barrel scoop.

"Not talking about rank," she replied. "I'm talking about respect. One's useful. The other's a curse. "

He paused. Thought about that.

Then asked, "You think the others will ever stop looking at me like I might burn the place down?"

Brannig studied him for a long moment.

"They will. One day you'll bark an order and no one'll remember why they were nervous. Just that you were the one who didn't flinch when it mattered. "

◉

The courtyard was quiet when Halfa arrived. Not the sacred quiet, the kind that meant most of the work had been done for the day. Scaffolding leaned tiredly against the sanctuary's inner wall, and a wheelbarrow lay tipped on its side like someone had lost an argument with gravity.

Halfa didn't announce himself. He never did. He picked up the barrow, brushed off the dust, and started moving bricks.

He heard footsteps soon enough, light ones, with a rhythm he recognised. Marin.

"You know we're not paying you for this," she called from the edge of the stone path.

"I know. "

She crossed to him, holding two mugs. One was steaming. The other was probably only called tea out of courtesy. She handed him the first. He took it without a word.

They leaned against the same half-rebuilt wall. Above them, a lantern swung lazily from a beam, its glow catching the dust in the air like fireflies that had forgotten how to leave.

Marin sipped her drink and squinted at the spiral courtyard. "They redid the curve this morning. It's crooked again. "

Halfa nodded toward the centre. "That corner's off. "

"They say it's tradition. That the spiral shouldn't be perfect. "

He took a long sip. "Or maybe we just keep getting it wrong. "

Marin shrugged. "Joy's not straight lines. It's scrapes and smudges and spilled mortar."

A silence settled between them that was not uncomfortable. Just real. They watched as a young acolyte tried to lift a too-heavy bucket near the herb beds and nearly fell over. A second child ran to help, neither of them noticing the scorch mark still faint on the nearby wall.

Halfa watched them for a long moment. "Do they remember?"

Marin followed his gaze. "The kids?"

He nodded.

She tilted her head. "Most of them do. Some of them have already rewritten it. In their version, you were ten feet tall and had fire wings."

He almost smiled.

"And Bilbin chased off six men with a flaming ladle," she added.

He looked down at his tea. "That part might be true."

Marin bumped his arm gently. "They remember joy, Halfa. Not just the fire."

He didn't answer. But he watched the children longer. Watched them laugh, tug at ropes, play tug-of-war with Bilbin's apron when he wasn't looking.

Eventually, he set his mug aside and stepped back toward the half-collapsed tool shed. The door still leaned on its hinges. It wasn't part of the official repairs, just an afterthought, too small for lists and too crooked for prayer.

He bent, picked up a hammer, and started adjusting the frame.

"You don't have to fix everything," Marin said softly behind him.

"I know."

"But you want to."

Halfa looked at the misaligned door, at the cracked hinge, at the places where old wood met new.

"Yeah," he said. "I do."

◊

The Watchhouse courtyard was quiet. The lanterns along the stone archway flickered faintly, too tired to ward off the deeper dark. No shouts. No merchants. No drunks singing lies to the sky. Only the creak of Grayspire's bones settling for the night.

Halfa sat alone on a bench near the outer wall, uniform still dusted with soot from the lower ward. The fabric no longer fought him the way it used to. Either it had softened, or he had.

In his hands, he turned over a small matchbox that was empty save for one last stick. He wasn't sure why he'd kept it. Perhaps it reminded him of something. Maybe because it hadn't failed him yet.

He hadn't heard a word. Not since that night. No sightings or whispers. No revenge killings. Gronk had vanished.

Halfa had walked every block of Blackjaw territory during and after his patrols, boots echoing through alleys that remembered too much. He asked questions without asking, letting pauses hang too long, letting glances say more than words. He lingered near the places Gronk once claimed, stood beneath the soot-stained eaves where orders used to be given, and waited for something, anything, to rise from the cracks.

He wasn't assigned there. No one had asked him to investigate. He just wanted to find his friend.

But there was nothing.

No rage or grief.

Silence and absence.

And that was worse.

He stood, his legs slow to straighten. Crossed to the alcove where the Watch stored spare patrol lanterns, plain brass things, all function and no poetry. He took one gently, filled it from the oil drum, and returned to the steps.

The match flared against the stone, then touched the wick.

A single flame bloomed.

Halfa watched it for a long time.

He thought of Gronk. Not the man who'd broken jaws and issued orders with a smirk, but the boy who'd once split stolen bread with him in the rain. The boy who laughed too loud and always walked a little ahead, like the world needed him to test the path first.

Maybe that boy was still in there.

Perhaps Halfa had failed him.

Maybe they'd both failed each other.

He placed the lantern on the edge of the steps, beside the Watchhouse threshold. Not hidden. Not announced. Just... there. Facing the street. Letting the city see what it wanted to.

He didn't speak at first. Just stood.

Then, softly, "So where the hell did you go?"

No answer, of course.

Just flame.

Steady. Small. Alive.

"I looked for you," Halfa said. "You know that, don't you?"

The wind didn't move. The flame didn't waver.

"I don't know if I'm supposed to hate you. Or miss you. Or thank you. "

He touched the lantern's side briefly. The metal was warm.

"I'm still here," he said. "I only wish I knew if you were, too. "

He turned to go.

Then paused, long enough to whisper over his shoulder, half hope, half warning: "Don't stay gone. "

He left the lantern burning on the steps, its glow catching in the cracks of the stone like a memory trying to root itself in something solid.

And behind him, the flame held steady.

Watching the street.

Waiting.

◉

There was no ceremony.

No formal parade of words, no brass band, no handshake beneath a flag. Just a cramped office that smelled like pipe smoke and old ink, and a captain with bags under his eyes and a pen gripped like a dagger.

Halfa stood silent while the captain stamped the parchment.

"Probation lifted," the man muttered. "Competency exceeds expectations. Brannig signs off, I sign off. Try not to burn anything unless you're told to. "

He didn't look up.

Halfa nodded once.

Across the room, Dot leaned against a shelf stacked with ledger books, his arms folded, his mouth a tight line. He didn't interrupt. Didn't protest. He watched like a man keeping track of a storm on the horizon, knowing it couldn't be leashed.

The moment the ink dried, Halfa stepped out into the courtyard, the parchment tucked into his belt, the late sun catching the faint shine of his newly issued badge. The uniform was adjusted finally to fit him, and it no longer pinched. It felt... worn in. Like something he could walk in without tripping over what he used to be.

Brannig Barrelshield joined him on the steps. She said nothing for a moment. Stood beside him, hands on her hips, scanning the yard like she expected it to fall apart if she blinked.

"So," she said at last, voice low. "What's next, lad?"

Halfa stared ahead at the bustle of the Watchhouse. Officers moving. Recruits shouting. The inaudible murmur of city life pushing up against the walls.

Then, simply, he said: "Steady ground. "

Brannig gave the smallest smile.

The sun dipped low as Halfa climbed the temple stairs. The bells in the market tower had finished their third chime, early evening. The air smelled of fresh bread and hammered copper, and for once, the city's noise felt distant. Behind him, his Watch badge caught the last glint of daylight. Ahead, the Temple of Thessira stood rebuilt, not whole, not as it once was, but undeniably alive.

Lanterns lined the entryway. Ribbons hung across the repaired arch, each dyed with clove and rose water, fluttering like breath returning after a long silence. And through the open doors came laughter.

It startled him. Joy always did when it came suddenly.

Inside, the temple had gathered around a low table stacked with offerings, fruit, warm root pies, and spiced tea. Serelion stood near the altar, speaking quietly with a pair of young acolytes. Bilbin barked instructions from the kitchen doorway, his apron freshly stained and his beard still scorched at one corner. Marin darted between guests like a dancing ribbon, barefoot and bright, hair tied back with a twist of temple silk.

Halfa didn't know who'd organised it. He only knew it wasn't for the Watch. It was for him.

As he stepped inside, Marin saw him first. She smiled—not a grin, not something for show, just that small, sideways smile that said *I'm glad you're here.*

"Look what the street coughed up," she said, drifting toward him with a cup of tea in each hand. "Crimson suits you. "

"You think so?" he muttered.

She handed him the tea. "I think you're walking like someone who belongs. "

Before he could answer, Bilbin called from across the room. "Oy! Barrelshield! You still owe me a rematch on onion dice!"

Brannig stood near the threshold, arms folded, armour dusted with flour from an earlier ambush by Bilbin. She didn't smile, but her presence said enough. She gave Halfa a curt nod.

"You showed up," he said quietly, stepping over.

"I hate parties," she replied. "But I came for the pie. "

A pause. Then: "You earned it. "

She didn't stay long. Long enough to share a cup with Serelion, mutter something unintelligible to Bilbin, and clap Halfa once on the shoulder hard enough to remind him she still outranked him.

When she left, the celebration carried on. The music was soft. The stories got louder. At some point, someone lit a small fire bowl in the courtyard, and the light danced across the rebuilt silk hangings. Halfa stood apart for a time, content just to watch.

Later, Marin found him again.

"Come on," she said, tapping his elbow. "I want to show you something. "

He followed her up a narrow staircase he hadn't walked in months—since before the fire. The stairs creaked, but held. At the top, the trapdoor to the rooftop opened without protest. Cool air spilled in.

They rebuilt the rooftop, not exactly as it was, but close. The stone parapet were straighter now, and the boards along the east edge had been reinforced. A blanket lay near the far wall. A lantern sat beside it, already lit.

Marin flopped down onto the blanket, arms behind her head. "They fixed the ladder last week," she said. "Brannig sent some off-duty Watch to do it. She said we'd need it again. "

Halfa lowered himself beside her, boots thudding softly against the stone. He didn't lie back. Sat with his legs drawn up, elbows resting on his knees.

The city stretched before them in all directions. There were domes, towers, and chimneys spitting smoke. It looked endless. But the stars were out tonight, and they blinked through the haze like even they were surprised the city had survived.

"It's strange," Marin said, "how something can burn and still be here after. Still be... itself. Just changed. "

Halfa didn't speak. But his chest rose and fell with the steadiness of someone listening.

She rolled onto her side to face him. "You've changed, too. "

"Did I lose myself in the flames?" he asked quietly.

She reached out and touched his hand, not grasping, resting her fingers atop his.

"No," she said. "You stayed. That's rarer. "

He turned to look at her.

For a long moment, neither moved.

The lantern flickered between them, and the silence was full, not empty.

Marin smiled. "Don't go catching feelings on a rooftop. It's cliché. "

"Wouldn't dream of it," he murmured. But he didn't pull his hand away.

They sat like that a while longer, the city humming beneath them, the stars blinking overhead. Two people who were scarred by fire and saved by something softer.

Not a question anymore.

Not a maybe.

But something real.

Something worth staying for.

A Quiet Flame

He tasted copper. Something in his nose was broken. Every breath burned like he'd swallowed smoke.

The cage wasn't much. Iron bars bolted into the stone beneath a tavern that had died two owners ago. Rust clung to the metal like moss. Blood pooled under his chin.

He didn't know how long he had been here. Time had blurred in between the beatings.

Boot steps came softly across the stone. Gronk didn't look up. He didn't need to.

Valka prowled in. All sharp edges, as usual.

She stopped outside the cage. Silence hung a moment longer than comfort allowed.

"You built me a ladder," she said. "And now you want to pull it down?"

Gronk grunted. His eye was swelling shut.

Valka knelt, folding like a blade set back into its sheath. "You brought me the Blackjaw captains. You bled for me. You killed for me. And when we won, when it was done, you turned. " She tilted her head. "That part confuses me. "

Gronk wiped his mouth on the back of his wrist. "Didn't turn. Just disagreed on hurting my friend. "

"You didn't take what we built seriously. "

"We built?" he croaked. "I was your spine. Now I'm just meat in a cage. "

Valka's eyes flicked toward the bars, then back to him. "You never wanted power. You wanted safety. Food. Respect. Something to outrun the look in Halfa's eyes when he left you behind. "

That stung more than the bruises.

"I gave you that," she went on. "Gave you the city's fear. And what did you do with it? You crawled back to the rats."

She stood again, slow and precise. Her silhouette against the hanging lantern didn't flicker. The fire inside the cage guttered low, like it knew better.

"You think the Temple can protect them? You think Halfa's fire will hold against me?"

Gronk didn't answer.

Valka smiled. It wasn't cruel. Just quiet.

"We brought down the magic users. My power, your strength, no one could stand against us."

The cage creaked as she turned.

"With you," she said, "we were unstoppable. Without you...."

She didn't finish the thought. Her voice had already moved on.

She paused at the edge of the light.

"What should I do with your fire-born friend?" she asked, like she was asking the air.

Then she left, leaving Gronk bleeding. Sweating.

Meat in a cage.

◉

He'd stopped counting the hours. Or maybe he'd never started.

Hard to count when your ribs throb like a second heartbeat. When every blink comes with a pulse of light behind your eyes.

No one had checked on him. Not since the last fists. That was the Blackjaw way—decide your sentence by how long they let you rot.

He lay flat, face to the bars, cheek against the stone.

Didn't matter if the blood was dry or fresh. The stink stayed the same.

He thought of Halfa.

Not the fire. Not the strength.

The way he carried himself, like he didn't ask for space—he just filled it.

Gronk had wanted that. Wanted to stand beside him and not feel like an afterthought. Wanted the city to see them both and not just whisper *"Fire"* when Halfa passed.

He'd told himself power would be enough. A title. A crew. A coin pouch that didn't jingle empty.

But it hadn't made him taller.

Hadn't made the mirror any kinder.

Voices drifted through the dark. A pair of Blackjaws, drinking near the stairwell.

"...Ash Rats got numbers, no direction. "

"...street rats with kitchen knives. "

"...would fold if someone pressed. "

Gronk didn't speak. Didn't move.

He knew that tone. That laugh. It used to be his.

He thought of the Rats. Scrappy. Disorganised. Hopeful enough to keep trying even when hope wasn't cheap.

He didn't pity them.

He envied them.

They didn't know what it cost to stand still. To look at what you've built and realise it's just scaffolding around someone else's throne.

He stared through the bars. Past the dark. Past the hurt.

And for the first time since the cage door slammed, he wished he'd run farther.

He didn't hear her until she was close enough to whisper.

"Still breathing?"

The voice was low. Calm.

Gronk blinked. The torchlight barely reached the cage, but her features cut clean through the dark—curved horns, deep crimson skin, and sharp-angled eyes like frost-glass.

"Rix. "

He'd heard the name whispered in corners. A tiefling who moved between gangs without kneeling to any. Eyes that saw things before they happened. A shadow with a knife.

She crouched by the lock, tools already moving.

"Didn't think I had a reputation with the bleeding elite," she muttered.

"You don't," Gronk said. "But I listen. "

The lock clicked once. Then again. She moved quickly, confidently.

"Why are you letting me out?"

"Because I don't like cages," she said. "And I don't like where this is going. "

"You don't even know me. "

"I know what you could be. "

He said nothing.

"You picked Valka," she went on. "Could've picked anyone. But you picked the one who turns mages to ash and wipes out her rivals. "

"I picked not starving. " It sounded weak, even to him.

"Didn't have to stay once the meal turned rotten. "

The final click came. Clean.

She met his eyes. Her gaze didn't accuse. It measured.

"You're not the man they say you are. "

"No. "

"Good. I wouldn't have come for him. "

She opened the door.

He stepped out slow. Knees shook but held.

"You gonna run?" she asked.

"Not this time. "

She handed him a knife. Plain steel. Well cared for.

"More where that came from?" he asked.

"If you earn it. " She didn't smile. "I have an idea for you. I think you'll like it. "

❦

Grayspire never truly rested. Even when its taverns dimmed their lanterns, and the watch bells stopped ringing, the city exhaled through alleyways and steam vents, smoke curling like whispers from rooftops, soft clatter from late-night gamblers, the low hum of a world that didn't believe in silence. It breathed like a thing alive. Loud. Cracked. Relentless.

Halfa Schoona walked the morning streets in uniform, his boots scuffing cobblestones slick with dew and soot. The crimson sash at his waist marked him as

Watch, but fewer people sneered now. Fewer averted their eyes or flinched when his shadow passed. Some even nodded, a silent gesture of respect, quiet as the dawn.

His probation had ended without ceremony. A scroll signed in triplicate. A grunt from the captain. And a paper badge replaced by a real one. The celebration at the temple afterwards was a stark contrast.

He kept the badge tucked in the left side of his coat.

Grayspire still snarled. Still lied. Still devoured the weak when no one watched. But Halfa wasn't bracing for its teeth anymore.

But part of him still flinched when someone called him Watchman without a sneer. He'd spent so long being the outsider, the brawler, the fire barely held back. Acceptance sat in his chest like a stone that hadn't figured out if it was a gift or a burden. Some nights, it felt like wearing someone else's peace.

Doubt still clung to him on some mornings like soot. When he passed alleys and saw Blackjaw marks etched in rust.

The Watch uniform finally fit.

Tailored to Halfa's massive frame, it no longer pinched his shoulders or threatened to split at the seams when he moved. It wasn't flattering, but it felt less like a costume now. Less like a borrowed title. More like... something he'd earned.

"You still walk like you're carrying a cathedral on your back," Brannig Barrelshield muttered as she buckled her vambrace, and then tossed a half-eaten pastry at him across the barracks.

He caught it without flinching.

"Relax the shoulders, lad. You're not hoisting the whole damn Watch."

Halfa took a bite. It was dense and flaky, filled with something that tasted like lemon and coal. "Not yet."

Brannig barked a laugh. "Ha! That's the spirit."

Her laugh was like a door slamming open, a little too loud, unexpected, but oddly welcome. She moved through the Watchhouse like a storm in steel, all squared jaw and rolling stride, the kind of woman who scared you *and* made you want to impress her. Halfa liked her more than he let on.

She had become more than a mentor. She was a constant. The rare officer who didn't lead from a pedestal, but from the mud beside you.

Brannig stood at her locker, back turned. Her other vambrace sat on the bench beside her, worn leather cracked from years of use. She reached for it, paused, and muttered something under her breath—too quiet to catch, but the rhythm of it was familiar. Old. A soldier's prayer, Halfa realised.

She fastened the vambrace, jerking the strap tighter than needed. Her breath hitched, not enough to draw attention, but enough to know it hurt.

Halfa said nothing.

When she turned, her face was already stone again. Helm tucked under one arm. Voice brisk.

"Pickbone Alley. Snake oil seller has been peddling fake healing potions. Sick folk are getting sicker. You feel like ruining someone's morning?"

"Always," Halfa said.

Brannig pulled on her helm. "Then let's make a house call. "

◊

Pickbone Alley lived up to its name.

It twisted behind the fishmongers' lane like a forgotten spine, narrow and crooked, flanked by leaning buildings that looked like they were conspiring to collapse. The stench of boiled bones and vinegar clung to every step. Halfa turned sideways to pass without knocking over a line of stained laundry.

Brannig marched ahead like she was daring the street to bite her.

"Place reeks like a troll's soup pot," she muttered, brushing aside a curtain of drying fish scales and beaded charms. "I hate when fake priests get creative. "

Behind the glitter curtain stood the man in question. Wiry. Pale. A little too smooth around the eyes for someone this deep in the gutter. His fingers were ink-stained from his fake potion labels, and he was already muttering some nonsense about "spirit-cleansing tinctures" when Brannig raised a brow.

"Run," she said flatly.

And he did.

Tried, at least.

Halfa stepped into the doorway like a landslide.

The man bounced off his chest with a soft "oof" and stumbled back, hands flailing. Brannig caught him in a spin, slapped irons on his wrists, and yanked him forward with all the ceremony of dragging out spoiled meat.

"Congratulations," she said cheerfully. "You've won a complimentary walk through the market square with your reputation tied behind your back. "

The man protested.

"Don't flatter him," Halfa said, stepping aside.

"I wasn't," Brannig replied. "I meant the sick folks will cheer when they see us hauling your bony arse to the cells. "

As they marched him through the alley, the neighbours peeked from behind shutters and market stalls. Halfa saw more than a few nods of approval. A woman clapped once and threw a wilted daisy onto the cobbles.

He didn't smile. But he walked a little taller.

They stepped out of Pickbone Alley into the pale midmorning light; the scammer squirming between them, his complaints falling on deaf ears. Brannig adjusted her grip on the iron chain and muttered under her breath.

"Ash Rats. "

Halfa glanced over. "What about them?"

She jerked her chin toward the alley behind them. "Heard their sigil was chalked on the back wall last week. Near the fish barrels. "

Halfa frowned. "You think this guy's one of them?"

"No," she said. "Too soft. But maybe he paid someone for protection. Or space. " She shook her head, sighing like someone remembering a bruise. "They're not all bad. Started out running couriers for old priests and blind cobblers, street kids carving out their own rules. But when the jobs dried up, some of them didn't stay harmless. "

Halfa's brow furrowed. "They've got structure?"

"Some," Brannig said. "Enough to worry me. Enough to make a mess if they grow teeth. "

The scammer tripped on a cobblestone. Brannig didn't slow down.

🔥

Halfa didn't drink after his shifts.

He didn't linger for dice games or follow the others to the taverns. He walked east instead, past the gutter stalls and soot-stained archways, through the twisting heart of Grayspire where laughter echoed louder than coin, and lantern smoke curled like memory.

He walked until the old temple found him again.

The courtyard was patched with new stone where fire had cracked the walk. Though faded and fewer, the silks still swayed above the garden, stitched by patient hands. The sanctuary roof had been replaced, the beams raw and pale against the soot-stained walls. The scent of clove lingered. A tambourine jingled faintly somewhere inside, off-rhythm, but not off-beat.

The Temple of Thessira was healing.

And Halfa came here because it helped him remember how.

Inside, voices hummed in quiet rituals. Children whispered in the prayer hall. Marin's laughter echoed once, quick and sharp, before trailing into the back kitchen. Bilbin's voice followed, grumbling about spoons and joy being "bloody unmeasurable. "

Serelion passed him in the entryway, robes singed at the hem but face soft. They said nothing, offered him a cup of citrus tea and a look that demanded nothing.

Here, Halfa wasn't the Watchman. Not the Wall. Not the fire walker.

Just Halfa.

He sat in the sanctuary long after the lamps were lit. No sermon. No music. Just the sound of a broom on tile and distant voices. He let it fill him.

Later, Marin found him beneath the central arch, where the spiral tiles had been cleaned and re-laid, half-burnt, half-restored, uneven but unbroken. She sat beside him, cross-legged, one hand tracing a line between tiles.

"Fire's quieter now," she said.

Halfa nodded. "So am I. "

She passed him a lantern. Small. Painted in laughing orange. The kind used for festival processions, once.

"This one needs a flame," she said.

Halfa held it in both hands. Closed his eyes.

No rage. No fear.

Just... intention.

A spark flickered in his palm. It curled into the wick and caught, gentle, golden, stubborn.

They watched it glow together.

Marin leaned against his shoulder. "You carry them with you, don't you?"

He didn't answer right away. Just watched the flame. Thought of Gronk. Of the men he'd burned. The ones who'd run. The ones who hadn't and those who never got to choose.

His voice was low when it came.

"I have to," he said. "If I don't... who else will?"

Marin didn't reply. She didn't have to.

"The ones I couldn't save. The ones I didn't understand. "

Marin didn't move. "I think most of us carry someone. "

"Do you?"

"My uncle. He taught me to dance. Said joy was a protest. " She smiled faintly. "He was arrested for helping a mage family escape the South Quarter. Back when they were outlawed. "

"What happened to him?"

"I never found out. "

They sat in silence a little longer, shoulder to shoulder.

"I don't want to just survive them," Halfa said. "The ghosts. "

"You want to honour them. "

"I want to outlive them. Rightly. "

Marin looked over. "Then you already are. "

◈

It started with whispers. A new gang. Young. Fast. Petty thefts and courier jobs. No territory yet, but ambition in spades.

"They call themselves the *Rats of Fortune*," Brannig said, chewing a roasted pepper as they walked through the winding lanes of the Midden Markets. "Cute, right? Until they cut purses instead of deals. "

Halfa raised an eyebrow. "Organised?"

"About as much as a drunk parade," she muttered. "But desperate kids get dangerous quick. "

They passed spice carts and sleeping beggars. The morning air was thick with smoke and the scent of cinnamon. Somewhere, a woman shouted about oysters and divine prophecy in the same breath.

The Rats had made a hideout behind a collapsed bakery. A cellar with a warped door, blocked by crates and a chalk-drawn symbol of a rat on a piece of slate.

Inside: six children, none older than fifteen. Ragged clothes, sharp eyes, improvised weapons. A butter knife. A splintered chair leg. One boy had painted a scar over his eye, though the real one beneath it was whole.

The girl in charge stepped forward, bold chin, tangled curls, a badge of bone and thread on her chest.

"We're a gang," she said defiantly. "We've got rules. "

Brannig raised a brow. "Really. What rules?"

"No stealing from temple boxes," the girl said. "No knifing kids. And no giving up. "

Halfa crouched to her level, resting his arms on his knees. "Rats of Fortune? Sounds a bit too close to the Ash Rats. "

The girl glanced at the others. "We like them, but don't want to join them. "

He reached into his pouch. Pulled out a single copper coin and placed it on the nearest crate.

"Buy bread," he said. "Next time I find you here, it'll be latrine duty in the prison yard. "

Brannig added with a growl, "With your toothbrush. "

The kids scattered.

Outside, Brannig exhaled and rolled her shoulders. "You're a strange kind of Watchman, Halfa. "

"I've seen worse," he replied.

And for a second, they both stood still, quiet, solid in the chaos of Grayspire.

◊

The temple was quieter at night. Not silent, but softer. The laughter faded to murmurs, the tambourines to heartbeat rhythms. Lanterns painted the mended walls in amber and rose, and the scent of clove hung low in the air like an old song remembered.

Halfa sat at one of the low tables near the eastern archway, his elbows on his knees, a single candle burning in front of him. The flame threw his shadow long across the tile.

Bilbin shuffled in from the kitchen, mug in one hand, biscuit in the other, and muttering something foul about tea leaves. He dropped onto the cushion beside Halfa with a grunt and no ceremony.

"Tea?" he offered. "Tastes like remorse and boiled twine. But it's hot. "

Halfa accepted it without a word.

They sat in silence for a while. The candle flickered once, as if it was listening too.

"I ever tell you," Bilbin said, "about the time I burned down my cousin's spice shed trying to impress a girl with fireworks?"

Halfa looked over. "No. "

"Good. Don't ask. Moron move. Never got the girl. Lost the shed. Gained a lifelong fear of coriander. "

The candle crackled. Bilbin took a bite of his biscuit and chewed like it owed him money.

"You've been lighting a lot of these lately. "

Halfa's eyes stayed on the flame. "Feels like I should. "

Bilbin shrugged. "Sure. Light's good. But don't let it fool you into thinking it pays off a debt. "

Halfa didn't answer. Just sat with it.

"You still carrying it all?" Bilbin asked. "The fire?"

Halfa flexed his hand. "It's quieter. But yeah. "

"Good," Bilbin said. "Keep it banked. Don't let it burn your damn eyebrows off again. "

Another pause.

"You're not the fire, lad. You're the bloke who pulled soup out of a half-burnt pantry and fed thirty scared acolytes. That's what I remember. "

Halfa blinked. "You remember that?"

"Course I do," Bilbin grunted. "Burned the onions, but you tried. "

He stood, brushed crumbs off his apron.

"This one's for Serelion," he muttered, nodding toward the candle. "Not 'cause they're gone. Just 'cause I'm still glad they're not. "

Halfa nodded. "Me too. "

Bilbin turned to go, then looked over his shoulder. "Don't sit out here too long. Moon's full of opinions. You'll start thinking you're poetic, and then I'll have to stage an intervention. "

"No lute," Halfa said.

"Good lad. Lutes are for men who've given up. "

And then he left, muttering about biscuits and the fundamental weakness of tea.

Halfa stayed.

The candle flickered.

And this time, it didn't feel like a weight.

Just... company.

⟡

Someone had updated the shift board in wet ink when Halfa arrived at the Watchhouse the next morning. His name had been slotted beneath a hastily scrawled heading: Special Patrol–Shambles District.

No initials from Brannig. No notes from the captain.

But Dot's signature curved at the bottom like a dagger with a curl.

The Shambles was Grayspire's broken rib. It was a place of slanted homes, leaking windows, and the gutters there ran past Burnmouth Square, where old statues leaned so far they whispered secrets to the cobbles. It was where smugglers and street crews clashed in whispers and knives, where the coin was lighter than breath and just as easy to lose.

Halfa scanned the roster. Two names he didn't recognise. Probationaries. Young. One that he recognised had been in a training drill last week. Thin, wide-eyed, nervous. The other? A boy with too-new boots and too many questions.

Halfa's gut turned to stone.

Dot stood in the room's corner, polishing a badge with a cloth that didn't need to be there.

"Just a little cleanup," he said without looking up. "Rumours of illegal shipments in a butcher's cellar. Go in quiet. Come out fast. "

Halfa didn't respond. He didn't need to.

Dot smiled. "You're not worried, are you, Stoneface?"

"No," Halfa said. "But maybe you should be. "

Dot's eyes flicked up. For a moment, something cold passed between them. No fire. No rage.

Calculation.

Then the moment passed.

Halfa turned away. But the knot in his stomach didn't loosen.

Something was wrong. He could feel it in the way Dot grinned. In the way Brannig's name was missing. In the way the city that never stopped breathing seemed to hold its breath when he stepped out onto the cobbles.

And somewhere ahead, The Shambles waited.

Smoked Out

The rain had barely begun when Dot summoned Halfa to the planning hall.

He caught his reflection in the window glass of the Watchhouse wall. His uniform pressed, boots shined, badge polished. He didn't quite believe the man looking back was real.

He thought of the flame in his hands the night before. Of the way it jumped too fast when all he wanted was a flicker.

If the Watch trusted him, why didn't he trust himself?

The room was empty, just the two of them and a map pinned crooked on the wall, curling at the edges. Candlelight flickered across the parchment, throwing shadows over the districts. Dot stood beside it, posture relaxed, expression unreadable.

"It's time," he said.

Halfa folded his arms. "Brannig's not on shift. "

"Exactly. " Dot gave a thin smile. "Which means you're acting lead. Congratulations. "

He walked to a side table and handed over a folded map that was thin and smudged. The ink bled through in places, blurring the alley names.

"No kits?" Halfa asked.

Dot shook his head. "Won't need them. Quick check-in. Quiet corner. The illegal shipments will be in the butcher's shop. In and out. "

Halfa stared at the map, then at Dot.

"You coming? "

Dot's smile widened, cold as winter steel. "Can't risk being seen. Politics, you understand. "

He clapped Halfa on the shoulder, then turned to leave.

"Just stick to the plan," he said over his shoulder. "Don't do anything... dramatic."

The door closed behind him.

Halfa stood alone, the map heavy in his hand. Outside, thunder rumbled somewhere over the rooftops.

He didn't like the way the air felt.

Not at all.

◉

The Shambles breathed rot and ruin.

Halfa led the patrol through its broken arteries, alleys too narrow for carriages, buildings leaning like drunkards propping one another up. The stones beneath their boots were slick with rain and worse. Fog clung low, thick as wool, curling around their ankles like a warning.

Halfa passed a shop window cracked with age and glimpsed himself in the glass. Big. Pale. Heavy in a world built for smaller people.

Gronk was the only one who looked like him, and even then, not quite. They had the same bones, the same weight behind their strides. But Gronk didn't burn. Gronk didn't question the fire's origin or its borrowed feeling.

He was the only Goliath he'd ever known. No tribe had claimed him. No elders had passed down stories. There were no songs to remind him who he was or where his fire had come from.

All he had were whispers in the dark, rumours spoken with fear, guesses made by men who had only ever seen his kind bleeding on a battlefield or dragging stones across scaffolding.

People called them monsters until they needed them. Then, they became tools.

People looked at him and saw a brute. They looked at Gronk and saw a threat. No one ever stopped to wonder if either of them might just be lost.

The fire didn't come with answers. Just heat. And silence.

Behind him moved three Watch recruits: Lasse, long-limbed and jittery, fingers never far from the hilt of his baton; Gorne, wide-shouldered and loud, his bravado barely concealing nerves; and Tallen, youngest, his crisp crest pin already dulled by rain, but still gleaming like the boy believed in it.

None of them belonged here. Not yet.

Halfa had walked places like this before, slums where the walls whispered murder and every window watched with hunger. But the Shambles didn't whisper.

It laughed.

The group passed shuttered stalls and boarded doors. Not a soul stirred.

"This doesn't feel right," Tallen muttered, glancing into the mist. "Where's the noise?"

"Where's anyone?" Lasse added, voice tight. "Smugglers don't hide in dead zones."

Halfa raised a fist to halt them. They froze.

Crooked Nail Lane lay ahead, just as the map showed. An old butcher's shop hunched in the corner. Its windows were boarded. No smell of meat. Not even flies. A crooked lantern hung above the frame, too clean. Too wrong.

Halfa's stomach tightened.

He turned to the others. "Circle left. Check the alley. Quiet. Stay close."

They moved, boots silent on wet stone. Halfa advanced toward the butcher's door, knuckles tight around his baton.

The silence deepened.

Then came the sound.

A bottle shattered. A hiss filled the air.

Thick, acrid smoke exploded from the alley mouth behind them.

The fog turned violent.

A glass bottle burst near Lasse's feet, spraying shards across the cobbles. Smoke poured upward—oily, choking, bitter as burned blood sausage. In heartbeats, the alley transformed into a trap.

Halfa barely had time to shout—"DOWN!"—before shadows erupted from the mist.

Four attackers. Fast. Masked. Blades in hand.

Tallen tried to raise his baton. He took a club to the temple and dropped like a sack of grain.

Gorne roared, drawing his short blade. He charged blindly into the haze, and was cut down. A smuggler slashed across his side, drawing a dark red arc that sent him staggering backward.

Lasse froze, looking over at Halfa for guidance.

"Retreat!" Halfa shouted, grabbing Tallen's limp form by the collar. "Fall back—signal flare—where's the gods' damned flare?!"

But no one answered. No flares. No smoke cloaks. Dot had said they wouldn't need them.

Dot had lied.

A smuggler came in low from Halfa's left. Halfa pivoted, catching the blade on his bracer. He struck with his elbow, bone to temple. The man dropped.

Another rolled a smoke bomb at his feet. It hissed, releasing a blinding veil.

Halfa coughed. Vision swimming. Choking. He could barely make out Gorne collapsing, blood smearing the cobbles like ink in the rain.

The fire stirred in his chest. It was rising, pleading, begging to burn. One burst would clear the smoke. One blaze, and the attackers would run.

No.

He forced it down.

Not here. Not yet.

He lunged toward Gorne, hoisting him with one arm, dragging Tallen with the other. Lasse stumbled into view, his eyes wide, face pale. Halfa barked, "Run! Cover! Now!"

They staggered through a side passage. Halfa kicked down a door. Splintered wood. A cellar. They vanished into it like ghosts into a tomb.

The smugglers didn't follow.

The cellar stank of mould and old blood. Gorne's ragged breathing echoed off the stone. Tallen's pulse was faint beneath Halfa's fingers. Lasse sobbed once, then bit it down.

Halfa didn't speak. He couldn't.

He stared into the darkness where the smoke still writhed, and for a moment, he hated the silence more than the danger.

And the knowledge that this was never supposed to be a fair fight.

The Watchhouse doors slammed open under Halfa's boot.

He carried Gorne over one shoulder, blood trailing down his back, and dragged Tallen by the arm—his tunic soaked, his head lolling. Lasse stumbled behind them, coughing, eyes raw from smoke. Not a single flare had been fired. Not a single healer had come.

Inside, the light blazed too brightly.

And Dot sat behind the front desk.

Neatly dressed. Clean gloves. Perfect posture. Not a speck of soot on him.

A folder sat before him.

Halfa lowered Gorne to the ground. Gently. Tallen, too. Then turned.

Dot didn't look up. "You're late. "

Halfa stared.

"Loss of control," Dot recited, tapping the report. "Acted without support. Bypassed fallback protocol. Disobeyed thresholds for The Shambles patrol. Result: critical injury of recruits and failure to apprehend suspects. "

"You wrote that," Halfa growled, "before I got back. "

"I anticipated the outcome. "

Halfa stepped forward. "There were no maps. No smog gear. You signed them out; I checked the log. "

"Then perhaps," Dot said, brushing invisible dust from his cuff, "you'll file a formal grievance. Or perhaps you'll realise you're lucky I'm not recommending expulsion. "

Halfa's fists curled.

"You set us up," he said. "You lied to me. "

"I gave you a chance to lead. " Dot finally looked up. His eyes were flat as glass. "You failed. Some flames just aren't meant to burn clean. "

For a breath, Halfa's chest expanded, not from rage, but from restraint. The fire clawed at him, a serpent in his lungs. But he held it.

He didn't speak again.

He turned.

And walked out.

◊

Halfa stood in the hallway outside the infirmary, fists clenched so tight his palms ached. Behind the closed door, Gorne groaned through his bandaged ribs. Tallen hadn't stirred once. And Dot—Dot sat inside the front office, *smiling like nothing had happened.*

The fire inside him surged.

He could feel it rising in his throat, sparking behind his eyes, burning along the edges of every breath. He saw flashes: smoke pouring from the Watchhouse doors, Dot's polished desk scorched black, words turned to cinders.

His body glowed.

One step. Just one, and he could let it out.

He took it.

And stopped.

His boots trembled against the stone floor. He pressed a hand to his chest. Not to hold himself back. Only to remember what was still there.

The temple of Thessira. It still stood and had been almost burnt to the ground because of his fire. He didn't want to lose control again.

Not here. Not now. Not like this.

The fire subsided. Not gone. Never gone. But obeying.

Just in time.

Somewhere behind him, a rookie's voice cracked in a training drill. The Watchhouse kept breathing. And so did he.

◊

Brannig stormed into the captain's office like a thunderclap, Halfa lurking behind her.

The door slammed hard enough to rattle the ink pots. She held a file in one hand and fury in the other. Dot stood behind the captain, casually leaning against a wall.

"Where were the kits?!" she shouted, slamming the folder down. "You sent rookies into The Shambles with no flare oil and no smog gear!"

The captain barely looked up from his ledger. "Dot said it was a clean sting. Low risk. "

"He lied. "

The captain flipped a page.

"He *forged* requisitions. "

"You can't prove that. "

Brannig took a step forward. Her voice dropped, low, cold. "You know what happened out there. One unconscious. One nearly bled out. Another too shaken to speak. "

The captain finally looked up.

"Dot's been reassigned. "

Brannig blinked. "What?"

"Effective immediately. Dock Yards. Senior Logistics Officer. "

"That's not punishment. "

"It's politics," the captain said. "Officers above are making noise. Someone had to take the fall. "

"And Halfa?"

"Demoted. Stable watch. " A beat. "Officially: 'Reassignment pending review of judgment and protocol adherence. '"

Brannig's eyes narrowed.

Dot tapped the edge of the captain's desk with two fingers, the motion casual as spilled ink.

"Told you that wall would crack. "

The word hit differently this time. No camaraderie. No respect. Just a label turned inside out.

Halfa didn't respond.

He didn't need to.

But he felt the weight of it. How a name could shift in someone else's mouth, lose all the warmth it once held.

Brannig clenched her fists. "He did everything right. "

The captain gave her a long, tired look. "This isn't about right. It's about quiet. "

Brannig turned and walked out—jaw tight, boots echoing down the hall.

Halfa followed on to the barracks steps. Rain fell in thin sheets.

"They gave him a god damned *promotion*," she muttered.

Halfa didn't answer.

"They're afraid of you," she said softly. "You scare them more than the smugglers or gangs ever did. "

He didn't look at her. Just whispered, "I did everything right. I didn't burn. Didn't lash out. I followed orders. "

"I know. "

"They still think I'm a threat. "

Brannig rested a hand on his arm. "You're not a threat, lad. You're a punishment they don't know how to justify on paper. "

He turned to her. Rain soaked his brow.

"So what now?"

She didn't answer. Because they both knew.

🜂

That evening, with the temple quiet and dusk crawling in, Halfa lingered near the back corridor where the eastern lamps were kept. One had burned out, a simple oil lantern, its wick damp with failed flint strikes.

He glanced around. No footsteps. No voices.

He raised his hand.

Focused.

"Just a spark," he muttered.

The fire came—too fast.

A burst, not a flicker.

The glass lantern cracked with the heat, and the oil inside hissed like a threatened animal.

Too fast again. Every time he tried with care, it slipped, like it didn't trust calm. Only anger opened the door. But Serelion said joy burns slower. Brighter. He just hadn't found the spark yet.

Halfa lunged forward, hands cupping the flame, forcing it down with breath and will. It guttered out, leaving the air stinking of scorched metal and smoke.

He stared at his hands, fingers red from the brief blaze.

Not enough to injure.

But enough to remind him that the fire wasn't tame. Not yet.

He exhaled slowly, rubbing his palms on his trousers as if he could scrub the heat away. The scent of scorched oil still clung to his sleeves. For a few moments, he stayed there, alone in the corridor's quiet hush, listening to the distant sounds of laughter echoing through the temple. Joy was alive, just beyond the wall. He could hear it in the music, in the rustle of silks, in the cadence of children's feet. But part of him still sat in the shadows, staring at his hands, unsure how to cross the space between fire and celebration.

He sat back on his heels, the hiss of the extinguished flame still sharp in his ears. The broken lantern guttered beside him, its cracked glass glinting with faint orange. He reached for a streamer that had fallen loose from the nearby shelf, a length of dyed silk meant for the courtyard festivities, and held it between his fingers.

The edge singed.

Melted where the fire had flared too fast, too hot. The blue and gold had turned muddy, crisped into ash at the fringe. He hadn't even seen it catch.

Halfa stared at it, shoulders curling in, the silence thick around him. He didn't mean to burn it. He didn't mean to ruin something meant for joy.

He hadn't noticed the footsteps.

Serelion knelt beside him, wordless at first. They didn't touch him. Didn't scold or soothe. Just watched the streamer in his hands, their presence as calm and inevitable as sunrise.

And then the courtyard sounds returned, laughter drifting in, music tuning, petals spinning in lazy arcs outside the open door.

Streamers and laughter filled the temple courtyard, petals fluttering like confetti in the breeze. Children were chasing coloured lanterns. Somewhere, Marin was tuning a stringed instrument far too large for her frame, and Bilbin shouted at the stew pot like it owed him money.

"I didn't mean to burn it," he muttered. "It was just joy. It felt bright. But it jumped. It... broke."

Serelion nodded gently, their eyes reflecting the candlelight.

"Your fire doesn't come from hate, Halfa. It answers emotion. Rage lights fast, but joy? Joy is a slower flame. Harder to summon. Stronger when it holds. "

Serelion knelt in front of him, their robe smeared with chalk dust and petal fragments. Their dark hair was pulled back, crownless today, a priest among people.

"Joy doesn't break," they said softly. "It changes shape. "

Halfa looked down at the ruined ribbon.

"Fire's part of joy too," Serelion continued. "But only if you choose *why* it burns. Rage will always be ready. But joy..." They touched his chest gently. "Joy needs to be invited. "

"How?"

They smiled. "Start with laughter. Start with something silly. "

They leaned back and pulled another ribbon from her pocket, bright pink, twice as long, with mismatched ends, like a snake that had lost a bet. They tied it around their wrist, knotting it once, twice, then thrice.

"Try again," they said.

"But I'll—"

"And if you do?" Their grin grew. "We'll light it on purpose next time and call it a festival. "

Halfa stared. Then, slowly, he opened his palm.

A spark bloomed—small, warm, steady. The pink ribbon fluttered but didn't catch.

Serelion's smile turned reverent.

"There it is," they whispered. "Joy fights back. Even from fire. "

◈

The hall smelled of herbs and boiled linen. Lanternlight flickered off polished brass, casting long shadows across the infirmary walls. Halfa stepped in quietly, his boots nearly silent against the stone. The weight of the patrol still clung to his shoulders, blood-soaked memories, smoke-stained thoughts.

Three cots lined the far wall.

Tallen lay in the first cot, a bandaged head and breaths shallow but even. His family crest pin still sat on the table beside him, wiped clean.

Gorne occupied the second, his ribs wrapped, one arm strapped to his chest. A healer had scrawled arcane runes along the bandages to numb the pain. He twitched in restless sleep.

And in the third bed, Lasse, uninjured but shaken.

His eyes were open.

Halfa stopped beside him.

"You look like someone fell down the gods' staircase," Lasse muttered. His voice was rough, but his grin flickered like an old flame. "Was it bad?"

Halfa didn't answer right away. He looked down at the bruises blooming along the boy's arms, the split lip, the clumsy stitch across his brow.

"I should've called the retreat earlier," Halfa said quietly. "Should've pulled you out before the first blade dropped. "

"You *did pull* us out," Lasse said. "That's why I'm still breathing. "

Halfa sat on the edge of the cot, silent.

"I've never seen anyone move like that," Lasse continued. "Through the smoke, through the shouting—like you were made for it. Like the rest of us were just playing Watch. "

Halfa looked at him. "We're not supposed to be made for it. "

Lasse's grin faded.

"I just wanted to be useful," he said. "First time I felt like I could be something more than a scribe's cousin. " He shifted slightly, wincing. "Didn't think it would get people killed. "

"It didn't," Halfa said. "You held formation. You followed orders. What happened wasn't on you. "

He paused.

Then added, "It was on Dot. "

Lasse closed his eyes. "Doesn't matter now, does it? I heard you got demoted. "

Halfa stood. "Titles don't matter. What we do does. "

He reached out, placing a hand gently on Lasse's shoulder—solid, steady.

"I'll come by tomorrow," Halfa said. "You're not alone in this. "

Lasse gave a tired nod.

Halfa turned to leave.

Behind him, Lasse whispered, "You didn't burn, did you?"

Halfa paused in the doorway.

"No," he said. "But I almost did. "

Then he stepped into the hall, where the scent of boiling herbs gave way to candle wax and rain.

◊

That night, Halfa didn't sleep.

He walked east, away from the barracks, the paperwork, the rain that still clung to his shoulders. Away from Dot's smile. Away from the silence that followed when the system decided a threat had no place in its ranks.

Through the veins of Grayspire he moved, past shuttered taverns and echoing courtyards, past candlelit windows and laughter that didn't belong to him. The city didn't notice his steps. But something beneath the stones seemed to shift as he passed, as if it, too, had been holding its breath.

He stopped at a violet-painted door between a bookbinder's shop and an old theatre, its frame cracked with time and its threshold humming with warmth.

The Temple of Thessira.

He didn't knock. He didn't need to.

Inside, the air smelled of rose oil and smouldering cinnamon. Music floated through the halls. It was not loud, not joyous, but gentle. Like comfort offered from across the room with no need to speak.

Bilbin was humming in the kitchen, loud, tuneless, and with enough flour in his beard to count as a fire hazard. Marin moved through the entryway with a tray of candles, her braid lopsided, her eyes bright, pausing to light each wick with a whispered blessing and a grin. Near the southern pillar, Serelion balanced on a low stool, painting a new joy symbol in sweeping gold strokes. Their robes were spattered with pigment, their expression serene, their fingers steady, each brushstroke a prayer that didn't need words.

No one turned when he entered.

They gave him space.

Halfa stepped through the spiral.

One step. Another.

Boots scuffed the tiled path, worn smooth from decades of prayers, of stories told without words. And those tiles were mixed with the new tiles recently laid. The incense made his eyes sting.

He let each step take something from him: the weight of the alley, the sound of Tallen's fall, the way Gorne bled, the smell of singed hair, the paper with Dot's lies. Each step bled it out.

At the centre of the spiral sat a shallow clay bowl, its surface rippling with water. Floating inside it: a glass charm, shaped like a flickering flame.

Serelion's flame.

Halfa knelt. The floor was cool beneath his knees.

He reached into the bowl and lifted the charm. Water slid down his fingers. He held it tight.

He let himself breathe.

This place... it never asked him to burn. Not to prove himself. Not to survive.

Here, the fire didn't need to roar. It could whisper. Rest.

He looked at the charm in his hand, the same spiral Serelion had worn through smoke and ruin, and realised it hadn't just survived the fire.

It had chosen to.

Serelion had been watching. They stepped closer, their voice soft as silk drawn through ash.

"Keep it," they said. "Let it remind you where you are, not only what you've done. "

◐

Halfa was still in a mood as he moved towards the back of the temple. That was until he heard Marin's laugh nearby.

Marin was laughing. Not loud, but enough to make any space warmer.

Halfa hadn't even meant to be there. He'd passed the storeroom after his time at the altar, and found her half-buried by some fallen crates.

"You all right?" he asked from the doorway.

She turned, a small pile of wax-stuck bundles in her hands. Her cheeks were flushed. "Define 'all right. '"

"Unbleeding. Untrapped under something heavy. "

"Then yes. " She wiped her brow with the back of her wrist. "I'm trying to find two dozen uncracked prayer candles before morning. "

"That sounds like punishment. "

"No, this is joy," she said with mock reverence. "Can't you feel it radiating off me?"

Halfa found himself smiling, quietly. "You're not as subtle as you think. "

"What gave me away?"

"The sarcasm. And the wax in your hair. "

She laughed again. "Come in, then. Might as well help. "

He stepped in. The room was cramped, shadowed, and smelled of cloves and oil. Marin's presence seemed to fill it.

She handed him a misshapen candle. Their fingers brushed.

She didn't move right away.

Neither did he.

"You're good at this," he said eventually.

"Candle sorting?"

"Making things less... heavy. "

Her smile didn't fade. "You make things feel solid. Like they'll hold, even when everything else doesn't. "

That struck deeper than he'd expected. He looked down at the candle, then lit it with a slow flick of his thumb. He seemed to have more control when he was around her, when he just felt right.

The light flickered between them.

Marin tilted her head. "You always do that? No flint, just flame?"

"Only when I trust what I'm lighting. "

She didn't respond for a moment. Then: "Good line. "

"Wasn't meant to be. "

"All the better. "

He met her eyes. They were sharp, kind, and a little curious.

"You're staring," she said.

"I know. "

She didn't look away.

The candle flame flickered. Not from wind. From something else.

Marin stepped closer, just half a pace. "Good. Then you'll notice this. "

She plucked the candle from his hand, held it between them, and smiled again. This smile was smaller, but unmistakably directed.

Then she turned and walked out of the storeroom, candle in hand, her shoulders straight, her braid swinging behind her. Joy radiated from her, as always. He didn't fully understand joy. But in moments like this, he knew exactly why it was worth protecting.

Halfa stood still for a moment, pulse steady but strange.

He smiled. Just faintly.

And grabbed the crate of candles.

Embers

Grayspire didn't sleep, but that morning, it came close.

The sky hung low, thick with bruised clouds that rolled like slow thoughts over the crooked rooftops. The usual chaos—street hawkers, cart-jammed lanes, barkers shouting over each other, felt dulled, like someone had thrown a blanket over the city's noise. Halfa Schoona walked through it without speaking, his cloak pulled high, boots slapping through puddles that steamed at the edges. The storm hadn't broken, but the air felt heavy with waiting.

He didn't know if the quiet came from the sky or from him.

The demotion still sat across his shoulders like a second badge, silent and unmistakable. He wore the uniform, still. Walked the beat. His presence held no sway. No more command assignments. No more chances to do anything meaningful, if the captains had their way. He was a shadow with a badge.

It had been just over six weeks since Brannig had signed him on, four since the alley fire. Time enough for the city to forget. Not long enough for the Watch to forgive.

Stable watch. Commons patrol. Lost goats and stolen pastries.

He should've felt relief. There were no knives in the alleys here. No smog bombs or smoke-slick fights in the dark. No young recruits bleeding on the stones because someone played politics.

But he hated it.

Because the rage hadn't left. It just curled up somewhere quieter.

Each night, after the shift, he walked east.

Past the taverns and brothels. Beyond the fish market, where the air turned metallic and wet. Past the old stagehouse with its crumbling arch. Until he reached the violet-painted door with no sign above it.

The Temple of Thessira smelled of clove and citrus again. The rebuilt sanctuary caught the afternoon light in its restored windows, and silk streamers drifted in the breeze from the high courtyard arches. It was smaller than it had been. Less grand. More human.

It had taken nearly two months to get the roof beams up. A miracle, really, Halfa thought.

Halfa found peace in the doing. Not sermons. Not songs. Just motion. Carrying crates. Mending floorboards. Fixing hinges that squeaked too loud during prayers. He helped Bilbin hang lanterns and scrub soot from the garden wall. He didn't speak much. He didn't need to.

Marin gave him tasks without asking. Serelion offered small nods of approval, their gaze lingering a little longer when Halfa worked near the front steps. No one treated him like a weapon anymore. He wasn't the Wall here. Wasn't the Watch. Just Halfa.

One quiet evening, as he swept up fallen petals near the herb beds, Marin approached, hands behind her back.

"Someone left this," she said, voice light. "No name. Found it tucked behind the breadbasket. Thought it might be for you. "

Halfa took the cloth-wrapped bundle. Inside: a sheet of cheap parchment, soft from damp fingers and creased at the corners. A drawing, rough but focused. A spiral flame circled in charcoal petals. Below it, two words, printed in uneven handwriting:

Don't stop.

He didn't speak. Halfa held the note and stared at it for a long while. Then, quietly, he folded it and slid it into his coat, right beside the charm Serelion had given him. The glass flame shimmered slightly brighter in the light.

Later, Halfa found Serelion repainting one of the joy symbols on the main doorframe. Their brush was fine-tipped, their movements slow and deliberate.

Halfa watched them for a while, then stepped closer.

"We should talk," he said softly. "About how to make this place harder to see from the street. Or harder to reach. "

Serelion didn't stop painting. But their head tilted slightly.

"You're not suggesting more walls, I hope. "

"I'd love more walls, but no," Halfa said. "Nothing loud. Just... a second latch on the garden gate. Don't relight the left-side sconces. Keep that wall in shadow. Anyone watching the courtyard from there won't see clearly—but we'll see them. Layers of defence. Quiet ones. "

Serelion paused at the edge of a golden swirl. Then nodded.

"We'll do it. Not because we're afraid. Because we want to stay. "

Halfa didn't smile. But something inside him loosened.

Later that night, he sat at the centre of the temple's spiral floor, surrounded by candlelight and drifting incense. His coat lay folded beside him. The flame charm rested in his palm. The note, too. He held them both.

His friends bled. Fire roared too loud to hear through. But tonight, the temple was quiet. His shoulders didn't ache from armour. His fists weren't curled in warning. He was here. Still.

"Don't stop," he whispered, not to the charm, not to the note, but to himself.

And the fire in his chest answered. Low. Steady. Alive!

◊

At first, he thought he was imagining them.

A smudge of soot under a rainspout. A jagged etching in the corner of a warehouse door. A mark drawn into the dust on a cellar window, three vertical slashes, one diagonal, rough but familiar. Kneeling, Halfa used his sleeve to wipe it away, his heart hammering.

He saw another the next day. Then, two more by the week's end.

They weren't new. Not exactly. Just more frequent. Blackjaw markings showing up all over.

But Halfa had learned to read them.

These were warnings.

And worse, invitations.

The Watch didn't seem to care. Or maybe they didn't notice.

He brought it up during morning rounds with another officer, who shrugged and said the kids probably saw a rat god in their soup again. Someone else told him the marks were old. "Been there for months," they said. "Don't mean nothin'. "

But Halfa had a memory of fire.

He brought it up with Brannig, too. Quietly, over tea near the armoury.

She listened. Drummed her fingers on the tabletop. Then, she shook her head.

"Don't borrow trouble, lad," she muttered. "Grayspire has enough. "

"But if it's them—"

"There's always a 'them. ' There's always smoke in the alleys. This city thrives on looking the other way. "

Her tone wasn't unkind. Just tired. She'd fought too many shadows already.

But Halfa had seen this kind of shadow before.

He'd watched it creep under doorways. He'd watched it drag people he loved into the dark.

He pressed a palm to the badge on his coat. It was just metal. A shape. But it meant something, or it should.

So when the next mark appeared bolder, clearer, and almost proud, Halfa didn't look away.

He stared back.

And he started carrying his flame charm on the outside of his shirt.

Just in case they were watching, too.

❧

The fog came in heavy that night, folding low, over the western lanes near the river district. It dulled the lanternlight, softened the edges of rooftops, and turned every sound into something distant. Halfa's boots struck puddles as he walked, the water dark with soot and runoff from the day's rain. The air smelled faintly of salt and old stone.

Behind him moved Tallen, his partner, for the evening patrol. The youngest of the Shambles rookies, now cleared for light duty. His temple wound had healed into a pale crescent, still visible beneath his cap. He carried himself better now. Shoulders higher. Steps far more confident. But his hand still hovered near his baton with each shadow they passed.

"This part of the route wasn't on our map," Tallen said quietly, voice muffled by the mist. "We're past the checkpoint. You want to double back?"

Halfa didn't answer immediately. The street felt ominous; something lurked. The houses here were too quiet. The lanterns were dimmer than they should have been. He glanced toward a nearby wall where the bricks were slick with moss and years of damp. His breath misted in front of him.

"No," he said finally. "A few more streets. "

Tallen nodded and kept pace.

They turned down a side lane. Ahead, beneath a broken streetlamp, two figures leaned against a wall, one smoking something wrapped in dark paper, the other tossing a small knife from hand to hand, the blade making soft clicks each time it touched stone.

Halfa slowed. Raised one hand to signal caution.

The figures didn't startle.

"You're out late," the smoker said, glancing over with a half-lidded stare. "Can't imagine you came all the way out here for the weather. "

Halfa stepped forward, eyes on the space between them. Not hostile, but not friendly either.

"Move on. "

The smoker exhaled a stream of thin grey smoke, then smiled without humour. "Just stretching our legs. Long night. "

The knife handler chuckled and nodded toward the wall behind them. "You'll like the art," he said.

Halfa's eyes followed the gesture.

Etched into the stone—fresh, unmistakable—was the Blackjaw sigil. A jaw-bone painted boldly in thick, chalky lines. No effort to hide it. No attempt to pretend.

Tallen stiffened beside him.

"You marked Watch territory," Halfa said. His voice didn't rise. It didn't need to.

"Seems to me," the smoker said, pushing off the wall, "some territories don't know who owns them anymore. "

He flicked the stub of his cigarillo into the gutter and stepped back into the mist. The knife handler followed. But before they vanished entirely, the smoker paused.

He turned just slightly, enough to let his voice drift back toward them.

"There's a temple near the theatre district," he said. "Painted ribbons. Laughing lanterns. You know the one. "

Halfa didn't reply.

The man's smile sharpened. "Would be a shame if someone mistook joy for weakness. "

Then they were gone. Swallowed by fog. No footsteps. No echo.

Halfa stood still for a long moment.

Tallen's voice was quiet. "Was that a threat?"

"Yes," Halfa said.

"Should we report it?"

Halfa's hand drifted to his chest, fingers brushing the glass flame charm beneath his coat. The fire inside him stirred. Not hot. Not wild. Stirring.

"We will," he said. "But not to Dot. "

Tallen hesitated. "Then who?"

Halfa turned, eyes scanning the mist behind them one last time. "To the people who need to be ready. "

◉

The Watchhouse felt quieter than usual. A tension clung to the air, not loud, not obvious, but real. Like a string pulled too tight between rafters.

Halfa entered through the side gate, boots dripping river mud. He moved past the drill yard, past the rookies sparring with dulled sticks, past Dot's old office, now empty, curtains drawn.

The archive chamber was tucked beneath the east wing. It was half library, half graveyard. Stone shelves sagged under ledgers no one had touched in years. Halfa had come looking for an old smuggler's logbook that had something about dock permits and back alley passphrases. A guess. A thread.

He crouched beside a crumbling crate marked *Confiscated Records–Undated*, fingers brushing brittle parchment when he heard the door creak behind him.

"Watchman Schoona?"

He looked up.

A junior clerk hovered in the doorway. Gangly. Sallow-skinned. Eyes darting like a bird that had flown into the wrong room. His name was Bern, if Halfa remembered correctly. Bern was barely out of training, mostly tasked with copying patrol logs and sorting lost property claims.

Halfa stood slowly. "Need something?"

Bern entered, closed the door behind him, and scanned the room like the shadows might be listening.

"You didn't hear this from me," he whispered, pressing a folded note into Halfa's hand.

Halfa frowned. "Why?"

Bern swallowed hard. "Because two of our street informants are missing. One turned up with broken legs and no memory of the last week. The other—Tarsi—just... vanished. "

"Tarsi from the Midden Runs?"

Bern nodded quickly. "She asked about sigils near Fish Row. Three days later, her flat was empty. No signs of struggle. Just gone. "

Halfa unfolded the note.

A name. A location.

"Reeve. Tallow Street. Midnight markets. Ask for smoke glass. "

Halfa knew the name. He had heard it before.

Yetta would've called it "the kind of name you whisper into a locked box and hope it doesn't answer. "

Halfa looked up. "Why are you helping me?"

Bern gave a shaky laugh. "Because someone needs to. And because if I disappear, I want at least one honest bastard to know why. "

Then he turned and walked away, the door shutting softly behind him.

Halfa stared at the note in his hand.

Then folded it and tucked it beside the child's drawing in his coat.

◈

Halfa brought the note to Brannig.

Brannig rubbed her temples, exhaling like she was breathing out a weight that wouldn't move.

"You're not the only one noticing things," she muttered. "There is something weird about the Ash Rats. Way too many Ash Rat symbols showing up. "

Halfa raised an eyebrow. "Kids. Street crew. Mostly harmless. "

"That's what they want you to think. Captains love the story, you know, rowdy orphans getting too clever. Blame 'em for a fire, a few missing crates, slap a curfew in the Market Ward, and call it justice. And meanwhile, the Blackjaws stay in the shadows. "

Her gaze hardened.

"But those marks on the stone? That's not kids with chalk. And those disappearances? The Ash Rats didn't orchestrate that. Someone's wearing their name like a mask, and I don't like who's behind it. "

Halfa leaned forward. "Blackjaw?"

Brannig looked away, jaw tight. Then, almost too softly to hear:

"She is fully in charge, we have heard. "

Halfa leaned in.

"Valka Thorne. "

Halfa's fire in him recoiled at the mention.

"She's not loud," Brannig continued. "Not like the thugs you've seen. She doesn't shout. Only whispers. She lets others do the bleeding. By the time you see her shadow. . . usually, it's already too late. "

She stood, adjusted her coat.

"We've all lost things to people like her. "

That night, Halfa lay in his bunk beneath the barracks eaves, arms folded behind his head, staring up at the warped wooden ceiling. Rain tapped gently against the shutters, slow and rhythmic, like a lullaby sung from a rooftop. The barracks creaked around him, quiet save for the occasional grunt or shifting cot from the rookies nearby.

He closed his eyes.

And the world broke open.

He stood in the mountains again.

Not in memory. Not in place. Dreamlike, with towering peaks, fierce winds, and a blood-red sky. Goliaths loomed around him, broad-shouldered, flame-marked, silent. They wore iron bands around their forearms, each etched with a spiral of molten light. Faces were painted in ash and gold. None looked at him. Nonetheless, they parted for him.

At the summit, fire cracked the sky.

He turned and saw himself reflected in the stone. Taller. Wreathed in flame. His arms were glowing like forges, and when he opened his mouth, the breath that came was molten.

Then, the mountain trembled and cracked.

He fell through the peak like a hammer through glass.

Below, there was darkness. Earth. Heat.

He landed in a cavern that pulsed like a heart. And in its centre stood Gronk.

Older now. Scarred. Wrapped in bone-coloured cloth and iron. He stood before a massive forge, not tending it, but speaking to it, whispering into the coals. Something moved behind him in the shadows. Larger than him. Listening.

"You always looked up," Gronk said without turning. "That was your problem. "

Halfa took a step forward. The stone burned under his feet.

"You never asked what was growing beneath you. "

Gronk turned. His eyes glowed the same orange as Halfa's fire. But they didn't burn. They hungered.

Then—

A shift. A flicker.

Halfa stood in the Watch courtyard.

It was wrong.

The air reeked of ash. The flagstones glowed orange beneath cracks that spider-webbed outward. His badge was gone. His sleeves were scorched. He saw Brannig on her knees, coughing through the smoke, one arm shielding her face.

"Tallen!" someone screamed.

The boy stumbled from the shadows, hand outstretched, reaching for Halfa.

And then it came.

The fire.

Too much. Too fast. It exploded from Halfa like a furnace kicked open, spiralling upward in a dome of destruction.

It hit Tallen square in the chest.

Brannig vanished into flame.

Halfa screamed, but the sound was swallowed.

And when the fire receded, nothing remained.

No Watchhouse. No stone. No sky.

Just him, alone in a field of embers.

And the voice.

Valka's.

Calm. Certain.

"You're still trying to burn like them. But you're not like them. "

"You're like me. "

Her voice followed him even into waking. Like it had always been there, beneath the quiet.

His sheets were soaked in sweat. His hands trembled.

Around him, the barracks were quiet. Still. The rain had stopped. No wind moved. The only sound was the soft creak of rafters settling.

Halfa sat up slowly.

He reached for his coat. Fumbled inside.

The charm was there. Serelion's flame.

But it was warm.

Just... aware.

He stared at it for a long time.

He had seen fire from above.

And fire from below.

And now, somewhere in between, he would have to choose what it meant to burn.

Morning came grey and sluggish, dragging clouds like bruises across the sky. Halfa skipped roll call and headed straight for the Watchhouse's upper floor, where the senior offices overlooked the street like stone-faced sentinels.

Brannig's door was half-open. Inside, the scent of ink, boiled leather, and cold tea filled the air.

She was hunched over a stack of logbooks, her braid tucked into the collar of her coat. When she looked up, one eyebrow rose.

"You look like you slept in a smithy. "

Halfa stepped inside, his voice low. "I need you to listen. "

That wiped the humour from her face.

She gestured to the chair across from her, but Halfa remained standing.

"I've been tracking the marks, Ash Rats graffiti, they call it. I think you're right about Blackjaws wearing them like a mask. "

Brannig didn't interrupt.

"They're hiding," he continued. "Behind the Ash Rats. The name's a mask, Brannig. A front. The real hands moving behind this? They're Blackjaw. I still believe the Ash Rats exist. We have seen them ourselves, but these movements are not all going to be from the Ash Rats. "

Brannig closed the ledger slowly. Her expression didn't change, but something behind her eyes went still.

"Go on. "

He told her about the riverside threat. the masked men, the sigil carved openly into stone. About the whisper in the fog: *Your little joy-club... would be a shame if it burned. "*

Brannig sat back, arms crossed.

"You're not wrong," she said at last. "We've suspected for weeks that the Ash Rats name was being used to cover something dirtier. It started with missing crates. Then missing people. Then silence. " She exhaled through her nose. "But we don't have proof. Not enough to take to the captains. "

"They won't move unless it's already on fire," Halfa muttered.

"No. They'll wait until it burns something *convenient*—a merchant guild warehouse, a tax collector's stable. Then it'll be an emergency. "

Her jaw tensed. "Not a temple. Not a slum. Those don't count until someone wealthy writes it down. "

Halfa folded his arms. "So what do we do?"

Brannig leaned forward, voice tight but steady.

"You keep watching. Gather everything you can. You build a picture so clear, even the worst bastard in the council chambers can't pretend it's a street gang with chalk and bravado. "

She paused.

"And when it's time, when you *do* move, you won't be alone. "

Halfa met her gaze. "They're coming for the temple eventually. They won't let it go. Even though they started it. "

"I know. "

The silence that followed wasn't empty. It was bracing.

Then Brannig nodded once. "You've already chosen your side. Now, choose your moment. "

Halfa gave a slow nod. Turned. And left.

Halfa made his way toward the Temple of Thessira, shoulders heavy, mind drifting between the embers of recent battles and shadows still looming. The Blackjaw threat was shifting—less brute force, more whispers. And Valka Thorne's name lingered in his thoughts like a wound that hadn't bruised yet.

He hated how much Valka haunted him. Not just her name, or her silence, but what she represented. Power with no warmth. Order without care.

And somewhere in the back of his mind, a darker fear: that his fire, if left unchecked, would make him into something not so different.

Not her, exactly.

But not himself, either.

He was almost at the courtyard gate when footsteps approached from behind, soft but certain, close enough to recognise.

He turned.

Tallen stood a few paces back. His uniform was cleaner than most recruits managed to keep by the end of the shift. Marin had likely scolded him into brushing it. At his side was Gorne, a fresh wrap visible under the collar of his coat. His usual scowl was absent. His eyes looked... lighter.

"Evening," Gorne muttered, rubbing his arm like it itched. "We were heading this way. "

Tallen grinned. "Bilbin said there was warm cider. " He held up a lopsided bun wrapped in wax paper. "And spicebread. Marin made it. I'm ninety percent sure it's edible. "

Halfa's brow lifted. "And the other ten percent?"

"Faith," Tallen said solemnly.

Gorne rolled his eyes, but there was affection in it. "We figured you'd be here. "

They walked the rest of the way together in quiet. The temple glowed ahead, lantern light spilling through the arches like golden breath. Laughter echoed faintly—a hymn with no chorus, just the rhythm of people who'd chosen to stay joyful.

At the steps, Tallen reached into his coat. "I made something," he said, suddenly awkward. "During recovery. It's not fancy. Just. . . it felt right. "

He handed over a small charm, with twine threaded through a scrap of polished wood, roughly shaped like a flame. Carved into the side: a spiral. Crooked. Honest.

Halfa took it carefully, like it might break from gratitude alone. "Thank you. "

"I've seen no one carry that much and still stand," Gorne said, rubbing the back of his neck. "Back in The Shambles, I thought we were done. You pulled us out. "

"You kept moving," Halfa replied. "That's all anyone can do. "

Tallen nodded. "I wrote your name in the temple's spiral the night I could get out of bed again. Didn't know what else to do. "

The words settled between them, quiet and real. Halfa looked at the charm in his hand, then at the two of them, scarred, healing, still here.

He tied the new charm next to Serelion's on his belt loop. Two flames. Both carried forward.

He used to think fire was only something that escaped, roared, consumed, destroyed. But these? These he chose to carry. Quiet flames. Named ones. Not loose sparks in the dark, but lights tied to memory. To meaning.

They walked into the temple together.

◈

Inside, the celebration had begun.

The sanctuary was strung with silk ribbons and painted lanterns, casting flickers of orange and violet across the tile. Bilbin presided over the refreshments with flour on his sleeves and a ladle he wielded like a baton. Marin tuned a long-necked stringed instrument from the back platform, her smile crooked, her braid coming undone. Someone had scattered flower petals along the spiral path, and children were scooping them up like treasure.

Serelion stood near the altar, lighting candles in a wide arc, their robe cinched with a threadbare sash that looked more ceremonial than practical. Their eyes found Halfa's as he entered. They didn't speak. Nodded once, slow, certain, present.

A child near the entrance whispered as Halfa passed. "They say Serelion never sleeps. That they just sit, watching the spiral, like they're waiting for something. "

"My mother's mother said that Serelion was here when she was a child, tending to Thessira. " Another child answered in hushed tones.

Halfa moved through the celebration, hands at his sides. He wasn't patrolling. Or wasn't guarding. He was just. . . there.

At the edge of the spiral, he stopped. The symbols underfoot had been scrubbed clean, the burn marks had faded, and been repainted with care. It wasn't the same temple.

It was better.

Because it had survived.

Tallen and Gorne melted into the crowd, pulled into some game involving painted stones and wild shouts. Marin laughed at something Bilbin said too loud. Serelion offered a candle to a passing child who cradled it like a secret.

Halfa stood alone, watching it all. Not apart from it. Just. . . aware.

His fingers brushed the two charms at his waist.

The fire inside him stirred, not in warning, not in grief, but in promise.

He didn't burn to destroy.

He burned to protect.

And that, finally, was a flame worth feeding.

◊

Later, the courtyard was quiet except for the sound of cloth being folded.

Halfa moved slowly, his sleeves rolled up, fingertips stained with oil and ash. A dozen brass lanterns lay in rows beside him, half polished, half soot-scarred. He worked methodically, cloth in one hand, soft-bristled brush in the other.

"You're scrubbing too hard," came Serelion's voice from the far end of the bench. "Let the soot come off. Don't tear the metal trying to win. "

Halfa didn't look up. "It's soot. It doesn't come off with kindness. "

"Neither does grief," Serelion replied. "But it still deserves care. "

They sat beside him without invitation, picking up the nearest lantern and setting it in their lap. Their movements were slow. Balanced. Rhythmic. Every stroke left a gleam.

For a long while, they worked in silence. Not the tense kind, but the kind that knows words aren't always necessary.

"You knew I was coming," Halfa said at last.

Serelion didn't pause. "The flame shifts when you're near. "

"That's not comforting. "

"It's not meant to be. "

Halfa finished another lantern and reached for the next. It had a cracked side; the metal warped from heat. He hesitated.

"Some can't be saved," he muttered. "Too far gone. "

"Then don't save it," Serelion said. "Reframe it. "

Halfa didn't look up. "That easy, huh?"

"Not easy," Serelion said. "Deliberate. "

They set their lantern down gently, as if to prove the point. "We fix what we can. What matters is the intent. "

Halfa's hand tightened around the warped metal in his own. "You think all this didn't leave a mark?"

"It did," Serelion said. "That's why you get to choose what happens next. "

"So what, I just carry it and smile?"

"No," they said, gently now. "But you're not meant to stay bent. If you hold fire the same way every time, it burns the same way. You choose the container. You choose the shape. "

He snorted. "What if I don't like the shape I'm becoming?"

"Then you let the flame soften it," Serelion replied. "That's what grace is. Not forgiveness. Re-shaping. "

He looked over. They were holding up their lantern, letting it catch the court-yard's flickering golds and violets.

"This one was damaged too," Serelion said. "We added ribbons. Now, it casts fire in spirals. Unintended beauty is still beauty. "

Halfa stared at the warped metal in his hands.

"Why do you keep letting me come back?" he asked quietly.

Serelion smiled. "Because you haven't stopped walking. "

The light caught their face just right, soft and steady. And for the first time, Halfa didn't feel like he needed to ask another question.

He set the broken lantern in his lap. Picked up a ribbon. Began tying it on.

There was still work to do. And he wasn't done walking.

❦

Marin was alone in the side gallery when Halfa found her.

The temple had mostly gone to sleep. Only a few lanterns flickered along the long windows, casting broken light on the polished tiles. Marin sat with one knee drawn up, elbows on the stone ledge, watching the city through the high, cracked glass.

Halfa hesitated at the archway.

She looked over her shoulder. "Didn't expect company. "

"Didn't expect to give it," he said.

She smiled faintly. "That's almost poetic. "

He moved closer, slow. Sat beside her, but not too close.

"You do this often?" he asked.

"Sometimes. " She nodded to the window. "The city's quieter from here. Still the same mess of rooftops and chimney smoke. But it feels... held. Like it hasn't slipped too far. "

Halfa looked out. "I love being up high. It feels right. "

"I've noticed," she said.

"You've been watching me?"

"Yes. "

A pause.

"But it's tiring, I imagine," she added. "Being down there, in the thick of it. . "

He nodded. "Feels that way. "

She looked at him carefully. "Do you ever wish you didn't care?"

"Sometimes. "

"Me too. "

He met her eyes. "But we still do. "

"We still do," she echoed, almost like a prayer.

For a while, they watched in silence. Somewhere far off, a bell marked the hour.

Marin spoke again. "I used to have a pendant I wore every day. It wasn't valuable. Just small. Silver. A sunburst. "

Halfa waited.

"My brother gave it to me. I lost it during the fire. I looked for days. Cleared rubble, ash, soot. Never found it. ".

"I kept telling myself it was just metal. Just something to wear. But losing it still hurts. Not because of what it was, but what it meant. "

"A tether," Halfa said.

She nodded. "Do you have anything like that?"

Halfa was quiet. Then: "Not an object. But people. Places. This temple, now. A few names. Yours. "

Marin turned to him. "Mine?"

"You don't pretend," he said. "You laugh, but it's never to hide. You see things and say them. Even when I don't. "

Her smile was slow this time. Earnest.

"Well," she said softly, "you're noticing. "

He didn't move. Didn't reach for her.

But something had already moved between them.

"I'm not fearless," he said.

"No one worth trusting is. "

She reached out, fingers brushing the back of his hand. They were light. Deliberate. Then she pulled back, unsure.

Halfa held still.

"Goodnight, Halfa," Marin said, voice gentle.

"Goodnight, Marin. "

She left him there, taking in the view. And for once, he didn't feel below it.

The Shape of Smoke

Grayspire had always thrummed with a crooked rhythm. Markets shouting over prayers, curses layered with music, steam, and smoke moving in tandem like dancers who'd forgotten the steps. But lately, the song felt wrong. Not off-beat. Off-key. Like a melody slipping from memory into something darker.

Halfa felt it first in the Midden Markets.

A pawn shop he'd passed a dozen times now had guards, two lean men with hard eyes, boots polished too clean for that part of town, and matching scars that mirrored like punctuation marks. They didn't look like protection.

Later that week, a merchant's cart had been tipped over in the Commons. Nothing stolen. No gold, no stock. A symbol carved into the splintered wood: a rat's skull with its jaw cracked wide. Not freshly made, but sharp enough to leave a splinter in the eye.

Halfa said nothing at first. Watched. Catalogued. Listened.

◉

"Walk with me," Marin said.

Halfa didn't argue.

They moved past spice carts and shuttered shrines through the crooked lantern paths of the Commons until the streets narrowed into a stairway that climbed toward the old quarter roofs. Grayspire groaned beneath them, the stones warm with old breath, the city low and glinting with scattered lantern light.

"You always bring your Watch projects here?" he asked, mostly teasing.

"Only the ones with decent shoulders and dangerous eyes," she said, bumping his hip with hers. "Don't get cocky."

"Too late."

She grinned, and for a moment it was easy to forget the weight they carried.

They reached the rooftop's edge. Marin pulled a wrapped bundle from her satchel. Two bowls of broth from a vendor Halfa didn't recognise, still warm, still fragrant.

"Bribery," she explained, handing him one.

"For what?"

"For showing up. Not exploding. For not letting the city eat you."

Halfa took the bowl. "I thought joy wasn't a transaction."

"It isn't," she said, settling beside him. "But soup is."

They sat shoulder to shoulder, feet dangling over the ledge. The broth was rich with lentils and lime, with a heat that lingered at the back of the throat. It reminded him of something he never had. A safe meal. A good memory. Something whole.

"How do you keep doing this?" he asked. "The rituals. The people. The softness. Doesn't it feel like building paper walls in a city full of fire?"

"Sometimes," she said. "But I've lived without it. And that world? That world is colder than this rooftop, and twice as empty."

Halfa didn't answer.

"Joy is stubborn," she said. "Like you. It stays where it shouldn't. Shows up in bad weather. And if you're lucky, if you're really lucky, it grows."

He looked at her. Really looked.

"You're not what I expected," he said.

"Good," she replied, smirking. "I'd hate to be predictable."

The wind swept past them, soft and sea-salted. Marin tugged her scarf tighter and leaned slightly against his side.

He didn't flinch. Shifted to match her weight.

"You ever think this could be it?" she asked. "A rooftop. Two bowls. The city at your feet and someone to share it with."

"I think I'd like it to be," he said.

She turned to him. Not surprised. Not smiling. Just... present.

He kissed her. Gently. No heat. No urgency. Just presence.

When they pulled apart, Marin leaned her forehead against his for a breath, then laughed, quiet and breathless.

"This," she declared, "is joy. "

Halfa smiled, an unguarded, rare thing.

"Took you long enough to say it," he murmured.

"Took you long enough to believe it," she shot back.

They stayed like that a while longer, shoulders pressed together, the city low and shimmering beneath them.

❦

The gulls were screaming at something dead in the canal when she appeared.

Halfa leaned against the rust-warped railing outside the old grain depot near the Fishbone Docks, one of the quieter Watch posts in Grayspire. Too quiet. A place they assigned to Watchmen when they weren't sure if they were assets or accidents. He didn't mind. Quiet gave him time to think. To breathe. To listen.

Then, a voice hit him like a pebble hurled through a stained-glass window.

"You still look like someone dropped a statue in a thunderstorm. "

He turned, slow, disbelieving.

Yetta stood behind him, boots caked in river muck, apron streaked with grease, one braid pinned back with too many clips and the other half-unraveling. She held a half-eaten meat pie in one hand and a folded parcel in the other like she'd been trying to hand it off to someone and finally gave up.

The smell hit him first. Savoury, spiced, and sharp with onion and something warm he couldn't name. His stomach twisted, his memory stirred.

"Yetta," Halfa said. Just the name. Relief washed over him, a feeling he hadn't known for weeks.

She grinned. "Took you long enough. I've had my cart two streets over since the last frost, and not once did your giant shadow come stomping by. Thought you'd fallen into the harbour, or worse, gotten promoted. "

He followed her nod. Parked beyond a crooked lamppost was a cart, low-built, painted a stubborn lavender, and lettered in her too-bold script: YETTA'S BITE. Someone had scratched a spiral flame into the side, cruder than any temple mark. A warning or a prayer. Maybe both.

"New cart," Halfa noted.

"New ward, new bruises, new clientele. You'd be amazed how much smuggling happens over soup. And you, badge and all, huh?" She glanced at the crimson trim on his Watch coat. "Didn't think you'd take to uniform work. "

He adjusted the collar slightly. "It fits better now. "

She tilted her head. "You happy?"

Halfa hesitated. He thought of the flame still coiled inside him, the temple's painted lanterns, Tallen's carved charm and Brannig's quiet defiance. He thought of Valka Thorne.

"Yes," he said. "I'm still standing. "

He hadn't realised it until now, but she'd always seen the fight in him. Not the fire, but the joy beneath it.

Yetta nodded, satisfied. "Stubborn joy. That's my favourite kind. "

She passed him the rest of the meat pie. "Last one. Eat it, or I'll throw it at a rat and call it charity. "

He took it. It was still warm, sweet on the first bite, sharp with pepper by the second. Her way.

As she turned to leave, she paused at his side, gave him a sidelong glance. "How's your girl?"

Halfa blinked. "What?"

She raised an eyebrow. "Marin, right? Candle-witch with the musician's hands. I've seen how you look at her like she's made of sunlight and glass. "

He coughed. "She's not — She's. . . we've been rebuilding the temple together. "

"Oh," Yetta said, dragging the word out like honey off a spoon. "Rebuilding. Is that what the kids are calling it now?"

He didn't answer. Yetta grinned and patted his arm like she'd won something.

"There's something in the air," she said, growing serious. "Not just damp and gull stink. Fear. I've seen it before. It moves quiet, like smoke. By the time you notice, it's already under your door. "

Halfa nodded once. Quiet.

Yetta looked up at him. "Keep your head on straight, Halfa Schoona. You've got more to lose than you used to. "

Then she melted into the early crowd, apron flapping like a flag in retreat.

Halfa stood alone, the pie cooling in his hand, the taste of onion and fire still on his tongue, and the feeling that something important had returned to his life, full of timing, trouble, and exactly the right words.

◉

The Ropeworks District was a city unto itself, tight, slouching buildings stacked like dice, rope lines crisscrossing overhead like spiderwebs, and children darting through alleyways like they owned them. The air reeked of salt, tar, and damp wool. Steam hissed from broken vents. The stones glistened like they had secrets to keep.

Halfa walked with purpose, boots thudding on uneven cobblestone. The mist curled around his ankles like something half-alive. He wasn't here on orders. No active warrant. No directive. Intuition and the weight of a sleepless night.

Lasse moved quietly beside him. He wore his uniform with pride now, though the crest pin was scuffed, and his belt had a nervous squeak.

"This place always feels like it's watching?" Lasse asked, glancing up at the sagging windows overhead.

Halfa didn't answer immediately. His eyes swept the alley, a narrow throat of rain-slick stone between a boarded tannery and the skeletal remains of a collapsed fence. It was quiet, except for the soft creak of rope overhead.

Then he saw it.

Etched into the lower brick of a crumbling wall at shin height, half-hidden by a leaking gutter pipe.

A rat skull.

Not painted. Not chalked.

Etched.

Halfa crouched, brushing away grime with a gloved hand. The grooves were deep and precise, the work of someone patient. Someone practised.

"Lasse," he said, voice low. "Here. "

The younger Watchman stepped beside him, squinting at the mark. "Ash Rats?"

Halfa didn't answer right away.

It looked like their sigil. But it felt wrong.

The Ash Rats were brash. Bold. They scrawled sigils with charcoal or smeared ink—quick, messy, performative. They wanted people to see them. But this?

This had been carved.

Deliberate. Hidden. Proud.

"Not their style," Halfa murmured. "Too clean. Too careful. "

"You think someone's copying them?"

Halfa's jaw tightened. "No. I think someone's wearing them. "

Lasse's brow furrowed. "You mean Blackjaw?"

"Maybe," Halfa said. "Or something worse. "

He stared at the mark a little longer. Something about the curve of the grin... it itched at the back of his memory. Something he couldn't place.

"You okay, Watchman?" came a voice.

They both turned.

A boy stood ten paces away, barefoot in the mist, a loaf of half-stolen bread tucked under one arm and a slingshot strung through his belt. Couldn't have been older than twelve. Hair stuck up in wild curls. Eyes sharp enough to cut wire.

Halfa straightened slowly. "Just watching for rats. "

The boy's grin was too familiar. Too wide.

"Then you're in the right place," he said, and darted off into the steam.

Lasse watched him go. "He one of theirs?"

"Not sure," Halfa said. "But he knew something. "

They turned back to the mark.

"Think they're planning something?" Lasse asked.

Halfa didn't answer right away. His hand drifted to the glass charm at his side, the one that still pulsed warm some nights. He stared into the fog, the way it swallowed rooftops like a mouth closing.

"They're not planning," he said softly. "They're already here. "

The mark grinned back at them from the wall, carved deep. Etched in confidence.

The Ash Rats might have started this.

But someone else was finishing it.

◈

Halfa stepped through the violet door, his shoulders still tight from the alley. The streets outside had felt thinner lately, every glance too sharp, every cart too fast. Even the fog had moved like it was following someone. But here, in the temple, the air softened. It always did.

Lanterns swayed on silk cords strung between columns. Incense spiralled from cracked dishes near the altar's base, and someone was gently tuning a harp in the next room, like they didn't want to wake the walls.

He paused in the entryway, letting the door swing shut behind him. His coat was damp from rain and stained with dust near the cuffs, but no one commented. No one ever did. A few children darted past, laughing with masked ribbons in their hair. Bilbin grumbled from the kitchen about missing herbs. Marin moved through the far corridor with a tray of warm rolls, offering one to a wide-eyed acolyte.

She didn't see him. Not yet. But Halfa saw her, soft light catching the smudge of flour on her cheek, her braid loose, her smile crooked but real.

"How's your girl?" Yetta had asked. Like an undeniable truth.

He hadn't answered. Not then. But now, watching Marin drift from person to person, laughter like music, presence like flame, he wasn't so sure. She wasn't his, not in the way Yetta meant. But he was hers, in ways he hadn't realised until now.

He didn't know if she knew. If she felt it too. Their kiss had made Halfa think she did. But he wasn't sure. He carried it now, like something he couldn't set down, even if he wanted to.

His hand drifted to his coat. Serelion's flame-shaped charm sat against his chest, warm through the fabric. He touched it, a reflex, a ritual, a grounding.

He crossed the entryway, nodding to Serelion, who was adjusting lantern placement near the garden windows. They nodded back, wordless and knowing.

As Halfa turned to leave, Serelion's voice followed him.

"You're not sleeping again. "

He paused, glancing over his shoulder. Serelion stood in shadow, one hand still on the lantern hook. Their robes caught the flickering light like water.

"What gave me away?"

"You fixed that holder three times," Serelion said. "It's not crooked. "

Halfa half-smiled.

"I don't know what to do with the quiet," Halfa said finally. "Not after everything. "

"Most don't," Serelion replied. "That's why they fill it with fear. Or fire. "

"Which am I?"

"You've been both. That's not a failure. It's a choice still being made. "

Halfa's hand drifted to the charm beneath his coat.

"What are you?" he asked. "You never burn. You never shout. You just. . . hold. "

Serelion tilted their head. Not smiling. Not denying.

"Maybe I've already burned. Maybe I've already shouted. Or maybe I remember what the world looked like before it forgot how to hold joy. "

The flame between them flickered.

"If you want to carry it," Serelion said, "then let it be a song. "

Halfa didn't answer. He bowed his head in deference and then continued on towards the altar.

Halfa moved by habit, straightening chairs in the prayer room, fixing the 'lopsided' candleholder with quiet precision. But his mind wasn't on the tasks.

There was a weight tonight. A stillness that didn't belong to silence.

When he reached the altar, he paused. The bowl at its centre shimmered with flame, its surface almost too still. He crouched beside it, letting the light wash over his face.

Then, the flame flickered.

And in that flicker, a shape formed in the far archway.

Broad shoulders. A stance he knew too well. Someone half-hidden in shadow, too tall to be Marin, too still to be passing through.

Gronk?

No, a trick of memory. The silhouette vanished with the next breath. Only silks shifted in the breeze now. Only candles crackled.

Still, Halfa didn't move.

Behind him, the temple breathed, laughter from the hallway, the rustle of festival streamers being gathered for tomorrow's blessing. The scent of clove and smoke. Life, in full colour.

And yet, all he could hear was Yetta's voice:

"You've got more to lose than you used to. "

He stood, steadied himself, and lit one of the offering candles with a whisper of flame. Gentle, warm, controlled.

He didn't know what was coming next.

But he knew where he'd stand when it came.

And who he'd stand beside.

He turned from the altar just as Marin entered the sanctuary, wiping her hands on her apron and humming something off-key. She paused when she saw him.

"Thought I'd find you here," she said, voice light. "There's a bowl in the kitchen that's refusing to cooperate with physics. Bilbin swears it's possessed. "

Halfa offered a half-smile. "Do we need an exorcist or a hammer?"

Marin tilted her head. "You're holding both, depending on your mood. "

She stepped closer, her fingers brushing a loose thread from his sleeve.

"You always come here when your fire's too quiet or loud," she said. "Which is it tonight?"

Halfa didn't answer immediately. He looked at her. Her cheeks flushed from the heat of the ovens. The way her hair had escaped its braid. The calm in her eyes, even when the city spun too fast.

"Both," he said finally.

Marin smiled, soft but steady. "That means it's working. "

She turned, walked away, then paused.

"Oh," she added, glancing over her shoulder, "I saved you a roll. And if you don't eat it, I'm giving it to the squirrel that lives in the roof beams. "

Halfa blinked. "There's no squirrel. "

Marin's grin widened. "Then you'd better eat faster. "

Halfa stood still, the flame behind him, the warmth ahead.

And for a moment, he didn't feel pulled between them.

He felt... held.

Halfa didn't mean to run into Brannig. Not exactly.

He was halfway through evening patrol, Gorne walking a few paces behind, when he spotted her, leaning against the cracked facade of a shuttered bakery, helm tucked beneath one arm, chewing a strip of dried mango like it was jerky and she was angry at it.

"You've got your shoulders up again," she said without turning. "Means something's stirring. "

Halfa slowed. Gorne raised an eyebrow behind him but stayed quiet, adjusting the strap on his coat.

Halfa stopped beside her. "How long have you been watching?"

Brannig shrugged. "Long enough to see you're not just walking a loop. And that you've got something twitching behind your eyes. "

She gave Gorne a once-over. "And you, rookie. How's the limp?"

"Better," Gorne said. "Worse when the weather smells like smoke. Which it does tonight. "

Brannig nodded. "You saw something. "

"Marks," Halfa said. "Three of them in the outer Ropeworks. And something strange near the temple. A shape. A feeling. Like being watched from the inside. "

"Blackjaw?" she asked, without hesitation.

Halfa paused. Then nodded once. "Yes. "

Brannig didn't flinch. She finished off the mango, looking quite satisfied.

"I've been hearing things too. Not enough to shout about, but enough to listen harder. Some Ash Rats have gone quiet. Others are showing up where they don't belong. The coin's moving weird, slipping through places it shouldn't. "

Gorne frowned. "You think someone's using the Rats?"

"I think someone's wearing their skin," Brannig said. "The way old wolves do, just long enough to walk through a gate without a question. "

Gorne shifted his weight. "And the rat skull marks?"

Brannig's mouth tightened. "Not just graffiti. That's a promise. The kind meant to remind you they've been inside your walls before. "

They stood in silence. The mist drifted low over the rooftops, curling like something listening.

Then Brannig pushed off the wall, tucking her helm under her arm again. "Whatever you're planning. . . don't get loud too fast. They're not coming in like before. They're seeping in. "

She turned, took two steps, then glanced back.

"Gorne," she said, "Don't let Halfa write me a eulogy unless he learns how to spell. "

And then she was gone.

Gorne let out a low breath. "I take it that wasn't just a friendly check-in. "

"No," Halfa said, already turning toward the street. "That was a warning. "

He thought of Gronk's voice from the dream—low, certain, unforgiving. *"You never asked what was growing beneath you. "*

He didn't head back to the Watchhouse.

◈

The streets between the Docks and the temple curled like smoke, narrow, twisting, always listening.

Halfa moved through them slowly, hood up, boots muffled by the slick stone. Not patrolling. Not investigating. Just... observing. Beside him, Gorne walked with his usual half-limp, stubborn pride in each step despite the lingering damage. His hand rested lightly on his baton. He didn't ask questions. Just stayed close.

A Watch patrol stood outside a pottery stall half-lit with oil lanterns. Three officers, two Halfa recognised. Dot's people. They weren't questioning. Just watching. The shopkeeper packed in silence, head low, hands trembling as she boxed goods too carefully. This wasn't enforcement. It was encouragement.

One officer nodded to Halfa as they passed. Not friendly. Not hostile. Just... noting.

"That was subtle," Gorne muttered. "Almost didn't see the threat under all that helpful silence. "

A few alleys on, they caught the scratch of stone on wood. A woman hunched by a lintel, drawing a symbol Halfa didn't recognise. When she saw them, she froze, then wiped it away with the heel of her hand. Gorne stepped forward to ask her something, but Halfa shook his head.

"She's scared," he whispered. "Not hiding something. Hiding from something."

Further still, they passed a small shrine wedged between two stacked homes, barely a ledge, just room enough for one bowl and a candle. A child, no older than eight, stood beside it, whispering into the flame.

No prayer. Not begging. Just... speaking.

Gorne glanced at Halfa. "You feel that?"

"Yeah," Halfa said. "Grayspire's bracing for something."

"And watching us while it does."

The alley beside the temple wasn't usually quiet.

Children played there in the afternoons, chalking hop circles and chasing streamers from the last Thessiran festival. Even the drunks knew better than to piss too close to the violet-painted door. The temple's joy extended outward, warding off the worst of Grayspire's shadows.

But tonight, the alley was wrong.

Halfa slowed first. He had heard something, sharp and low. The sound people made when they didn't want to be heard at all. Gorne noticed, too. He tapped Halfa's elbow and nodded ahead.

They rounded the corner.

Four figures in heavy coats. Faces half-covered. Pressed against the wall, barely holding their ground, were two teenagers. Ash Rats, by the look, scrappy, soot-faced, and very much outmatched.

Halfa stepped forward. Not fast. Not aggressive. Just deliberate. The way storms roll in when they've already decided what they're going to break.

The nearest thug shifted. "Watchmen."

Gorne drew up beside Halfa, voice even. "Evening. You look overdressed for candlelight and ribbons."

One thug raised a hand casually. "A simple misunderstanding. These kids picked the wrong pockets."

"Then you've reported it to the Watchhouse?" Halfa asked.

Silence.

"Temple territory," he added. "You know what that means."

The one with the ring smiled, slow and sure. "Didn't realise we'd stepped into a shrine."

"You do now," Halfa said. His tone didn't rise. But the fire behind it was unmistakable.

A pause stretched long enough to let Gorne roll his neck and adjust his stance.

Then, one by one, the Blackjaw men stepped back. Not in panic. But in awareness. Like wolves backing away from a larger one that had just shown its teeth.

They slipped into the dark.

The Ash Rats didn't thank them. Didn't speak.

They ran.

One dropped something.

Halfa knelt and picked it up. A carved bone charm. A rat's skull, painted in thick strokes. Not black. Red.

He turned it in his hand.

"Deliberate," Gorne said. "They wanted us to find that."

"Yeah," Halfa murmured. "It's not just a warning anymore. It's an invitation."

Red. The colour of fire. The colour of war.

Halfa stood, the token heavy in his palm.

Gorne glanced toward the temple door. "Still glowing."

"For now." Halfa replied.

They didn't speak as they walked back into the streetlight. But Halfa's hand curled tight around the charm.

He turned to walk into the temple, Gorne beside him.

❧

Halfa knew something was off the moment he opened the temple door, and the noise stopped.

Not just quiet, purposeful silence. No laughter from the herb kitchen. No off-key humming from Bilbin. No Marin shouting for more light. Just... silence.

Then a muffled sneeze.

Then, a louder shush.

Gorne, one step behind, raised an eyebrow. "That didn't sound sacred. "

Halfa pushed the door open fully.

The main hall waited in suspicious stillness. A crooked circle of children huddled in the middle of the spiral floor, trying very hard to look casual and failing completely. A pile of ribbons lay beside them. A makeshift sign leaned against a bowl of fruit: CEREMONY IN PROGRESS–DO NOT INTERRUPT.

Bilbin stood behind the children, wearing a pink sash tied diagonally across his apron. He was also holding a copper mug like it was a scroll.

"Citizen Halfa Schoona of the Watch and Temple-Aligned Logistics Support," Bilbin declared, voice far too formal for his usual muttering tone, "we hereby bestow upon you the ceremonial honour of—" he glanced at the back of the mug "—Torchback of the Spiral Flame. "

A tiefling boy stepped forward. His horns curled tightly above his brow, his eyes bright with effort and nerves. He held out a lopsided crown made of braided ribbons, paper flowers, and what looked suspiciously like a teacup handle glued to the side.

Halfa blinked. Gorne crossed his arms and said, "That's bold craftsmanship. "

The boy added quickly, "We were gonna make you a cape, too, but someone burned it by accident. "

From the back of the group, a girl hissed, "He said it was a ceremonial sacrifice!"

"I lit it on purpose," the tiefling protested. "That counts. "

The room cracked with giggles.

Halfa looked at Bilbin. Then at the children. Then at Marin, who was trying, and failing, to pretend she wasn't lurking inside the curtain with a paint-stained towel over her shoulder.

Near the edge of the spiral, Serelion stood with their arms folded, watching with the long-suffering patience of a teacher who'd stopped trying to control anything except the outcome. Their only reaction was the faintest tilt of the head.

Tieflings were rare in Grayspire's central wards. Not forbidden, not driven out, but always watched. Always whispered about. Born of long-forgotten infernal bloodlines, their horns and glowing eyes drew both awe and suspicion. In the Ropeworks or back-alley tenements, people called them luck bringers or curses. But here, in the temple, they were merely children. Loud. Chaotic. Welcome.

Halfa took the crown gently in both hands. Didn't put it on. Just held it.

Halfa didn't know what to say. He wasn't good with thanks. Or with being seen. But something cracked inside him, quiet, clean. Not pain. Not fire. Just... warmth. They'd made this for him. Not because he asked. Not because he'd fought for them. Because he'd stayed. Because sometimes, joy didn't come from the grand gesture. Sometimes it was a crooked crown, and a room full of people who thought you were worth the effort.

"You missed a spot," he finally said.

The kids swarmed him with cheers and glitter. Someone dumped flower petals on Gorne, who sputtered in half-hearted protest. Another child started beating a tambourine completely out of time. For the next five minutes, joy absolutely desecrated the spiral floor.

Halfa stood still in the middle of it, his coat dusty, his boots sparkling, his arms full of ribbon and reverence. His fire didn't stir in warning.

It stirred in gratitude.

He smiled, quiet and full, and let it burn.

◈

The dream arrived slowly, a creeping flame, unseen. It curled at the edges of Halfa's mind, smelling of smoke and old ash, whispering truths he hadn't asked for.

He was in Grayspire.

But not the Grayspire Halfa knew.

This city burned slowly. The rooftops sagged under the weight of heat. The streets shimmered with steam rising from stone. And everywhere, embers. Floating, drifting, catching on banners that used to bear joy symbols but now hung in tatters.

A different Marin was there, devoid of mirth and light. This Marin stood in a narrow alley soaked with old rain and older fire. Her cloak was torn, her hair matted, her eyes like open doors, no longer watched. She didn't speak. She just pointed.

All around her, the walls pulsed with symbols. Burnt into brick. Etched into windows. Painted in something darker than ink. Blackjaw. Over and over. One mark layered on another until the shapes bled into something unnatural, something hungry.

Marin turned, and for a moment, Halfa saw her mouth move. No sound. Just the shape of a word.

And then she disappeared.

The Temple of Thessira loomed crooked in the haze, its spiral path warped, the candles melted down to blackened nubs. Above the door, someone had carved a symbol into the stone.

At first, Halfa thought it was the Blackjaw mark.

But it wasn't.

It was something new.

The familiar jawbone remained, but now it was ringed in fire. Not drawn. Not etched.

Burned into the wall, the flame licking and alive. Inside it: a spiral. Not Thessiran. Something tighter. Crueler. It collapsed inward like a snare.

He stepped toward it.

And Valka was there.

Neither standing nor waiting. Woven from the smoke, her shape shimmered into being, gown trailing embers, eyes lit with reflection, not light. She didn't speak at first. Watched him, like she already knew what choice he would make.

"Your fire still hesitates," she said, voice low and full of iron. "Why?"

Halfa tried to answer, but the dream held his throat shut.

"You fear becoming what you are," she continued. "But I don't. I've already become it. "

Behind her, the forge flared. Not the city forge. His forge, the one he carried in his chest. She walked through it without burning. The flames bowed around her.

"You light candles," Valka said, circling him now. "You carry charms. You beg the fire to be gentle. And still, people bleed. "

She stopped behind him. Whispered in his ear.

"Give it to me. "

He turned, fire surged at his back, reflexive and wrong, and she caught it. Held it in one hand like silk, her fingers untouched by heat.

"See?" she said. "You don't know how to hold it. But I do. "

The ground cracked.

He saw Brannig coughing in the smoke. Gorne, limping through ash. Marin, backlit by flame, reached toward him, and soot, not blood, covered her hand.

Valka looked at him from within the inferno. "Joy can't stop me. Faith won't stop me. You're the only one who might. But not with fire. "

She stepped forward and placed a single finger over his heart.

"You burn for others," she said. "I burn for change. I burn for power. That makes me stronger. "

The spiral at her feet ignited.

The flame rose too fast and too high, consuming the temple, city, and sky.

◊

Morning in Grayspire broke like rust peeling from metal.

The clouds had settled into a low, heavy blanket over the city, muting the usual hue of sunrise into something the colour of ash. The streets hadn't fully woken. A few shopkeepers rattled shutters. A pair of children darted past the fountain, laughing too loudly for the hour. The world pretended to be normal.

But Halfa could feel it.

Something was shifting beneath the cobblestones. In the way dogs refused to bark. In how the pigeons kept to higher roofs. Silence, like a secret too heavy to speak, was carried on the wind.

He stood outside the Temple of Thessira, cloak drawn against the cold, steam rising from his breath.

The violet door behind him was locked for the morning. But the warmth from within, laughter, music, the scent of cardamom and chalk, still radiated through the stones.

The charm on his chest hung heavy. Not burning, not glowing.

Just present.

In the distance, the bells of Grayspire began to toll.

Once. Twice.

A call to morning. A warning of fog. Counting of time.

But today... they felt different.

As if they were counting down.

Bilbin appeared across the square, boots scuffing wet stone, jaw tight. He didn't call out. Nodded once when their eyes met. He nodded back.

The smoke was rising.

The song was changing.

And Halfa Schoona, a man of fire and memory, stood at its edge, no longer waiting.

Just ready.

Beneath the Surface

Grayspire didn't sleep.

It turned in its restlessness, a beast of brick and breath, coughing up steam through crooked vents and whispering names in the alleys. Even now, past midnight, when other cities might dim, Grayspire only smouldered. The gas lamps still flickered. The markets never quite closed. Somewhere, always, someone was shouting.

Halfa walked into the Ravel Ward with his cloak drawn tight against the drizzle, the air damp and metallic on his skin. His boots echoed on uneven cobbles, a slow and steady rhythm, like a war drum softened by rain.

Beside him, Brannig moved with the compact surety of someone who had never once slipped on these stones. Her braid was tucked into her collar. Her badge hung slightly crooked like it dared not ask for attention. She held her baton like a hammer that had seen too much use.

"This ward always smells like boiled regret," she muttered, glancing toward a gutter where something steamed.

"Only when it's wet," Halfa said.

Brannig grunted. "So... always. "

They walked in silence for a time. The lamplight smeared across puddles like stained glass gone feral. From a nearby stoop, someone hummed a broken lullaby. A paper lantern floated by, half-deflated, like the city was trying to forget its holidays.

On his belt, Halfa's badge swung heavily. But heavier still was the red-painted rat skull charm tucked into his coat. The talisman hadn't left him since the alley near the temple. Wood, he kept telling himself. Carved bone and cheap pigment.

But every time he touched it, it felt warm.

Warmer than it should be.

"You keep fingering your coat like it owes you rent," Brannig said.

He looked at her. "You believe in cursed things?"

"I believe in stupid people doing dangerous things. That covers most curses. "

He didn't answer. Halfa reached inside his coat again, fingers brushing the edges of the charm. Jagged. Twisted.

"They've changed," he murmured.

Brannig raised a brow. "Blackjaw?"

He nodded. "They don't bleed loud anymore. They wait. Watch. They want to make the Ash Rats disappear and then reappear quieter. Meaner. More organised. "

They turned a corner near an old spice stall. The shutters were closed, but something sharp lingered in the air, nutmeg, cinnamon, blood.

"You think the Rats are working for them now?" she asked.

"No, but I think they are losing. "

They passed a burned-out candle shrine. Melted wax pooled like bones beneath the soot. A message had been scratched into the wall behind it, half-rubbed away, but still readable.

"WE WERE HERE. "

They kept moving. The city exhaled through a nearby vent, steam rolling across the cobbles like breath from something ancient.

"I've seen this rhythm before," he added. "The silence, then the smoke. After that.... "

Brannig looked sideways at him. "You think flame comes next?"

He didn't answer immediately.

Instead, he stopped beneath a crooked eavespout, listening to water drip beside him in a slow rhythm.

"Not think," he said. "Know. "

Brannig didn't argue. She stood beside him for a while, baton loose in her hand, gaze scanning the mist like it might speak first.

Far off, the city coughed. Somewhere, a laugh cut short. A gutter clogged.

The signs were there. First came the silence. Then, the smoke.

And after that?

Only flame.

✦

The Watchhouse smelled of old sweat, burnt coffee, and ink, a morning bouquet that settled into the lungs and stayed there. The gruel in the corner kettle was more paste than porridge, and the half-circle of officers looked like they'd been chewed on by the night and spat back into their uniforms.

Halfa sat near the edge of the table, arms folded, a smear of alley dust still clinging to his cloak. He hadn't slept, but then again, sleep had become a formality lately, something he mimed more than practised.

Brannig Barrelshield stood near the wall-length map of Grayspire, chalk in one hand, a short baton in the other. Her tone was clipped and clear, slicing through the morning fatigue like a whetstone against steel.

Someone had scrawled a note on the map. Brannig pointed at it. "Third cart this week left gutted on Tallow Street," she said, drawing a line across the southern quarter of the map. "No footprints. No blood. Just this. " She tapped the chalk against a small symbol hastily drawn on parchment – a rat skull, mouth agape.

A rustle of murmurs followed. One Watchman, a lean man from Eastgate, cleared his throat. "Just tagging?"

"No," Halfa said, quiet but firm.

The room turned. Brannig didn't interrupt.

Halfa leaned forward, elbows on knees. "It's probing. Pressure points. They're testing response time, visibility, Watch habits. This isn't vandalism, it's recon. "

Brannig gave a curt nod. "Agreed. We've seen it before. Different gangs, different tactics. But this. . . this feels methodical. "

Another Watchwoman raised a hand. "Blackjaw?"

"Not as we knew them," Brannig said. "But it's the same stink under different cologne. "

Laughter rippled weakly, forced, brittle.

She pointed to a knot of alleys in the western quadrant. "We've also seen repeat sightings near the Ropeworks and Spires. Keep an eye out for young runners. They're not just delivering messages anymore. "

Halfa felt the weight of her words land heavier on his shoulders than most. He knew who she meant. The Ash Rats were no longer a curiosity.

Brannig paused, then turned fully toward him.

"Anything to add, Schoona?"

He hesitated. The rat-skull talisman sat like a secret in his coat pocket, red paint chipping where his thumb had rubbed it raw.

"They're watching us," he said at last. "Not avoiding patrols. Tracking them. Matching routes. Playing games with our timing. That means discipline. Leadership. And worst of all. . . patience. "

A silence settled over the room. No one enjoyed hearing that.

"Don't engage unless necessary," Brannig broke the silence, her tone firmer now. "No lone chases. No heroics. And no investigations off the books. We've already lost good people. "

There was no judgment in her gaze.

Only memory.

Halfa nodded once. "Understood. "

The others filtered out, chatter low, nerves fraying at the seams. Halfa stayed behind, staring at the chalk lines and the ink-stained pins. Each one a wound waiting to reopen.

He hadn't changed his uniform since yesterday. No time. Or maybe no point.

Brannig remained at the map, her fingers smudging old borders, drawing new ones.

Neither of them said it out loud.

But they both knew:

This wasn't a resurgence. It was an evolution.

◊

The interview room in the east wing had one table, two chairs, and no illusions left.

Halfa sat across from a boy, twelve, maybe thirteen, with a dirt-smudged face, scar down one temple, and a bandaged knuckle he kept picking at like it itched too deep to heal. His wrists were unbound. There was no fear in his posture. Only stillness.

"Name?" Halfa asked.

The boy shrugged. "Doesn't matter. "

"It will if you end up with broken teeth in a gutter. "

He smiled, small, deliberate. "You think that scares me more than *her*?"

Halfa tilted his head. "Who?"

The boy's grin widened, but his eyes stayed flat. "They say she walks through walls. Hears a rat breathe through stone. Say her name wrong, and your shadow forgets you by morning. "

Halfa's voice dropped. "Her name. Say it. "

Silence.

"Is it Valka?"

A pause. Then, almost gently:

"You don't say her name. Makes the walls nervous. "

Halfa leaned in. "You're just a runner. You don't know what you're caught in. "

The boy's expression didn't change, but his voice sharpened. "That's where you're wrong, Watchman. We're not caught. "

He turned slightly, one foot already in the mist. "You think this is your city. But it's *hers* now. "

Halfa didn't follow. Didn't answer.

And for the first time that day, the badge on his chest felt heavier than the coat beneath it.

◊

The Midden Markets were never quiet. Even in the drizzling hours after peak trade, the air buzzed with motion, vendors haggling over dented crates, cats yowling beneath fish stalls, children darting between boots like practised thieves in training.

Elves with tight braids and gilded rings haggled beside dwarves in soot-dusted aprons, their voices cutting through the mist like song and gravel. A halfling woman balanced a tower of lanterns atop her head, each flickering a different hue. Two tieflings argued over spice weights in a cracked shrine to Draveth, their horns glinting wet in the lantern light. Grayspire never mixed cleanly, but here, in the market's throat, the world pressed elbow to elbow. It didn't always speak the same language. But it listened. And watched.

But tonight, the rhythm was wrong.

Halfa moved through the heart of the market with deliberate steps, his greaves clinking faintly, the drizzle beading across the shoulders of his cloak. His badge caught the light beneath a flickering lantern. Two hawkers lowered their voices. Not out of respect. Out of calculation.

Beside him, Tallen kept pace, his eyes sharp, one hand resting on the grip of his baton. His uniform was tidy, the creases stubborn despite the rain. He scanned the edges of the stalls, posture alert.

"Feels tight tonight," Tallen murmured. "Like everyone's waiting for something."

Halfa nodded once. "They are."

A cart that usually sold smoked oysters sat abandoned. Its canopy sagged, torn, flapping like a wounded wing in the mist. Beneath it, partially obscured by a loose net, Halfa saw it, a mark.

He crouched. Brushed the net aside.

Rat skull. Open mouth. Etched cleanly into the wood.

No paint. No signature. But deliberate.

Tallen crouched beside him, frowning. "That wasn't here last week."

"No," Halfa said. "It wasn't."

He scanned the nearby vendors. A woman with a basket of onions avoided his gaze. A cobbler muttered to a passing apprentice without looking up. The silence wasn't open hostility. It was careful. Coiled.

"Should we ask around?" Tallen said.

"No one's ready to talk. Not yet."

Ahead, a child stood near a stall of dried herbs, cradling something in both hands. A carved rat skull. Red-painted. The moment Halfa's eyes met his, the child froze.

Then, a hand reached out. His mother, maybe, and snatched the token away, stuffing it into her cloak with a hiss.

"It's just a story," she muttered. But she didn't meet his eyes.

Halfa didn't respond.

Didn't move.

Beside him, Tallen exhaled. "They're afraid of something."

"They should be."

They moved on, past a baker who didn't offer a greeting. Past a spice vendor who shuffled her wares too loudly, pretending not to see them. Past a vacant beam where a wind chime used to hang. A small thing, but Halfa remembered its sound, bright and defiant in the breeze.

Gone now.

They turned down a side lane tucked between a fishmonger's stall and a mossy alley shrine to Draveth. The air was colder here, the stones slick and green. Halfa stepped around a ragged tarp and stopped.

A figure rounded the far corner.

Cloaked. Rushed. Deliberate.

Tallen saw it, too. His baton twitched in its loop.

Halfa signalled silence with one hand, and they followed, two paces faster, boots quiet against the damp. The alley bent sharply left, then dipped, where runoff from the upper terraces drained down.

They passed a shattered mirror propped against the wall.

Caught a motion, a flicker of cloak.

And then, nothing.

The alley was empty.

No doors ajar. No crates disturbed. No sound but dripping water and a lone pigeon flapping overhead.

Tallen looked to Halfa. "Backtrack?"

Halfa stood still for a long moment. Watching. Listening.

"No," he said at last. "Not tonight. "

"You think it was a tail?"

"I think it was a message. " He turned slowly, glancing once over his shoulder. "They're watching how we respond. "

Tallen's voice was low. "And we're not ready. "

"We will be. "

They retraced their steps without haste. The silence followed. So did the eyes.

Whatever moved in Grayspire's veins now, it wasn't chasing.

It was waiting.

And for once, so was Halfa.

The Watchhouse was quieter than usual when Halfa returned. Not silent, Grayspire didn't do silence, but subdued. Unsolved reports yielded silence. Too many boots without their usual swagger.

He passed the bunks near the east wall. Tallen's was cluttered with ribbon scraps, Gorne's had a dented practice helm perched on the corner. Back in place. Breathing easier. Still here. Lasse was snoring in his bunk.

Brannig was in the side chamber that passed for her office, a half-storage, half-sanctuary, filled with old patrol maps and worn practice gear. Hunched on a low stool, scrubbing her boots with more force than finesse, cursing under her breath when the brush caught on a loose strap.

Halfa lingered in the doorway.

"They're getting bolder," he said.

Brannig didn't look up. "No. They're getting comfortable. "

She dropped the boot, flexing her wrist like it had betrayed her, then grabbed the second and resumed her assault.

"That's worse," Halfa said.

She glanced at him. "You ever see a fire settle in too deep? Burns low, eats through the walls before anyone smells it. People think a bright blaze kills you. But it's the ones that smoulder, quiet and patient, that take an entire block down. "

Brannig grunted, rubbing her jaw. "You notice we keep hitting the same crews? Doesn't matter what corner they're on. "

Halfa nodded. "Grayspire's underworld isn't big. It's deep. Same names. Same grudges. They just echo louder in the dark. "

Brannig dropped the brush into the bucket. "This isn't the Blackjaw we knew," Brannig said. "It's cleaner. Quieter. This feels like someone new is running the script. "

Halfa didn't respond right away. He looked past her, to the corner of the room where an old lantern hung unlit....

A relic from before his time. Before hers, too.

"Kids are trapped by it," he finally said.

"They always are," Brannig muttered. "The city bleeds from the bottom first. That's where the pressure builds. Where it tests the seams. "

She stood, stretching her shoulders. Her armour creaked like tired bones. "You thinking of doing something stupid again?"

Halfa tilted his head slightly. "Define stupid. "

"Running into a smuggler den with rookies and no backup," she shot back. "Acting like you're alone. "

He didn't deny any of it. "I'm not looking for a wall to throw myself against. "

"Good," she said. Then, more softly, "this City needs no martyrs. It needs shields. And maybe, when it's lucky, someone who knows how to burn right. "

Halfa's jaw tightened. He remembered Serelion once saying, *Joy isn't the absence of fire. It's choosing where it burns. "*

Brannig's words weren't the same. But the shape of them felt familiar, like an echo carried through smoke.

Halfa looked at her.

"Burn right?"

Brannig met his gaze. "Yeah. Controlled. Hot enough to keep the darkness at bay. Not so wild it takes the temple with it. " She grinned. "Again. "

He gave the slightest nod.

"I'm trying. "

Brannig exhaled. "Good. Try harder. "

She walked past him then, back into the main hall, her boots leaving wet prints on the stone.

Halfa remained in the doorway for a moment longer, staring at the place where the lantern hung.

He didn't need to see it lit.

He just needed to know it was there.

◊

The Watch mess hall still stank of boiled turnips and damp wool. Even with half the benches empty, the room felt cramped, its stone walls crowding closer with every shift change. Halfa sat at the edge of one long table, hunched over a chipped mug of lukewarm tea. He didn't eat. He didn't talk. He listened.

Across from him, a trio of North Ward recruits joked over a bowl of stewed beans. They wore their nerves poorly, with too many laughs, and too much noise in their swagger.

"You hear about the rat gang in the Ropeworks?" one of them said, poking at his food like it might bite back. "Little brats playing enforcer with tin daggers and war paint. "

"They call themselves Ash Rats," said another. "Sounds like a bad bard's idea of a threat. "

"They've got a 'rat king' now," the third chimed in with a snort. "Supposed to sit on a throne made of broken crates. "

Laughter rippled across the table.

Halfa didn't join in.

"They're not a joke," he said quietly.

The table stilled.

The first recruit, broad-shouldered, scar on his cheek, smirked and leaned forward. "You sympathising with pickpockets now, Stoneface?"

"I'm saying," Halfa replied evenly, "they're gathering under something. Or someone. And they're afraid. But not of us. They're afraid of the Blackjaws. "

Another beat of silence. The recruits shifted uncomfortably. The tension had a smell now, old sweat and something colder beneath.

The second recruit, with a lighter voice, fidgeting fingers, cleared his throat. "I heard something," he said. "Couple nights ago. Friend of mine from Split Alley Patrol. Went missing. Just… didn't show for the shift. His bunk was made. Boots still lined up. "

The first recruit scoffed. "Ran off, probably. Tired of garbage duty. "

"Maybe," said the second, looking doubtful.

"They say the one giving orders now never speaks above a whisper," one recruit muttered. "But when she does, people vanish. "

One of the older officers, Jovik, from the Wharf detail, spoke without lifting his eyes from his tea. "They say her name's Valka. "

The others stilled.

Jovik looked up. "And now she speaks. Quiet. Careful. Just enough for people to think the fire was their idea. "

Halfa didn't blink. But the name sat in his mind like soot, refusing to wash off.

Valka.

Halfa stood, pushing the mug away. "Valka is the leader of the Blackjaws. Next time you see that mark, don't make noise. Just remember: smoke comes before fire."

He walked out, the weight of silence trailing behind him.

The Ravel Spires district always felt a half-step out of sync with the rest of Grayspire. Narrow streets folded over each other like a stack of forgotten books, and the smell of ink, old leather, and rainwater clung to the air like memory. Halfa's patrol took him through its spine, crooked cobbles, shuttered kiosks, and paper lanterns that hadn't been lit in days.

Today he was on patrol by himself. None of the usual recruits or Brannig could come, and others weren't that keen to be seen with him.

He moved quietly. Not because he had to. Because the street demanded it.

Then he felt it.

A shadow at his back. A breath behind his ear.

He spun, hand hovering near his baton.

Tap.

He turned again, this time to find a tiefling girl no taller than his waist, arms folded like she owned the street.

"You jump easily for a big man," she said, eyebrows raised.

Halfa blinked. She wore a tunic two sizes too big, patched at the elbows. Her boots had been stolen and re-stitched from three others. Her eyes were bright and unblinking.

"Name's Rix," she offered. "You're Halfa Schoona."

"Am I?"

"You are. The temple likes you. So do the spice hawkers. And the Blackjaws want your teeth in a pouch."

Halfa tilted his head. "You always deliver news this blunt?"

She shrugged. "Only when it's true."

There was a pause. She dug into her sleeve and pulled out a folded scrap of parchment. "Got a message. From someone important."

Halfa didn't take it.

"Split Alley," she said. "Old tannery. Basement door. If the lantern's lit, it's safe. "

"What name?" he asked.

Rix chewed her lip. "Didn't give one. Said it's someone with history. Someone who knows you. And that if you want to stop what's coming, you need to listen instead of just lighting fires. "

Halfa frowned. "What are you, a courier?"

"I'm a lot of things," she said. "Courier's the safest today. "

She extended the note again. This time, he took it.

"Are you going?" she asked.

"Not yet. "

She smiled, wide and toothy. "Didn't say *now*. *Soon*. "

And with that, she spun on her heel and vanished down a side alley, leaving behind only a faint echo of laughter and the dusty imprint of boots far too small for the weight she carried.

Halfa stared after her, then down at the note.

The seal was a smear of soot. The parchment smelled faintly of tallow and charcoal.

He didn't open it.

He just tucked it into his coat beside the coral flame.

The city was shifting. And the rats, Ash or otherwise, weren't running.

They were building something.

And someone was calling.

The word *tannery* lodged in his chest like a splinter.

He didn't know why, only that the last time he smelled boiled hide and iron oil, it was mingled with ash and fear.

And Halfa had never forgotten the stench.

◊

The streets glowed amber by the time Halfa reached the Temple of Thessira. The sky had bruised into rusted copper. The dusk that made colours run and shadows stretch long. The air smelled like rain on stone and the fading sweetness of pressed flowers from some earlier celebration.

His boots were sore. His spine ached in that slow, creeping way that came from too much caution and not enough rest. The day had dragged him through fog-drenched alleys and tighter Watch corridors, where silences held teeth. But the temple? The temple never flinched when he arrived.

The violet door stood open.

Inside, warmth greeted him, not the kind that came from firelight and closed windows, but the kind that came from presence. From music drifting in from the courtyard, voices that didn't rise in anger, and from incense that clung like memory.

Children played near the sanctuary's edge, stringing ribbons between the prayer benches. Bilbin was mid-rant about someone misusing the cinnamon again, his apron stained, his ladle waving like punctuation. A new lantern flickered above the spiral basin, its flame caught in a swirl of glass and etched with a joy symbol that was just slightly crooked. Someone had tried, and that mattered.

And across the room, Marin.

She moved like someone caught mid-thought, wiping flour from her hands as she crossed the entryway. Her braid was slipping again, and her tunic bore streaks of candle wax and ink. Her laughter sparked across the space like a struck match, too loud, too real. It made something in Halfa's chest loosen.

She saw him. And didn't smile right away.

Instead, she crossed to him, steady. Stopped close enough that the scent of citrus oil on her wrists mixed with the ash on his cloak.

"You're late," she said.

"I didn't know we had a time. "

"You're still late. "

He gave a tired exhale. "Had to walk past something. Decided not to follow it. "

Her brow furrowed, not in judgment, but in curiosity. "That's new. "

"I'm trying things," he said. "Not lighting everything I touch. "

Marin looked at him for a long moment. Then, slowly, she reached up, fingers brushing soot from the edge of his collar. Not gently. Just... deliberately. Like it was something she was allowed to do now.

"I like the quiet you carry," she said softly. "Even when it wants to scream."

He didn't speak. Not right away.

So she took his wrist lightly, and tugged.

"Come with me," she said.

She led him through the sanctuary, past a pair of dozing cats and the broken prayer tiles they always slept on, through the side hallway and up a narrow stair. The rooftop garden hadn't fully recovered since the fire, but someone had replanted the herbs. Someone had strung bells between the beams again.

The stars were faint tonight. The city glowed beneath them, Grayspire's windows blinking like uncertain eyes.

Marin sat first, cross-legged on the rooftop's edge. She patted the stone beside her. Halfa sat.

She always moved with purpose. Even the way she sat felt deliberate. Grounded.

She didn't fill the space with noise. She filled it with her presence. And somehow, Halfa felt smaller around her, not because he was less, but because she let him set something down.

And gods, he wanted to.

For a while, they just breathed.

Then she said, "Yetta stopped by."

Halfa tilted his head.

"Said you got a bit flustered the last time you spoke to her," Marin said, a faint smile curling her lips. "Something about 'How's your girl?'"

He laughed, just once, under his breath. "I panicked."

"I know."

Silence again. Not awkward. Just full.

Halfa shifted, hands braced behind him. His coat fell open slightly, revealing the two charms at his neck—Serelion's flame, and the one Tallen had given him.

Marin reached over. Touched the newer one. Ran her finger lightly along the curve of the flame.

"You're not who you were in the fire," she said.

"No," he said. "I'm... trying to be who I want to be next."

"And who's that?"

He hesitated. Then, quietly: "Someone who doesn't lose the people he loves trying to protect them. "

She looked at him, and her gaze wasn't soft. It was steady. Focused.

Then she leaned in.

Not fast. Not shy.

Just sure.

Her forehead touched his first,an old Thessiran gesture. Shared breath. Shared space.

Then she kissed him.

It wasn't a blaze. It wasn't a spark. It was heated like coals, banked and quiet and real. The kind of fire you lit when you knew you'd be staying a while. Halfa knew then that his earlier worries were ungrounded.

When they pulled apart, neither said anything right away.

But Halfa's hand found hers, and didn't let go.

And above them, the wind moved through the rooftop bells, ringing slow and low and sure.

◈

The barracks were quieter than usual.

Halfa's boots made no sound on the stone floor as he crossed to his bunk in the far corner. Most of the other Watchmen were out, drunk, or asleep. A single oil lamp burned near the door, casting long shadows across the empty cots.

He sat down heavily, joints stiff from the day, but not from exhaustion.

From weight.

The same weight that had haunted his steps since the alley.

Since the girl.

Since the note.

It lay on the wooden table beside his bunk, exactly where he'd left it: a scrap of parchment, folded neatly, the corners beginning to curl. He hadn't opened it again. He didn't need to.

He remembered every word.

Basement under the tannery on Split Alley. Lantern in the window means it's safe.

No signature.

He stared at it now, the surrounding silence deepening.

No wind tonight. No city hum. Just the lamp. Just the note.

The pulse in his chest, slow and steady until it wasn't.

Because when he closed his eyes, he didn't see the sigil.

He saw Marin.

Not the kiss itself, though he could still feel it, impossibly soft and quietly devastating, but everything surrounding it. The sound of her breath, steady and close. The way her hand found his before he even realised he needed steadying. Their lips met, not as a question, but the answer to one he hadn't dared ask.

She had kissed him like she saw the man beneath the fire.

And for once, he hadn't flinched. He hadn't pulled away. He hadn't ruined it.

His fingers found the flame charm at his neck, closing around it with practised ease. It was smooth and warm in his palm, a weightless thing shaped to carry burdens without breaking. Somehow, it steadied him more than it should have.

A part of him had always believed that the fire would keep him alone, that carrying it meant being set apart. But Marin had stepped into the blaze not as a warning, not to douse it, but with quiet certainty, as if she'd chosen the flame and everything that came with it.

He didn't light the lantern. Didn't reach for his coat. The night pressed soft against the windows, and the silence held.

But within that stillness, something shifted. A breath. A ripple beneath the surface. A pause in the tide that felt less like calm and more like a coiling motion, like the moment before a city burns or a war begins.

Grayspire was stirring.

Brothers in Ash

The morning fog clung to Grayspire like a guilty conscience. Low, wet and watchful. It oozed through the gutters and alley mouths, swirled beneath market awnings, and pressed like a breath against the grime-frosted panes of the Watchhouse commons. Inside, the iron-bellied stove snapped and crackled, spitting heat into the cold stone chamber like a cornered dog baring teeth.

Halfa Schoona stood before the briefing board, tin mug in hand, steam curling from its rim. He didn't drink. He rarely did. Just let the heat seep into his fingers and remind him that, for now, they were steady.

The warmth steadied him, but it explained nothing. The fire inside him wasn't always rage, not anymore. Sometimes, it answered grief. Sometimes fear. At times... he didn't even know what he felt when it came. And sometimes, it didn't come at all. There were no books about people like him. No mentors. No stories passed down. Just the heat, and the questions it never answered. He wasn't even sure if it was magic. Maybe it was something older. Something broken. Something his blood remembered, but he didn't.

But he was starting to understand one thing: rage might summon the fire, but choice could shape it. That was the difference. The fire listened when he was calm.

The board was a mess, pins, strings, names, half-torn reports. Fires. Thefts. Disappearances. More every week. A thin red string traced from Pickbone Alley to the Ropeworks District, then looped back to a dockyard bar known for under-the-table dealings. Someone had scrawled *"ASK DOT?"* in sharp charcoal beside it. The question mark looked more like a threat.

Brannig Barrelshield was already there. Arms folded across her broad chest. Jaw locked. Eyes flicking with practised calculation over the incident map. Her cloak, dusted with fine moisture from the fog, dripped a slow rhythm onto the floor behind her. It sounded almost like a clock.

"Another alley fire in Pickbone," she muttered, not looking at him. "Third one this tenday. "

Halfa grunted low in his throat. It wasn't much, but it said enough.

Brannig peeled a fresh parchment off the board and jabbed a callused finger at the hand-drawn sigils inked across it. "Ash Rats are claiming it wasn't them. "

"Blackjaws?" Halfa asked, finally taking a sip. The tea was bitter. Oversteeped. Just how he liked it.

"Maybe," Brannig said. "Could also be some gutter spark trying to throw smoke and start a turf war. But the flames, they're too clean. Intentional. Someone's making a point. "

She pulled another sheet, voice dropping to a low rumble. "Thing is, Halfa... the Rats have rules now. They might be a pack of street pups, but they've got a spine. They don't shake down grannies for temple coin. They don't torch bakeries for turf. "

Halfa raised a brow. "You sound like you respect them. "

Brannig gave him a sidelong glare. "Don't be thick. I *don't* like them. But I know worse. Organised is dangerous. Especially when the city's too distracted to notice. "

She flipped the page in her hand and showed him a folded internal memo. The ink was official. Too official.

"Dot's record," she said. "Clean as a consecrated chapel. No mention of those failed patrols. There is no report on Tallen or Gorne's injuries. No record of The Shambles ambush. "

Halfa's grip on the tin tightened. "He had it cleared. "

Brannig nodded, slow and grim. "Quiet pressure. Someone pulling strings from higher up. And now, Dot's circulating talk of 'efficiency reviews' on the lower ranks. Trying to weed out 'problematic personalities. '"

"Like me. "

"Like us. "

They stood in silence. The only sound was the stove spitting in the corner and the shuffle of boots in the hallway beyond.

Brannig sighed, finally leaning her weight against the board like it might hold her up. "We've got good folk out there. But something's shifting. The air's heavier. Don't know if you've felt it. "

"I have," Halfa said quietly. "Every morning, it takes longer to breathe."

Brannig glanced over at him, then back to the board. "Dot's not just ambitious. He's *connected*. And whoever's pulling his strings? They've stopped pretending the Watch is about justice."

Halfa didn't respond. He looked at the red strings. The pins. The little fire-shaped symbols are now too many to count. A spreading pattern. A sickness.

Brannig pushed away from the board. Her eyes met his.

"Stay sharp, Halfa. And watch your back. You're the wrong kind of big for them to ignore."

He nodded once. Quiet. Focused. But inside, he felt the heat stirring again. Not the rage. Not yet.

But the warning before the boil.

❦

The fog hadn't lifted. It only grew bolder with the morning sun, thickening like curdled milk in the gullies and winding tighter around Grayspire's bones.

Halfa moved through it slowly, the dull weight of his boots echoing down narrow flagstone corridors. His uniform bore the city's sigil, but his presence carried something heavier now, expectation, resentment, potentially fear.

Beside him, Tallen walked with a quieter rhythm. Shorter than Halfa by over a head, the younger Watchman kept his crossbow slung, but his hand never far. His eyes flicked from doorways to rooftops, tension in every glance.

"Too quiet," Tallen muttered. "Even for fog."

Halfa grunted.

Patrols were routine. Or used to be. These days, they were quiet in all the wrong ways.

They passed through the Commons, down a sloped avenue lined with squat homes and shuttered windows. The usual morning noises, bakers calling out prices, children shrieking at nothing in particular, were conspicuously absent.

A dog barked from behind a gate. No one hushed it.

"Feels like the entire city's holding its breath," Tallen said. "Or like it's already exhaled, and we missed the moment."

Halfa didn't answer. He didn't need to. The streets were already answering for him.

At Lantern Street, he paused. A group of children used to play marbles here, two human boys, a dwarf girl, and a lanky half-elf who always cheated. Today, the cobbles were bare. A chalk circle marked where they'd been. Rain had half-washed it away.

Tallen followed his gaze. "Kids don't stop playing without a reason. "

"They do if someone makes them," Halfa said, and kept walking.

At the mouth of a side alley, Mrs Valbryn, the elderly halfling who ran the corner pie stand, was sweeping ash from her awning. When she saw them, her eyes darted nervously. She gave a tight nod and vanished back inside.

Tallen frowned. "Used to love her crusted rhubarb. She always had a slice waiting. "

"She didn't forget," Halfa said. "She's scared. "

"Of us?"

"Of what follows us. "

They turned down Groat's Corner, where a fruit vendor was arguing with a tall, overdressed boy in a noble's tabard. The lad was red in the face, barking about "ruined reputation. " The vendor looked ready to swing a stall leg.

Halfa didn't intervene. Not yet. He watched. Measured.

Tallen glanced at him. "You always wait like that?"

"Only when I'm learning. "

Then Halfa stiffened.

A flicker of motion, low to the ground, quick as a breath, ducking behind a laundry cart. A glimpse of reddish skin. A sharp glint of eyes.

"Rix," he said softly.

Tallen turned, alert. "That the tiefling you mentioned?"

"Yeah. She's trouble. "

They both moved, but she was gone. Smoke through fingers. Vanished into a side lane.

Then the shouting started. Two streets over. Near Candle Row.

Halfa was already moving. Tallen matched him stride for stride, one hand on his weapon.

They turned a corner as a wooden crate crashed to the cobbles, splitting open and sending candied plums skittering like glass beads. A merchant cried out.

Three figures towered over a man lying on the ground. Blood at his mouth. One hand raised in a plea. A boot pressed into his ribs.

"Tax collection," said the half-orc enforcer, delivering another kick. "City's gotta eat. "

Halfa's voice cracked across the stones like a thunderclap. "Grayspire doesn't tax through fists. "

All three enforcers turned. Leather jackets with crimson stitching. Bracers carved with snarling wolf heads.

Blackjaw.

Tallen swore under his breath. "They're not even hiding anymore. "

The half-orc cracked his knuckles. "Maybe we're the new government. "

Halfa stepped forward, slow and unflinching. Fog coiled around him like smoke before a bonfire.

The other two enforcers shifted. One adjusted his grip on a hidden blade.

"This man under your protection?" the half-orc asked.

"No," Halfa said. "He's under Grayspire's. "

The silence that followed tasted like blood and copper. One thug twitched toward his belt.

"Don't," Halfa said, eyes narrowing.

The half-orc raised a hand. "Not worth it. Another time, Watchman. "

They turned. Walked away.

The fog swallowed them.

Tallen exhaled slowly. "They're getting bolder. "

Halfa crouched beside the merchant, helping him up. The man's breath was ragged.

"You alright?"

The merchant nodded, wincing. "They're everywhere. "

Halfa looked after the enforcers. His hands were still clenched.

Tallen stood beside him now, watching too. "You gonna write this one up?"

"No," Halfa murmured. "I'm gonna remember it. "

Halfa stood still for a long moment after the enforcers vanished into the fog, his eyes fixed on where they'd disappeared.

Tallen hovered nearby, scanning rooftops and windows. His jaw was tight, but he didn't speak.

The merchant leaned against the wall, cradling his side with a wince. A trail of crimson trickled from his lip to his chin. His cart lay overturned nearby, wood splintered, plums scattered and trampled, sugar glinting like glass in the gutter.

"Thank you," the man said hoarsely. "They've come by twice this week already. Said I owed for 'street use. ' Last time, they took the cart. This time..." He didn't finish.

Halfa helped him upright, careful with the man's bruised ribs.

"Go see Old Beska on Stonethread Way," Halfa said. "She's no healer, but her poultices smell awful enough to work. "

The merchant gave a weak smile. "I'll manage. Just... be careful, Watchman. They don't fear the law anymore. "

Tallen muttered, "They don't even pretend to. "

Halfa didn't answer. His gaze drifted upward, past the rooftops. Somewhere above, the morning sun fought a losing battle against the fog, turning the world the colour of old pewter. He felt the weight of his coat on his shoulders, the badge over his heart, and something deeper, hotter, coiling in his chest like a live coal.

A soft click echoed nearby, boots on stone.

They turned together.

A small crowd had gathered at the edge of the square. Not many, six or seven people. A woman holding a sack of onions. A boy with a splintered lute. Two tradesmen. None of them spoke. None of them stepped forward.

They watched.

Halfa could feel it in their eyes, not just the fear, but the calculation. Some saw a Watchman. Others saw a monster barely leashed. He was used to that look. Big. Pale. Silent. Grayspire didn't have a word for what he was, so it settled for whatever made people feel safest, tool, brute, threat. He wondered, not for the first time, if they would've stepped forward if someone smaller had stopped the thugs. Someone familiar. Someone like them.

Halfa nodded to the merchant and walked toward the crowd. Tallen followed half a step behind. The crowd parted, eyes lowering. No cheers. No thanks. Just the sound of retreating boots and fear hanging in the air like smoke.

As they reached the corner where the alley met the wider lane, an older man with sun-browned skin and a mason's apron cleared his throat.

"You'll make yourself a target, Watchman," he said, not unkindly. "Folk like them, don't forget being embarrassed. "

"I'm counting on it," Halfa replied.

The man didn't smile. He nodded, disappearing into the mist.

They resumed the patrol in uneasy silence.

Tallen didn't speak until they'd passed two whole blocks. Then, quietly: "That was... bold. "

"Necessary," Halfa said.

"You think they'll come back?"

"They never left. "

They moved through the Ropeworks District, where the fog mingled with tannery stench and salt from the harbour winds. Nothing stirred beyond the usual beggars and stray dogs. But Halfa knew better.

The Blackjaws weren't gone.

They were repositioning.

And they weren't the only ones watching.

Back near Ironhook Street, Halfa inspected a flickering gas lamp. The city had stopped maintaining them regularly, too many "budget reallocations. " The flame inside this one sputtered and guttered, casting uneven light across a red symbol scrawled in chalk on the brick wall behind it.

A jagged sigil.

Behind them, footsteps approached, quick, light, and stopping just short of careless.

They turned together.

Rix.

She stood across the street, leaning against a crumbling archway, arms folded tight over her chest like she was holding herself together.

"Nice speech. " She said.

Halfa blinked. "I didn't give a speech. "

"You didn't have to," Rix said. "You stood there, and they walked away. That's rarer than it should be. "

Tallen shifted his weight beside Halfa, glancing between them. "Friend of yours?"

"No," Rix said.

The air between them stilled. Tallen didn't interrupt again, but stayed close, watchful.

"You following me?" Halfa asked.

Rix snorted. "Please. You're loud enough to follow yourself. I just... wanted to see what kind of Watchman you were. "

Halfa didn't reply. The street between them felt wider than it was.

Rix's expression shifted. "You're bleeding fire. I can feel it. "

Tallen gave Halfa a sharp look, but said nothing.

"Maybe I should let it burn this time," Halfa muttered.

"No," she said. "Not yet. "

She turned and walked off into the fog.

No goodbyes. No promises.

Just the sound of her boots fading into nothing.

Tallen waited until the silence stretched too long. Then, gently: "She knew you. Knew about your fire. "

Halfa's jaw flexed. "She knows too much. "

Tallen looked back at the sigil on the wall. "Funny. They're organising. And we're still just reacting. Wish we knew how to catch up. "

Halfa said nothing. But the heat in his chest stirred again, no longer restless.

Now, it had direction.

◊

The fog had thickened by dusk.

It slithered down the alleys like a second skin, soft and suffocating, draping Grayspire in a hush too complete to be natural. Even the gulls fell silent, their usual squawks swallowed by the murk.

Halfa walked alone through the narrowing streets, his coat damp, the edges of his boots leaving no impression on the wet cobbles behind him. He had taken no direct path. His feet moved on memory, not intention. Somewhere along the way, he'd passed the site of the fruit stall again, now abandoned. The plum juice had stained the cobbles dark, like bruises beneath the stone's surface.

He didn't look back.

Eventually, he arrived at the temple.

It was quiet now, past evening prayers, but not yet midnight. The lights inside were dim, enough to cast a golden warmth through the tall arched windows. The carved reliefs over the doorway, depicting dancers, fireworks, a rising sun held in open palms, were worn smooth by time, but Halfa ran a hand along them anyway. He found comfort in the texture. Something unchanged.

Inside, the spiral waited.

Each walk was unique, yet familiar.

Each step around the mosaic path brought a recent memory to the surface. A laugh that no longer echoed. A song hummed on a quieter night. The heat of a meal shared with someone long gone.

He walked slowly.

The flame-shaped brazier at the spiral's centre flickered gently, casting light in rhythm with the beat of his heart, or maybe the beat of something deeper, something sacred.

He reached the spiral's centre and stood still.

The flame burned steadily here, low but fierce. It danced in its bowl, surrounded by iron petals. The light touched his face in waves.

He didn't kneel. Not today. He stood, the silence pressing in around him like smoke without fire.

His hand drifted to his coat.

He pulled out the note.

The parchment was worn now, edges curled. Rix had folded it three times, and each crease was sharp enough to cut if held too tight. The ink was rushed and slanted, a message not meant for ceremony but for urgency.

He hadn't gone the night it arrived. He hadn't been ready.

But now?

Now, the city had started coughing smoke again. And the Watch needed some information. Halfa needed some information.

Halfa stared at the flame.

He thought of Serelion, arms outstretched during a festival. Of Marin's fingers catching his wrist as he walked past. Bilbin laughing around a mouthful of lemon tart. Of the temple in Grayspire burning in the rain.

"Thessira," he murmured. "I know what joy feels like, thanks to you. But I also know what its absence feels like. "

The flame stirred.

Or maybe it was just a draft.

Behind him, quiet footsteps approached, soft leather on stone. He didn't turn.

"Too late for prayer," Marin said gently.

He let the silence stretch before replying. "Not too late for truth. "

She stepped beside him, her coat still damp, her curls haloed in the temple light. For a while, she said nothing. Just looked into the flame, same as he did.

Then: "You're heavier these days. "

"I'm carrying more. "

"I know. And I'm tired of watching it grind you down. "

He didn't respond. Marin sighed and reached into her sleeve, drawing out a small curved, sea-pink shaped object, like a curling flame.

"Found it in the offering bowl," she said. "Bilbin says it's coral. Serelion says it's symbolism. I say it's a gift. "

Halfa took it. The charm was smooth, warm from her hand, and lighter than it looked.

"You think I need reminding?"

"I think," Marin said, "you've forgotten how to float. "

Across the hall, Serelion moved quietly among the votive shelves, tending candles that had long since burned out. His presence brought no interruption, only a steadiness, like a stone in a stream.

Bilbin leaned in a doorway nearby, pretending not to watch. His voice floated over. "If you're going somewhere interesting, I'd appreciate a pastry when you get back. None of that jam-filled rubbish. "

Halfa gave him a look. Bilbin shrugged. "What? Spiritual clarity requires snacks. "

Marin smiled faintly. "Where are you going?"

Halfa looked toward the doors. "Stonehook Lane. "

"Then come back," she said. "Don't disappear. "

He nodded once. "If I can. "

No one stopped him. Serelion bowed their head as Halfa passed. Marin pressed her hand briefly to his arm, then let go.

Outside, the fog no longer felt heavy. Just necessary.

He pulled his coat tighter, stepped into the dark, and followed the ghost of a memory toward the smoke.

🔥

Night in Grayspire had a scent to it.

Not the usual alley soot, dockside brine, or the rot-sweet reek of old fish guts, but something sharper, more ancient. Like stone remembering fire. Like the breath before a scream.

Halfa moved through it with quiet steps that didn't ask permission. His boots knew the way even when he didn't. Gas lamps sputtered overhead, their flames casting long, uncertain shadows that danced against walls like ghosts playing out a memory.

He didn't walk with purpose.

He walked with weight.

The note, creased and familiar, rested in the inside pocket of his coat. He hadn't reread it since the temple. He didn't need to.

The alleyways narrowed as he walked. Buildings leaned in like old conspirators, windows shuttered, doors double-bolted. Somewhere far off, a bell rang, midnight tolls echoing thinly through the fog.

Stonehook Lane waited like a held breath.

Once, it had been a warehouse district. Now, it was rotten wood and whispers. Crates stacked where carts once rolled. Rope ends fluttering like limp flags. Forgotten corners where the Watch rarely patrolled, not out of fear, but neglect.

The entrance wasn't marked, but Halfa knew it when he saw it: a slanted alley to the left of a collapsed loading dock, and a symbol, a rat curled around a flame, scratched just low enough on the wall that most would miss it.

He stopped, let his breath slow, then stepped through.

The alley narrowed until it became more of a suggestion than a path. Half-broken crates leaned against the soaked walls. Rainwater trickled in a thin stream down the centre. Moss had begun its quiet conquest here, thriving in the places light forgot.

Rix was waiting.

Perched on a crate, one foot dangling and the other drawn up close, elbows resting on her knees, she looked like a child trying not to seem nervous. She wasn't smiling. Just watching.

"You took your time," she said.

"I had a long week. "

She tilted her head. "You always do. "

A flicker crossed her face. Not quite amusement, not quite relief. Just... something human. Without another word, she slid off the crate and started walking.

Halfa followed.

They didn't speak as they wound deeper, down stairwells littered with old rope, through boarded alleyways that peeled like scabs, across rusted catwalks hanging over forgotten wells. The scent changed too: smoke giving way to cedar, damp wood, and faint hint of vinegar. Somewhere far below, someone was cooking onions in a cracked pan.

Rix glanced over her shoulder once, to make sure he hadn't vanished. "I expected you sooner," she said.

"I wasn't sure if I was ready. "

"Well," she muttered, "you're here. So you are. "

They passed a room lit by jars of glowing lichen, a dozen teens sharpening knives, sorting food into old tobacco tins, or tracing chalk routes on fraying parchment maps. None of them looked up.

"Used to be a butcher's," Rix said without slowing. "Then a theatre basement. Now it's ours. " She gestured vaguely at a wall. "Don't lean on the plaster behind the crates. It's held up by hope and two nails. "

Halfa didn't smile, but something in his shoulders eased.

It was warmer down here than he had expected, not the heat of fire, but of presence. Of movement. Of shared breath in close quarters. A quiet hum, like a heart beating in the city's ribs.

They passed a sparring ring, ropes tied around barrels, where a halfling and a tiefling moved through slow strikes under the eye of an old goblin smoking a pipe carved from bone. Nearby, two children carted boxes labelled LARD and NUTS that clinked with metal inside.

It wasn't a gang's hideout. It was a den, but not a lair. Lived in. Watched. Protected. A home.

Halfa slowed as they reached a weathered canvas curtain dyed a rusty red. A single candle burned beside it, its flame shielded by a glass jar.

Rix stopped. She turned to him, voice quieter now. "You sure you're ready?"

Halfa tilted his head. "Should I not be?"

She didn't answer. Studied him for a moment, like she was trying to read something beneath the skin, then pushed the curtain aside.

Warm light spilled through the gap.

Halfa stepped through without flinching. And as the curtain fell closed behind him, the heat inside him stirred.

🔥

It was simple: bare stone walls, no chairs, and one table pushed off to the side. A candle burned low on a crate near the back, casting flickering light across the tall figure at the far end. Hooded. Still. Goliath-tall.

The figure turned, and even cloaked in shadow, Halfa knew. He didn't need to see the face. He didn't need to hear the voice. The shape was enough, the weight of him, the memory.

"Gronk," he said. Not a question. A name dropped into the world like a stone breaking a frozen lake.

"Gronk. "

The name fell like a hammer, not loud, but final. It echoed in the stone chamber as if the room itself recognised the weight of it.

The figure standing near the far wall didn't flinch. He simply reached up and pulled the hood back.

There he was.

The face was leaner now, the cheeks hollowed, the lines around his eyes deeper. A long scar traced his collarbone. His tattoos, once haphazard, meant to intimidate, were sharper now, precise, inked with purpose rather than pride.

His hair was shorter. His presence wasn't.

Gronk.

The boy who once raced Halfa barefoot through Grayspire's alleys, carrying loaves they hadn't paid for.

The teen who beat him bloody in a dockside ring, then helped him walk home.

The man who stood beside him when the fire met joy, and chose neither.

Now, he stood still. Measured. Not surprised.

"I figured you'd find your way down here," Gronk said, his voice that same gravelled murmur, like stone rolling through coals.

"You didn't exactly hide," Halfa replied.

Silence stretched. A silence carved by shared history. Not hostile. Not warm. Just heavy.

Rix stood in the doorway behind Halfa, uncertain.

Halfa didn't look back, but he lifted one hand slightly. "Go. "

She hesitated. Then slipped away.

The curtain swayed once.

Then fell still.

Halfa took another step into the room. His boots rang against the floor like distant thunder.

"You're leading the Ash Rats?"

"They lead themselves. I just keep the fire lit. "

Halfa crossed his arms. "Didn't think you liked fire anymore. "

Gronk's mouth twitched, just slightly. Not quite a smile.

"Depends on what you burn. "

Another silence. Longer this time.

Halfa studied him. Gronk still stood like he was in a ring, feet wide, weight centered, always ready to move or strike.

"You're not with the Blackjaws anymore," Halfa said.

Gronk gave a dry, almost amused exhale. "Not for a while now. "

"They cast you out?"

He shrugged, the motion stiff. "More like imprisoned, and then escaped. "

"Because of the temple?"

"Because of you," Gronk said. "I pulled you out of the fire. Told them to stand down. Thought I was buying time."

Halfa's jaw tightened. "You saved me."

Gronk met his gaze, steady. "No. I made a choice. That's not the same."

A beat.

Then Halfa asked, "And now?"

Gronk's jaw worked, slow and deliberate. "Now I do what they couldn't. I make something that survives."

"By stealing? Recruiting kids?"

"They came to me. Just like you did once. Hungry. Angry. Looking for something bigger than running."

Halfa's expression tightened. "You think this is bigger?"

"It's not about size. It's about shape." Gronk turned, pacing slightly. "We watch corners the Watch ignores. Stop worse gangs from moving in. We give them structure. Meaning."

"You sound like Serelion," Halfa said, cold and quiet.

Gronk stopped.

The silence hit harder this time.

"The elf at the temple? Never thought I'd be compared to them."

"And you think you're better?"

"I think I'm different."

Halfa took another step. The space between them was smaller now. Charged.

"You're building something down here. I see that. But what happens when the fire gets bigger than you can control?"

"Then we burn."

"That's not noble."

"It's honest."

They stood there, years stretched taut between them like a rope over a flame. Neither pulled. Not yet.

Finally, Halfa asked, "What's your plan?"

Gronk exhaled slowly. "To stop the Blackjaws. Before they turn the whole of Grayspire into another Dock Ward."

Halfa stepped in closer. "And Valka? What's her role in all this?"

Gronk's jaw flexed. He didn't answer right away. Just looked toward the far wall like he was remembering the weight of fire.

"She runs them," he said at last. "Blackjaw's bones rebuilt under her hands. She reshaped what was scattered and weak. "

Halfa narrowed his eyes. "So she's the leader?"

"She doesn't lead like they used to. No speeches. Just certainty. And enough fear to make the old wolves kneel. "

"And you?"

Gronk's voice was low. "Even now, part of me's still waiting to hear her whisper. "

Halfa let the silence stretch, then asked, "Her powers? She snuffed my fire out like it was nothing. How did she do it?"

Gronk turned to face him fully. "She can suffocate someone's magic. Seen her take down multiple mages this way. There's a reason magic is so rare in Grayspire these days. "

Halfa's breath caught slightly. It hadn't just been a trick or timing. She'd reached into the core of him and closed her fist around it.

He thought of the spiral flame guttering. Of the heat in his chest, dimming to an ember under her gaze.

"So this, your Ash Rats, this is what? Resistance?"

"It's a firewall," Gronk said. "The last one I know how to build. "

Halfa studied him. "You want to work together?"

"I didn't say that. "

"But you knew I'd come. "

Gronk's lips twitched. "I left the symbol. Had Rix drop the note. "

Halfa nodded slowly. "You wanted to see if I'd remember. "

Gronk met his gaze. "Did you?"

Halfa looked around the room. At the stone. The flame. The silence.

"I remember a lot of things. "

He turned toward the curtain.

"Halfa," Gronk said, stopping him.

Halfa paused, hand on the canvas.

"I don't expect forgiveness. "

Halfa didn't turn. His voice was low. Steady. Tired.

"Good," he said. "Then you won't be disappointed. "

He pushed through the curtain and walked back into the tunnel.

Behind him, the fabric fell shut like a guillotine.

But the quiet didn't leave him.

He moved past the sparring ring, the banners, the jars of light. The scent of cedar clung to his coat. Somewhere behind a wall, someone laughed.

And it struck him, not with rage.

But with something heavier.

Gronk was building something.

And it was working.

Halfa wasn't sure what they saw in him. Protector? Spy? Ghost? The children hadn't flinched. But they hadn't smiled either.

Halfa wasn't sure if that made him angry, sad, or scared.

Maybe all three.

Maybe that's what the fire was now.

Not destruction.

Not vengeance.

But the slow-burning ache of *possibility.*

The kind that made you question where loyalty ended, and legacy began.

The stairs felt steeper on the way back up.

Each step echoed differently now, less hollow, more resonant, like the stone had listened in on the conversation below and wasn't sure how to let it go.

Halfa emerged from the Ash Rats' tunnels. The curtain of fog still blanketed Grayspire, thicker now, swollen with the weight of night and secrets. Gas lamps flickered in uneven rhythms, some dimmed to embers, others flaring like startled eyes.

He paused beneath the alley's overhang, letting the cold air bite at his sweat-damp skin. The surface always felt colder after being down there. Not just in temperature.

In truth.

He looked up.

The rooftops loomed like silent sentinels, sharp-edged silhouettes against a sky too cloudy to show stars. Somewhere far off, a dog barked once. Then silence reclaimed the streets.

Halfa reached into his coat and pulled out the coral flame charm Marin had given him. It sat warm in his palm despite the small, smooth and gentle chill.

A contradiction.

Just like the Ash Rats.

Just like Gronk.

He turned it over once. Then twice. Then tucked it back into the folds of his belt and exhaled.

"I remember a lot of things," he had said.

It was true.

He remembered how it felt to run beside Gronk, not against him. When their shared strength had meant protection, not escalation.

He stepped out of the alley, his boots landing solidly on the cobblestones. The fog swirled around him like smoke that refused to rise. The city had a way of swallowing moments like this, burying them beneath the noise of the next crisis.

But Halfa felt it in his bones:

Something had shifted.

The fire hadn't gone out.

It had changed direction.

He didn't know yet if he would stand beside Gronk again, or stand against him. But either way, they were brothers in ash. And the fire was moving.

Part 3 - Without a Match

Embers in the Stone

They walked without speaking for a while. The streets of Grayspire were in one of their rare in-between states, too late for morning bread carts, too early for noon drunks. A few shopkeepers swept their thresholds. A stray dog slept in the shadow of a shuttered inn.

Brannig kept at a brisk pace, boots clicking with sharp punctuation marks on the uneven cobbles. Halfa matched her stride.

"There's talk."

Halfa raised an eyebrow. "Talk?"

"Dockside Captain," she said. "Shaking hands with Reller Barsh."

That name hit like a sour note.

"Barsh?" Halfa echoed. "The enforcer from Hardby?"

Brannig nodded. "Burned down half a tavern because someone shorted a crate of amberleaf."

"And now he's shaking hands with city brass."

"Aye. Promotions handed to cowards. Patrol routes shuffled. Watch reports going missing. Dot's every word attracts a growing audience. 'Efficiency,' they say. 'Stability.'" Her voice dropped. "You know what I see?"

Halfa waited.

"I see rot. Dressed in polished boots."

They stopped at a high wall marked with faded Watch insignias. Chalk graffiti stretched across it, layers upon layers of old slogans, gang signs, even a child's attempt at drawing the Grayspire crest.

Halfa stared at it, then asked, "What's the Watch turning into, Brannig?"

She didn't answer right away. Just looked up at him, face carved in quiet resolve.

"You already know the answer," she said. "Question is, what do you do when your house is catching fire... and the captains are locking the doors?"

Halfa didn't answer.

He looked at the cracked stone.

At the worn motto.

At the city beyond.

❦

Halfa sat on a half-broken bench outside what used to be the old East Market wall, now a stretch of rubble and ivy, half-swallowed by time. Moss crept between the stones like it was reclaiming the city one silent inch at a time. The stall behind him had collapsed months ago, a painted sign for honey dates now hanging askew like a drunk trying to stay upright.

He rested his elbows on his knees, fingers laced, staring at nothing.

Trying to build the map in his head.

The Ash Rats. The Blackjaws. Dot's spotless reports. Barsh's too clean smiles. Merchants folding under "new partnerships. " Even the Watch wasn't walking like the Watch anymore, boots too polished, gazes too blank. He tried to draw the threads between them.

They didn't form a net.

They formed a fuse.

He didn't hear her approach. But the city did. The air shifted, and there she was.

Arms behind her head. Legs kicked out. No hello.

"You look like you're thinking too hard," she said.

Halfa's jaw didn't move, but his eyes slid toward her. "You always sneak up like that?"

"Only on people who need a push. "

They sat for a moment without speaking.

The wind picked up. It dragged paper scraps across the stones and stirred the vines clinging to the broken wall. A gull cried overhead, then went quiet.

Halfa turned to her, brow slightly furrowed. "Something on your mind?"

Rix didn't smile. "He's planning something. "

The words hung there. She didn't need to say the name.

"Gronk?"

She nodded.

"He won't tell me everything," she continued. "But I see it. Smarter recruitment. Strategic placement. The Rats are shifting. Doing quiet drills in the tunnels, new symbols being scratched on warehouse corners. He's taking corners the Blackjaws haven't even touched yet. "

Halfa didn't know how Gronk had done it. He had given the Ash Rat's structure. Purpose. He'd learned to build this disorganised band into something almost formidable.

Halfa's voice was careful. "Expansion?"

"More like... preparation. " She scratched at her jaw. "He says it's defence. We're just keeping the Blackjaws boxed in. But that's not how it feels. "

Halfa didn't reply immediately. His eyes stayed on the cobbles.

Gronk hadn't burned the temple. But somehow, Halfa felt the smoke in every word Rix didn't say.

"And you're telling me this," he said finally, "why?"

"Because I don't know if it's smart..." She shifted, voice lower now. "...or if it's war. "

Halfa looked at her. Rix was rarely unsure. She'd survived on instinct, on gut and grit. This was different.

"He says he's protecting Grayspire," she said. "But sometimes... I catch that look in his eyes. Like he's trying to prove something. Or bury something. I've known him a while now, and that look?" She shook her head. "That look's older than the Ash Rats. "

Halfa said nothing.

The silence that followed wasn't distant. It was crowded. Thick with memory, neither of them wanted to name.

Rix leaned forward, arms resting on her knees, mimicking Halfa's posture.

"I know you two have history. And I know it's not clean. But whatever's coming? It's going to hit fast. And hard. "

She stood.

The bench groaned with her absence, then settled into stillness.

"I figured you deserved to hear it from someone who doesn't want the city burning. "

Halfa watched her go. She didn't look back.

A breath rose in his throat but didn't escape. He held it there, somewhere between sorrow and resolve.

The fire didn't flare like it used to.

But it was there, quiet and patient. Beneath his ribs, it curled inwards instead of out. A reminder.

He still feared what it could do.

Halfa stayed on the bench for another minute after she left, elbows on knees, breath tight beneath his coat.

Then, a flicker of movement caught his eye across the square.

Tallen was tightening the wrappings on his forearm, slow and deliberate. Gorne stood beside him, practice blade in hand, offering it without a word. No formal drills. No Watch instructors barking orders. Just two survivors moving in rhythm, cautious, quiet, careful. Training in a public square.

They didn't see Halfa watching.

But he saw them.

Still here. Fighting. Scared.

And for the first time that morning, the fire in his chest didn't flicker with warning.

It burned with purpose.

◊

The next street over should've been quiet. It usually was. It was just a tangle of laundry lines, cracked tiles, and one half-forgotten shrine tucked between two dye shops.

But today, Halfa stopped.

The shrine was boarded up.

Not just closed. Transformed.

Fresh paint, cheap and rushed, covered the outer stonework, bleeding into the old carvings. The name of Elaran had been scraped from the lintel. Fresh signs hung unevenly from the doorframe. "Coming Soon: Grayspire Cultural Resource Centre. "

Halfa stared at the defaced shrine, stomach knotting.

The old Blackjaws never scraped names. They burned them. They didn't rebrand sanctuaries; they levelled them. This was cleaner. Quieter. Almost *respectful*, in the way predators sometimes are before they bite.

A woman stepped through the doorway, robes faded but familiar. A temple worker, young, maybe twenty, with a box of incense jars clutched tight to her chest. Her eyes darted left, then down, as one of the suited men murmured something and held the door for her with a rehearsed smile.

Halfa didn't hear the words. But he saw the posture. Not violence. No threat.

Permission. The kind that made you complicit if you nodded.

He kept walking. Behind him, the resource centre swallowed the girl whole.

Resource centre.

He could still smell incense inside. Beneath the paint, the old prayer marks were visible. Half-scraped. Half-ash.

Two men stood outside.

Clean clothes, clean boots.

One looked up as Halfa passed. He didn't smile or nod, just watched, his face giving away nothing.

Halfa moved on. But the breath he let out felt like it had teeth in it.

Blackjaw.

◉

He didn't mean to find her.

Halfa was walking back to the Watchhouse, boots heavy with the silence Grayspire had been wearing more and more lately. Every window shuttered a little too early. Every alley mouth watched a little too long. He was lost in thought after the conversation with Rix.

Then the scent hit him, grease, pepper leaf, and something aggressively charred.

He turned the corner, and there she was.

Yetta had a new cart again.

Sort of.

It looked more like an old grain drum mounted on wheels, with a chimney pipe belching steam from the back and three sauce bottles hanging from a chain like alchemical flasks.

She was ladling something thick and red into wooden bowls, one hand on her hip, the other wielding a spoon like a fencing foil.

Two dockhands were laughing nearby, steam rising off their bowls. One coughed. The other cried. Both kept eating.

Yetta saw him and grinned.

"Well, look what the crows dragged in. The Goliath Ghost of the Guard. Still brooding professionally, I see. "

Halfa raised an eyebrow. "Thought you'd retired. "

"I did. From reason. " She tossed him a bowl. "Still owe you a pie for that night. This is what you get instead. Call it even. "

Halfa caught the bowl. It smelled like something that could strip paint. He didn't question it. He had enjoyed enough of Yetta's stews.

Yetta leaned on her cart, and wiped her hands on a towel that had clearly lost the war weeks ago.

"You feel it?" she asked, quieter now. "City's breathing is wrong. "

Halfa nodded. "Yeah. "

"Too many good people looking tired. Too many bad ones looking rich. "

She handed a sauce bottle to a teenager who darted off without paying. Didn't stop him.

"I know I'm just the soup lady," she added, "but I know the shape of fire when I smell smoke. "

Halfa looked at her.

She shrugged.

"I've been burned before. This time, I'm not waiting for the roof to catch. "

He handed her a silver piece. She pushed it back.

"Don't insult me. "

"You need to eat. "

"I do," she said. "But not at your expense. You've already paid. "

Halfa nodded once. Tucked the coin away.

Yetta called after him as he turned to go.

"You ever torch this place, torch it clean. "

Halfa glanced back, half a smile under his hood.

"Only if I get to eat first. "

The streets narrowed as Halfa moved, his steps slower now, like his body was moving through water, while his thoughts sprinted ahead. Rix's voice lingered behind his ears, but it wasn't her warning that echoed.

It was the uncertainty in it.

He wasn't used to that.

He turned off the main road and ducked through a low stone archway that once marked the outer bounds of Watch territory, before the district maps were redrawn, before new captains shuffled streets like cards.

The courtyard beyond, had been forgotten.

No patrols walked here anymore. No merchants set up stalls. Only cracked flagstones, a broken fountain, and the ghosts of uniforms long faded. The only sound was the soft creak of ivy climbing through the gaps in old walls and the distant tick of a loose gutter tapping against a shuttered window.

A Watch emblem had been carved into the wall. It was once proud, but now chipped and buried in soot. Halfa studied it. The symbol was faded but familiar: a rising sun over a crossed sword and scroll. Someone had drawn over it in charcoal. A cracked jaw.

He stared at it for a long time.

Then, slowly, he knelt.

From his coat pocket, he pulled a stick of pale chalk; the kind used by Watch instructors during training. He hadn't even realised it was still there.

On the stone beside the defaced emblem, he sketched.

Not art. A map.

Lines. Arrows. Names.

Dot circled in one corner, clean, distant, untouched by dirt but surrounded by voids.

Barsh near the docks, radiating outward like a cracked bottle.

Blackjaw marks growing west of the Ropeworks.

Ash Rat signals drawn tighter, denser, more organised.

And in the middle, between two flames—

Gronk.

Halfa stepped back.

It didn't look like a battle plan.

It looked like a fuse waiting to catch.

He sat down on the cold stone and stared at the diagram.

He retraced the name Gronk. Then, reluctantly, added another line, one that led from Gronk to himself.

No one else would've made the connection.

But the city would feel it when it blew.

A rustle of movement caught his ear.

He glanced up. A child skipped through the archway, chasing a ribbon tied to a stick. They froze when they saw him. Halfa didn't move. Just watched.

The child hesitated. Then smiled widely.

"Watchman," they said, not with fear. With pride.

Halfa nodded. "Afternoon. "

The child twirled the ribbon in the air, then darted away again, laughing as it fluttered behind them like a streamer in the wind.

When the echoes of their footsteps faded, Halfa turned back to the wall.

He stood.

He looked at the map one last time.

Then wiped it away with his hand.

The chalk smeared across his palm in white smudges. Names vanished. The arrows disappeared into the dust.

All that remained were the cracks in the stone.

Fractures older than this moment. Deeper than the diagram.

He left the courtyard without looking back, heading to the temple of Thessira.

◉

That evening, as Grayspire dimmed into a gold-edged shadow, Halfa stepped through the violet door.

The city vanished behind him like steam on cold stone.

Inside, the temple was warm without flame. Candlelight pooled in shallow bowls. Incense laced the air, orange blossom with a sharper undertone, maybe clove or cinnamon. The scent made you notice your breathing.

He didn't take off his boots. But he walked quieter here, like the floor had earned it.

He passed through the quiet hall, catching glimpses of small things: someone had polished the offering bowls. The spiral path had been swept. A fresh stitch mended the frayed edge of one curtain. Joy lived in those details. The joy no one demanded thanks for.

Near the mural wall, Marin was painting alone.

Her sleeves were rolled to her elbows, one cheek smudged with blue. A ladder stood nearby, unused; she balanced on the balls of her feet as she filled in a cascade of dancing figures spilling from a sky of ribbons and fireworks. Her brush moved with calm precision, but there was nothing passive about her.

"You always show up when the paint's still wet," she said without turning.

Halfa paused. "You say that like I planned it. "

"You do that too. Show up late enough to avoid helping, but early enough to look sentimental. "

He stepped closer, his gaze following her hand. "The mural's changed. "

"So have we. "

She rinsed her brush, then glanced at him. "Want to walk the spiral?"

He hesitated.

"I wasn't asking for you," she added. "The flame's been quiet today. I think it misses you. "

Halfa gave her a look, half scowl, half surrender, and moved toward the spiral.

The candlelit path wound inward through black stone and coral tile. Each slow turn tugged a thought from his shoulders.

The tension in the Watch.

Dot's buried reports.

Rix's silence.

Tallen's scar.

The fire that still pulsed under his ribs, waiting for something it couldn't name.

He reached the centre and stood still, facing the flame. Gold and red flickered in its bowl, laced with brief flickers of blue. Serelion had once said blue meant *joy remembered,* and red meant *joy lost.*

He couldn't remember what gold stood for.

Behind him, footsteps approached, soft, careful, familiar.

Marin joined him without a word. Not close enough to touch, but close enough to anchor him.

For a long while, they watched the flame in silence.

Then she said, "You've been patching things again. "

"I haven't—"

"The pantry shelves. The comb by the tea corner. The back gate. "

He looked at her. She didn't smile.

"Those weren't work orders," she said. "That was you. Fixing things no one asked you to fix. "

Halfa's voice was rough. "Someone had to. "

"And who's going to fix you?"

He blinked. The flame shifted.

"I'm serious," she said, quiet but not soft. "You keep carrying everything like it's your job to rebuild the entire city one beam at a time. But you can't do it alone, and you can't keep pretending it doesn't cost you. "

Halfa exhaled slowly, his gaze on the flame. "I don't want it to cost anyone else. "

"It already does. " Her voice caught just slightly. "I see it every time you come back from patrol. Every time you walk through that door, you're more tired than the day before. "

Silence stretched between them. The flame flickered. A thread of blue danced.

"You want to talk about it?" she asked.

He shook his head.

She nodded. Not as permission, but as acknowledgment. Then, after a beat:

"You know what Serelion said to me once? That joy is like a flame in cold hands. You either warm people with it—or burn yourself trying. "

Halfa's gaze stayed on the fire.

"I didn't understand it," Marin went on. "I thought they meant you had to choose. Warmth or pain. But now. . . I think they were talking about you. "

Halfa's brow tightened, but he didn't speak.

"You walk into every fight like the only way out is through fire. Like hurting is how you prove you're still trying. But that's not what this place is about. It's not what you're about either. "

She turned slightly, facing him. "You don't have to burn to be strong, Halfa. You just have to stop doing it where no one can see you fall."

He didn't speak. Couldn't.

"I'm not asking you to stop burning, Halfa," Marin said. "I'm asking you to stop doing it alone."

His breath hitched, not from pain, but from recognition.

He remembered Serelion's voice. The dances. The temple spirals. Marin's hand catching his wrist when he faltered. Her gaze, was steady even now.

The fire didn't retreat.

But for the first time, it felt... quiet. Held.

Halfa looked at her, truly looked.

"You're not afraid of me?"

"I'm terrified," she said, and smiled. "But only because you matter."

Halfa didn't speak. But his hand, calloused and rough, shifted, one knuckle brushing the side of her arm, then her wrist. She didn't pull away. Instead, she slid closer, just enough that their shoulders touched.

The warmth wasn't sudden. It had always been there.

This was the moment they stopped pretending otherwise.

She leaned her head against his shoulder. He let it happen.

Outside, the city breathed fog, stone and quiet.

Inside, two people sat side by side, saying nothing, and saying everything.

◈

The next morning, the fog had lifted, but Arcanist's Walk still carried its weight in the air. The market buzzed with a half-hearted rhythm. Vendors called out deals with practised cheer, while spell-flickers pulsed inside potion vials like trapped stars. A pair of illusionists juggled shimmering birds overhead, more for themselves than the crowd. But beneath the colours, the city felt like it was holding its breath.

Halfa walked down the lane with Gorne at his side, boots crunching on uneven cobbles. Gorne moved like a man used to longer shadows, broad in the shoulders, heavier in the steps, but sharp-eyed despite the calm.

"Feels off," Gorne muttered. "Like a festival with no laughter."

Halfa gave a faint nod. "Too many stalls. Not enough smiles. "

This part of town always blurred charm and desperation. Sellers hawking love charms beside burnt-out alchemy wagons, incense smoke curling above rust-proof cloak racks. It should've felt alive. Instead, it felt strained.

They passed a row of rune weavers and old scroll-peddlers before a flicker of movement caught Halfa's eye.

Two men stood at the edge of a charm vendor's stall. Charcoal-grey coats. One tall, one thicker through the arms. The vendor, an elderly woman with a blue kerchief pressed flat around her silver hair, clutched a small lockbox with both hands. Her fingers had gone pale.

One man leaned in close, voice low. The other tapped the corner of her table with three slow fingers, like a clock counting down.

Halfa didn't rush. He just straightened.

Gorne followed his gaze, eyebrows tightening. "You want left or right?"

"I'll take the one smiling. "

Halfa stepped forward, pace steady. He didn't shout. He didn't need to.

"This is Watch jurisdiction," he said, voice low but cutting.

Both men turned.

The one with the lockbox offered a pleasant smile, thin, smooth, practised. The other stepped just slightly forward, coat shifting enough to reveal a sheathed knife along his belt. Not drawn. But visible.

"Just resolving a dispute," the smiling man said. "Lady forgot our arrangement. "

"I saw no agreement," Halfa replied. "Only intimidation. "

A ripple passed through the market. Conversations hushed. A street mage paused mid-gesture, her illusory sparrow flickering out. A bard nearby held a final note in the air a little too long.

The man holding the box tilted his head. "You planning to draw on us, officer? In front of all these good citizens?"

Gorne stepped up beside Halfa, arms at ease but jaw tight. "Funny how often people say that when they're hoping we will. "

Halfa didn't respond. He simply stepped between the men and the vendor, planting his boots and folding his arms.

"You'll hand that back now," he said.

The taller man glanced around, not at Halfa, but at the crowd. A few shoppers were still pretending not to watch. Most weren't bothering to hide it. The street had stilled.

After a long pause, the second man leaned in and muttered something low.

Halfa caught one word.

"Watchdog. "

Then they turned and walked. Not quickly. Not like they'd lost. Just... not interested in pressing further.

The vendor stayed frozen. Her knuckles hadn't loosened from the lockbox. When Halfa turned to her, she startled slightly, then exhaled.

"Thank you," she said.

He nodded. "Stay near the open stalls today. They won't try twice where people are watching. "

She looked like she wanted to say more, but Halfa was already moving.

He and Gorne passed a row of potion stands. A little girl crouched near a mural wall, scribbling stars over old graffiti with a chalk nub. She looked up, wary at first, then hopeful. Halfa gave her a small nod.

She smiled and kept drawing.

"Didn't think you'd let them walk," Gorne said once they were out of earshot.

"They wanted attention. Not blood. "

"And if they wanted both?"

Halfa didn't answer right away. The heat in his chest had never surged. But it had waited. Watched. Fire didn't need to speak to be present.

"They'll be back," he said at last.

Gorne grunted. "Then so will we. "

The market slowly returned to motion, voices rising again, haggling resuming, the rhythm stitching itself back together.

◊

The rooftop outside the Watchhouse was quiet.

The city below murmured. Carts rolling, bells chiming, someone shouting about pickpockets down near Wickerhook, but none of it reached this high with urgency. Up here, the stones were warm with sunset, and the railing creaked just slightly when the wind changed.

Halfa leaned back against the stone ledge, legs stretched out, one hand wrapped around a tin cup of spiced tea that had long gone cold. He had brought it with him from the temple.

Brannig sat beside him on an overturned crate, coat unbuttoned, boots muddy, eyes narrowed at the skyline like it owed her an answer she couldn't quite phrase.

Neither of them spoke for a while.

They didn't need to.

Eventually, Brannig lifted her cup and sniffed. "Bilbin's heavy on the clove this week."

Halfa grunted. "Tastes like medicine."

She sipped anyway. "Better than nothing."

They sat in that comfortable silence for another minute. Then:

"The Ash Rats are moving differently," Brannig said, low and steady. "More organised. More surgical. They're not just shoving the Blackjaws off corners anymore. They're *claiming* them."

Halfa didn't look at her. "I've seen it too."

Brannig exhaled. "Someone's training them."

A beat.

Halfa sipped his tea.

"They're cleaner," he said. "Less blood on the stones. Less coin taken from the weak. They're... not like the old gangs."

Brannig raised an eyebrow. "Doesn't mean they're saints. Just means they're good at pretending."

She waited a beat.

Then added, "You hear anything from that old friend of yours? The Ash Rat girl?"

"Rix."

Brannig nodded. "That's the one."

"She led me to Gronk. She says Gronk's planning something," Halfa said, eyes still on the horizon. "Bigger than turf. Something with reach. Strategy. Maybe even intent."

"Thought he was long gone?"

"He's not. "

"Does he want peace?"

Halfa didn't answer right away.

A gull passed overhead. Somewhere across the rooftops, a glass bottle shattered and someone cursed in three languages.

At last, he said, "He wants control. "

Brannig made a quiet sound. Neither a laugh nor a scoff.

"Control's not peace. It just wears quieter boots. "

She leaned back, folding her hands behind her head. Her knuckles cracked.

"I've been on these stones a long time, Halfa," she said. "Seen gangs rise and fall. Watched the Watch clean its blade with one hand and open its purse with the other. But this?" She gestured vaguely at the city. "This is different. "

Halfa's grip tightened slightly on his cup.

"It's not war yet," he said.

"No," she agreed. "Not yet. "

A breeze passed, and the sound of the city fell away for a moment.

Halfa looked out at Grayspire.

The rooftops were undulated like scales, golden at the edges, rust-coloured in the shadow. The city looked peaceful, maybe even beautiful, from up here.

But he knew better.

He could feel it in his chest.

The fire was building.

Waiting to breathe.

Untold Truths

Night brought quiet to Grayspire's streets.

The real quiet. It wasn't the tense silence preceding a battle, but the exhausted quiet of a city that had endured the day and chosen to rest, at least for the moment.

Boots clicked in rhythm along the stone walk. Brannig walked ahead, lantern swinging at her side like a pendulum, counting the time neither of them kept.

Halfa stayed a step behind.

Not because he had to.

Just because it felt right.

"You're heavy-footed tonight," Brannig muttered. "Something on your mind?"

Halfa didn't answer right away. He let the sounds fill the space between them, the creak of shutters; the wind brushing alley dust, the faint drip of some far-off pipe.

Then he said, "They call me quiet."

Brannig smirked. "Aye. Among other things."

"But I've worked beside you for months. Nearly died beside you. And I couldn't tell someone a single thing about your life outside that desk."

That earned a raised brow.

"You've never mentioned a family," Halfa continued. "A partner. A home. Not even a favourite drink."

"I told you I like bitterleaf tea."

"You drink it. That's not the same."

Brannig grunted. "Didn't realise this patrol came with soul-mining."

Halfa offered a rare smile. "Just seems uneven."

They walked another block before she spoke.

"I grew up in Cragmere," she said at last. "Little fortress-town northeast of Stonevale. Tighter than a drum. Every dwarf knew every other. It wasn't a town; it was a mirror. You either liked what you saw, or you ran. "

"Which were you?"

She snorted. "I ran. Or tried. Joined the merchant guard at fifty. Wanted to see more than granite and gossip. Ended up on a salt barge, caught between orc raiders and a winter that didn't end. "

Halfa didn't interrupt.

Brannig went on, her voice a little softer. "Met someone out there. Another guard. Human lad. Too tall, too kind. Taught me how to whistle through my teeth and bluff a die hand. "

"What happened to him?"

She was quiet for a moment. "War happened. "

Halfa's jaw tightened. "I'm sorry. "

Brannig shrugged. "It was a long time ago. I came to Grayspire after that. Swore I'd hold a line somewhere. Make sure people had *one* good wall left standing. "

She glanced sideways. "Didn't expect the wall to fight back. "

Halfa looked down at his boots. "I don't always know how to be part of something. "

Brannig gave a soft chuckle. "Neither do I. But we're not bad at holding each other up, are we?"

"No," Halfa said. "We're not. "

They reached the corner of an empty square; the lamp light catching the edges of a merchant cart long since packed away.

Brannig stopped. Looked up at the stars just barely visible above the rooftops.

"I don't say it much," she said. "But I'm glad you're here. "

Halfa blinked. "You said you vouched for me out of guilt. "

"I said that once. " She squinted. "I've grown since then. Not taller. But wiser. "

He smiled, just faintly.

She nudged him with one elbow. "Alright. Your turn next time. I want one wonderful secret, or I guess. "

Halfa nodded. "You'll get one. "

Brannig raised her brow.

"Doesn't mean it'll be good. "

◈

Halfa didn't knock. The temple door was always open.

But that night, it still felt like trespassing.

The spiral path was empty, the flame low. Most of the lanterns had been doused. Only one figure remained in the mural chamber, kneeling near the centre tiles with a spool of thread in her hands.

Marin.

She didn't look up when he entered. Her hands were working quietly, re-stitching the hem of one of the ceremonial banners that hung near the prayer wall.

Halfa stayed near the doorway, unsure.

Marin spoke first. "You ever notice how we only find time for peace when the city's too tired to argue?"

He stepped forward slowly. "You always sew this late?"

"Only when I can't sleep. " She paused. "Or when I need to think. "

The thread slipped through the fabric with a soft whisper.

Halfa hesitated, then sat beside her.

For a while, the only sound was needle, thread, breath.

Then she said, "Do you know how I got here?"

He looked at her. "To the temple?"

She nodded, but didn't stop sewing. "Everyone assumes I was raised here. Born into prayer, or rescued in some noble gesture. But that's not how it happened. "

Halfa didn't speak.

Marin kept her eyes on the stitch. "I grew up in a merchant house. Not wealthy, not poor, just sharp-edged. Rules for everything. A consequence of every wrinkle. My father believed in obedience. My mother believed in silence. "

Her fingers paused. The thread tugged tight.

"I was good at being quiet," she said softly. "Too good. Until one day I wasn't. "

Halfa waited.

"There was a boy. Older. Trusted by the family. He said I should be grateful for his attention. " A beat. "I wasn't. "

She tied off the stitch. Hands shaking only slightly.

"I told my mother. She told me not to ruin things. "

Halfa's breath caught.

"I packed a satchel the next night and walked to the river. Didn't even know where I was going. I just wanted to be somewhere that no one had the power to tell me to stay. "

She set the finished banner aside, folding it with care.

"I slept under a ferry dock for three nights. Didn't speak to anyone. Ate stolen apples and crusts from temple bins. On the fourth night, Serelion found me. "

Her voice softened at the name.

"They didn't ask what I was running from. Just asked if I wanted to breathe. I followed them back to Thessira's temple, expecting rules. What I found was... rhythm. Light. Rooms that weren't locked. "

She looked at Halfa now. Fully. "You think the temple saved me?"

He didn't answer.

Marin shook her head. "It didn't. *I did.* I chose it. Chose joy. I chose breath. Chose escape from a set and boring fate. "

A long silence passed.

Then she added, "But sometimes I still dream of the spoon drawer. Lined up like knives. Of the perfect folds on the tablecloths, in the clothing. And when I wake up, I'm angry that I still flinch. "

Halfa's hand closed gently around hers.

"You don't flinch now," he said.

She squeezed his hand once, then let go.

"I just patch banners," she replied.

"Not just. "

She looked at him, not smiling, but whole.

"And you?" she asked.

He tilted his head.

"When you wake up," Marin said. "What do you still burn for?"

Halfa didn't answer right away.

The flame in the spiral bowl flickered red, gold, a single lick of blue. The silence stretched, not with hesitation, but with weight.

Finally, he said, "I don't know where I come from. "

Marin looked at him, brow softening.

"I mean that literally," Halfa continued. "No name. No family. Not even a memory of someone calling me theirs. I was big early. Strong. So, people assumed I belonged somewhere. But I didn't. I just... was. "

His voice didn't shake. It didn't need to.

"For a while, I thought I was just a mistake. Something someone left behind because they couldn't lift the weight of what I might become. "

He stared into the flame, eyes distant.

"When the fire came, when it first burned, I thought it was punishment. A curse. Proof that I wasn't meant to last long. Maybe I'd explode, and the world would be better for it. "

Marin didn't speak. She listened. Not with pity. With presence.

"I kept waiting for something. A sign. A scroll. A name. Anything to explain why I was like this. Who left me? Where the fire came from?" His hands curled slowly. "But it never came. "

He exhaled, not heavy, but hollowed.

"So I stopped waiting. I started surviving. One day, one coin, one fight at a time. Until..."

He hesitated.

"Until I stopped fighting *for* survival and started fighting *for* others. For the quiet ones. For the hungry. For people like I used to be. "

He looked over at Marin.

"Until I found the temple. "

She met his gaze, steady.

"Until I found *you*," he said.

That caught her breath. Not with surprise, but with truth.

"I still don't know where the fire comes from," Halfa said, voice low. "Maybe I never will. But when I protect something, when I *choose* joy, when I walk into a place like this and feel like I belong, I don't care as much. "

He looked down at his hand, the one that had brushed hers earlier.

"I still wish I had a name. A story. Just *one lead* to follow. One link. But if I never get it... I think I could be alright. "

The flame burned low, casting their shadows long across the stone.

Marin reached out and took his hand again.

"You have a story," she said. "You're still writing it. "

He didn't smile.

But the fire in his chest settled. Not silenced.

Just still.

They stayed a little longer beside the spiral flame. Then Marin tugged his hand once, wordless, and led him through the quiet halls, up the back stairs, past the sleeping cats, to the rooftop garden that still smelled faintly of rosemary and ash.

Halfa sat beside her on the edge of the low wall, boots dangling. The city glowed beneath them, oil lamps, hearth fires, the faint shimmer of life too stubborn to go out.

"I used to think I wouldn't live long," he said.

Marin glanced at him, but didn't speak.

"Not just from fights. From inside. From the fire. I thought it would break me or hollow me out. Or burn too bright one day and leave nothing. "

She didn't offer comfort. Just presence.

"Now I think... maybe I'm afraid it won't. " He looked down at his hands. "I'm afraid I'll live a long time. And never know what I'm meant for. "

Marin slid her hand over his palm, warm, steady. "You're not meant for one thing," she said. "You're meant for every moment you choose. "

"What if I choose wrong?"

"Then we fix it," she said. "Together. "

He didn't answer. But when he turned to her, the fear in his eyes had shifted. Still there, but no longer alone.

◈

The patrol had been quiet.

Too quiet.

Halfa moved like he always did, steady, watchful, eyes tracking corners more than streets. Tallen kept pace beside him, a half-step behind, still favouring his healing shoulder but hiding it well.

They rounded a bend near Copper Alley, where fishmongers argued over salt rations, and fog crept along the gutters like old smoke.

That was when he saw him.

The man leaned against a post beside a shuttered bar. Blackjaw colours, but muted. Grey coat, sharp cuffs, a knife hilt barely visible under one arm.

He looked up when Halfa passed.

And smiled.

Not the threatening kind. Not the cocky kind, either.

The *recognising* kind.

"Well," the man drawled. "Didn't think you made it out of that temple. Last I saw, you were walking through fire like it owed you something. "

Halfa stopped cold.

Tallen nearly walked into him.

The man didn't move. He didn't reach for a weapon.

He didn't need to.

"Funny world," he said. "You torch a few people in a temple, wind up wearing a badge. Maybe the gods *do* have a sense of humour. "

Halfa didn't reply. Didn't blink. Just stepped forward once, enough to close the space between them. Close enough to speak low.

"If you're smart," Halfa said, voice flat as stone, "you'll forget you ever saw me. "

The man's smile didn't change. But something behind his eyes shifted.

Fear? Or calculation? Hard to say.

He tipped an invisible hat and disappeared into the fog.

Tallen waited until the footsteps had faded.

Then: "Friend of yours?"

"No. "

"Sounded like he knew you. "

"He didn't. "

A pause.

"Temple fire?" Tallen asked, careful, quiet.

Halfa didn't answer. Not right away.

Then: "A few days before I joined the Watch. Thought Dot had made that public knowledge. "

Tallen looked at him, really looked.

Then nodded. "I'd always rather trust the source. "

Halfa glanced at Tallen's grip on the hilt, steady, squared, no tremor in the wrist. Not perfect. But practised. Still there. Still fighting.

They walked on, boots soft on damp stone.

Nothing else was said.

But something between them had shifted.

◊

The patrol ended early.

Nothing to report but a drunk vendor arguing with a chicken and a loose shutter flapping like a bored ghost. Brannig signed off the shift at the Watchhouse and made for the back steps, where the stone bench caught what little warmth the gas lamps had left.

Halfa was already there.

He said nothing when she sat down beside him. He nodded, his silence a weight.

They sat in companionable silence. The city exhaled around them.

Brannig waited.

After a long moment, Halfa spoke.

"I knew him before all of this. "

Brannig blinked. "Who?"

"Gronk. "

He didn't look at her. Just at his hands, callused, steady, resting like weights on his knees.

"We were young then. Just bruises and bones. Fought for bread. Slept under crates. The Dock Ward doesn't keep track of gutter kids. "

Brannig didn't interrupt.

"He was faster. Louder. Always smiling like he knew a joke I didn't. We fought almost every week. He gave as good as he got. But he never—" Halfa stopped. "He never hit to end it. Only to prove something. "

"Sounds familiar," Brannig said gently.

Halfa's mouth twitched. Not quite a smile.

"I really hope some of the boy Gronk was is still in the man Gronk has become. Look at him, the leader of the Ash Rats. "

"How did he get there?" Brannig asked.

"Rix said she saved him from the Blackjaws after the Temple fire. Took him to the Ash Rats. He spent the first few months protecting everyone. He was everywhere. It didn't take long for them to love him, or to fall in line behind him. "

"Let's hope that's a good thing," Brannig mused.

❦

Halfa had made his way back to the temple after his musings with Brannig, and had found himself watching Bilbin cook.

Bilbin was stirring a pot of something sharp and savoury. "You're watching way too intently. " He said, not lifting his eyes from the pot. He scraped the bottom, then added softly, "What are you doing here, Halfa?"

"Wanted to end my night here. The patrol finished early. "

"No," Bilbin looked up. "What are you *really* doing here?"

"I keep coming back here," Halfa said after a short silence. "I have a bed at the barracks; no one asks me to be here. Yet, here I come. "

Bilbin continued to stir. "I can think of one long-haired beauty who might disagree. " He smiled. "That doesn't answer the question. "

"Im tired of being used by the Watch, by my own fire. I don't want to just react anymore. "

"So, what do you want?"

Halfa took a breath. "I want to protect. I want that choice to matter. Not because someone gave me orders, or because I'm angry. Because it is right. "

"But why here? Why Joy?"

Halfa looked down at his hands, thinking. "It isn't trying to prove itself. Joy just... is. It doesn't justify itself. It hasn't got a uniform, or a fight in it. "

Halfa paused, the words slower now. "Maybe that's what makes it worth fighting for. "

Bilbin nodded once, stirring still. "Ok, Serelion. "

Halfa grinned and reached forward to grab a bowl. "Enough of this talk. "

◉

The next night, Rix met Halfa beneath the old winch station on Salthook Rise, silent, hunched, eating something wrapped in brown paper that crinkled with every bite. She didn't offer him any.

"You said you wanted truths," she muttered, voice muffled by food. "I've got one. But you'll owe me after. "

Halfa raised an eyebrow. "Owe you what?"

"Don't know yet," she said. "That's how favours work. "

She led him up a side staircase choked in vines and old rust. They climbed until the city opened below them, lanterns smeared across rooftops like spilled light. Grayspire at dusk.

"There," Rix said, crouching by a broken archway and pointing down.

A courtyard sat behind what used to be a shipping guild, half-collapsed, its outer wall swallowed by ivy and soot. But someone had cleared the debris. Rebuilt a gate. Hung banners.

And in the middle of the courtyard, standing before a row of kneeling figures, was a woman.

Tall. Composed. Unarmed. Human.

Her coat was plain but tailored, grey trimmed in dark red. Her brown hair was cropped close. She was small and skinny. But even from this distance, Halfa could tell—she *commanded*.

The way the kneelers tilted toward her. The way the guards stood back, not bored, but reverent.

She didn't shout. She didn't gesture.

"That's her," Rix whispered. "Valka. "

Halfa watched in silence. Hard to forget the woman who had been haunting his dreams. The woman who had snuffed out his fire.

"First time I saw her," Rix said, "she was sitting on a wall above a riot. Eating an apple. Watching people tear each other apart like it was music. "

"Did you follow her?"

Rix's jaw twitched. "I didn't. Not at first. " She hesitated, then added, "She found me. After my older brother died. He was Ash Rat first. Thought he could carve out a space where we didn't have to run. He bled, trying. I didn't know where to go, so I ran. Again. "

Halfa looked at her.

She didn't look back.

"Valka didn't promise safety," Rix said. "She promised clarity. Said she doesn't build walls. She burns them. And if I wasn't ready to do the same, I should leave. "

"And you stayed. "

Rix exhaled. "I thought fire meant pain. I didn't know it could mean *purpose*. "

Down below, Valka turned. Her eyes passed briefly over the rooftops, almost like she'd seen them.

Rix pulled back first.

"That's all you get," she said. "Next time, I ask the questions. "

Rix turned slightly, the rooftops still glowing behind her. "I've still got friends in that pit, you know. People who stayed when I didn't. Not loyal. Some of them send word when they can. Others don't know they're helping me. "

She glanced at Halfa. "But don't expect names. I burn my bridges after I cross them. "

Halfa didn't respond.

He watched the woman below as she walked between the kneeling figures. Silent. Steady.

And the fire inside him didn't burn with rage this time.

It watched.

The Ash and the Oath

The temple was quiet at this early hour.

Halfa sat on the cold stone steps near the spiral's edge, elbows on knees, watching the flame bowl flicker against the dark.

Serelion approached from the shadows with no ceremony.

"Still asking?" they said.

"Still not sure what to ask," Halfa replied.

They sat beside him. Close enough to share breath. Not close enough to impose it.

"The flame doesn't answer questions," Serelion said after a while.

Halfa looked at the spiral. "So, what am I doing here?"

"Letting it remember you. "

He shifted. "You talk like it's a god. "

"No," they said. "But it's the closest thing I've ever seen to one. "

"Then what are you?"

Serelion didn't blink. "A steward. A witness. Maybe the first time someone laid their fear down and found warmth instead. "

"And does it help?"

"Not always," Serelion said. "But it holds the ones who want to be held. Even when they don't know how. "

They stood. The light caught the edge of their robe.

"You're not a soldier, Halfa. You're a spark. Find where you're meant to catch. "

Then they were gone. No footsteps. Just a ripple of warmth as the spiral flame curled slightly higher.

◈

The Ash Rats' tunnels always felt colder when the city above was quiet.

Halfa couldn't remember what had drawn him down there this time. Maybe it was instinct. Maybe it was a habit. Perhaps it was just the fire inside him needing somewhere it wouldn't set anything important alight.

He moved through narrow halls where children whispered in code and candles flickered behind hidden walls. He wasn't expected. But he wasn't unwelcome.

Gronk didn't call him.

But the silence knew he'd come.

The training ring wasn't really a ring.

It was a cleared space in the back of the Ash Rats' den, lit by cracked lanterns and warmed by the breath of twenty half-muted conversations. No one shouted. No one jeered. Just the scrape of boots and the thud of padded blows.

Halfa leaned against a load-bearing beam, arms crossed, watching.

The floor was chalked in crude lines, boundaries, forms, maybe old runes half-rubbed away. A tiefling girl ducked under a halfling's hook. A human boy shifted his weight like he'd seen a Watch drillmaster do it once, then did it again, smoother.

They weren't playing. Weren't mimicking. They were learning.

Gronk wasn't in sight, but his fingerprints were all over it.

The stance corrections. The footwork. The way the taller kids kept scanning exits while the shorter ones kept low. Not just street-fighting. *Tactics.*

Halfa didn't move.

He recognised some drills. The kind used to keep rookies alive on their first patrol. Slow pivots, quick breaks, partner rotations. The kind Brannig had barked into his bones a hundred times.

Someone was teaching them how not to die.

One of the younger kids, a wiry boy with a ragged scarf and mismatched boots, caught Halfa's eye mid-swing. Froze. Stared.

Halfa stared back.

The boy didn't flinch. He gave the smallest of nods, like he was clocking the shape of the room, and acknowledging that it had changed.

Then he went back to work.

Nearby, two girls ran through a defensive formation. One wore a sash tied with old temple beads, half of them scorched. Halfa caught a spiral scratched into one lantern beside her, a Thessiran symbol. Crooked. Earnest.

Rix passed behind them, silent and watchful. She flicked her gaze toward Halfa but didn't speak. Just moved on.

He let himself exhale. Not relief. Not tension.

Something in between.

The Ash Rats weren't soldiers.

But they weren't just strays anymore, either.

And whatever they were becoming, it wasn't Gronk's alone.

❦

Gronk had changed little.

Not in the ways that counted.

He still stood like the room owed him space. Still spoke like every word had to pass through grit and gravel to be heard. Still watched Halfa like he expected a punch, and was deciding whether to duck or take it.

The Ash Rats' hideout was quiet. Too quiet.

It wasn't silence; it was stillness, the kind that hung in the corners of an old battlefield or a church right before a sermon turns sour. The room they sat in was part stone cellar, part converted undercroft. Moss clung to damp walls where lanterns hadn't warmed. The ceiling dripped with the patience of old wounds. The air was thick with coal smoke, wet stone, and something else, burnt rope, maybe. Or singed hope.

A low brazier stood between them, its fire licking lazily at a stack of dry pine and resin-soaked timber. The flames didn't roar. They whispered.

Half a dozen Ash Rats lingered on the edges of the room. Not quite guards. Not quite spies. Just... eyes. Kids barely old enough to shave. Veterans too broken to be soldiers. A tiefling girl sat near a stack of crates, whittling a sliver of wood into something sharp. A halfling leaned against a pillar, eyes darting constantly toward Gronk like he was waiting for permission to breathe.

Gronk hadn't told them to leave.

Just waved them back.

They hadn't really gone.

Halfa sat across from him, arms folded, his bulk half-lit in the brazier's flicker. His expression hadn't changed since he arrived. As usual, he was stone-faced, unreadable. But the air between them held static, and the fire threw shadows that danced like memories neither wanted to name.

"I figured you'd punch me," Gronk said finally. His voice was low. Dry iron dragged over old stone.

Halfa didn't smile. "I figured you'd lie. "

A corner of Gronk's mouth twitched. Not quite a smirk. A crack refusing to morph into a smile.

"Maybe we're both disappointed. "

Silence stretched. The fire cracked. A single loud snap, like a bone settling into place.

Gronk stared into it. "I meant it when I said I was out. After the temple... after the Blackjaws left me bleeding in that alley and shut the door behind them..." His voice slowed. "I walked away. "

"Your 'protection' nearly cost me everything. " Halfa said. His tone was level, not angry. Just *remembering*.

Gronk didn't flinch. "I followed orders. Valka's orders. "

Halfa's eyes narrowed. He hadn't known that. The fire in his chest roared, nearly drowning out his thoughts.

"Until you didn't. "

Gronk's jaw tightened. "And you always had the luxury of standing on your principles. Must be nice, carrying the moral high ground when you never had to live in the mud. "

Halfa leaned back. "I lived in the same streets as you. "

"No," Gronk said. "You *survived* the same streets. You never let them make you into what they needed. "

A pause. The fire hissed. Something dripped into a nearby bucket with a slow, metronome rhythm.

"You always had a convenient line between duty and choice," Halfa said.

"And you always thought you were above consequence," Gronk snapped back. Their eyes locked.

And in that stillness lived everything they hadn't said.

The ruined temple.

The blood on the stone.

A torch thrown. A door slammed. A brother left behind.

Halfa breathed deeply and composed himself. His shoulders eased a fraction.

"Why here?" he asked.

Gronk surveyed the room, not just at the walls and the flickering shadows, but at the Ash Rats watching from the gloom. One youth sat with a bandaged hand, sketching on the floor with a bit of charred wood. Another rolled dice beside a crate marked for trade but clearly filled with weapons.

"Because Grayspire forgets the right people," Gronk said. "The Blackjaws threw me to the dogs, Halfa. Said I was weak for letting you live. " Gronk looked up, jaw hard. "So I made something else. "

He leaned forward, elbows on his knees.

"The city left them behind. Street kids. Orphans. Ex-soldiers no one wanted to feed. Mages who burnt out their spark on side jobs for noble brats. I didn't build an army, I caught a fire before it turned wild. Gave it shape. Gave it purpose. "

Gronk's fingers tapped once, twice, against the table, like he wasn't sure if the sentence was finished.

His eyes drifted, briefly, toward a boy near the far wall, wrapping his arm in a too-big sling.

When he looked back at Halfa, something had shuttered behind the eyes.

"All of this," Halfa said quietly. "All of this was to survive?"

Gronk's jaw ticked. "No. This is to protect. "

He stood, slowly, deliberately. Not looming. Just rising.

"The Blackjaws are moving," he said. "You know it. I know it. And now they don't slit throats in alleys. They buy tables. They clean their boots. Shake hands with captains and call it civic investment. "

"I've seen it," Halfa said.

"They don't *take* power. They inherit it. And buy silence. People let them in because they offer order, just not the kind anyone should trust. "

Halfa leaned forward. "Dot's rise isn't an accident. "

"No. It's strategy. Dot's not working with them, not directly. But he sees what they bring and calls it efficiency. He likes numbers that balance and streets that stay quiet, even if the cost is something rotting under the boards. Even if thousands die. "

"So your answer is what? Build your own empire?"

"My answer," Gronk said, "is to stand in the gap. To keep people from falling in. You think I like this? I didn't want a flag. I didn't want a cause. I wanted quiet. I wanted out. But someone had to do something while you were polishing boots for a Watch that stopped watching. "

Halfa stood, too.

He didn't speak right away.

They stood across the brazier now. The fire between them. The years between them. The weight of what they almost became between them.

"You want me to work with you?" Halfa asked.

Gronk didn't answer right away. He stared into the fire as if it had asked a different question.

When he finally spoke, his voice was softer. Not smaller, just more careful.

"I want you to survive what's coming. "

Halfa's jaw flexed.

"I can take this to Brannig. "

"I'm not asking you to," Gronk replied. "I'm asking you to stand where you always stood. Between the fire and what's worth saving. Or in the fire itself. "

A long beat.

Halfa looked at the Ash Rats in the shadows. The rough shelter they'd built from nothing. At the strange, misshapen hope taking root underground.

"What happens if you win?" he asked.

Gronk looked at the embers.

"Then I hold the line," he said. "Until someone better takes it from me. "

Halfa studied him. Not his stance. Not his scars. But the wear in his voice. The callus on his conscience.

"I know what you were," Halfa said. "What we both were. I remember what it felt like to be feared. "

"I remember what it felt like to be helpless," Gronk replied.

That, more than anything, hung in the air.

Then, without ceremony, Gronk extended a hand.

Not as a challenge.

As an invitation.

Halfa looked at it.

He thought of Serelion. Of Brannig. Of the silence in the Watchhouse. Of Dot's clean boots and colder eyes. Most of all, he thought of Marin.

He took it.

Their grips were rough. Uneven. Real.

"You work clean," Halfa said. "No threats. No children harmed. You answer to me if it goes sideways. "

"And if it burns?"

Halfa's eyes lit with something ancient.

"Then I put it out. "

Neither of them said more.

The fire hissed low between them, half-forgotten but still watching.

Halfa held Gronk's eyes for another second, and let go of his hand.

He hadn't joined.

But he hadn't stopped it either.

Not yet.

Gronk shifted his weight like he might say something, then didn't.

The silence that followed wasn't heavy. It was hollow.

The quiet that only holds things you're not ready to say.

✿

They stayed behind after the others cleared out: Halfa, Gronk, and Rix. Long enough for the lanterns to burn lower and the quiet to feel intentional.

"There's one more thing," Halfa said, voice low. "I don't think I can take her. "

Gronk raised an eyebrow.

"Valka," Halfa said. "She snuffed my fire like it was smoke in her lungs. Even my strength felt sapped. If it's just me against her... I lose. "

"She doesn't just kill mages. She shuts them down. Cuts the fuse before it lights. " Halfa continued.

Gronk didn't look surprised. Just thoughtful.

"She needs to face someone she can't manipulate. Someone who doesn't rely on magic. Someone who fights like a wall. "

He looked at Gronk.

"You. "

The room was still. Rix didn't speak. Gronk rolled his neck once, slow and deliberate.

"If I get the chance," he said finally, "I'll take it. "

"This isn't just about brawn," Halfa said. "She'll try to break you. With words. With fear. "

"She's tried before," Gronk replied. "Didn't work then. Won't work now. "

Rix stepped forward, gaze sharp. "You sure?"

"No," Gronk said. "But I'm sure of this, she built something that scares people. I'll break it if I have to. Or die trying. "

Halfa nodded once. "You won't be alone. "

"Wouldn't matter if I was," Gronk said. "I'm the only one she can't silence. "

◈

Halfa didn't head straight for the stairs.

The handshake still echoed in his bones, like a bell struck once and left to hum. As Gronk turned to give quiet orders to a nearby lieutenant, Halfa stepped away from the brazier and moved through the tunnels.

No one stopped him.

But everyone watched.

He passed beneath a rusted archway, its stones blackened with soot and age. The corridor beyond opened into a warren of connected chambers. Storage, sleeping cots, makeshift kitchens. The Ash Rats had carved out an entire second life down here. A shadow city beneath the real one.

The floor was uneven, patched with stone and scavenged tile. The walls were reinforced with old scaffolding, hammered sheet metal, and even torn banners from merchant houses that had long since ceased to exist. One bore the faded sigil of a noble family Halfa vaguely remembered seeing them investigated for tax fraud. Another had once been a Watch flag.

Now, it served as a curtain between rooms.

He kept walking.

In one chamber, two teens sat cross-legged, arguing over a hand-drawn map. Their fingers moved like dancers across the paper, tracing alleys and corners and symbols Halfa didn't recognise. One paused when he passed, eyes widening, mouth tightening like they'd just seen a ghost from a childhood story.

In another room, a halfling woman was organising supplies. Jars of pickled roots. Bundles of kindling. Weapons. She caught his eye, then returned to her work without a word.

There was discipline here.

Not just survival.

Structure. Purpose. Belief.

That unsettled him more than chaos would have.

He turned into what looked like an old storeroom, now converted into a sparring pit. A wooden ring had been marked on the floor with rope and chalk. Inside, two young Ash Rats exchanged cautious blows, nothing fancy, nothing flashy. Just repetition. Precision. They weren't fighting for dominance.

They were training.

An older dwarf watched from a low stool in the corner, pipe between his teeth, arms crossed. His gaze flicked to Halfa briefly. Then, back to the fighters.

A third kid, maybe ten, maybe younger, stood just outside the ring holding a chipped wooden sword. He wasn't watching the match. He was watching Halfa.

When their eyes met, the boy straightened.

Like he expected to be addressed.

Or inspected.

Halfa gave him a nod.

The kid returned it, hesitant, but proud.

He moved on. The tunnel curved and narrowed, leading him into a quieter hall, older stone, less adorned. The air felt heavier here. Not darker. Just deeper.

A small alcove was carved into one wall. Inside, a single candle burned beside a strip of parchment pinned to the stone with a nail. Names were written on it. No titles. No marks of rank. Just names.

Ash Rat dead.

He reached out and placed a hand gently on the stone beside it. The candle flame trembled, but didn't go out.

Behind him, someone cleared their throat softly. He turned.

Rix stood just outside the alcove, arms folded, one eyebrow raised. "You wandered," she said.

"I walked," he replied.

"Same thing down here. " She stepped into the light, her expression unreadable. "He meant what he said, you know. About holding the line. "

Halfa nodded. "I know. "

"He doesn't sleep well. Wakes up sweating. Says it's the pipes, but he doesn't say it like he means it. " She glanced at the wall. "That list started with three names. Now it's eighteen. "

He looked at her, measured. "You glad you joined the Ash Rats?"

"My turn for questions next," she said, and something in her voice softened the edge.

From her belt, she pulled a small leather pouch and tossed it to him. He caught it by reflex.

"Copperleaf salve," she said. "For bruises. "

He loosened the tie and opened it slightly. The scent of pine and crushed mint rose from the cloth, sharp, familiar. Memory.

Halfa nodded. "Thanks. "

Rix gave him a crooked grin. "Don't make me regret trusting you, Big Watch. "

"Don't make me regret shaking his hand. "

For a beat, her expression didn't shift. Then she said, quieter, "You know, they're scared. Half of them think you're here to spy. The other half think you're going to bring the Blackjaws right down on us. "

Halfa met her gaze. "Maybe I am. "

She didn't laugh. Looked at him a moment longer, then turned and walked away. Her boots echoed against the stone as she disappeared into shadow.

He stood there a little longer, watching the candle flicker beside the names. Then he turned and followed the tunnel's curve back toward the long stair, where fog and lamplight waited above.

Later that evening, Halfa emerged from the underground.

The fog had thickened since he'd gone below, it was rolling low over the cobbles, curling through gutters and gas lamp halos like breath held too long.

He moved through it like a shadow with weight, cloak drawn close, the scent of coal smoke and damp stone still clinging to his skin.

The Watchhouse stood like a stubborn tooth in the mouth of a crumbling district, its edges worn, windows barred, its old crest still painted above the entry, despite years of graffiti attempts. It hadn't changed. But tonight, it looked smaller somehow. Like the world around it had grown too fast.

Inside, the warmth was thin but welcome.

Oil lamps hissed softly in their wall brackets. A pot of over-steeped tea simmered near the dispatch desk. The scent of parchment and old sweat lingered in the air. The kind of smell you stopped noticing after enough years on the job.

Brannig was still inside.

She sat in the corner of the Watchroom, boots off, one foot soaking in a chipped basin of herbs. Her coat was draped across a wall hook. Her brow was furrowed, one eye squinting down at a ledger spread open beside a rolled-up map. A half-eaten pear perched atop a stack of unfiled citations. Her teacup balanced precariously on a chipped ceramic lid.

She looked up as he entered.

"You look like you just shook hands with a bear," she said.

"I did," Halfa replied.

He shut the door behind him with a soft *click* and dropped into the chair opposite her. The cushion wheezed under his weight.

Brannig raised one eyebrow.

"Gronk?" she asked.

Halfa nodded once. "I spoke with him. "

She snorted. "So you're trying to get demoted again. "

"I don't think I can get demoted anymore. " He sighed.

"He's not lying," Halfa said. "He's got discipline. The Ash Rats... they're not just scavenging anymore. They're moving with structure. With intent. They don't want blood. They want a chance. "

Brannig picked up her tea and swirled it absently, watching the leaves cling to the edge of the cup.

"And you trust him?" she asked.

"Not quite," Halfa said. "But I understand him. "

She didn't speak right away. Just watched him. Weighing.

Then: "You know what they'll say if this leaks?"

"That I'm working with a terrorist," Halfa replied.

Brannig shook her head, slow and sharp. "No. That you forgot which side you're on. "

She watched him. Weighing.

Outside, the fog clung to the windows. A cart creaked by, it's wheels shrieking slightly against the wet stone.

"This isn't a tavern brawl, Halfa," Brannig said finally. "It's politics now. Corruption in the bones. You know how high this goes?"

"I don't care. "

"You *should*. "

"I *can't*," he said, voice low, fire banked but present. "If I think about the whole system, I stop moving. I freeze. That's not what we're here for. "

Brannig took a long sip, then let the cup rest on her knee.

"You think you're going to fix this?"

"No," Halfa said. "I think we're holding the line. Long enough for someone else to figure out how to fix it. "

"And in the meantime?"

"We survive. "

Brannig leaned back, letting her foot rise out of the water. The basin sloshed, a single drop spilling onto the floor. She stared at Halfa, questioning.

Halfa nodded his head. "I still believe in law. I just know now it's not the same as justice. "

A beat.

Brannig looked at him. Really looked.

He was tired. But not broken. Something in his posture had changed since the last time they'd talked like this. Not weariness. Not pride.

Resolve.

She set her cup aside and leaned forward, elbows on her knees.

"This doesn't touch the ledgers," she said. "Not one footnote. Not one initials code. You work with him; you speak for him. That's your oath. I won't cover it. I won't clean it up. "

"If it burns," Halfa said, "I'll burn it with him. "

Brannig exhaled slowly.

"You're lucky I don't sleep much," she muttered.

He smirked faintly.

She reached into the drawer behind her and pulled out a sealed parchment. Passed it across the table without fanfare.

"That vendor you saved in Arcanist's Walk," she said. "Filed a commendation. "

Halfa blinked.

"She said you didn't draw steel. Wrote that you stood like a wall between her and the storm. "

He didn't open it.

Didn't need to.

He just held it in his hand for a moment and felt its weight. The warmth of it. The strange shape of a world where people still noticed. Still named what was good.

Brannig leaned back again and closed her eyes.

"Still mad I vouched for you," she murmured.

"You'd miss me," Halfa said.

"I'd miss the quiet," she countered.

But there was warmth in her voice.

Not laughter. Not relief.

But belief.

The kind you only gave to someone who'd already earned it.

◈

In the early morning, just before dawn, the air around the temple was thick with the heat of too many bodies and too much tension.

The Ash Rats had arrived without warning, two of them, teenagers barely out of boyhood. Grimy and wired, they tracked mud and desperation across the spiral floor. One clutched a bruised arm; the other carried a sling of stolen medicine. The commotion stirred everyone in the temple from their sleep, scattering the usual stillness.

Halfa met them first. One word from him and they'd have been turned away.

But he didn't say it.

Because trailing behind them was a child, no older than six, barefoot, soot-streaked, shaking like a leaf in a thunderstorm. She was smeared with ash and blood, clutching nothing but herself.

Marin reached her first.

She crossed the room without a word. No rush, no questions. Her robes were loose and sleep-creased, but her presence was solid, steady.

She knelt.

Met the child's eyes.

And held out her hands.

The child froze. Then collapsed into her arms like she'd been waiting for that silence her whole life.

One teen muttered, "We didn't mean to—"

Halfa stepped forward. The room stilled. But it was Marin who turned, calm and heavy with presence. She met the older boy's gaze, no anger, no command. Just weight.

She touched her hand to her heart. Then to the spiral inlaid in the floor. "Sit."

The teen swallowed. Nodded. Didn't run. Didn't argue. He sat.

Later, as the child slept in the back room and the temple exhaled back into its rhythms, paint brushes tapping against stone, flour settling in the air, hymnals humming soft and imperfect, he found Bilbin in the kitchen.

He didn't greet him. He just handed over a plate, three slices of sugared bread, a smear of dried fruit jam, and a mug of something dark and sharp with cloves.

Halfa stared at it.

"Take it," Bilbin said. "You look like someone who forgot what breakfast is. "

Halfa took the plate and sat on the bench near the big spice barrel, where the kids liked to stash pouches and secrets. The mug was hot in his hands. The bread smelled faintly of memory.

Bilbin returned to his prep work, chopping ginger with a short, scarred blade. He hummed—nothing sacred, nothing cheerful.

The silence hung long enough to soften the edges of Halfa's breath.

Eventually, Bilbin spoke without turning. "You ever notice how a fire burns clearer when the oven door stays open a crack?"

Halfa looked up.

"Too much heat, it warps the bread. Too little, it goes flat. But steady heat, just enough space to breathe, that makes something worth sharing. "

He set down his knife and wiped his hands on his apron. "Joy's like that. You don't need to force it. You just give it room. "

Halfa didn't respond at first.

But he stayed.

And ate every slice.

When Bilbin finally looked over, he grinned around a piece of candied ginger. "You don't have to be all blaze and bellow all the time, you know. "

Halfa raised an eyebrow.

"We already like you," Bilbin added. "Might as well enjoy it. "

Strike and Silence

The Watchhouse roof always creaked in the wind. That night, it sounded like it was thinking too hard.

Halfa stood at the edge of the overlook, hands on the stone rail, eyes scanning the district below. Tanner's End. Dockward fringe. Quiet lately, too quiet.

Footsteps approached.

"You wanted us?" Tallen's voice. His voice had an eager tinge to it.

Tallen stood beside Gorne and Lasse, all three out of uniform, but still visibly Watch members. Still carrying the tension of too many unanswered orders. Too many silences where orders should be.

Halfa nodded once. "I've got a target. "

Lasse raised an eyebrow. "Sanctioned?"

Halfa looked at him.

Lasse didn't ask again.

"Rix fed me something solid," Halfa said. "Short run. Blackjaw convoy. Resource crates headed west that are disguised as laundry export. "

Gorne snorted. "They really used that? Laundry? That's lazy crime. "

"No banners. This is a coin run," Halfa said.

"Hit it clean?" Gorne asked, arms folded like he already knew the answer.

"Fast. No uniforms. We break carts, not skulls. If it gets hot, we pull back. "

Tallen grinned. "Old-school Watch justice. Love it. "

Halfa met his gaze. "Not justice. Pressure. We're not toppling the house; we're rattling the windows. "

Lasse exhaled through his nose. "And if someone hears us?"

"Then we run. Or we hold. Depends on who shows up. "

The recruits exchanged a glance. Gorne cracked his knuckles once.

"Fine," he said. "But if this ends in paperwork, I'm blaming all of you. "

"I'm in," Tallen said, already adjusting his belt like he was prepping for a parade.

Lasse didn't move at first. Then: "No steel unless drawn on?"

Halfa nodded. "This isn't war. "

A pause.

Then Lasse said, "Yet. "

The city creaked beneath them. Somewhere below, a cart wheel squealed like a warning.

"Alright," Lasse said. "Let's break something worth fixing. "

Halfa didn't grin. But something behind his eyes flickered.

Tallen laughed first, a short, surprised, nervous burst that made Lasse snort and Gorne crack his knuckles like a drumbeat. They were bruised, sure. Tired, always. But in that moment, they stood straighter. Sharper. The promise of action had lit something in them that the Watch had nearly snuffed out.

And Halfa? He'd given them that. Not with orders. Not with fire. Just with trust. And maybe that was enough.

◆

The alley stank of oil. Lantern light flickered over rusted chains.

Halfa crouched behind a stack of empty crates, watching the convoy emerge from the side passage near Scalders Row. Just three wagons, made of wood reinforced with iron, no banners, no city seal. Two drivers, a pair of runners with short weapons and no armour, and one "guard" pretending not to be asleep. That was it.

It looked like nothing.

Which meant it was something.

Behind him, Tallen shifted, checking the length of his truncheon. Gorne held his breath like he was back on parade, body taut, eyes locked. Lasse muttered a prayer, something from Elaran, Halfa thought, all tide and mercy.

Halfa raised a hand. Waited. Counted six paces from the last wagon's wheel to the arch.

Then: *Go.*

They moved like shadows.

Tallen went wide, looping behind the rearmost wagon to cut off escape. Gorne and Lasse burst forward with quick, silent efficiency. One of the drivers saw movement, opened his mouth to yell out, but Gorne hit him low, knocking the breath out of his lungs before a sound could rise.

Halfa moved in last, bulk looming out of the fog and lantern light, and planted his weight between the second and third wagons.

"Off the carts," he growled.

The guard went for his hip.

Halfa hit him once, an open palm to the chest, and sent him crashing into the alley wall with a noise like dropped furniture.

The others dropped their weapons without hesitation.

It should have ended there.

"Fast," Tallen said, binding one of the runners. "Too fast. "

Halfa turned toward the first wagon, tugging at the tarp. Beneath it: crates. Stamped with inked sigils. There was coin, bolt, meal, and salt. Munitions disguised as food relief. Their markings didn't match any official aid distributor. Rix was right. This was Blackjaw logistics disguised as charity.

"We torch the axles, not the crates," Halfa said. "We want the Ash Rats to get this—"

A yell. Tallen's.

Halfa spun.

The fog at the end of the alley moved. No, not moved—*parted*.

Eight shapes came through.

Not Watch. Not rats. Blackjaws, armoured in mismatched leather and chain, faces masked or painted with flaked ash symbols. Fast. Coordinated. One already had steel drawn. Another carried a sledge with blood on the hammer.

And at the centre—*her*.

She didn't wear a mask.

She didn't need one.

Valka moved like smoke wrapped in threadbare silk, her cloak trailing just behind each step. Her hair was bound high and tight, and her eyes swept the wrecked convoy with surgical precision. She was unbothered, unreadable.

Halfa's flame surged.

He felt it crack inside him, wild and hungry.

She stopped five feet from the outer wagon. Didn't raise her voice. Didn't raise a weapon.

She simply said, "Break them. "

The alley exploded.

Flame ripped from Halfa's chest before he could stop it, upward and outward, a heatwave of memory and rage. He wouldn't let Valka snuff it before he got one attack in. The carts splintered, the tarp igniting in streaks of gold and orange. Timber cracked. Crates burst open. Shockwaves flung the Watchmen and Black-jaws alike backward.

Tallen, Gorne, and Lasse hit the cobbles in a tangle of limbs. Valka staggered, cloak aflame at the edge. The others rolled, scrambled, swore. Halfa stumbled to one knee, breath torn from his chest.

Most of the fire had gone skyward; thank Thessira for that. But it had been close.

Too close.

He hadn't released that much fire since the Temple of Thessira battle. And now, just like then, he could feel it coiling behind his ribs, unsatisfied. His hands shook. His head rang. He knew he'd pay for it later.

But there was no later now. He reined it in; Halfa could not let the flame hurt his friends.

The Blackjaws regrouped. The Watchmen did too, bruised, bleeding and fu-rious.

And then they charged.

Gorne caught a blade on his vambrace and slammed his attacker into the broken cart. Lasse rolled through the ash and came up swinging with a shattered plank. Tallen found the wall, braced himself, and fought like a cornered animal.

Halfa surged forward, fire still humming in his limbs. He dropped one Blackjaw with a shoulder-check, grabbed another by the coat, and hurled them into a half-burnt crate.

The convoy was now a battlefield, boxed in, burning, unforgiving.

And above it all was Valka, still standing, still watching.

Not joining.

Not yet.

Halfa felt it, her gaze was dissecting him. Learning from him.

Then she moved.

Fast. Too fast.

She crossed the space between wagons like water over cobblestone, blades drawn from dual sheaths at her lower back, thin, elegant twin knives, grooved and gleaming, whispering as they cut the air. She ducked under Gorne's swing and sliced the strap off his shoulder as he tried to lurch away.

Halfa turned to face her.

Valka met his eyes. And smiled.

A small smile. Professional. Knowing. She made the same gesture she had made back at the Temple of Thessira, and Halfa felt the flame in him stop burning. He stumbled.

Then she vanished again into motion, springing toward Gorne, who was still trying to get into position to defend against her and the other Blackjaws.

Halfa moved, but not fast enough; the snuffing of his flame had cost him again.

Something knocked Valka off course. Halfa couldn't see what it was until they stopped. Gronk had entered the fray.

He had come from the end of the alley like a battering ram hurled down a hallway. No warning. No war cry. Brute force and boots on wet stone. He collided with Valka mid-step, forcing her sideways into the base of the wagon. She rolled, recovered and landed low with one hand braced on the street.

Her smile widened.

"Of course it's you," she said.

Gronk cracked his neck. "Still slippery."

Valka launched first.

She moved like a shadow with knives. Gronk blocked one, ducked the other, and swung wide. She rolled backward, blades scraping against metal. The alley pulsed with their clash—*precision vs. weight, grace vs. anchor.*

Valka twisted, one blade locking with Gronk's arm, the other tracing a line across his coat. Not deep. Just a warning with teeth.

Gronk grunted, driving her back with raw mass, but for every step she gave, the alley closed tighter.

Blackjaw shadows moved in.

A chain whipped past his ear. Another hand reached for his leg. He stomped down, boot crunching bone, but the next blow came low, sharp and aimed. Valka ducked under his guard and drove a knee into his ribs.

He staggered.

For a breath, the alley was hers.

More Blackjaws pressed forward, circling him like carrion.

And Gronk, for the first time Halfa had ever seen, looked overwhelmed.

Halfa shoved a Blackjaw off Tallen and joined the fray.

It was like falling back into an old rhythm.

He and Gronk didn't speak.

They didn't have to.

Gronk swung wide, Halfa struck low. One Blackjaw fell. Then two.

Valka leapt onto a wagon roof, crouched. Assessed.

"You'll lose this city," she said.

Gronk wiped blood from his chin. "You'll choke on it first. "

She leapt again, over them, flipping once midair and landing just beyond the alley mouth.

The remaining Blackjaws retreated with her.

Silence, except for breath and bruises.

Halfa turned. Tallen was leaning against a crate, bleeding but upright. Lasse knelt beside Gorne, who was holding his arm and cursing softly.

"We good?" Halfa called.

Tallen nodded. "Still standing. "

Gorne grunted. "Arm's not broken. Just pissed. "

He began wrapping the elbow with a torn sleeve. "Tell me again why we don't wear helmets?"

Lasse, scanning rooftops, didn't miss a beat. "Because then we'd look like we knew what we were doing. "

Gorne snorted. "Remind me to forget this tomorrow. "

"Already forgotten," Lasse said.

"Then secure the wagons," Halfa said.

Halfa looked toward the alley mouth.

No sign of Valka.

The alley was still humming from the fight.

Not noise, but *resonance*. The kind that settled into the stone and bones and boots. Halfa could feel it in the back of his teeth.

Tallen wiped blood from his cheek and slid down the side of a crate, breathing in short bursts. Gorne flexed his wrist, muttering something bitter about knives and theatre kids. Lasse was checking straps, scanning corners, already watching for the next move.

Halfa looked toward the wagons.

The "laundry exports" were in splinters. Broken crates exposed wrapped bundles. There were blades, ration packs, rust-coloured flasks marked for field alchemists. Blackjaw gear, no question.

"You alright?" Halfa asked without turning.

Behind him, Gronk cracked his neck.

"I've had worse days," he said.

There was blood on his jawline. Not his, Halfa thought. Probably. He didn't ask.

They stood in silence for a beat.

"You always show up just in time?" Halfa asked.

Gronk shrugged. "Rix had someone watching the tail end of that convoy. When it diverted early, she sent a runner. "

"Good timing. "

"Good bait. "

Halfa raised an eyebrow.

"You," Gronk said. "You're predictable, Watchman. If something needed hitting, you were going to hit it. "

"Wasn't planning to play hero. "

"No?" Gronk asked.

He looked around at the shattered cargo, the bruised Watch recruits, the blood-streaked stone.

"Nice work," he said. "Messy. But honest. "

"Valka?"

"Slippery," Gronk muttered. "I clipped her once, maybe twice. Didn't land clean. "

"She was quick. "

"She's worse than I remembered," Gronk said. "But she didn't kill anyone today. "

Halfa frowned. "She wanted us scared. Not dead. "

Footsteps echoed from the alley's mouth.

They weren't rushed. They weren't armoured.

They came in waves, boots on stone, whispered signals, flickers of movement behind crates.

The Ash Rats.

Rix emerged first, coat pulled tight, a short staff across her shoulders. Three more followed, young, quick, and quiet, faces half-shadowed by soot. One of them was the boy who'd delivered Halfa the scorched token. He wouldn't meet Halfa's eyes.

Rix scanned the wreckage. "You broke the wagons. "

"We broke their day," Gronk replied.

Tallen stood, wincing. "You're welcome. "

One of the Ash Rats laughed, a quiet, breathless sound. Rix silenced him with a glance.

Halfa gestured to the crates. "Yours, if you want them. "

"We want them," Rix said.

Two Rats moved in instantly, opening packs and rolling salvage cloth. Another climbed the wagon and began counting aloud. Thankfully, the display of fire had only damaged the outside of the wagons.

Gronk turned to Halfa.

"You could've run. "

"So could have you. "

They didn't smile. But something shifted in the air between them.

Respect. Maybe memory.

Gronk nodded to the Watch recruits. "They held well. "

"They've never seen anything like that," Halfa said, thinking of his explosive fire. "And I hope they don't again. "

The last of the Ash Rats disappeared into the fog beyond the alley, crates and bundles slung over shoulders, boots muffled by layers of ash-soaked rags.

Rix paused near the exit.

She looked at Gronk, then Halfa. Then: "You know this won't hold, right? They'll respond."

Halfa nodded. "We want them to."

She didn't reply. Vanished into the streetlight.

Gronk didn't move right away.

"You'll need to decide soon," he said quietly. "How much fire you're willing to carry."

"Soon," Halfa agreed.

Gronk reached down, picked up a small broken chain link from the alley floor, turned it once in his fingers, then dropped it.

Then he left.

No ceremony. No goodbyes.

Just boots and silence.

Halfa turned back to the others.

Gorne had the last of the wagons stabilised. Tallen was walking now, if crooked. Lasse was watching the rooftops.

"Back to the Watchhouse," Halfa said.

The four Watchmen watched the Ash Rats and Gronk leave, and turned back towards the Watchhouse.

❧

The Watchhouse had changed.

Halfa knew it the moment he stepped through the front gate. The warmth was gone. The familiar clatter of dice on the common room table, the scent of coffee from the shared pot, Brannig's off-key singing from the strategy room, all were missing. Replaced by icy silence and polished boots. Tallen, Gorne and Lasse all peeled off from Halfa before the main courtyard, going their separate ways, which, as it turned out, was lucky.

There were unfamiliar faces in uniform. Too many. Men and women who didn't look like Watch recruits. They had clean armour, spotless collars, blank eyes. They moved like shadows, and none of them smiled.

Halfa passed two of them in the hallway. One nodded, the other didn't. He glanced at their belts. They were issue-standard, but unused. Not a scratch on the bracers. Not a crease on the scroll cases. Ghosts in grey.

Brannig was in the map room, pacing.

She didn't look up when he entered. Just tossed a parchment onto the table with enough force to slide it into his chest.

"Read it. "

He picked it up. An official decree, ink still drying. New appointments. New precinct shifts. Three sergeants reassigned to outlying districts without explanation. A Watch quartermaster quietly dismissed. And Dot....

"Liaison to Dockward Enforcement?" Halfa read aloud. "Never even heard of that before. "

Brannig snorted. "More like free rein to move assets and personnel without oversight. "He's been laying this groundwork for months," she added. "I didn't think the brass would hand him the keys so soon. "

She pointed to a different name, Lieutenant Hess of the South Gate. "Hess reported that Dot's men were interfering with a customs inspection. That same night, Hess gets reassigned to supply audits. "

Halfa set the parchment down. "He's consolidating. "

Brannig finally looked up. Her eyes were red-rimmed, but blazing. "He's carving the Watch into his own bloody knife. And the city brass are letting him. "

She dropped into the nearest chair, pinching the bridge of her nose.

"I've written five memos this week. No replies. The Captain's been in meetings behind locked doors for three days. Half my reports disappear. One came back rewritten, with my signature forged. "

Halfa's jaw clenched. "What do we do?"

Brannig laughed without humour. "You think there's still a 'we' in this?"

He didn't answer.

She leaned forward, voice dropping. "They want us to break. Or bend. I won't do either. But I'm one dwarf against a tide. "

"You're not alone. "

"No. I've got you. " She grinned wryly. "One flaming Goliath and a few rookies too scared to speak. "

She stood abruptly, pulling on her coat. "You're exhausted. Let me walk you out of here. "

"I burned too bright tonight," Halfa replied, "Starting to feel it. "

Halfa followed her through the halls. The air was wrong, too still, too clean. Posters had been removed from the walls. Notices rewritten. A bulletin board near the mess hall now bore an emblem he didn't recognise, a stylised flame wrapped in chains. Not Watch standard.

"What is that?" he asked.

Brannig didn't slow. "Dot's new division. Calls it 'Stability Command. ' Says it's for civic coordination. "

"Militia. "

"Worse. It's law with no oath behind it. "

They passed an office Halfa didn't recognise. Inside, a man in a city tabard spoke quietly with two ghost-faced recruits. Something about the way they nodded. They were too eager, too immediate. It sent a chill down Halfa's spine.

When they reached the front doors again, Brannig stopped and looked up at him.

"I hope you're ready, lad. "

"For what?"

She didn't blink.

"For the moment that the Watch forgets what it's meant to watch over. "

Halfa didn't respond. Just a nod, small, stiff, and slow.

He left the stairs without a goodbye. Brannig didn't ask where he was going. She could see it in his shoulders.

He barely made it back to his bunk.

Halfa moved through the Watchhouse like a shadow, wearing boots too heavy for his bones. His legs ached. His hands shook. His ribs still carried the echo of the fire that had torn out of him.

His door groaned when he opened it. He didn't light a lantern.

The cot was harder than he remembered, but he didn't care. He collapsed onto it, still half-dressed, armour straps loose around his chest, boots still on.

For a while, he lay there. Letting the dark hold him.

The fire had *wanted* to come out. The moment he saw Valka—everything in him had gone hot. And it hadn't been careful. It hadn't been clean. It had nearly burned everyone.

He hadn't lost control. Not entirely.

But he'd let go.

And even now, as tired as he was, he could feel it behind his ribs. Waiting. Smouldering. It didn't take long for it to come back after it was snuffed out.

He shifted onto his side. The cot creaked.

He didn't have answers.

Just heat behind his eyes, the weight of burned wood in his lungs, and the memory of Valka's sharp, knowing, fearless gaze.

His fingers curled.

Then relaxed.

Sleep claimed him; his last feeling, a fire's echo where once he breathed.

◊

The Blackjaws weren't subtle anymore.

The next morning, Halfa's patrol passed through Copper Row and found new graffiti scorched into the brickwork, Blackjaw symbols etched deep, as if carved with acid instead of paint. Nearby vendors had stopped setting up stalls. One flower seller said her crates were stolen. Another simply didn't come back after a warning was nailed to her door.

It wasn't the warnings that stood out.

It was how the Watch didn't respond.

Halfa reported the symbols, the threats, and the missing vendors. Nothing. The paperwork went up the chain, vanished into silence. He visited one of the shuttered stalls himself, a spice merchant named Delra, who used to hum while scooping saffron.

Her door was gone. Just splinters and scorch marks.

The woman next door whispered, "They came at night. Not a word. Just torches. She didn't fight. Still vanished. "

Halfa stepped into the empty stall. Ash still clung to the corners.

He could feel the fire inside him stir.

When he got back to the Watchhouse, Brannig was waiting.

"They've moved into Tanner's End," she said, jaw tight. "Two taverns now run by known enforcers. Coin changing hands faster than complaints can be filed. "

"Where's Dot?"

"Assigning recruits to 'community patrols. ' They don't go where they're needed. They go where the Blackjaws don't want us. "

Halfa folded his arms. "They're playing us. Framing the Ash Rats as chaos, so they can be the solution. "

"They've got city officials in their pockets now. Remember Deputy Malren? Used to be a drunk with a loud mouth?"

"Still is, from what I hear. "

"Just landed a post as an Inspector of Dockside Conduct. Guess who signed the appointment?"

Halfa didn't need to ask.

It got worse that evening.

Word came from Rix. Delivered by a boy with soot-streaked cheeks and a hollow voice. The boy handed Halfa a folded cloth. No note, just the familiar red-rat insignia stitched in the centre. Halfa unwrapped it and found a sliver of scorched metal inside. The top half of a rat skull badge cracked.

"A warning?" Brannig asked.

"No," Halfa said. "A marker. The Blackjaws torched a cache. "

"Which one?" Brannig asked.

Halfa's jaw tightened. "Westward run off Salter's Arch. Medic storage. Looks like they're hunting now. "

"Then we need to run faster," Brannig said.

Halfa didn't speak. But in his chest, the flame stirred again, stirred with resolve.

◈

The temple had always been a sanctuary. That night, it felt like the last dry stone in a rising tide.

Halfa stepped through the violet-painted door and into the quiet glow of lantern light. Music drifted from the back hall. The soft lutes and clumsy drumbeats were off-tempo, but full of life. The scent of cardamom and fresh bread curled through the air, threaded with citrus oil and candle smoke.

The faithful moved gently through the space, slower than usual. Laughter came in smaller bursts. Children danced between hanging silks while elders lit candles with trembling fingers. The air wasn't heavy, but it was aware.

Halfa lingered near the spiral, scanning the room. He didn't see Marin at first. But he felt her before he heard her voice.

"Didn't think we'd see you tonight. "

He turned.

Marin stood beside the inner column, sleeves rolled, a tray of bread and plum slices balanced on one hip. A smudge of flour clung to her temple. Her voice was warm, but her eyes were searching.

"I needed quiet," he said. "And bread that doesn't taste like whatever it is the Watch feeds us. "

She arched a brow. "Is that a compliment?"

He stepped closer. "A compliment to Bilbin. Is that fresh cardamom?"

Marin set the tray on the edge of a low table. "It is. And you're stalling. "

He hesitated, then nodded. "The city's shifting. The Blackjaws are buying Watch captains. Dot's rise isn't a coincidence. "

She didn't speak for a moment. Then: "You knew it wouldn't stay quiet forever. "

"It never does," Halfa said. "But it's louder this time. Closer. "

She reached for one of the candles nearby, checking the wick, adjusting it. Her hands didn't shake. "You didn't come here for food or warning. You came because something cracked. "

He didn't deny it.

They moved toward the side garden, where lanterns swayed gently from tall poles. Painted ribbons fluttered, each marked with a prayer, a name, or a moment someone wanted to remember. The mural on the wall was half-finished and still damp; it depicted a flame stylised like a dancer's skirt, rising in arcs of gold and red. It was joy given shape.

Marin sat on the edge of the planter box and nodded for him to join her. He did.

They sat in the stillness. The garden was quiet except for the brush of silk and a soft hum from the temple's back hall. The scent of wet pigment clung to the air.

"She painted it through a Blackjaw tag," Marin said, nodding at the mural. "Didn't scrub it away. Just covered it in colour. "

"A message," Halfa said.

"A reminder," she corrected. "That fear doesn't win unless you let it. "

Halfa looked down at his hands. "I keep thinking the fire will settle. But it's louder lately. Closer to the skin. "

Marin looked at him, steady. "Then don't hold it alone. "

He glanced sideways. "I don't want to burn the things I care about. "

"Then let someone help you shape it. "

She didn't reach for his hand.

He reached for hers.

Calloused fingers brushed warm palms. She didn't flinch. He didn't pull away.

"Every time I come back," he said, voice low, "I wonder if I've already stayed too long. If this place deserves better than me. "

"It doesn't need better," Marin said. "It needs you. Not for the fire. For the way you carry it. "

Their fingers laced slowly. Deliberately. No urgency. No doubt.

"I never had something to lose before," Halfa said.

"Now you do," she replied.

And for the first time in days, the flame in his chest didn't feel like a warning.

It felt like warmth.

Their fingers remained tangled, resting on the wood between them.

Neither of them moved to fill the silence. They didn't need to.

The garden held them in a hush, broken only by the rustle of ribbons and the soft crackle of a distant lantern wick. The mural's colours deepened in the dusk, red over gold, a flame growing into something that looked almost like wings.

Halfa turned toward her.

Marin met his gaze, and for a moment, they didn't speak. But something passed between them, something quieter than fear, heavier than safety.

"I don't know how to do this right," Halfa said. "But I know what it means to burn for something that doesn't hurt. "

Marin's voice was softer than the wind. "Then stop waiting. "

She leaned in first.

Not far. Just enough.

Halfa closed the distance.

The kiss was slow. Steady. No sparks, no rush. Just warmth that unfurled like a breath held too long. His hand slid to her cheek, carefully. Her fingers curled into his coat. She wasn't pulling him closer. She was just anchoring him there.

The kiss lingered like a held breath.

When they parted, neither of them spoke. They didn't need to.

But before the silence could settle into something sacred, a voice cut through the garden from the far archway.

"Well, it's about damn time!"

They turned in unison.

Bilbin stood a few paces away, arms crossed, one eyebrow raised with theatrical satisfaction. He held a plate of rolls in one hand and a mug in the other, as if he'd come to deliver snacks and accidentally walked into this.

"You've been circling each other like moody moonbeasts for *weeks*," he continued. "I was starting to think I'd have to draw up a chart to get you together again. "

Marin groaned softly, hiding her face against Halfa's shoulder.

Halfa, still holding her hand, just closed his eyes.

"I brought plum rolls!" Bilbin added cheerfully. "But I see someone already got dessert. "

Marin laughed first, quiet, muffled, but it cracked the tension like kindling underfoot. Halfa chuckled next, shoulders loosening, and finally let out a real, full sound that warmed the corners of the courtyard.

Bilbin grinned like a man very pleased with himself. "Don't mind me. I'll just be over here, not watching the epic slow-burn finally catch fire. "

He ambled back toward the hall, muttering about romance, timing, and how no one ever listens to him.

Marin shook her head, still smiling. "He's impossible. "

Halfa gave her hand a gentle squeeze. "He's not wrong, though. "

She bumped her shoulder against his. "Don't let it go to your head. "

"I'll try. "

And beneath the ribbons and lanterns, they sat together, quiet again, but lighter this time. Not burdened. Just... finally, joyfully seen.

◊

The rooftops of Grayspire turned copper in the late light, the city shifting into evening with the slow ache of an old bruise. The Watchhouse was quieter now, all the reports filed, barracks half-emptied, the last shift prepping for night patrol. Halfa had returned to make sure Brannig was okay and had found her on the upper balcony, sitting back, bottle in hand.

She said nothing when he joined her, she just passed the bottle without looking.

He took a sip, coughed once, and handed it back.

"It's been nearly four months since your demotion," she said. "Long enough for the brass to forget your name. Not long enough for them to forgive your choices. "

Halfa shrugged. "I didn't ask them to. "

"Good," she said. "Because you've earned trust in the only place that counts out here, with the ones still standing. "

Brannig took another swig.

"Temple folk still dancing?" she asked.

"Trying," he said. "They're holding joy like a shield. "

Brannig stared across the city. "Feels like it's all slipping between the cracks. "

"It is," Halfa said. "And some of those cracks were carved intentionally. "

Brannig leaned back against the wall, her silhouette outlined in torchlight. "Dot's reports come through flawless. Too flawless. But every time I bring up inconsistencies, I get shut down. 'Lack of hard evidence. ' 'Misplaced suspicion. ' They've neutered oversight. "

She rubbed her eyes with the heel of her palm. It wasn't just exhaustion. It was grief—quiet, professional, buried too deep to name. But it was there.

Halfa folded his arms. "The Blackjaws aren't kicking in doors anymore. They're walking through them. "

Brannig chuckled without humour. "When I joined the Watch, I thought the worst thing I'd face would be some drunk with a knife. Turns out it's my own damn colleagues. "

He looked at her. "You ever think of leaving?"

"All the time," she admitted. "But I still believe in what the Watch *could* be. Not what it is. And who else would be here to look after you?"

Halfa grinned, but said nothing in return.

They sat in silence for a while; the wind whistling faintly between chimneys and stone.

Finally, Halfa said, "Gronk's right about one thing. The Blackjaws are going to burn this city from the inside out if no one stops them. "

Brannig didn't flinch. "And you think you're the one who will?"

"I think I might be the spark," Halfa said, eyes distant.

Brannig turned to him. "You're walking a razor's edge, lad. Between justice and vengeance. You fall too far into either, and you're not coming back. "

Halfa looked down at his hands. "What if they're the same now?"

Brannig shook her head. "They're not. One builds. The other breaks. "

He didn't respond right away.

Then: "There's a storm coming. I can feel it. "

Brannig raised the bottle again. "Then we better start boarding the windows. "

◊

Brannig called Halfa and the recruits into her office the next morning before they started their patrols. There was no hint of the night before's drinks and worries on her face.

Brannig laid the city map across the table, weighed down by lanterns and cracked mugs. Halfa stood across from her, arms folded. Tallen hovered nearby, nursing a bruised jaw and looking more focused than usual.

"Valka's a suppression mage," Brannig said. "Not a traditional caster. She doesn't throw fire. She silences it. Unmakes it. "

Halfa nodded slowly. "She shut mine down like it was nothing. Not resisted. Snuffed. "

Tallen blinked. "Wait. You're saying she... turns it off?"

"If it burns, she can bend it," Brannig said. "If it glows, she can gut it. She does it with presence, not power. The more you rely on flame, the more she controls the battlefield. "

"Then what?" Tallen asked. "We let her walk in?"

Brannig shook her head. "We let someone in who doesn't burn. Who doesn't rely on anything she can twist. Someone who fights like a fist, not a flame. "

Halfa's thoughts turned to his conversation with Gronk. Almost this exact conversation.

"It's not just fire. Gronk told me she can do this to any magic caster. " Halfa said.

Tallen was the first to say it. "Gronk. We have already seen him go against her. He could be the one. "

Brannig didn't flinch. "He's chaos. She's in control. Let them meet. "

Halfa's jaw tightened. "If we let Gronk take her down, we don't just end her. We start something else. "

Brannig nodded once. "Better the flame we know than the shadow we don't. "

The map crackled softly as Brannig pressed her palm over the central district.

"Let him be the one she can't silence. "

What We Let Burn

The meeting place wasn't the same cellar Halfa had visited before. This time, Rix led him through a series of side alleys in the Merchant's Quarter, past shuttered tailors and dye houses with their windows painted shut. A cracked fountain whispered nearby, forgotten beneath a leaning statue of some merchant prince whose name no one remembered.

"Merchant quarter," Rix muttered. "No one expects rats in silk alleys. "

She tapped twice on the side of a wrought-iron grate and muttered, "For ash, not smoke. "

It creaked open. A narrow stair led them down into silence.

This place was different; it was cleaner than the Ash Rats' usual haunts. Storage crates lined the walls, marked with merchant brands Halfa didn't recognise. Supply drop? Or something more carefully curated?

Gronk was waiting at the far end, seated at a rough-hewn table surrounded by candle stubs. The faint smell of chalk and sweat lingered in the air. A city map stretched before him, its surface cluttered with tokens, chalk lines, and faint blood smears.

"You came," he said, without looking up.

Halfa folded his arms. "You called. "

Rix peeled off and leaned against the wall, arms crossed but alert.

Her knuckles were wrapped in fresh linen, tinged faintly with blood. She didn't mention how.

Gronk gestured to the opposite seat. "Sit. It's time you saw the entire board. "

Halfa didn't move right away. Then, quietly, he took the chair.

Gronk picked up a small wooden token, a rat skull etched into the base, and placed it over a point near the Fishbone Docks.

"That warehouse? Blackjaws have it under a merchant proxy. We tried to hit them last week. Got stonewalled by legal permits and two bought Watch officers. "

He moved another token, this one scorched black, to a point near the Midden Markets.

"This one? They're funnelling coin through a laundry coop. Charity front. Looks legitimate. It's how they're bankrolling pressure on small vendors. "

Halfa frowned. "You're mapping corruption. "

"I'm watching the fire spread," Gronk said. "And where the Watch isn't watching. "

He turned to Halfa, voice quieter now. "You think they're coming with blades and masks again? No. They've adapted. They don't torch temples. They lease them out, one name removed. Don't kill priests. They discredit them, pay for scandals, and vanish evidence. That's worse. "

Halfa's jaw flexed. "What do you want from me?"

"Pressure. Legitimacy. If you can't shut down the Blackjaws at their roots, you make noise. We squeeze from both sides. We lost three this week, kids barely old enough to shave. Burned out of a side den in the Midden slope. No one even filed a report. "

"We hit what they hide, while you choke off the sunlight they're trying to grow under. " Gronk continued.

"That makes this an alliance. "

Gronk nodded. "A tactical one. You don't owe me loyalty. You just need to keep the ground from rotting. "

Halfa leaned over the table. "What about Dot?"

"Not him. Yet," Gronk said. "Cut him now and the Watch doubles down behind him. He's clean on paper, and dangerous in shadow. He won't get involved in open battle. "

Halfa glanced at the map again. "You've got eyes in more places than the Watch. "

"We don't wear badges. We don't need to. "

He stood and pointed to a point near the Temple Row. "That's your corner. Mine's the Shambles and the Market's throat. You keep your people safe. I'll keep mine. And if we're lucky—"

"We burn out the Blackjaw rot," Halfa finished.

They stood there for a moment, two giants of different wars tracing fault lines in the same city.

Gronk offered no handshake this time. Just a nod.

"Watch yourself, Halfa. You're still one fire away from falling. "

Halfa's voice was steady. "Then it's a good thing I've learned to walk through smoke. "

◉

Halfa turned the corner from the alley and entered the Watchhouse courtyard with his shoulders still heavy from the meeting. Gronk's map still lived behind his eyes, chalk lines and rat skulls and all.

But here, behind the old stables where broken wheelbarrows rusted and pigeons nested under the eaves he heard movement.

Practice.

Tallen spun through a quick parry, feet slipping slightly on the mossy stone. Gorne called out corrections from the wall, and Lasse stood poised nearby with a wooden baton, eyes sharp despite a faint bruise darkening his eye.

"Arms up," Gorne barked. "You're guarding like someone asking to be robbed. "

"I am robbed," Tallen grunted. "Of rest. Of dignity. And decent armour. "

"Tell me again why we don't wear helmets?" Gorne muttered.

"Because then we'd look like we knew what we were doing," Lasse said flatly, without missing a beat.

Halfa leaned against the doorframe, arms folded, watching.

It was raw. Sloppy. But the effort was definitely there.

Tallen noticed him first. "Commander," he said, pausing mid-swing.

"I'm not your commander," Halfa said.

"Still," Tallen replied, adjusting his stance, "you keep showing up right when it matters. "

"Yeah, well. Bad habits die harder than I do. "

Gorne wiped sweat from his brow. "Thought we were street rats and washouts. "

"You were," Halfa said, eyeing their form. "Now you're street rats with decent footwork. "

Lasse chimed in from the corner. "With praise like that, I may actually start believing in us. "

Halfa grinned. "Don't get cocky. "

Lasse smiled and gave a short, practised nod.

Then the light shifted.

Not much. Enough for Halfa to notice he wasn't the only one watching.

Serelion stood near the wall beside the half-dead vine clinging to the stone. Their robes were darker than usual. They were plain, unadorned. Their presence didn't startle. It simply *was*.

Halfa stiffened.

He had never seen Serelion outside the temple. Not like this. They belonged to spiral paths and incense, not training yards and Watch stones.

"Didn't expect to see you here," he said quietly.

"I didn't expect to be here. " Serelion replied.

Tallen froze mid-stretch. Gorne straightened. Lasse bowed faintly, awkwardly, but reverently.

Serelion's eyes swept across the recruits, then settled on Halfa. Their gaze wasn't cold. It wasn't warm either. Just knowing.

"The city is stirring," they said. "The kindling's laid, and the wind is shifting. What comes next will not wait for permission. "

Halfa's jaw tightened. "You came to warn me?"

"I came because the flame feels... restless. "

They stepped closer, not looming, present. Their eyes dropped to the soot on Halfa's coat, the bruises on the recruits.

"You're carrying weight that doesn't belong to you," they said softly. "Let it go, or shape it before it shapes you. "

Serelion turned to the recruits. "Hold your lines," they said. "Someone will need to rest behind them. "

Then, to Halfa again: "And you, remember, the flame is not your burden. It is your mirror. Now, I need to see that Brannig about some tea. "

Without fanfare, Serelion turned and walked through the Watchhouse's front doors, silent as a breath.

Tallen exhaled slowly. "Is it just me, or do they always leave a riddle behind instead of a goodbye?"

"That's their gift," Halfa murmured. "And their curse. "

"Keep training," he continued.

"Why?" Lasse asked.

Halfa's voice was soft, but unshaken.

"I'll need you all standing in that line with me. "

Gorne raised an eyebrow. "Where are you going?"

"I've got to get back to the temple. "

◓

Halfa had left Gronk with a knot in his chest. Plans had been made. Orders set. The city was inching toward something sharp, and none knew if they were holding the blade or falling on it.

The recruits had held their line well, but he could see the tension in their shoulders, the way they watched him when they thought he wasn't looking. Even Serelion's calm had carried an edge. Not fear. Not prophecy. Just... pressure. Like the world was leaning in.

That pressure didn't ease as he walked.

It followed him. Beneath the cobblestones. In the silence between footsteps. In the faint scent of ash that seemed to cling even now.

He followed instinct, the same pull that had guided him the first time he stepped through those violet-painted doors.

The Watch had given him structure and some semblance of purpose. Brannig had offered belief. Tallen, Lasse, and Gorne had given him a line to hold. But it was Serelion's stillness, Bilbin's laughter, and Marin's quiet strength that had reminded him there was something worth protecting, not just with fists or flame, but with heart.

The temple had never asked him to be more than he was. It had simply welcomed what he brought, and helped him carry the rest.

Somewhere between duty and defiance, between fire and restraint, Halfa had found something he hadn't known he was looking for. A place to return to.

And as before, he was drawn back to that violet-painted door that had grown to mean so much to him.

He turned the corner toward the Temple of Thessira and stopped.

A cloaked figure stood near the doors.

Motionless. Like a statue waiting to be noticed.

Halfa stepped forward, cautious. His breath caught, not from fear, but from recognition.

The nearest flame lantern guttered sideways despite the still air.

"Excuse me—"

The figure turned.

Valka.

She appeared unnervingly calm.

Halfa's fists clenched.

"No weapons?" he asked.

She smiled faintly. "None I need. Not for you. "

The fog behind her didn't move like fog. It curled at her heels, slow and thick, like it didn't want to leave.

"What do you want?"

"Conversation," she said. "And for you to listen. "

He didn't move. The temple door was just steps away. The light inside flickered violet. Warm. Real.

"I have people in there," she added. "Behind the curtain. One word from me, and joy dies screaming. "

Halfa didn't flinch.

A moment passed.

"I came here once," she said, stepping aside from the entrance. "Watched children draw spirals in chalk. I watched your temple hand out bread to anyone who wanted it. It was beautiful. "

"Why threaten it?"

"Because it's fragile," she said. "And because of you. You burned my people. Took what was ours. You call it justice. I call it a tally. One I intend to settle. The first sparks are never the last. You lit yours; I'm just answering. "

She glanced at the door. "You're trying to save something delicate in a city that eats glass for breakfast. I admire it. I really do. But it's a losing game, Halfa. "

"I'm not playing games. "

"No," she said. "You're walking into fire and calling it joy. "

She turned. The light near her bent slightly. Like something in her pulled at it.

She walked three steps into the alley. Over her shoulder:

"If you want to protect something soft, you must be willing to scorch the ground around it. "

She didn't wait for an answer.

Halfa let her go, turning to get in to the temple and remove any Blackjaws Valka had stashed in there.

But when he entered the temple, he found only warmth. Incense. Laughter. Valka had been bluffing.

But the warning still burned.

The temple was louder than usual. Or perhaps it felt that way after Halfa's meeting with Valka.

The scent of cardamom hung in the air, warm and spiced.

Bilbin was near the entry, balancing a tray of unbaked loaves with one hand and stirring a pot of spiced butter with the other. He didn't look up right away, but when he did, his eyes crinkled in greeting.

"I'm about two seconds from burning the glaze again," he said. "Stay long enough and you might witness greatness or disaster. "

Halfa offered a small smile. "Can't tell the difference in your kitchen. "

"That's the point," Bilbin muttered, returning to his work.

The temple's central flame burned low but steady, its glow reaching far enough to soften the edge of the night waiting outside.

Halfa moved toward it, slow and quiet. As he passed the woven curtains into the spiral chamber, he spotted Marin kneeling beside the mural wall. She was repainting a chipped section, her fingers stained with crimson and orange, her sleeves rolled, a smudge of colour streaked across her cheek.

She didn't speak at first. Turned slightly, watching him without rising.

"It's louder today," she said. "Like the city's trying to warn itself and nobody's listening. "

Halfa stepped closer, the street noise trailing after him like smoke. "Feels like it's holding its breath. Not in fear—just. . . waiting to exhale wrong. "

Marin gave a dry smile. "Grayspire's good at that. Pretending the tremors are just footsteps. "

She looked at him, finally meeting his gaze. "You felt it too, didn't you? That shift in the air. Like something important already broke, and we're all still pretending it's whole. "

He stepped into the spiral. Each step along the candlelit path felt heavier than the last.

Brannig's warning still rang in his ears. Gronk's makeshift order. Dot's controlled chaos. Valka, just Valka.

He reached the centre and knelt beside the flame.

From inside his coat, he drew out two small tokens. The first was Serelion's flame-shaped charm, smooth and amber-coloured. The second was the crude, red-painted rat skull taken from the alley's aftermath.

One had guided him toward joy. The other had left him with questions.

He held them in his palm, side by side. Balanced. Unburned.

Marin approached, stepping into the spiral, wiped her hands on a cloth streaked with orange, and crouched opposite him. She didn't speak at first. Watched the flame catch the edges of both tokens.

After a moment, she asked, "You alright?"

Halfa didn't answer right away. "Close enough to matter. "

She nodded. That was enough.

He leaned forward and placed both tokens into the bowl. The fire curled around them but didn't consume. They sat there, quiet, part of the flame now. Or watching it.

Marin rose first. "Come on," she said. "Bilbin's about to set butter on fire. "

Halfa looked at the flame one last time, then followed her out.

The air felt taut again. It wasn't heavy, and it wasn't loud.

It was ready.

The Line in the Sand

The city hadn't yet stirred.

Outside the Watchhouse, Grayspire was still wrapped in fog and sleep, the air heavy with sea salt and chimney soot. Inside, the lamps burned low, casting a golden glow across the stones like tired eyes.

Halfa moved through the quiet corridors, his boots echoing like questions with no answers.

He moved stiffly, his chest sore from the fire nights ago. It hadn't faded. Just cooled, for now.

A message had arrived before dawn: *Come to my office. No uniform.*

He found Brannig Barrelshield at her desk, bent over a map. Her armour sat beside her, unbuckled and dusty. Her boots were off, one foot soaking in a tin basin of herbs, the other resting on a stack of case reports. A half-eaten roll of bread sat forgotten on the corner of the desk.

"Close the door," she said, without looking up.

Halfa did. The latch clicked like a verdict.

Brannig tapped on the map. A circle had been drawn beside a cluster of warehouses. "Interception report. Courier intercepted near the river quay. Shipment expected within the week, origin unconfirmed, destination clear. "

"Blackjaws?" Halfa asked.

She nodded grimly. "High-value. Weapons, maybe coin, maybe something worse. "

Halfa leaned forward. "We can act. "

Brannig held up a hand. "That's not the problem. " She reached beneath the desk and produced a sealed envelope, sliding it across the table.

He didn't open it.

"Missing persons report," she said. "Three informants. All disappeared after submitting evidence against local smugglers. Two were last seen in the company of Watch officers. Officers with commendations. "

"Dot. "

Brannig didn't answer. She didn't have to.

"I don't have proof," she said. "But I have a gut. And this city's belly is turning. "

The brazier crackled softly behind her, its warmth doing little to soften the air.

"I've made my choice," she said at last. "We can't beat this from inside the lines. We need allies. You've built some. "

Halfa blinked. "You're backing me?"

"No. " She smiled, bitter and proud. "I'm backing what I see in you. If this goes wrong, if the Ash Rats burn the city to cinders, you will walk away clean. I'll take the fall. "

Silence pressed between them like iron.

"I won't let you—" Halfa began.

Brannig slammed her palm against the desk. "I'm not asking. "

She stood slowly, joints cracking. Her face reflected a life of hardship and concessions. She set down her empty tea cup forcefully.

"Listen to me, Halfa Schoona. I joined the Watch because someone like you pulled me out of the gutter and said, *We're better than the world says we are.* That someone died with a blade in her gut and no badge on her chest. If I have to go down making sure there's still one good wall standing in this city, I'll do it. "

Halfa looked at her for a long time. Then, quietly, "Thank you. "

Brannig poured herself a cup of bitterleaf tea. "We plan today. No paperwork. No uniforms. Just results. "

She raised the cup in mock salute.

"Welcome to the real Watch. "

The training yard behind the Watchhouse was mostly empty. Just some discarded staves, a cracked shield leaning against the far wall, and the sound of distant boots on stone.

Halfa stood in the doorway, arms folded, watching.

Tallen was out there. Alone.

He moved through the forms slowly. His shoulder was stiff, his face was tight with focus. His footwork was solid. His strikes controlled. Not flashy. Not perfect.

But steady.

The way Halfa had once taught him.

After a few minutes, Tallen turned toward a rack of gear. Spotted Halfa. Froze.

Halfa raised an eyebrow. "Didn't mean to interrupt. "

"You're not. " Tallen wiped the sweat from his brow with a sleeve. "Just. . . trying to get in shape. "

"You're further along than you think. "

Tallen snorted. "Still can't sleep without hearing boots behind me. I still flinch when someone shouts too close. The Shambles, I can't get rid of it. "

"Good. "

Tallen blinked. "Good?"

Halfa stepped into the yard.

"If you're scared, it means you remember. And if you remember, you learn. "

Tallen nodded slowly. "So. . . I keep going?"

Halfa looked him in the eye. "You're still here, aren't you?"

There was a pause. Not awkward. Just full.

Then Tallen said, "I ran drills for the rookies this morning. Brannig had too much going on. Figured someone had to. Lasse helped. "

Halfa's expression didn't change.

But something behind his eyes softened. Just a little.

"You think they listened?" he asked.

"They will," Tallen said.

It wasn't bravado. It was belief.

Halfa reached for a practise staff and tossed it toward Tallen. The younger man caught it, ready without flinching.

Halfa gestured toward the centre of the yard.

"Then show me what you taught them. "

By sundown, the plan was in motion. Quiet signals passed through alleyways. Safehouses opened. The war didn't start with a trumpet, just a nod, a map, and old debts coming due.

The Ash Rats didn't meet in taverns or alleyways anymore.

Not for this.

Their new war room was deep beneath the cobbled bones of Grayspire, carved into the old maintenance tunnels where the foundations sweated and the stone walls remembered when the city was smaller. The light came from low-burning braziers and scavenged lanterns, their glass tinted red and amber. The air tasted of damp metal and burning oil.

Halfa followed Rix through the winding passage, her stride quick and sure.

"You're late," she muttered.

"You told me the meeting was after sundown."

She glanced back. "It is. Barely. Besides, Gronk's cranky when people make him wait."

"He's always cranky."

Rix smirked. "Yeah. But now he's *important* and cranky."

They stepped into the council chamber. What had once been an old cistern was now cleared of debris and filled with makeshift tables, maps, and crates of supplies. The Ash Rats had grown. No longer just runaways and scrappers. They had tacticians now. Scouts. Quartermasters. Veterans with scars that told entire histories.

At the far end stood Gronk, arms folded, looming over a table marked with chalk lines and pins.

The moment Halfa entered, the room quieted, just for a beat.

Then Gronk waved him forward. "We're past pleasantries. You ready?"

Halfa stepped up beside him. "That depends. Ready for what?"

Rix joined them, pulling her hood down and planting her hands on the map. "Three confirmed safe houses. Two unconfirmed. Shipment lands in less than four days. Blackjaws are arming up like they're preparing for a siege."

"We heard of the shipment, too. Do you think it's weapons?" Halfa asked.

Gronk nodded. "And coin. Enough to buy loyalty in five districts. Maybe ten."

A wiry man with a knotted beard and tattoos on both hands, one of the Ash Rats' new logistics runners, pointed at the eastern quay on the map. "We intercepted chatter. They're using a falsified merchant ship. Same name as a grain hauler that sank last winter. Classic shell game."

Halfa frowned. "Smart."

"Smarter than they used to be," Rix said. "They're not just recruiting muscle. They're buying politicians. Merchants. Watch captains. They stopped trying to win fights. Started trying to win systems. Someone taught them the rules of the bigger game. "

"If this shipment lands clean, they take the whole southern slope. " She continued.

"And if it doesn't?" Halfa asked.

"Then we've got a shot," Gronk said. "But we must move fast, and we can't do it alone. "

He turned to Halfa. "I want the Watch. Or at least what's left of it that still gives a damn. "

Halfa thought of Brannig's desk. The fog in her eyes. The tired edge in her voice when she said, *I'll take the fall.*

"I can get us a team," he said. "Small. Quiet. You won't see uniforms. " He thought of Brannig's offer. Tallen, Gorne and Lasse had already shown they were in with the last raid.

Rix folded her arms. "And you think that'll stop a street war?"

"I think it'll delay one. And if we hit the Blackjaws hard enough, if we torch the shipment or steal it, if we break their play, we take out their teeth. "

Rix leaned in. "I still say we need to be careful. Push too hard, too fast, we become them. "

"I'm not asking for a war," Gronk said. "But if it comes? We bleed smarter than they do. "

The room was silent for a moment, the maps flickering in firelight, the hum of tension crawling up the stone walls.

Halfa placed a hand on the map. "One hit. One chance. You send the signal; we strike fast. "

Gronk met his eyes. "Agreed. "

Rix tapped the northeast corner of the map. "We'll need overwatch here. Too many angles. "

Gronk nodded. "I'll take it. Third wave. Rooftop vantage. Somewhere I can insert myself if needed. "

Halfa raised an eyebrow. "You sure?"

"If I'm going to lead this mess," Gronk said, "I might as well bleed where they can see me. "

"And if it burns too hot?" Halfa asked.

Gronk cracked a faint grin. It reminded Halfa of Gronk, the boy, all of those years ago. "We've both danced in fire before. "

Halfa nodded. "Then let's light the match. "

Rix lingered at the edge of the table as the others turned away, her arms still folded. The candlelight sharpened the angles in her face.

"We're not building a second Blackjaw," she said, voice low. "You know that, right?"

Gronk didn't look at her. He was already sketching new movement routes on the map, eyes hard, jaw locked.

"I said we'd hold the line," he muttered.

"That line keeps shifting," she replied. "And you're the one moving it. "

Still no answer. Just the scratch of chalk on old stone.

Rix watched him a moment longer, then turned and walked out.

Halfa didn't say anything.

But he heard it, too.

Something fraying at the edges.

The temple wasn't silent. Halfa had been silent as he walked back with Gronk and the Ash Rats.

No, silence didn't suit it. Even on nights like this, nights where the city pressed close, where the air outside carried the weight of fog and coming fire, Thessira's halls refused to be still.

There was always music. There was always the rustle of fabric or the soft clatter of someone stubbornly living.

Halfa stepped through the side arch like someone returning from the edge of something sharp.

His boots echoed on the polished stone, each step too loud for a place built on laughter and song. The door shut behind him with a whisper, sealing out the city's roar.

And Marin, of course, noticed him first.

She was perched halfway up a ladder in the central hall, brush in hand yet again, red pigment streaked along one forearm. The mural she worked on, a ribbon of fire curling through a dancing figure, was more than halfway complete. She was adding details to the hands. Careful lines. Joy given fingers.

"You're walking like a man who thinks the world's already burned," she called down. "You planning to announce the apocalypse, or sulk until someone feeds you bread?"

Halfa stopped at the base of the ladder. "Do I get a choice?"

"Of course," she said. "You can also patch the window stool again. Bilbin sat on it wrong. "

"He's been sitting wrong since last autumn," came a voice from the corridor. Bilbin emerged carrying a bowl of spice-glazed almonds, his apron bearing signs of both triumph and disaster.

"You're welcome for the snacks," he added. "They're joy-flavored. "

Halfa took one. Chewed. "Tastes like rebellion. "

Marin laughed from her rung. "That's the chilli. And the cinnamon. And then I made Bilbin bless the pan with a prayer of joyful vengeance. "

"I did no such thing. "

"You muttered it while stirring. "

Halfa leaned against the nearby column, watching her descend the ladder with grace that belied how tired she must have been. Her sleeves were rolled, her curls pinned back messily. She wore the same temple whites as always, but the colour didn't diminish her edge.

Marin wasn't soft. She was sharp in places where no one expected it.

"You smell like smoke," she said, stepping close. Not accusing. Just noticing.

"It's in the air now," he said. "Every street. "

They walked together toward the spiral, where the votive candles burned in loose concentric arcs. Someone had rearranged them tonight, each flame reflected in a polished mirror set behind the altar. It looked like the fire had doubled.

"You know," Marin said, settling beside him on the edge of the step, "I used to think this place only mattered because of the rituals. The walks, the murals, the songs. "

"It doesn't?"

"It does," she said, then added, "But only because we decided it does. Joy isn't sacred on its own. It's sacred because we protect it. Choose it. Bake it into bread and scrape it onto murals with bleeding fingers. "

Halfa was quiet for a moment. "And if the people who protect it are busy?"

"Then someone else picks up the torch. Or we take turns carrying it. "

She nudged him lightly with her shoulder. "I see you trying to carry it all at once. That's not bravery. That's just bad math. "

"I don't even know what that is. "

"Clearly," she said dryly.

For a moment, they sat like that, two people whose silence meant safety instead of absence. The candles flickered in the mirrored light, and from the kitchen, Bilbin's voice floated out again. Something about flour, joy, and disrespectful ovens.

"You know," Marin said quietly, "you don't scare me. "

Halfa glanced over. "I should. "

"No," she said. "You burn loud. But the people who scare me most are the ones who smile while cutting things down. You? You fight to build. "

He didn't answer right away. His hand shifted just enough to brush against hers. She didn't pull away.

"You carry fire like it's a curse," she said. "But you forget, it's also warmth. And light. And joy, if you let it be. "

Halfa's voice was low. "I don't know how to let it be anything. "

"Then start by not being alone in it. "

She reached out first this time.

Their hands met. No urgency. No ceremony. Just presence.

And for a moment, Halfa didn't feel like he was walking into war.

He felt like he was choosing the reason not to.

Outside, the wind whispered against the violet-painted doors. Inside, the fire burned on.

The temple wasn't invincible.

And if Valka and the Blackjaws ever chose to strike it, there might not be another warning.

The next morning, Halfa went back to the Ash Rats.

He was passing through the deeper corridors of the Ash Rats' hideout, checking exits, mapping blind corners, doing what the Watch had trained into him. The air was heavy with the scent of salt and iron. Somewhere above, someone was laughing.

He turned a corner and stopped.

One of the younger Rats approached Gronk from the side. He was ten, maybe eleven, dragging a clipboard too big for his frame.

"He's late for drills again," the kid mumbled. "Said his foot's acting up. "

Gronk didn't scold. Nodded once.

"Adjust his watch duty. Let him rest tomorrow. I'll talk to him. "

The kid nodded, turned—but Gronk reached out and gently straightened the boy's collar.

The gesture was awkward. Hesitant. Like it had meant to be firm but turned out gentle.

The boy blinked, then ran off. Gronk watched him go. Didn't say a word.

Halfa watched from the hall. He didn't step forward. Didn't speak.

But the fire inside him stirred. In memory.

Gronk sat down on a crate in a low tunnel room, his back to the wall, the glow of a lantern guttering beside him. One of the younger Rats lay curled up beside a makeshift bedroll. Bandaged leg. Soft snore.

Gronk wasn't watching the kid.

He was working.

A boot sat in his lap, half-torn at the heel. Gronk held a curved awl and a strip of thick thread. His hands moved slowly. Carefully.

One wrong tug would ruin it.

Halfa didn't move. Just stood.

After a moment, Gronk spoke without looking.

"You ever patch a shoe?"

Halfa shook his head. "No. "

Gronk grunted. "It's harder than it looks. Easy to pull too tight. Easy to make it look fixed until it splits again on stone. "

He tied the thread. Checked the seam. Trimmed it clean.

"He'd never ask for a new pair," Gronk added, nodding to the boy. "Wouldn't even tell me they were falling apart. Kept limping quieter every day. "

A pause. "They don't ask for much. Not the ones who've already survived more than they should. "

Halfa stepped closer.

"You think this is glory, Halfa? That I want a throne? I'm just building walls faster than the city lets them fall. "

His eyes found Halfa's. No fire. No fury.

Just tired honesty.

"I don't care if they remember me as a leader. I want them to remember how to survive. "

Halfa nodded once and said nothing.

But the image stuck with him.

Gronk.

In the dark.

Fixing a boot for a kid who didn't ask.

That night, Halfa slept soundly.

He dreamed, but it wasn't a peaceful dream. It was a warning.

He stood in the Temple of Thessira, but it was different this time. The painted glass was fractured, bleeding firelight instead of the sun. The spirals on the floor were burning. Candles melted upward. Walls cracked as if trying to hold back something too large, too hot.

Flames danced where incense once curled.

Marin stood at the centre of the spiral. She looked the same, paint on her fingers, wind in her curls, but her face was lit by fire. Real fire. The kind that didn't belong in the temple.

She was shouting. But he couldn't hear her.

Smoke billowed behind her. Two shapes collapsed through it, Gorne and Lasse, their backs to the flame, trying to hold the door. One raised a weapon. The other threw a punch that never landed.

The door burst open.

Valka stepped through.

She wasn't shouting. She didn't draw a blade. She simply raised her hand, and the fire obeyed her.

It twisted toward her fingers like it missed her. Bent like ribbon. She shaped it like a sculptor shaping clay.

The temple cracked. The flame bowl shattered. The murals caught. Marin screamed, but not in pain. In fury. In defiance.

Halfa tried to move. His legs were molten. His breath caught in his throat.

He looked down. His hands were alight, his arms glowing with sigils he'd never seen. Bloodlines.

From the smoke, other shapes appeared. They were tall. Broad. Glowing. Fire Giants. Or something older. Something watching.

Valka turned toward them and smiled.

Abruptly, he was falling, the ground breaking apart below him.

"The flame remembers its first spark," Serelion whispered. Their outline shone, light pouring from them in waves in front of Halfa as he fell. "But memory doesn't win wars. You'll have to burn with purpose. "

Halfa reached out to grab Serelion—

—and woke before his hand found theirs.

He woke just before dawn.

Sweat soaked through his shirt, but the room was cold.

The fire inside him wasn't raging, but it wasn't calm either.

Halfa sat up slowly, the shadows of the dream still etched behind his eyes. Valka bending fire like it had always been hers.

He rose and crossed the room, pulling his coat from the hook. On the table beside it sat a small velvet pouch; Marin had tucked it into his things after the temple gathering. He hadn't opened it until now.

Inside, the two charms waited. One, old and scorched, edges blackened from the Temple's spiral fire. The other, smooth and whole, shaped like a flame rising instead of flickering.

He held them both in his palm. Opposites. Or perhaps parts of the same thing.

Then, quietly, he strung them together on the same chain. Unburned and burned. Joy and warning. Past and becoming.

As he opened the door to the Watchhouse hallway, he paused by the crooked wall shrine near the stairs. One lantern flickered, guttering in the breeze. He lit another candle with a shaking hand.

"For the ones who might still fall," he said softly. "And for the fire they carry. "

Then he stepped into the cold.

The city glistened after an early evening drizzle, cobbles slick with the reflection of lantern light and stars caught in puddles. Halfa walked the narrow stretch between Watchposts near Fisher's Row, coat collar raised against the wind, hand never far from the badge tucked beneath his belt.

He wasn't in uniform tonight.

But Grayspire still watched him, the same way it always had, suspiciously, hungrily, like a beast judging its next meal.

He crossed into the quieter lanes where carts were stacked for morning deliveries, and the air smelled of salt and cut rope. The sound of gulls had died down, replaced by the creak of ships moored in the dark.

Dot stepped out from beneath an archway, gloved hands folded behind his back like he'd been waiting all night.

He had been quiet for weeks. Watching. Waiting. Dot was good at that.

"Well," he said, too casually. "Didn't think I'd find you here. Off shift, aren't you?"

Halfa didn't stop walking. "Taking the air. "

Dot fell into step beside him, hands still behind his back.

"You've been busy lately," he said. "Talk in the barracks is that your boots get little rest. "

"Rumours. "

Dot smiled faintly. "Funny, though. Blackjaws slipping. Ash Rats growing teeth. And all this happening just as a few old fires flare again. "

He leaned closer. "Makes a man wonder... who's holding the match?"

Halfa said nothing.

Dot's smile was thin. "You know, I've been told I'm too clean. That nobody likes a man who doesn't bend. "

"I've seen you bend. Just never when it counted. "

"Careful, Officer. " Dot's tone never shifted. Still conversational. Still friendly. "Wouldn't want you walking into something you can't walk out of. "

They reached a crossing and paused beneath a gas lamp. Halfa turned to face him fully now.

"You going to report me?"

Dot shook his head. "I'm not your keeper. If you want to waste your career chasing shadows with street rats, go ahead. But this city's a meat grinder, Halfa. And you..." He stepped closer, voice low, "You're still soft in the middle. You remind people of things we can't afford, Stoneface. Compassion. Hesitation. Men who hesitate get people killed. You're not a hero; you're a variable. And I don't like variables. "

Halfa didn't flinch. "You think softness is weakness?"

"I think idealists die younger."

Dot leaned in, close enough for Halfa to smell the ink on his gloves.

"I don't know what you're planning," he said. "But whatever it is… you're not as quiet as you think."

He stepped back, straightened his coat, and offered a final, almost polite nod.

"Good evening, Officer."

Then he walked off, boots clicking neatly as he disappeared into the fog.

Halfa watched him go.

Dot didn't need to arrest him.

He'd already done what he came to do.

Warned him.

Let him know: I see you.

And Halfa knew then that this would not end in silence.

The warehouse squatted near the old river quay like a dying animal, ribs of timber showing through rotted walls, a thick fog clinging to its sides. From a distance, it looked abandoned, another piece of Grayspire decay. But the Ash Rats said otherwise.

Inside, the Blackjaws were moving something big.

Too big.

Halfa crouched in a shadowed alley behind the warehouse with Brannig, Tallen, Lasse, and Gorne. None of them wore uniforms. Brannig had insisted.

"No badges tonight," she'd said. "We don't wear the law. We are the line."

She scratched the building's layout on the alley wall with chalk. There were three floors, a rear stairwell, and two lookouts, minimum. A trapdoor beneath the main cargo platform. It stank of an ambush, but it was also a chance. If they waited, the shipment would be gone. If they acted, it had to be now.

"Halfa takes point," Brannig whispered, shouldering a sap. "Tallen, you cover the rear. Lasse, Gorne, be quick, quiet, and no noise unless someone screams. We're here to clean up."

The others nodded, faces pale but focused. Lasse checked the wrappings on his cudgel. Gorne adjusted the leather strap over his shoulder, hiding his blade.

Halfa flexed his hands once. The fire didn't stir. Not yet.

They moved.

The roof was sagging in the centre, but still held their weight. Halfa led the way, slipping through a half-broken skylight into the upper gantry. The warehouse below was dim. Lit by a few oil lamps and the soft blue glow of a crystal lantern near the cargo stack.

There, he saw crates marked with false shipping seals. Long. Heavy. Too narrow for grain. Too many for coincidence.

One guard dozed by a brazier. Another paced near the stairs.

Halfa motioned.

Tallen dropped silently through a hatch, landing behind the pacing guard and wrapping an arm around his throat. The man struggled once, but Tallen held firm. Then he went still.

Brannig crept along a support beam, dropped behind the other sleeping guard, and clipped him behind the ear with her sap. The man slumped. Brannig caught him before he hit the floor.

No alarms. No shouting.

Perfect.

They fanned out. Lasse and Gorne lifted a crate lid.

Inside, there were crossbows. Dozens. Modified. Smuggled.

Beneath that was Watch-issue armour.

Halfa's stomach turned. "They've been hijacking shipments. "

Brannig rifled through a ledger nailed to the wall. "Look at this. " She passed him a scroll, unsigned but neat, precise block lettering in brown ink.

Halfa read the schedule. Names. Routes. "This is Dot's handwriting. "

No signature. But it was his.

They stared at each other.

Brannig lowered her voice. "You still think he's just convenient?"

Halfa said nothing.

A footstep.

A young Blackjaw, barely out of childhood, had returned from a latrine run. He froze when he saw them. Reached for his belt.

"Don't—" Halfa began.

Too late.

The boy drew steel.

Halfa lunged forward, caught the boy's wrist before the blade cleared its sheath, and twisted, disarming, not breaking. The boy yelped and dropped the weapon. Tallen darted in, binding the boy's hands with a cloth. He whimpered but didn't resist further.

"We're not here to kill you," Halfa said, crouching. "Just walk away. Tonight didn't happen. "

The boy nodded rapidly, eyes wide.

Brannig looked around. "Time's up. Burn it. "

They doused the crates with lamp oil from a broken barrel. Brannig struck a match and handed it to Halfa.

He hesitated.

Then dropped it.

Flames swallowed the weapons in seconds, black smoke billowing upward. Halfa unceremoniously dumped the unconscious and bound Blackjaws out a window on to the soft ground below.

The group slipped out the side before the fire drew eyes.

At the end, Brannig paused. Took a bit of soot from the wall and drew an old symbol, an unadorned eye, the mark of a Watch long gone.

"We see you," she muttered.

Outside, in the dark, they didn't speak until they were blocks away.

Tallen finally broke the silence.

"It finally feels like we're the good guys. "

Halfa didn't answer.

Because in his chest, the fire wasn't satisfied.

They still had a lot of work to do.

Grayspire burned quietly.

Not with flame, but with tension. It wound tight through its alleys and arches like a wire pulled taut. The moon hovered low and swollen, casting silver on slate rooftops and cracked tiles.

Halfa crouched on a rooftop near the docks, wrapped in shadow and watching the road.

Below, a Blackjaw convoy crept through the warehouse quarter, six carts under guard, no sigils, no colours, but the scent of wrongness rolled off the steel like smoke. Halfa didn't need flags to recognise what was coming.

In the distance, three fires flared in sequence. Midden Markets. The tanneries. Rivergate.

Signals. Just as planned.

The Ash Rats were moving.

Halfa's pulse thudded steadily, a war drum. Somewhere, Brannig was heading to a nearby Watchhouse to try and get some more support. Somewhere else, Gronk watched through smoke and silence. The line they'd drawn was holding, for now. He only had to hold it a little longer.

A rat darted past his boot. He didn't flinch.

He touched the weapon at his back, then the flower charm under his collar. Still warm.

Rix appeared beside him on the rooftop, silent as mist.

"They're splitting," she whispered. "Half to the docks, half to Fishbone Alley. You take the second?"

He nodded.

Her hand rested briefly on his arm. "Don't die. "

"I'm too stubborn. "

She smiled, then disappeared into the dark.

Below, the convoy turned. Halfa moved.

His boots struck the next rooftop with purpose. The city didn't stir, yet. But it would.

Because tonight, they didn't wait for orders.

Tonight, they answered a signal. And the fire no longer flickered in secret.

It had teeth now.

And it was ready to bite.

The Spark and the Storm

The alleys of Old Quay were already thick with movement. Lasse and Gorne flanked Halfa, armour hidden beneath brown cloaks, eyes scanning the shadows. Tallen trailed behind, eyes scanning.

"We'll sweep north to Bramble Row," Halfa said. "Clear looters. Protect who we can. Leave judgment to tomorrow. "

"And if someone draws steel?" Lasse asked.

Halfa looked back. "Then we draw steel. "

The others nodded.

The city howled around them with distant clashes, the shriek of glass, the hiss of alchemical flames.

They moved as one.

At the corner of Dustmill Lane, a gang of youths, barely older than children, were looting a spice vendor's stall. Sacks of saffron, cumin, and dried lemon peel burst across the cobbles. The vendor, a wide-eyed man in his forties, cowered beneath his cart, hands over his head.

Halfa didn't shout.

He stalked.

The first youth turned and froze. The others followed his gaze, and then scattered like leaves in a gale.

Halfa crouched beside the vendor, gently lifting the broken wheel from his shoulder.

"Go home," he said. "Board your door. "

The man nodded, dazed.

Gorne lingered behind, eyes distant.

They passed through two more alleys, dispersing a group of arsonists and guiding a mother and child to a makeshift shelter in a wine cellar. No arrests. No speeches.

Just protection.

But every street brought more smoke.

Every corner held another blaze.

Halfa paused at the edge of Breaker's Square. A signal fire burned atop the tailor's guild tower, Ash Rat flame, wrapped in violet cloth.

The uprising was in full swing.

He looked at his hands.

Felt the ember under his ribs stir.

And knew the fire inside him was no longer something to bury.

It was something to aim for. It wasn't fuel anymore; it was a weapon.

The city cracked open.

Not all at once. Not with a thunderclap. But in bursts, like knots of pressure releasing across a map, coordinated but chaotic. The Ash Rats had planned it for weeks. Maybe longer.

And now the strikes began.

Three districts lit up at once: Old Quay, Midden Markets, and Candlewalk.

From rooftops, fires signaled movement.

From cellars, armed shadows spilled into streets.

From alleys, whispers became war cries.

Grayspire flinched, and the Blackjaws bared their teeth.

Halfa crouched behind a crumbling stone fence at the edge of the warehouse district, breathing through the smoke and sweat already clinging to his collar. His team of Lasse, Tallen, and Gorne were with him, proving yet again their loyalty. Each wore ash-smeared cloaks with armour underneath, no Watch insignia, no sign of rank. Just grit and resolve.

Across the way, a fortified storage compound squatted beneath the red light of dawn. Blackjaw sentries patrolled its walls, crossbows slung low. A flag with their twisted insignia hung from a balcony, brazen.

According to Rix's intel, they were holding dozens of crates, smuggled weapons, magical contraband, and alchemical vials capable of lighting a city block.

And people.

Rumours whispered of captives. Leverage. Or worse.

Halfa exhaled.

Gorne tightened the bandage on his own shoulder. "No time for quiet entries now, is there?"

"Not today. " Halfa said.

"Same plan as before," Lasse muttered, checking his grip on a blunted mace.

They moved fast.

Inside the compound, chaos had already arrived.

Ash Rats hit from the western side, Rix among them. Her cloak was torn, lip bloodied, but she still shouted orders. A rooftop detonation created a breach. Crossbow bolts flew, and knives flashed in the light.

Halfa's team stormed the eastern entrance.

The first two guards went down hard, Tallen took one down with a vicious swing. Gorne drove another into a stack of barrels. Halfa disarmed the third, catching a blade on his armour before wrenching it free and tossing it aside.

They pushed through the compound, room by room, clearing corners, over-turning crates.

"Here!" Lasse called. "Watch gear, stolen. Some marked. "

Halfa moved to the crate. Inside, he saw shields etched with faded city seals... and beneath them, something worse.

Blackjaw armour, freshly made. Symbols of fire interwoven with cracked jaw symbols.

He turned toward Rix, who limped through the blasted hallway, eyes wild.

"This isn't what we planned," she said. "This wasn't supposed to be full war. "

Halfa helped steady her. "You knew it might come to this. "

"Not like this," she whispered. "Not fire on every roof. Not children hiding from what we lit. "

A scream echoed down the hall.

They turned, just in time to see Gorne fall, struck across the ribs by a desperate Blackjaw. Halfa rushed forward, and in one quick motion, slammed the man into the wall, knocking him out.

Gorne coughed, trying to stay upright. "Still breathing," he managed. "Barely. "

Tallen dragged him behind cover.

Ash Rats surged past them, chasing the retreating Blackjaws through a broken door.

Halfa stood in the smoke.

He hadn't yet unleashed the fire.

But it was closer now. Closer than he would have liked.

And it was listening.

Then the smoke shifted.

And Valka stepped through.

Her coat was scorched, her blades bloodied. One arm hung lower, perhaps injured. But her eyes? Bright. Focused. Watching Halfa like flame studies kindling.

"There you are," she said, voice low and velvet. "I wondered how long you'd hold out before the spark took you."

Halfa raised his weapon towards her. His fire surged in his chest, wild and unfocused.

Valka smiled. "About time."

She stepped closer. Behind them, the battle still raged, but in this ruined corridor, everything slowed.

"You don't have to be torn in half anymore, Halfa," she said. "No more broken Watch creeds. Free from temple guilt. No more Rats and rules. Only fire. Yours. Unleashed. I can help. I can burn your temple too, really set you off."

He said nothing. The fire inside raged.

She circled him now, slow and coaxing.

"You burn so well. Don't you want to feel whole again? Let me bring it forth."

The flame inside him roared.

But then—

"Step away from him."

Gronk.

Valka turned. Didn't flinch. "Gronk. Still alive, I see."

"You won't be for long if you keep talking," he said, stepping between her and Halfa.

"Oh, please. You were always too noble to kill me quickly."

She struck first, her blades flashing like twin tongues of lightning. Gronk caught one on his bracer, the other on his shoulder. Blood sprayed.

He swung back, wide, heavy, meant to maim. She danced around it, slicing at his side. They moved like shadows and wrecking balls. Every blow echoed. Every dodge left burns on the air.

"You're not a saviour," Valka hissed, blocking his next blow. "You're just another boss. Another brute pretending he's better than the last. "

Gronk's breath was ragged. His foot slipped in ash. "Better to try than to let you have it. "

"Then let's see how you try. "

Their blades locked. Fire flared in the cracks of the wood. Somewhere, Halfa shouted, but neither looked away.

Gronk headbutted her.

She staggered. He swung.

One clean hit, centre mass. The impact sent Valka flying into the wall. Her armour had saved her.

Her blades fell to her side.

She dropped to one knee.

Blood soaked her coat.

She looked up at him.

And smiled.

"You'll become me," she whispered. "You already are. " And she fled, into the smoke.

Gronk stood there, bloodied and breathing, and didn't deny it.

He didn't linger. He sheathed his blade with a grunt, cast one last look toward the scorched hallway where Valka had vanished, then turned on his heel. "Rix!" he barked. "Take the right flank. We move now. " Orders flew from his mouth like hammer strikes. Within moments, he'd gathered a second wind and vanished into the fog of war, dragging the fight with him. Gronk was gone, absorbed into the command.

Halfa looked around for his friends. Gorne, behind him, clutching his ribs. Tallen and Lasse were unhurt but covered in soot, ash and blood.

Time to move on.

Halfa reached the street and looked up. Nearby, on a scorched rooftop overlooking the square, Gronk stood like a statue carved from war. His cloak snapped in the wind, his voice barked over the battle. He yelled orders, redirections, fallback points. The Ash Rats moved to his rhythm. They carved through resistance with terrifying precision.

He met Halfa's gaze for a moment across the battlefield.

No smile.

No nod.

Fierce firelight in his eyes.

And then he turned, issuing the next wave.

Halfa couldn't help but feel a flicker of awe, but beneath it, a tingle of unease.

Not for the first time, he realised something bone-deep: Gronk might be the one who could face Valka and win.

Not because of magic.

Because of will.

And suddenly, that felt more dangerous than fire.

The Watchhouse on River Street was quiet.

Too quiet.

Brannig Barrelshield entered through the front doors without knocking, boots tracking ash across the tiled floor. Her armour was scorched, a fresh slice across her left pauldron. The dust of the city clung to her like war paint. She walked with purpose, each footfall a drumbeat, down the hall toward the command chamber.

Inside, Captain Jorith was sipping wine from a silver goblet.

Two lieutenants flanked him, stiff-backed, eyes hollow.

Brannig didn't wait for permission. She threw a bundle of papers onto his desk, scattering his ledgers and knocking over the wine.

Jorith arched a brow. "Sergeant Barrelshield. What is this?"

"Proof," she said. "Smuggled manifests. Intercepted messages. Names of Watchmen who turned the other way while the Blackjaws bought blocks of this city."

She stabbed a finger at the top sheet. "Your name's not on there. But I found three of your patrols guarding Blackjaw convoys this week. You either didn't know. . . or you let it happen."

Silence.

The lieutenants exchanged a glance. One shifted his weight.

Jorith set the goblet down. "These are. . . heavy accusations. And they're unsupported by official reports."

Brannig leaned over the desk. "That's the point. The official reports were scrubbed. Buried. Like everything else that stinks in this house. "

Jorith's smile thinned. "You're angry, Brannig. But anger doesn't make you right. And this... this looks like sedition. "

Brannig's hand dropped to her belt to rest on the leather strap of her ledger case.

Her voice, when it came, was low and clear. "You know me. You know I don't scare easily. And I don't bluff. "

She pulled out another smaller parchment, sealed with her personal sigil.

"My resignation. If you push back. But if you stand down, and let me make this right, I'll forget the part where your cowardice nearly sold this city. "

A long silence.

One of the lieutenants stepped forward. Young. Nervous. Voice shaking. "I've seen the manifests too. I'll vouch for her. "

The other didn't move. But he didn't stop his comrade either.

Jorith leaned back. Measured his options. Measured the fire in Brannig's eyes.

And folded.

He waved a hand. "You have temporary command of your district. Do what you must. But when the dust settles, this will come back to haunt you. "

Brannig turned to leave.

Paused.

Then looked over her shoulder.

"You don't get to talk about haunting Jorith. The innocents you've let die will haunt you enough. "

Outside, the Watchhouse doors slammed shut behind her.

A younger officer met her at the corner. "Orders, ma'am?"

"Send everyone. Contain this gang war. Don't let it spread to the innocent. And anyone not willing to draw steel for the city... gets reassigned to the outhouse shift. "

She walked on without waiting.

The city was burning.

But for the first time in weeks, she felt like someone was striking matches for the right reasons.

Halfa crouched on the rooftop of a crumbling warehouse, soot smudged across his jaw, watching the chaos unfold below.

Ash Rats and Blackjaws clashed in the smoke-choked alleys, steel ringing, spells flickering, bodies hitting stone. The city screamed beneath it all: a feral, wounded sound.

From his vantage, Halfa saw the moment the tide should have turned.

But didn't.

A company of Watch officers stood at the district's edge, shields polished, boots lined in perfect order.

They didn't move.

They watched.

Their commander stood ahead of them, hands folded neatly behind his back, not a speck of ash on his uniform.

Dot.

His expression was unreadable. Almost serene. A statue carved from cynicism and ambition.

Halfa slid down the roof's slope, boots thudding softly on the ledge below, eyes never leaving him.

Dot turned, as if he had sensed him. He didn't flinch. Offered a tired smile.

"You look awful," Dot said.

"Busy night. "

"Apparently. " He turned back toward the fire. "This? This happens when the wrong people are given too much faith. "

Halfa didn't answer.

"You're wondering why I'm not jumping in. " Dot gestured lazily toward the melee. "Why I'm not sending my men into that slaughter?"

"I'm not wondering. "

Dot chuckled. "Clever boy. Then maybe you've already guessed. "

He waved a hand.

"This isn't a Watch fight anymore. It's a gang war. We're letting the filth clean itself. "

"And when it spills over?" Halfa asked. "When it eats the rest of the city?"

"We'll be there," Dot said. "Fresh, unbloodied, ready to restore order. The people will thank us for it. "

His voice was calm. Smooth.

Practised.

Halfa stepped closer. "You saw the Blackjaws rise. You let them. Helped them. And when it's all over, you control the docks. "

"I let the city correct itself," Dot replied. "I'm not here to be a hero, Halfa. I'm here to survive long enough to make an actual change. Sometimes, that means letting bad things happen to worse people. "

"They're hurting civilians. Thousands have died because of you. "

His fingers twitched near the hilt. Not yet. The fire inside also rose, sniffing the air.

"They're hurting each other. "

Halfa's jaw clenched. His hand itched toward the hilt at his belt, but he didn't draw his weapon.

Dot noticed. "Smart. This rooftop doesn't need more fire. "

He glanced once more at the burning skyline, then turned to go.

Over his shoulder, he added, "Be careful which fires you start, Halfa. Some don't go out when you're done. "

He walked off into the smoke, trailed by quiet guards who never looked back.

Halfa stayed on the roof a moment longer.

Below, two Ash Rats dragged a wounded friend out of the crossfire. A child darted past them, barefoot, carrying a bucket of water too small to matter.

They met in the shadow of a cracked fountain off Wicker Alley. Smoke drifted between the stones like breath held too long. The broken statue of an old Sea Warden loomed above them, sword raised in rust and moss.

Halfa arrived first, cloak heavy with soot, fire still guttering beneath his ribs.

He glanced east, past the smoke. Nearby, the temple still stood. Still lit candles. Still sang.

Brannig stepped from the fog like she'd never left it.

She was back in armour. Not full regulation, scorched, scuffed, with one pauldron repaired in haste. Her stride was steady. Her presence was iron.

"I heard you flipped Jorith's desk," Halfa said, not quite smiling.

Brannig rolled her neck. "Didn't have to. He folded like a bad pastry. I've got command, temporary, unofficial, and already causing ulcers. "

"How long will it hold?"

"Long enough," she said. "I've sent what's left of the loyal Watch to choke the alleyways. Rivergate. Tanner's Row. Even sent a squad to hold the bridge in case someone tries to slither out. "

"And the ones who weren't loyal?"

Her mouth twisted. "Outhouse shift. Or worse. "

They stood in the pause.

Then she added, "Gorne?"

"He's alive," Halfa said. "And nothing is going to stop him from helping us now. "

Brannig's jaw tightened. "Then we finish this fast. "

He looked at her, firelight flickering in his eyes. "You sure you can still kick down a door?"

"I'm not here to watch it swing," she said.

She drew her weapon and nodded toward the rising smoke behind the rooftops. "One last rot-hole. You ready?"

Halfa adjusted the strap on his vambrace, his fingers brushing the twin flame charms beneath his collar.

"No. "

Brannig grinned, and for a second, just a second, she looked younger.

"Then let's pull the last tooth. "

The warehouse stank of pitch, sweat, and fire.

Brannig kicked in the door first, short legs moving like a siege ram, shield raised. Halfa was right behind her, with Tallen, Lasse, and Gorne fanned out behind them. The old timber creaked underfoot as the squad fanned into formation.

This Blackjaw stronghold was among the final ones. What hadn't fled, burned, or bent the knee had barricaded themselves in here, Grayspire's rotted tooth waiting to be pulled.

"Keep tight!" Brannig barked. "Watch your corners!"

The first floor was chaos, barrels overturned, beds ablaze, the air thick with acrid smoke and grit. A Blackjaw lurched from a side hall, blade raised.

Tallen dropped him with a shield bash before the man could speak.

Halfa caught movement above, someone scrambling across a wooden gantry overhead. "Upstairs," he said.

They moved fast, cutting through resistance like a knife through damp bread. These weren't soldiers. These were rats in a trap.

But the trap hadn't finished springing.

They reached the upper floor, what passed for a command hub. Maps, notes, a crate of half-burned coin.

And then the floor groaned.

A whistle. Then, a *crack*.

A rigged charge, and alchemical fire set beneath the beams. The floor erupted in sound and heat. Halfa was thrown backward by the blast.

He slammed into the wall, dazed. Smoke swallowed the room.

He coughed and struggled to rise. Flames danced around the splintered beams. The heat was rising. The air shrieked.

And through it, he heard Brannig's voice.

"Halfa!"

He stumbled forward. Gorne lay crumpled against the far wall, unmoving. Lasse was dragging Tallen out of a collapsed doorway, blood streaked across the boy's temple.

Brannig was pinned beneath a thick beam, one leg twisted unnaturally beneath the rubble. She was propped up on her elbows, grinning like a lunatic.

She grimaced, shifting her elbows to brace herself more upright. Every movement cost her. Her breath came in hitches, her jaw clenched against the pain, but her voice didn't waver.

"Told you not to let me lead the charge," she rasped.

Halfa dropped to his knees beside her. Tried to lift the beam, but it wouldn't budge.

"I can—"

"No time," she said. "They're regrouping. You need to finish this. "

"I'm not leaving you. "

"You are," she snapped. "You've got a fire burning in you that doesn't come back twice. Use it. Get them clear. "

Behind them, the outer walls cracked from heat and impact. Shadows danced beyond the flames.

Then Halfa let himself feel it.

The pressure in his chest. Anger. Grief. The *flame*.

He closed his eyes.

When he opened them, fire licked along his arms. The fire was bright, hungry, alive. His body *absorbed* the heat and the flame from around him.

This wasn't rage. Not this time. It was grief. Loyalty. Purpose. He let that lead. And the fire came, not as a scream, but as an answer.

With a roar, he heaved the beam off Brannig, sending sparks screaming through the air. He stood tall, flames coiling from his shoulders—and turned toward the breach in the wall.

He *burned*.

And the remaining Blackjaws scattered.

Gorne still didn't stir, but Lasse slung him over his shoulder without hesitation. Tallen kept pressure on Brannig's wound with one hand, his other gripping Halfa's belt to steady himself.

Brannig, pale but grinning, reached up and grabbed Halfa's sleeve.

"You were always fire, boy," she said, voice cracking. "But that's the first time I've seen you burn for someone else. Go. Finish this. "

Halfa's fire extinguished. His skin still steamed, but he felt rejuvenated, but wary. He reached down and picked Brannig up. "Not without you. "

The battle still raged beyond, but this place was done.

They left no badge behind.

But the ash marked where they had stood.

And where Brannig had fallen.

Halfa stepped into the street, Brannig's weight still heavy in his arms. Smoke rose behind him like a mourning banner. Lasse and Tallen flanked his steps. Gorne groaned faintly as Lasse put him down off his back, but he was breathing. He stood up slowly, ready to go on.

A figure was waiting near the far corner, half-hidden by smoke, hood pulled low, cloak torn.

Rix.

She stepped forward without ceremony, her voice rough, urgent.

"They're hitting the temple. "

Halfa stopped cold.

"What?"

"Blackjaws. They didn't strike during the chaos. They waited. And now they're moving."

"Where's Marin?" Halfa asked, his throat already dry.

Rix met his eyes.

"Still inside."

The fire in his chest surged, not in rage, but in terror.

He looked down at Brannig. Her eyes fluttered open just enough to see his face. She nodded, just once.

"Go," she rasped. "Go now."

Embers and Ascension

They ran.

Not marched. Not advanced.

Ran.

Halfa tore through the winding lanes of Grayspire like a man chasing the last spark of something holy. His breath thundered in his ears, boots striking cobblestone in a punishing rhythm. Behind him, Tallen, Lasse and Rix sprinted hard, sweat and soot on their faces, fear and resolve in their eyes.

Gorne lagged. Brannig had remained behind, hidden in cover, unable to move herself.

His shoulder was still bandaged, his gait uneven. But he didn't fall. He didn't call out. He just ran, jaw clenched, breath ragged, like the pain was an afterthought. The adrenaline pushed him harder than any command ever could.

They turned the last corner before the temple, and Halfa's heart dropped.

The Temple of Thessira was burning. Again.

Smoke billowed through its broken windows, thick and black, tinged with flickers of rose-coloured flame that had once been sacred. The painted walls were scorched, charred at the edges like a prayer caught in a furnace. The walls were cracked. Lanterns shattered. Silks torn.

And outside the temple, a war was already raging.

Blackjaws swarmed like hornets, hundreds of them, their sigils dulled with ash, many bleeding from other battles, pushed out of strongholds, cornered in side streets, funnelled here like rats into a dying nest.

Some were organised. Most were not.

But all of them were dangerous, angry, and armed.

Ash Rats and Brannig's Watch held the flanks, pushing from alleyways and balconies, trying to contain the wave. Many had fallen. More would fall. The temple, once a beacon of colour and calm, had become a siege point.

And at its front, at the violet-painted door, stood Gronk.

He held the line like a fortress.

Blood streaked his arms. His bracers were cracked. One eye was swollen. But his stance didn't waver. He roared orders between blows, striking with a rusted halberd like it was an extension of his body.

Each Blackjaw that tried to breach the threshold met him first.

None made it through.

But the line wouldn't hold forever.

Halfa froze mid-step, chest heaving, the heat of the temple fire already washing over him.

"Marin," he whispered.

There was no sign of her. There was no flash of white robes.

Smoke. And fire. And the unspoken truth that he might already be too late.

Tallen came up beside him, his face pale beneath the grime. "Orders?"

Halfa didn't answer.

He was staring into a nightmare made real, the place he'd found purpose, found peace, found her, already half-consumed.

"Gorne's slowing," Lasse said, panting. "We need to regroup. "

"No," Halfa said, his voice low and hard. "We go now. "

He tightened the straps on his belt. Felt the twin flame charms beneath his collar. One whole. One charred.

He looked at the temple again.

A scream echoed from within its walls.

He didn't know if it belonged to a priest or a Blackjaw, or someone too young to carry a weapon.

He just knew it wasn't going to be the last.

He drew his weapon.

"Cover the flank," he barked. "I'm going through that door. "

No one stopped him.

They couldn't.

He moved, blade ready, fire rising.

The fire wasn't just behind his ribs now. It coursed through his blood.

Because this wasn't just another battlefield.

This was his home.

And it was burning.

The Ash Rats and Brannig's Watch were holding the line, but only barely. They'd formed a semicircle outside the Temple of Thessira, pinned against the old canal wall with nowhere left to retreat. Smoke poured from the shattered dome. Firelight spilled through the violet-painted door like a promise broken.

And then, Halfa came through.

He ran straight through the Ash Rat flank like a storm in boots. They parted instinctively, no orders needed. Cloaks whipped aside, blades dropped slightly. Even the wounded stepped clear. They didn't see a man; they saw a fuse burning.

And then he hit the Blackjaw line.

Steel rang. Bone cracked. The first enforcer never even saw the blow coming. Halfa's shoulder smashed into him with a sound like thunder, sending him into two others. A second lunged with a jagged pike. Halfa caught the shaft with both hands, twisted, snapped it in half and drove the splinters into his gut.

The third tried to draw steel.

Halfa ignited.

Fire burst from his chest, wild and radiant, a geyser of fury that howled outward like a dragon's scream. The heat lifted stones, peeled paint, and sent half a dozen Blackjaws tumbling like leaves in a gale.

The temple doors flared in reflection. The stained-glass spiral above them shattered inward from the heat, raining violet shards across the stone.

The Ash Rats surged forward behind him, roaring. What had been a line became a wedge. They pushed forward, Rix among them, blades glinting, orders flying. The tide had turned.

Halfa didn't look back.

He carved through the chaos like a blade made of grief. Every strike burned. His flames arced outward in pulses, burning the air but never the innocent, searing banners and weapons, but not flesh. His control wasn't perfect.

But it was enough.

A Blackjaw tried to flank him.

Halfa didn't strike. He detonated. A burst of pure, silent flame threw the man backward a dozen paces, still breathing, but smoking.

And then he reached the doors.

Gronk stood there, back to the frame, halberd braced across the entrance. Blood ran from a gash on his temple. His chest rose and fell like a bellows, his eyes hard as volcanic stone.

They locked eyes.

No words passed.

Gronk just nodded.

And Halfa charged through the flame-framed threshold into the burning temple beyond.

◈

The moment Halfa crossed the threshold, the sight nearly buckled him. Not from fire. From memory.

The great mural wall was cracked down the centre. The spiral bowl was shattered. Smoke curled through the prayer hall like fingers searching for names.

Bodies lay scattered, Ash Rats, Blackjaws, faithful caught in the crossfire.

But none of them were her.

He stepped forward. Boots crushing shards of glass that once held the flame. His fire dimmed. His breath hitched.

And then—

Near the base of the inner flame, beneath a half-fallen tapestry, he saw her.

Marin.

Her robes were scorched. One side of her face streaked with soot. Her hand still clutched a child's arm, small, trembling. The girl was alive, wide-eyed, tucked against Marin's chest like a prayer.

Halfa knelt beside them, heart pounding like fists on a locked door. "Marin," he whispered, voice hoarse. "Marin, look at me. "

Her eyes fluttered open, dim, but focused. "Halfa," she murmured, a flicker of a smile. "You found me. "

He touched her cheek, careful not to press too hard. "You're hurt. "

"Everyone is," she whispered. "But... we held. The children—they... I couldn't let them fall. "

Her hand, weak but determined, pressed against his.

"You saved me long before tonight," she said, barely above the crackle of the still-burning silks. "You were everything I wished I had. Everything I still want to have. "

He tried to speak, but his voice caught.

"I saw your fire," she went on, coughing. "It brought me so much joy to know you were out there, to know you were coming to me. "

Behind them, a familiar shape stepped into the fractured light.

Bilbin. His apron torn, blood streaked down one arm, a kitchen knife still tucked in his belt like a defiant prayer. He knelt opposite Halfa and touched Marin's shoulder gently.

"She pulled them from the side hall," Bilbin said. "Carried two of them herself. Would've done more if I hadn't tackled her behind the altar. "

Halfa's eyes burned. "We need to get her out. "

"Already working on it," came a voice from the hall.

Gorne. Limping, one arm in a sling, soot smudged into every line of his face. Lasse and Tallen flanked him, weapons still drawn. Their eyes widened when they saw Marin, but they didn't panic.

"I'll stay," Gorne said, stepping forward. "I'm already half out of commission. I can hold this ground until the rest catch up. "

Lasse nodded tightly. "We'll form a perimeter. "

And near the broken archway, half in shadow, half in flame—

Serelion.

They didn't speak. They didn't need to. Just met Halfa's eyes and offered a single, solemn nod. A moment of old magic and unbroken faith.

Marin shifted. Her voice was weaker now. "They'll try again, won't they?"

Halfa leaned closer. "Let them. "

And for the first time in hours, the fire in his chest felt like a shield.

The light inside the temple had dimmed. Not the fire, there was still plenty of that, but the weight of it. The smoke curled gentler now. The screams were further off.

Halfa had left Gorne and Bilbin with Marin, who was gravely injured but not in any immediate threat. Serelion had disappeared from near the arch.

Halfa stepped through the violet-painted door, the stone arch half-collapsed above him. His boots scraped glass and soot as he moved, and his breath came shallow, ragged. Each step was a small betrayal of how much the fire inside him had taken.

Outside, the square still burned.

But the tide had turned.

His explosion, pure, unshaped, born of terror and grief, had torn through the Blackjaw line like a hammer through a stained-glass window. The Ash Rats, surging behind it, had not wasted the moment. They drove the Blackjaws back, out of the temple courtyard, into the alleyways where resistance thinned, and courage frayed.

Bodies lay scattered. Blood soaked the cobbles. Fires burned all along the courtyard.

And at the edge of the temple steps stood Gronk.

His cloak was burned through at the shoulder. One gauntlet was missing. His eyes scanned every street like a tactician in the middle of a chessboard still in play. He didn't turn when Halfa approached.

Halfa raised a hand and clapped him on the shoulder. Hard. It was a thank you that he couldn't find the words to convey.

Gronk turned his head just enough to glance sideways. No smile. Just understanding.

And then he moved forward, fast. Bellowing orders, gathering his flank, driving toward the western breach where Blackjaw banners still flickered.

As Gronk left, Halfa looked for Lasse and Tallen, and went to go and help Gronk finish this.

But as he did, his gaze caught something a little bit away from the battle.

The smoke there was thicker. As he watched, the smoke parted, and she walked through.

Valka.

She didn't march like a general. She didn't charge like a soldier.

She just walked towards Halfa.

Smoke curled around her heels. Her coat was torn, streaked with soot. It trailed like a memory that refused to die. Her hair was tied back, her posture relaxed, but her eyes...

Her eyes were sharpened glass.

She stepped over the bodies like they weren't there. Like they were already forgotten. Like grief was a language she had never needed to learn.

Halfa turned toward her. His limbs were heavy. His breath burned.

But he stood.

Valka tilted her head at him.

"Well," she said, softly. "Here we are. "

The temple still burned behind him.

And in that moment, before anything else happened, Halfa knew:

It wasn't over yet.

◈

The battle surged beyond them, steel clashed in alleys, cries rang out like broken hymns, but the square in front of the temple had gone still.

Halfa stood between Valka and the scorched temple steps, shoulders squared, boots firm in ash. To his left, Tallen, already bloodied but unshaken. To his right, Lasse, face grim, mace tight in one hand.

Gronk had vanished into the thicket of war again, a distant shape of rage and muscle driving back the Blackjaw line. His absence had left Halfa at the point of the blade.

Valka didn't flinch.

She stood five strides away, framed by broken columns and smoke-smeared sky, her hands bare, her coat hanging in torn ribbons. Her eyes burned brighter than her blades ever had.

"I was hoping it would be just us," she said. "No armour. No orders. Just truth. "

Halfa didn't reply.

He felt the fire inside him. It was coiled, wary. It knew fear now. It knew her.

Valka smiled like she could taste it.

"You think the fire inside you makes you powerful, Halfa," she said, taking one slow step forward. "But you forget who showed you what it could do. "

She opened her hand.

The flame *moved*.

Not from Halfa, but from everywhere else.

Lanterns sputtered out. Torches extinguished. Braziers across the square shuddered and died. A wave of darkness collapsed around them as Valka drew all the flame forward, coiling it in front of her, a spinning orb of light, heat and hunger.

It floated above like a sun cut loose.

"I don't only control *your* fire, Halfa," she yelled. "I command all fire that forgets its purpose. "

Halfa's dread landed like a weight in his gut. The heat of her power brushed his face.

Tallen stepped forward. "She's going to—"

Valka moved before the sentence finished.

She turned toward the temple, arm outstretched, and *hurled* the fireball.

It arced like a comet.

Straight toward the crumbling arch of the temple of Thessira.

"No—" Halfa's cry ripped from his throat.

But it was already flying.

Already burning.

Already coming.

The fireball screamed across the square, a streak of molten fury drawn from every flame Valka could reach. It lit the air like a second sun, spinning, roaring and wild.

Halfa's fire surged by instinct, not channelled, not controlled, just *launched*. A wall of golden heat burst from his chest, colliding with the oncoming inferno midair.

The two forces twisted—flame battering flame. But Valka's magic held stronger. Her fire bent. Curved. Absorbed.

It continued straight toward the temple.

"No!" Halfa shouted, the sound torn from his chest like a wound.

And then—

Above the violet-painted door, framed by curling smoke and broken banners, standing atop the cracked arch, was Serelion.

They did not shout. They did not flinch.

Their arms rose, palms open, as if welcoming the fire.

And the fire came.

The ball of blazing fury curved downward, then halted, inches from Serelion's hands, as if caught by invisible threads.

Wind screamed through the square. Debris lifted. The air itself *held its breath*.

Serelion's eyes glowed, not with power, but with peace.

They whispered something no one could hear. They locked eyes with Halfa, eyes full of peace and joy. A smile on their lips.

Then, the fire folded in.

Collapsed.

Drawn into Serelion's chest.

A burst of light exploded outward. It wasn't destructive. It was radiant. The flame became gold. Heat became a song.

And when the flash cleared—

Only ash remained.

A perfect spiral of it, slowly drifting to the temple steps.

Tallen took a step toward Halfa, then stopped. Lasse's hand dropped to his side. The firelight flickered across their faces, raw, quiet and changed.

Halfa fell to his knees.

No words. No scream.

Deafening silence.

Behind him, even the Blackjaws paused. Even Valka stopped smiling.

The fire had been claimed.

And its price had been paid.

He didn't know how long he stayed there, on his knees, surrounded by the stillness that followed the sacrifice. Wind scattered the ash. The fire in his chest didn't burn. It mourned.

Serelion was gone. But what they had done... it lingered. A line drawn between fury and faith.

◈

Halfa could barely see; his vision was blurred by smoke, sweat, and the raw sting of grief. His lungs burned. His arms trembled. The hollow left by Serelion's absence ached louder than the flame still coiling through his bones. But through the haze, he caught movement. Gronk. Shoulders squared. Jaw set like stone. The brute moved toward Valka without fanfare, without war cries. Just *intent*. And as he stepped between the embers, Halfa realised something terrifying: Gronk wasn't going to stop her. He was going to *end* her.

Valka, half-burnt, one sleeve torn, her left eye swollen shut. She stood in the centre of the courtyard, blades reversed in her hands, dripping with blood that wasn't hers. Around her, Ash Rats and even some of Brannig's Watch, lay still.

Gronk stood across from her. Breathing hard. One arm limp. His face was a mask of smoke and blood.

Valka saw Halfa over Gronk's shoulder. She grinned. "Just in time. He should see this. "

"You're finished," Gronk said.

She laughed. It was hoarse, cracked, but still full of flame. "Am I? You think if you kill me, it ends? You're a fool. You'll need me after this. My methods. My people. "

"They're not yours anymore," Gronk said.

Valka lunged.

She moved like a dying star, bright, erratic, full of gravity. Gronk caught her blade with his forearm, the metal biting through old scars. He didn't flinch.

He didn't hesitate.

They crashed together in the heart of the courtyard. One beast.

She was faster than she had any right to be.

Gronk's first blow landed, barely. She twisted with it, used the impact to roll over his shoulder, kicked off his spine mid-fall, and landed crouched. Her blade nicked his calf as she passed. Not deep. But precise.

Gronk staggered. She was on him again.

A knife at his throat was deflected. A second to his ribs, dodged. Her movements were precise. Not wild, but meant to feel wild. To unnerve. She danced like a storm and struck like a surgeon.

He caught her arm and drove a knee into her side. She buckled, but didn't break.

"You think this is control?" she spat, blade flashing across his collar.

"No," Gronk growled. "This is the end. "

She bled. So did he. They circled, panting. Gronk limping, Valka hunched. Her smirk cracked, but it didn't fade.

Then she faked a stumble.

Gronk stepped in, and she spun low, cutting into his thigh with the last of her strength. He dropped. One knee down. She raised both knives overhead, screaming—

And he drove upward like a piston, head-butting her clean across the mouth.

She reeled. Gronk surged. Grabbed her wrist. Broke it.

She screamed. Stabbed with the other hand.

He caught it. Slammed her into the pillar.

The blades dropped.

She fell.

She rose again.

He hit her harder.

This time, she stayed down.

Valka collapsed against the edge of the pillar, spitting blood onto the cracked stone. She looked up at Gronk. One eye still blazing.

"I hope you choke on this throne," she said.

He said nothing.

"You'll sit where I sat. You'll look out across this city. And you'll see me. In every desperate face. In every corner that you can't control. You'll become me. "

Gronk didn't respond.

He just reached down, grabbed her by the collar, and dragged her across the stones, past the wounded, past Halfa, past what was left of the old temple walls.

Halfa watched her limp blade trail through the dust like a fallen torch.

And Valka?

She smiled all the way to the square.

No one spoke. No one moved. The fight was over, but the air still crackled with the echo of her presence. Halfa looked at the blood she left behind and wondered if it was hers or the city's. Gronk stood tall, but even he didn't raise his voice. As the smoke thinned, Halfa realised something he hadn't dared name before: her body might fall, but her words had already planted roots. In fear. In anger. In the need to control. She'd lost, but she'd left a map for anyone willing to follow. And Gronk... he held the compass now.

Halfa looked at Valka as she was dragged away.

He could've chased her. Could've thrown fists, curses, fury. The rage burned, even without flame. No one would've stopped him. Some might've cheered.

But Halfa stood still.

His fire was gone, all expelled from him as he had tried to stop Valka's fireball. He could feel cold inside his chest. But the heat behind his ribs wasn't all that made him dangerous.

And it wasn't all that made him matter.

He looked toward the temple. Toward the spiral. Toward Marin's laughter on some forgotten morning, and the children's paper crowns, and the bread still warm in his chest. He looked up at the scorched arch where Serelion had stood for his last stand.

"Not like this," he said.

He knelt beside a fallen Ash Rat and helped him sit upright. Tallen and Lasse joined him.

No fire. No vengeance. Just hands. Just healing.

Just joy, stubborn and alive, refusing to be silenced.

◊

At the centre of the square, under a makeshift canopy of torn silks and tarpaulin, Gronk stood before the last of the Blackjaw leadership.

They knelt.

Some from wounds. Others from fear. A few from choice.

Their sigils had been slashed through. The reign of the Blackjaws in Grayspire was done.

But they weren't dead.

Not all of them.

Rix stood near the steps, one arm hanging unnaturally, face bloodied but alert. She didn't cheer. She watched.

Halfa pushed forward through the ring of Ash Rats and loyal Watchmen. His boots crunched glass. His heart burned. Tallen and Lasse, ever loyal, flanked him even now.

Gronk saw him. Nodded once.

Then turned back to the kneeling gang lords.

A beaten and bloodied Valka was on her knees, staring up at Gronk with a smirk, eyes firing with malice.

Gronk looked down at her, contemplating. His jaw clenched with resolve.

Valka coughed, blood flecking her lips. She stayed on her knees, her hands at her sides, blades forgotten in the dust.

The Ash Rats stood frozen. Even the wind seemed to hush.

She looked up at Gronk and Halfa in turn, half-laughing through the ruin of her breath.

"You think they'll cheer you?" she rasped, voice ragged. "You think they'll hang flags for the next butcher who gets a seat at the table?"

Gronk said nothing.

"You're just me in a new uniform," she continued. "King and knight. Pretending this isn't just another slaughterhouse with better drapes. "

She leaned forward, hand gripping a cracked stone for balance.

"This city doesn't want saving. It wants control. And you—" she looked at Gronk, "you gave it control with a friendlier name. "

Her gaze shifted to Halfa.

"You—fireboy. Temple boy. You still dreaming of joy in a world made of ash?"

She grinned wider, cracked teeth and red spit.

"Tell your goddess: joy doesn't last. Fire does. "

Then, gazing skyward, her voice softened.

"You'll remember me when the streets run red again. And they will. "

She raised her chin—proud, defiant, unbroken.

"Thrones don't rot from pressure. They rot from comfort. "

She closed her eyes.

"I built mine from ash. At least it never lied. "

Gronk raised his weapon and brought it down. Hard. Once. Twice.

There was a pause. No cheering, no shouting.

For a heartbeat, Gronk hesitated. Not before the blow, but after. A breath. A flicker. Then it was gone. The new throne waited.

"Your time's over," Gronk said, voice loud but calm. "Your brand dies here. But your strength doesn't have to. "

One man looked up. "What are you saying?"

"I'm saying you can live. You can work. You can serve. But not as Blackjaws. " Gronk spread his arms. "As Ash Rats. "

A murmur rippled through the crowd. Rix stepped forward.

"That wasn't the plan," she hissed.

"It's the new one. "

Halfa stood beside her. "You said you were holding the line. "

Gronk turned. "I am. I just moved it. "

Rix shook her head. "You don't absorb poison, Gronk. You bleed it out. "

Gronk met her eyes. "The city's bleeding already. I'm putting a tourniquet on. "

Halfa looked around. The square was ringed by survivors. Ash Rat lieutenants with cracked blades. Brannig's Watch with missing badges. Civilians peering from doorways, too afraid to cheer, too tired to run.

"This won't hold," he said. "You're building peace with bricks of rot. "

"I'm building something we can defend," Gronk said. "We control the streets. We control the flow. We stop the chaos. Dot and the corrupt of the Watch won't stop us, not now. We've got power. "

He looked past Halfa then, past the wounded, the crumbling walls, the temple now smudged with ash. "Maybe I'm not building peace," he said, quieter. "Maybe I'm just building something I can control. But sometimes that's all you get, the shape of the fire, if not the warmth. "

Halfa stared at him. "You sound just like the ones we burned. "

Gronk didn't flinch. "I learned from them. "

He turned back to the crowd.

"This is the Ash Throne now," he shouted to the gathered crowd. "And anyone who wants a place in the new Grayspire better decide fast. "

"This isn't victory. " Rix turned and walked away. Gronk watched her go, but remained silent.

Halfa stood there, flame coiled behind his eyes, watching the torch be passed from one tyrant to another.

Gronk raised his hand, and the Ash Rats cheered. The remaining Blackjaws looked around, not believing their luck.

But Halfa didn't join in.

His fire had flared, been spent, and now only the smoke remained.

Halfa didn't kneel, didn't cheer.

Instead, he turned toward the ruin behind him.

The temple was broken. Silks shredded. Stones cracked. Smoke still curled from the spiral path.

But the violet door?

It was still standing.

Charred at the edges. Soot-grimed. But upright. Defiant. The spiral symbol above the arch had been blackened nearly out of sight, yet Halfa swore he saw its shape glint in the firelight. A quiet mark of something that had not given in.

And somehow, that mattered more than the hollow victory.

The door still stood.

So would joy.

The Ash and the Ember

The temple was no longer burning, but it had begun to heal.

A few days later, Halfa stepped into the ruined sanctuary as morning light seeped through holes in the wall where stained glass had once caught the colour. The roof was mostly gone. Smoke-blackened timbers jutted overhead like broken ribs. Rainwater dripped through the cracks and pooled in the corners, mingling with ash.

The spiral path was shattered, the cracked stones scattered like teeth, but someone had swept the worst of it clean. The flame bowl at the centre had been replaced with a dented lantern, lit anyway.

He wasn't sure who had done it. But the gesture mattered.

He moved past the rubble in silence, boots crunching glass and burnt wax. The air smelled of damp stone and old incense. No song. No laughter.

Marin was elsewhere, still recovering from injuries, but still helping place the others. Bilbin had been seen carrying beams like furniture, cursing under his breath. No one rested. Not yet.

Halfa made his way toward the far alcove. What had once been Serelion's study was now barely a corner. It held a collapsed desk, a shelf warped by heat, and a few scattered pages left untouched by flame.

A cracked journal lay beneath a pile of half-burnt ribbon cords.

He crouched. Brushed aside the soot.

Inside the journal, pressed between two warped pages, was a folded letter. Its edges were singed, but the ink hadn't run.

Just one word on the front.

Halfa.

His throat tightened. He had not expected this. With trembling hands, he opened the letter.

Halfa,

You carry fire like a man who thinks it is borrowed. But it's older than you. Older than me. And it remembers.

I was never your teacher, not in the true sense. Only a mirror. Only a witness.

There is a place, north of the Shatterspine Mountains, beyond the fog and the frost, where the fire still speaks. Where Goliaths walk without chains. Where your name might mean something more than survival.

They call it the Emberdeep.

It is just past the flooded city of Marrowdeep. I would stop there to get the lay of the land, to resupply.

I do not know if either place still lives. I do not know if Emberdeep ever did.

But if the fire inside you ever grows quiet...

Follow the smoke.

It will know you.

—Serelion.

Halfa folded the letter carefully. Slid it into the inside pocket of his coat with the old charm and the torn badge.

He stood for a long moment, staring at the broken spiral. At the ruined roof. At the lantern, still burning in defiance.

Then he turned, stepping out of the ruin.

There were still people to see.

Still hands to hold.

Still debts to count.

And the first belonged to those who had bled beside him.

Outside, the temple walls groaned in the shifting morning air. Halfa adjusted his coat and walked south, boots silent through the rubble-strewn alleys. The path to the infirmary was half-barricaded with debris and old furniture, but someone had cleared a narrow gap through the centre.

He ducked through it.

The city was quiet again. But it was busy, never staying still for long.

And as he approached the Watch infirmary, the scent of mint leaves and blood greeted him like an old memory, and one more truth waiting to be faced.

The infirmary still smelled like blood and mint leaves. Less smoke than before. More silence. But Halfa didn't feel peace.

He ducked under the low lintel, boots scuffing the stone floor, nodding at the nurse who barely looked up. The far beds were filled with men and women in Watch colours, bandaged, bruised, and asleep.

Lasse looked up first.

He was seated at the side of a narrow cot, one arm in a sling, his face swollen but proud. His battered breastplate lay at his feet, burnished with grime and soot but newly polished around the edges.

"You made it," he said.

Halfa nodded. "So did you. "

Tallen stirred on the bed beside him, one eye cracking open. His head was wrapped in linen, and a deep cut ran from his temple to jaw, stitched with care.

Halfa hadn't seen the injuries in the moment. Neither had they, probably, not through smoke, blood, and adrenaline.

"I swear, Halfa," he croaked, voice dry but grinning, "you've got a talent for getting me injured. "

Halfa chuckled softly. "You volunteer for the hardest jobs. "

"You say that like I get a choice. "

Lasse snorted. "He doesn't remember half the fight. Keeps asking why the roof exploded. "

"I remember flames," Tallen muttered. "Big ones. "

Halfa didn't respond. Nodding once, eyes drifted towards the far bed.

Gorne lay there unconscious, his chest rising shallow and slow. A bandage wrapped tight across his ribs, another around his leg and his shoulder. But colour had returned to his cheeks. His sword lay on a chair nearby, polished and placed with quiet respect.

"He'll make it," Lasse said, catching Halfa's glance. "The healer said so. He needs time. "

Halfa exhaled through his nose. Relief hit his chest like a hammer.

"You all fought well," he said.

Lasse looked away, as if embarrassed. Tallen gave a weak thumbs-up.

"Word is," Lasse added, "we've been... promoted. Commendations. Bravery in the line of fire and all that. "

Halfa blinked. "Seriously?"

"We didn't expect it either. Thought they'd hang us up by our boots for what we did. "

Tallen grinned again. "Guess they ran out of boots. "

Halfa managed a smile, but it didn't reach his eyes.

"Have you heard anything?" Lasse asked. "About... you?"

Halfa shook his head. "Nothing yet. "

He didn't say it, but they all knew what that meant. No letter. No reassignment. No orders. Silence. And silence in the Watch wasn't safety. It was waiting for the hammer to fall.

He rose.

"Let Gorne know I checked in. "

"We will," Lasse said. "Halfa?"

He paused.

"You did good. "

Halfa nodded once, then left without another word.

But as he stepped out into the morning light, he could feel the city exhaling, slow and uncertain. Something had changed.

And so had he.

◈

The old Watch office was too quiet.

It was never loud to begin with, Brannig Barrelshield didn't like racket, but this quiet was different. Hollow. Final.

Halfa stepped inside and saw her immediately. She was seated behind her desk, one leg stretched out on a stool, the other... gone. The fabric of her trousers was neatly folded and pinned just below the thigh. A walking cane leaned against the far wall. A fresh pot of ink steamed beside a stack of unsigned reports.

She didn't look up.

"Took you long enough," she muttered, dipping her quill. "I was starting to think you'd forgotten your favourite dwarf. "

Halfa closed the door behind him. "Didn't want to interrupt your paperwork. "

"Interrupt away. Most of this is nonsense anyway. Final clearances, forms for medical leave, resignation letters. " She scratched her name on a parchment and tossed it aside. "Never thought I'd leave this place by quill. "

He stepped forward. "You're sure?"

Brannig finally looked at him.

Her eyes were tired, but sharp. As sharp as ever.

"You saw me, Halfa. Back there. I can't chase thieves. Can't jump fences. Can barely lift my axe without gritting my teeth. "

"You don't have to fight to lead. "

"Aye. But I've bled for this Watch too long to let it turn me into a symbol. "

She folded her hands over the desk. The knuckles were still scratched; the nails chipped. Warrior's hands.

"I'd rather leave on my own terms than be paraded around like a broken banner. "

Halfa said nothing.

Brannig stared at him for a long moment, then sighed. "You know... when I first vouched for you, I thought you'd get thrown out in a tenday. Too much fire. Too much storm. I figured you'd punch the wrong noble or burn down a barracks. "

"You weren't wrong," Halfa said quietly.

"No," she agreed, smiling faintly. "But gods help me, I'm glad you stayed. "

She leaned forward, pulled open a drawer, and withdrew something wrapped in cloth. She slid it across the desk to him.

He unwrapped it carefully.

A badge. Not his old one.

Brannig's.

"Not for show," she said. "Not for duty. A reminder that someone believed in you. "

Halfa closed the cloth again.

"I don't know if I'm staying. " he admitted.

"I figured," she said. "This city... it eats the good ones. Or turns them into something else."

He looked at her, brow furrowed.

"Do you regret it?" he asked.

Brannig chuckled, then grimaced and pressed a hand to her leg. "Every damned day. But that's the job. You regret, and you keep walking."

She stood slowly, leaning on her cane, and came around the desk.

"I don't get to keep walking, Halfa. But you do."

He nodded, once.

They didn't hug. They weren't the hugging type.

But when she placed a hand on his shoulder, firm and steady, it was all the farewell he needed.

"Watch your step," she said. "And if you ever find a place where the fire doesn't follow you..."

He waited.

"Don't trust it. Fire's part of you now."

Then she turned away, limping toward the door, leaving the badge and a silence full of meaning behind her.

◊

The Watchhouse boardroom had once been a storage room. It had thin walls, cracked plaster, and a crooked window looking out onto an alley filled with broken crates and stray cats. They'd cleared the boxes and called it official.

Captain Jorith sat at the head of the table, back straight, uniform crisp. Dot leaned in the corner, arms folded, mouth twisted into something between amusement and triumph.

Halfa stood opposite the desk, silent.

There was only one chair. He wasn't invited to sit.

Jorith tapped a parchment in front of him.

"Your record's been updated," the captain said. "Effective immediately, you're stripped of patrol duties. Your rank is reverted. Probationary reinstatement under limited command authority."

Halfa didn't flinch. "Understood."

"You led an unauthorised operation. Distributed intelligence to known criminal affiliates. You engaged in a coalition without chain-of-command approval. " Jorith's tone was clinical, but sharp. "You've given us... a unique problem, Officer Schoona. "

Dot stepped forward, a little too eagerly. "He acted on personal bias. Prior gang affiliations. Emotional recklessness. This wasn't justice; it was vigilante theatrics. "

Halfa met Dot's gaze, waiting for the smug grin or the sneer.

"You talk a lot for someone who's never bled for the people he files reports about," Halfa said. His voice wasn't loud. It didn't need to be.

Dot tilted his head, amused. "I don't need to bleed to make things work. "

"No," Halfa said. "You just keep things running while people disappear. That isn't freedom. "

"Freedom is a story people tell themselves when they're desperate," Dot replied. "Order is what keeps the corpse from rotting faster. "

Dot's face was still. Calm.

"You want mercy in this city?" he continued softly. "Build your own kingdom. Buy your own guards. Feed your own rats. Until then, you take what order you can get, and you pray it doesn't gut you in your sleep. "

He stepped forward, voice lowering. "I didn't choose this. I adapted to it. You think you're better because you lit some candles and punched the right people? Fire dies out. But systems, corrupt or not, they last. "

He looked down at the badge on Halfa's chest. "At least until someone comes along with a better system. Which you haven't. "

Jorith raised a hand to silence him, but didn't correct the record.

"Fortunately," the captain continued, "your actions, however disruptive, resulted in the dismantling of one of the largest criminal organisations in recent memory. Civilian casualties were lower than expected. Blackjaw presence in Grayspire has been effectively neutralised. Political pressure... is mixed. "

Dot didn't like that.

"But," Jorith added, leaning forward, "if we reward this behaviour, we lose control of the Watch. We set a precedent for chaos. So we won't. "

He pushed a sealed document across the table.

"Your probation begins at first bell tomorrow. You'll report to Officer Harvins in the Commons precinct. Training post. New recruits. They're green. Undisciplined. "

"Like I was," Halfa said.

Jorith blinked once. "Yes. Exactly like you were. "

Dot smiled wide.

"Any questions?" the captain asked.

Halfa looked at the seal. Didn't touch it.

"No questions," Halfa said. "But if the city drowns in the blood you ignored, don't say I didn't warn you. "

He didn't touch the document.

"I won't be here to clean it up. "

And with that, he placed his badge down on the desk and walked out.

❦

Halfa's quarters were spare.

A cot. A trunk. A battered lantern. His watch gear sat neatly in the corner, clean, polished, and untouched since the final battle.

The room still smelled faintly of smoke.

He wasn't sure if it came from the city, or from himself.

The envelope was waiting on his bunk. No name. No wax seal. Just parchment, folded once.

He picked it up and sat slowly.

The handwriting was rough, but deliberate:

You're still slower than me in a fight.

I still punch harder.

But you've grown up.

And I guess I have too.

The Blackjaws were rot. Now they're mine. And I'll carve something useful out of what's left.

You want to stop me, come try.

You want to change the world, don't wait for it to ask.

You were never meant for the walls, Halfa.

Keep your fire aimed forward.

—G

Halfa stared at it for a long time.

Then folded the letter, tucked it inside his coat and stood.

He turned, and found Yetta leaning in the doorway, arms folded, scarf half-tugged around her neck like a half-made decision. This was the first time he had seen her away from her cart.

"Thought I might catch you," she said.

Halfa blinked. "You're still here?"

"Not for long. " Her smile was small, but real. "I've booked passage north. Greyrock, maybe further. This city's full of smoke and ghosts. Time I stopped chasing both. "

He nodded, unsure what to say. "Thank you. For... everything. "

"Don't get sentimental on me," she muttered. "You still owe me a drink. And a decent sunset. "

He managed a dry chuckle. "Next time. "

"There'll be a next time. " She stepped closer and pressed something into his hand —a tiny, silver button, tarnished but familiar. "From the coat you ruined. I've kept it. Seemed... lucky. "

Halfa turned it over in his palm, heart thudding once. "I'll keep it safe. "

Yetta nodded. "You always do. "

Yetta paused just before the door. Her fingers hovered at the edge of her scarf, then dipped into the lining. She turned back and crossed the room in three quick steps.

"Almost forgot," she muttered, and pressed something into Halfa's hand.

A slip of parchment. Old. Creased. Smelled faintly of salt and charcoal.

"What's this?"

"Piece of a registry," she said. "From an old mercantile ledger. Found it years ago on a trade run past Kallik's Reach. I wasn't looking for anything, but the name caught my eye. "

Halfa opened the parchment slowly. A name was scrawled in faded ink. He couldn't read it. Beside it, a column labelled *"Origin. "* A sigil he didn't recognise. And under it, a single word:

"Ashborn. "

He looked up. Yetta's eyes were steady.

"I don't know what it means," she said. "Could be a place. Could be a title. But it wasn't nothing. And it didn't feel like a mistake."

Halfa stared at it. "Why give it to me now?"

"Because I think it matters now," she said. "Because I've watched you spend your whole damn life protecting people."

He folded the paper slowly. Tucked it into the pouch with the button and the blessing.

"Thank you," he said.

Yetta gave him a tired grin. "You were never just built for this city, Halfa. You were built for something older. Bigger. You find it, and don't forget who you are when you do."

Maybe she wasn't just a cook or a clever mouth. Perhaps she'd been guarding his path longer than he knew.

She saluted, this time with actual weight behind it, and disappeared into the corridor.

Halfa watched her go.

He didn't stop her.

But he was certain they'd cross paths again.

The room felt emptier without her. Halfa stood for a long moment, the button warm in his hand, then slipped it into the pouch beside the blessing and the spiral mark. One more ember to carry. One more reason to keep walking.

His boots thudded softly down the barracks hall.

He passed Brannig's old office without looking in.

Passed the sparring yard.

Passed the new recruits, who straightened as he walked by, even now, still trying to figure out if he was a myth or a warning.

◊

The safe house was quieter now.

No guards at the door. No maps pinned to the walls. The war room looked more like a storeroom again, except for a few broken crates and a splatter of dried blood someone had tried to scrub clean.

Rix sat on a bench in the corner, one arm in a sling, her cloak draped over her lap like a forgotten flag. She was peeling an apple with a small hooked blade, the slices landing neatly on a dented tin plate.

Halfa ducked under the low beam as he entered. He didn't speak right away.

Rix didn't look up. "Thought you'd be halfway to the Eastern Gates by now. "

"Thought I'd check on you first. "

She gestured with the blade. "Still here. Still beautiful. "

Halfa gave a small smile. "You okay?"

"I've got one good arm, three cracked ribs, and a city that smells like charcoal. So... could be worse. "

He leaned against the wall nearby, arms crossed. "You fought well. "

"So did you. " She tossed an apple peel into the corner. "Didn't expect the Temple to survive. Glad it did. "

He nodded, thinking of Serelion. "It barely did. "

They sat in the pause for a while.

Finally, Rix said, "Gronk's consolidating fast. More than half of the old Black-jaw members are now Ash Rats. They're rebranding, but it's the same claws underneath. Just cleaner armour. "

"And you?"

She looked at him, expression unreadable.

"I'm stepping back," she said. "At least for now. I did what I came to do. Helped the right people win the wrong war. But I'm not ready to be a queen of ashes. "

"You think he'll hold it?"

"He'll try. And he'll be better than the last lot... for a while. But you know Gronk. He always wanted to build something. Never said what he'd do once it was done. "

Halfa let that settle.

Rix reached into her cloak and pulled out a worn charm, half-burned, half-painted. The old Ash Rat symbol. She handed it to him.

"For luck," she said. "Or for memory. Whichever you need more. "

He took it. "Thanks. " Another keepsake to carry with him.

She stood slowly, wincing, and faced him.

"You saved me more than once, you know. "

Halfa shook his head. "I just stood where I had to. "

"Exactly. "

She smirked, softer this time.

"If we see each other again, don't let it be on opposite rooftops. "

"I'll try. "

She turned toward the door, but paused in the frame.

"Oh, and if Gronk ever forgets the line, you know what to do. "

He nodded. "I do. "

Then she was gone, boots quiet on the cellar steps, leaving behind a plate of apple slices and a silence that tasted like farewells.

◉

The Violet Door welcomed Halfa home.

Halfa knelt near the centre of what had once been the main hall, now half-exposed to wind and morning light. The spiral had been swept, but not restored. Still, it could be walked. Still, it led to a flame.

He placed the two charms on the altar ledge, one scorched and blackened, the other smooth and whole. Side by side. Not replaced. Carried.

Behind him, soft steps approached.

Marin.

Her robes were dusted with ash and paint, sleeves rolled to the elbows, curls pinned back with a sliver of glass. She looked tired. Whole. Fierce in that quiet way only she could be. Her wounds were healing, but she was still not quite back to her usual self.

"You're not leaving," she said.

It wasn't a plea. It wasn't a guess.

Halfa rose and turned toward her.

"No," he said simply. "Not yet. Not while this place still needs hands. "

Marin stepped beside him, gaze drifting to the broken spiral underfoot.

"This city doesn't deserve you," she said.

"I'm not staying for the city. "

She looked up at him, something fragile and bright in her eyes.

He went on, voice low. "Not until the temple stands again. Not until you can rest. And if that takes weeks, months..."

"It won't," she said, a soft smile rising. "Not with you helping. "

He returned it, tired, warm, real.

"Good. Because when we go, we go together. "

Marin reached for his hand. Paint-streaked fingers met calloused ones. The grip was firm. Familiar.

"I'll finish what needs finishing," she said. "Then we find the road. Together. "

"Together," he echoed.

She leaned into his side, cheek resting against his shoulder. "We don't have to run anymore, do we?"

Halfa exhaled, his breath catching briefly on memory. Serelion standing alone, sacrificing themselves for everyone in the Temple. The fire that had nearly taken all of it.

"No," he said. "We build. Then we go. "

"Wherever we go," she said, voice low but steady, "we bring the joy with us. "

Halfa looked at her, not in surprise, but in agreement.

Not because the city was fixed. Not because the fire was gone.

But because she was right.

Outside, wind threaded through the missing wall, carrying temple incense and fresh dawn in equal parts. Somewhere, someone hammered a support beam into place. Bilbin's voice barked orders from the back hall. The sound of life returning.

The temple wasn't finished.

Neither were they.

But they would be.

And when it was time, the world would have to make room.

Epilogue - One Good Wall

That night, out in the wilderness, Marin asleep at his side, Halfa dreamed.

He stood, back in the temple at Grayspire.

The world shimmered like smoke held in suspension. The stars above him were not stars, but spirals of light, and the ground pulsed beneath his feet like the breath of something ancient. He wasn't burning. He wasn't cold.

He was waiting.

Serelion emerged from the light like a truth remembered too late. Their eyes carried every candle the temple had ever lit. Serelion was bathed in light, but not too bright.

"You made it to the centre," they said.

Halfa blinked. "I don't remember walking the spiral. "

Serelion smiled faintly. "That's because this time, it walked you. "

A pause.

"I saw you," Halfa said. "When you took the fire. When you—"

"I didn't take it," Serelion interrupted gently. "I *held* it. So you could learn to carry it. "

Halfa's fists clenched. "But you're gone. "

"Gone is not the same as lost. " They stepped closer. "Joy lives in memory, too. It burns there. Bright. Quiet. Waiting to be chosen again. "

Halfa looked down at his hands. "The fire still scares me. "

"Good," Serelion said. "Fear means you respect it. But love it, Halfa. Let it dance. Don't just survive it. "

A breeze moved through the field. Spirals of ash curled and lifted.

"You're not Thessira's blade," Serelion said. "You're her spark. "

Halfa opened his mouth to speak, but the light was already fading. Serelion's outline blurred, then scattered into drifting spirals of gold.

Only their voice remained:

"Burn wisely, my friend. Burn with joy. "

Her new leg clicked softly on the cobblestones. Metal joints, custom-fitted, a little too smooth to trust at first. Now, it moved like an extension of her old stride—just with a different kind of weight.

She didn't limp anymore.

She *walked.*

She'd resigned, once.

Turned in her badge. She had told herself and others that she was done.

Too many fires. Too much rot in the walls. Too many nights wondering if the uniform meant anything at all.

But something had stayed.

A stubborn ember. A voice.

"We're not fixing this from the inside. We're holding the line until someone can. "

So she came back.

Not with fanfare. Not with a speech.

With a pen, a prosthetic, and a list of rookies who needed someone to yell at them properly.

Inside, the new recruits were louder than they should've been. They always were. Tallen had yelled once. It hadn't worked. So now, he just outlasted them.

Brannig watched him now from the side hallway.

He stood in the centre of the commons, arms crossed, steady as stone. His voice was calm, measured. When he spoke, they listened.

Not because he demanded it.

Because he'd earned it.

"Keep your corners tight," Tallen said. "You don't watch each other, and you'll bleed alone. We don't do that here. "

One of the rookies muttered something.

Tallen raised an eyebrow. He didn't speak.

Brannig smiled to herself.

Later, they sat together on the old bench outside. The same one Halfa used to sulk on when things got a bit tough.

Brannig poured two cups of tea. Bitterleaf. Not spiced. No sugar.

"Got a commendation today," she said, handing him the cup.

Tallen raised an eyebrow. "For what?"

"For not decking Captain Mallor during his speech. "

Tallen chuckled. "Personal growth. "

"Don't get used to it. "

They sipped in silence for a while.

Then Brannig reached into her coat pocket. Pulled out an old parchment. It was creased, weathered, and still sealed.

She passed it to Tallen.

"Vendor filed this. After Halfa stopped a shakedown. Never opened it. "

Tallen turned it over in his hands. Didn't break the seal.

"Why not?"

Brannig shrugged. "I already know what it says. "

The city stretched before them, fog hanging low like breath on glass.

"You think he'll come back?" Tallen asked.

Brannig didn't answer right away. Her eyes drifted toward the gates beyond the barracks, where the morning fog clung like memory.

"He's not wandering," she said at last. "He's searching. And maybe when he finds it, whatever he's chasing, he'll light another fire worth following. "

A gust of wind stirred the courtyard dust. Somewhere down the street, a burst of laughter rang out.

She smiled. "He's out there. I can feel it. "

Tallen nodded.

But he didn't put the letter away.

He just held it.

Like it mattered.

Brannig leaned back against the stone.

"I was wrong about you, you know. "

Tallen blinked. "About what?"

"Thought you were too soft. Too green. "

"And now?" She smiled faintly. "Now you're the one I trust to keep the wall standing. "

Acknowledgements

Well, where do I start. To finally publish a book is still a surreal feeling, and one I wasn't sure I would ever have.

Once I had Halfa's story in my head, it came out in waves.

I'd like to thank my wife and my daughter for their unwavering support throughout the whole process, especially the sleepless nights where I wouldn't even notice the time.

To the rest of my family and friends who knew that I was writing and were encouraging, thank you! (not you Ben, who spewed in his mouth.)

Penny, you were amazing as an editor, and I will be reaching out for Book 2 and hopefully many more. Thanks so much for finding all the things I overlooked (there were many), and thanks for sharing your contacts.

Igor, love the cover design, thanks again for your help bringing it to life.

If you are reading this as a Beta or ARC Reader, I appreciate the support so much. And to all readers, can't believe you have made it this far, thank you so much.

Halfa and Marin's journey is not over. Gronk has won the gang war in Grayspire. The three "recruits" are now veterans and Brannig returns to the fold, with a nice prosthetic. Rix has gone to who knows where. What is next? The Halfaverse (cringe) awaits! It is much bigger than the city of Grayspire.

Find me on Socials or at Halrowan. com

Keep reading for the first scene of Book 2: Currently Unnamed

From the Next Book in the Halfaverse

The schooner heaved in the dark, its hull groaning as if it, too, had grown tired of holding on. Halfa planted his feet wide and leaned into the wind, both hands wrapped around a rope that burned against his palms. Rain lashed his skin, saltwater blurred his vision, and every heartbeat felt borrowed.

Another wave slammed the side of the vessel. He staggered but didn't fall. The mainsail snapped above him like a whip. One rope had given way. He couldn't see which. Someone shouted forward, but the storm took the voice and shredded it into nothing.

The crew were outlines in the grey, hunched shapes moving with practiced desperation. They scrambled up the rigging or slipped across the deck, hands groping for knots, knives, anything that might keep them afloat for another breath.

Halfa moved toward the mast. The sky was black above, pulsing with flickers of light that didn't quite become lightning. Clouds churned. Rain hammered the deck boards, spilling through gaps and flooding low corners where ropes and barrels drifted like wreckage.

He reached for the closest line and pulled it tight, steadying the half-torn staysail. Fire prickled in his fingers for a moment, but he clenched his fist and smothered it. There was no use for flame here. This storm would only laugh at it.

The schooner pitched again. Halfa threw his weight backward to counter it, boots skidding across slick timber. He caught himself on the rail, teeth gritted. Somewhere behind him, something heavy tumbled and smashed. He didn't look.

Then came a hand on his arm.

He turned to see Rout beside him, soaked to the skin, seawater dripping from his sharp-featured face. The sea elf met his gaze and nodded once. He didn't speak, but he didn't need to. He tapped his chest, then pointed up to the torn rigging above. One finger hooked in the air. A question.

Halfa gave a short nod and stepped aside, handing over the coil of line. While Rout climbed, Halfa worked fast to brace the lower rope. His fingers ached, and the saltwater had turned the rope stiff and rough. But the motion helped. It gave his mind something to hold onto.

Above, Rout moved with inhuman grace, hands and feet flowing through the rigging like he was born to it. He reached the break and began to splice in the replacement. Halfa kept tension below, eyes flicking between the elf's silhouette and the restless sea.

Captain Irvell passed him a moment later, shouting into the wind. "Drop the foresail! If it tears, we lose the mast!" Her voice was hoarse, barely cutting through the storm. She didn't wait for confirmation, just barreled on toward the wheel, slipping once but catching herself.

The ship pitched again, harder than before. Halfa slammed into the mast and held tight. He felt the wood shudder against his shoulder, the deep strain of a vessel fighting to survive. A younger version of himself might have panicked. Might have shouted or cursed the sea.

But he stayed quiet now, grounded in the weight of the storm and the feel of the rope in his hands.

The rain hadn't let up. If anything, it came harder now, falling sideways, thick as river water. The deck became a river itself, and he found himself wondering how much lower it could sink before the sea decided to finish what it had started.

They weren't through it yet. Not even close.

But the line held. Rout was descending. The crew still moved. And Halfa stayed upright, eyes on the dark, waiting for the next wave.